continued . . .

"An engaging urban fantasy . . . a bravura finale."

—SF Reviews.net

"[An] entertaining contemporary fantasy mystery with a hard-boiled druid detective . . . a promising start to a new series."

—*Locus*

"Masterfully blends detective thriller with fantasy . . . a fast-paced thrill ride . . . Del Franco never pauses the action . . . and Connor Grey is a very likable protagonist. The twisting action and engaging lead make *Unshapely Things* hard to put down."

—*BookLoons*

"The intriguing cast of characters keeps the readers involved with the mystery wrapped up in the fantasy . . . I look forward to spending more time with Connor in the future, and learning more about him and his world."

—*Gumshoe*

"A wonderfully written, richly detailed, and complex fantasy novel with twists and turns that make it unputdownable . . . Mr. Del Franco's take on magic and paranormal elements is fresh and intriguing. Connor Grey's an appealing hero bound to delight fantasy and paranormal romance fans alike."

—*The Romance Readers Connection*

"Compelling and fast paced . . . The world-building is superb . . . Fans of urban fantasy should get a kick out of book one in this new series."

—*Romantic Times*

"A very impressive start. The characters were engaging and believable, and the plot was intriguing. I found myself unable to put it down until I had devoured it completely, and I'm eagerly looking forward to the sequel."

—*Book Fetish*

"A wonderful, smart, and action-packed mystery involving dead fairies, political intrigue, and maybe a plot to destroy humanity . . . *Unshapely Things* has everything it takes to launch a long-running series, and I'm very excited to see what Del Franco has in store next for Connor Grey and his friends."

—*Bookslut*

Ace Books by Mark Del Franco

UNSHAPELY THINGS
UNQUIET DREAMS
UNFALLEN DEAD

unfallen dead

mark del franco

ACE BOOKS, NEW YORK

THE BERKLEY PUBLISHING GROUP
Published by the Penguin Group
Penguin Group (USA) Inc.
375 Hudson Street, New York, New York 10014, USA
Penguin Group (Canada), 90 Eglinton Avenue East, Suite 700, Toronto, Ontario M4P 2Y3, Canada
(a division of Pearson Penguin Canada Inc.)
Penguin Books Ltd., 80 Strand, London WC2R 0RL, England
Penguin Group Ireland, 25 St. Stephen's Green, Dublin 2, Ireland (a division of Penguin Books Ltd.)
Penguin Group (Australia), 250 Camberwell Road, Camberwell, Victoria 3124, Australia
(a division of Pearson Australia Group Pty. Ltd.)
Penguin Books India Pvt. Ltd., 11 Community Centre, Panchsheel Park, New Delhi—110 017, India
Penguin Group (NZ), 67 Apollo Drive, Rosedale, North Shore 0632, New Zealand
(a division of Pearson New Zealand Ltd.)
Penguin Books (South Africa) (Pty.) Ltd., 24 Sturdee Avenue, Rosebank, Johannesburg 2196,
South Africa

Penguin Books Ltd., Registered Offices: 80 Strand, London WC2R 0RL, England

This is a work of fiction. Names, characters, places, and incidents either are the product of the author's imagination or are used fictitiously, and any resemblance to actual persons, living or dead, business establishments, events, or locales is entirely coincidental. The publisher does not have any control over and does not assume any responsibility for author or third-party websites or their content.

UNFALLEN DEAD

An Ace Book / published by arrangement with the author

PRINTING HISTORY
Ace mass-market edition / February 2009

Copyright © 2009 by Mark Del Franco.
Cover art by Jaime DeJesus.
Cover design by Judith Lagerman.

ISBN: 978-0-441-01689-1

ACE
Ace Books are published by The Berkley Publishing Group,
a division of Penguin Group (USA) Inc.,
375 Hudson Street, New York, New York 10014.
ACE and the "A" design are trademarks of Penguin Group (USA) Inc.

PRINTED IN THE UNITED STATES OF AMERICA

10   9   8   7   6   5   4   3   2   1

To my sister Jody,
who hears all and makes coffee.
And to Jack, as always.

acknowledgments

Thanks to Anne Sowards, my editor, whose enthusiasm and insight are deeply appreciated, as well as to her assistant, Cam Dufty, who remembers what I forget. Sara and Bob Schwager make my writing presentable with their deft red pencils and even defter ability to call me out on made-up words.

Melissa and Jeaniene inspired me with their advice and writing, and their understanding and wit when things got strange.

And many, many thanks to Francine Woodbury, who pokes things with sticks and giggles when she does.

1

When I find myself walking through dark, unlit hallways in an abandoned warehouse in the middle of the night, it means one of two things: I am on my way to an after-hours party—or to a death. Since Detective Lieutenant Leonard Murdock wasn't prone to inviting me to parties, I knew the only music I'd be hearing shortly was the squawk of police radios.

When Murdock called me out of a nice, quiet dive down on Stillings Street because he had something interesting for me, I didn't think it meant feeling like a rat in a maze. The warehouse had been easy enough to find because of the police and ambulance out front. Once inside, though, I made a wrong turn and found myself wandering a series of corridors that led back onto themselves.

I put my cell phone to my ear. "Which way, Murdock?"

"I have no idea, Connor. Get to a window and tell me what you see," he said.

Amusement colored his voice. I knew what he was thinking. Connor Grey, the great druid and former investigator for the Fey Guild, had gotten himself lost. In a building. Surrounded by police officers. With cell phones and radios. I may no longer have the ability to manipulate essence on a grand scale, but I didn't think I'd lost my sense of direction, too.

Using the silvery blue glow from the cell phone as a flashlight, I managed to find a window with frosted chicken-wire glass. I pushed at the frame, but years of paint refused to budge. I swore under my breath and put the phone down. Breaking the glass wouldn't help because of the safety mesh. It's moments like this that I find particularly frustrating.

I used to have the power to do things humans could only dream of. Essence made it possible, the essence in everything, including myself. The superstitious call it magic. I've had some mystical moments, especially lately, but in general I don't tend toward that kind of thinking. I like things to make sense, to be able to quantify them and apply rules. Essence is no exception.

Back in the day, I manipulated essence and caused it to flow out of my hands, my body—even my eyes—and it did things I intended it to do. Good things and bad things, but powerful things either way. Not anymore. Since the accident that caused the loss of most of my abilities, a dark mass in my brain blocks me from doing what I used to be able to do. Painfully so.

"Are you there?" Murdock's voice sounded tinny in the small phone's speaker.

"Yeah." I had probably been stuck on the same floor for twenty minutes. I decided enough was enough and didn't want the further humiliation of asking Murdock to send someone to find me.

Everyone has body essence to a different degree depending on their species. I can still access my own to an extent, but the thing in my head kicked up a storm of pain when I did. I avoided it most times. I put my hand on the window frame and shot a quick burst of body essence into it. Several things happened simultaneously. The window cracked; the frame cracked; and I'm pretty sure my head cracked. I clutched my temples as a searing pain shot behind my eyes.

"Connor?" Murdock's voice was now flat with police concern.

I picked up the phone. "I'm good." I pushed the window

up, fighting its years of inertia, and stuck my head out. "I'm on the third floor, looking at an air shaft."

"Hold on."

The full moon sent a faint light into the shaft, illuminating it enough for me to see another window ten feet across the way. I craned my head up and saw more windows. The silhouette of a head leaned out above me.

Murdock's voice echoed from behind me on the phone and above me in the shaft. "I see you. You need to come up two floors. There's a stairwell about fifty feet to the right as you face the air shaft."

I startled at a cold touch on the back of my neck. Jumping back from the window, I dropped the phone. The blue screen winked out. Complete darkness surrounded me. I crouched and picked up the phone, feeling cracks on the screen. It didn't light up at my touch. I'd managed to disconnect Murdock, too.

Something moved in the dark, soft and silent. I sensed more than heard it. I slid to the side of the open window so that my head wouldn't be a nice handy target against the dim moonlight behind me. When you're in a dark building with a dead body, you think of these things. I stilled my breath, listening. Nothing moved, at least nothing that I could hear. An afterimage of light from the air shaft cluttered my vision, but I couldn't see anything in the darkness anyway. I opened my essence-sensing ability, trying to perceive whether anyone was in the room with me. As a druid, I was naturally good at sensing essence. I was better at it than most. It was one of the few remaining abilities I had.

Faint white light coalesced in my inner vision, faint hints of ambient essence creating the shape of the hallway. Here and there along the edges of the floor, pinpricks of light showed evidence of insects, probably roaches. I made out the pathway. I stepped to the left toward the stubbornly hidden stairwell. Two doors opened to the right, dark and empty. As I passed the second one, cool air fluttered over me.

I froze. Just inside the door, essence shimmered in the

shape of a man. His indistinct face looked stricken, strange creases crisscrossing his forehead like deep worry lines. He lifted a hand toward me, an innocuous gesture that, under the circumstances, made me recoil.

"Who are you?" I asked.

Confused, he peered at his hand. Blinking slowly, he tilted his head and stretched his hand toward me again. He took a step, then evaporated like pale smoke in the dark. Gone. Even his essence was gone. He wasn't there, but he had to be. It's nearly impossible to mask your essence completely, especially from me. I focused my sensing ability tighter, like turning up a dial, but still couldn't register him. I held my hands out to ward him off if he came at me. Flattening myself against the wall, I slid away from the empty doorway, glancing quickly to the left to be sure I was going the right way, waiting for him to jump me. At the end of the hall, I realized why I kept missing the stairwell. An odd jog in the wall made the hall seem like it was a dead end. I stepped around the partition, pressing myself against the opposite side. I took shallow breaths, straining to hear if I was being followed.

A bright light shone in my eyes, and I startled. The light found me again, and someone said, "Connor Grey?"

Embarrassed, I held my hand up against the beam. "Yeah?"

The flashlight swept down, and a puzzled young police officer observed me in the backwash of the light. "Detective Murdock sent me down to get you."

Murdock was not going to let me hear the end of this. I pointed into the darkness of the hall. "There's someone down here."

The kid's training kicked in, and he went for his gun. In that coordinated way police have, he held the flashlight focused into the hallway and used the same hand to call for backup on the radio on his shoulder. I stepped behind him out of the way. I may be able to hold my own in a fight, but I had no idea what the mystery man had with him. Being cautious wasn't the same thing as being afraid.

"Stairwell's right behind us," the officer said in a low

voice. I backed into it and heard the clatter of running feet on the stairs above me. Another officer joined us, gun drawn.

I leaned away from the door to let him pass. "He's all yours, guys. First door on the left is where I saw him."

I mounted the stairs. Police officers get flashlights with their uniforms. I forget that not every building is going to have electricity. One long flight up, white light spilled into the stairwell. In my rush up the stairs, I had turned off a couple of floors too soon.

At the landing, the fifth floor opened as a wide space. The warehouse had been used for some kind of manufacturing, uniform workstations marching across the floor in two rows. I didn't recognize the rusted machinery, some of it obviously vandalized, all of it coated with dust. About halfway down the aisle between the rows, several police officers with flashlights gathered in a circle. The beams of almost blue light arced in the dark space whenever someone moved.

As my footsteps crackled against the dirty floor, Murdock's half-shadowed face turned in my direction. He gave me a faint smile, the one he reserves for those moments when my dignity has taken a hit. "Nice to see you."

I twisted my mouth into a smile. "You could have left bread crumbs for me to follow."

"Hey, I sent help. It's not like I just left you lying on a tomb somewhere."

Murdock and I have had a little disagreement as to the appropriate course of action I had taken on our last big case. "I told you, Murdock, the paramedics were there. I checked your essence before I left. You were fine."

"Uh-huh." He nodded toward the center of attention. I joined the group to check out my latest potential paycheck. When I lost my abilities and the Guild kicked me out, I picked up consulting gigs with the Boston P.D. They're not always equipped to handle cases involving elves or fairies, or most other kinds of fey from Faerie. I know a lot, so they call. At least Murdock does. Hence, paycheck.

While Murdock and the officers held their lights on the

body, I crouched for a closer look. An emaciated man lay sprawled on his back, his head smooth of hair. Not shaved. You can tell a naturally bald man. Someone who shaves his head gets a five-o'clock shadow. I'd seen it on myself recently. A few weeks earlier, I had lost all my hair in the backlash of a major spell. It started growing back immediately, but I wore a black knit cap against the late October chill. The dead guy didn't look like he was into a daily hygiene routine that included shaving.

Carved across his forehead was the reason Murdock called. Someone had used a sharp object, a knife being most likely, to make a horizontal gash from temple to temple. Across the sharp line of the gash, several hash marks had been made. Ogham runes, six of them, the old alphabet of the Celts. Deep red marks split the skin with little blood, which meant they were probably made postmortem. The victim's lingering body essence tickled at my senses, and I pulled back in surprise.

Murdock caught my movement. "What's wrong?"

I frowned. "I just saw this guy downstairs."

Murdock shook his head. "Not possible. I've been here at least an hour. He's been here longer."

I pursed my lips. "Have they found anyone downstairs?"

Murdock jutted his chin at one of the officers, who muttered into his radio. A static of muddled words came back, and he shook his head.

Interesting. A puzzle piece for the investigation. Turning my attention back to the body, I sensed that the guy was a human normal. Nothing about him registered as fey. If he were someone from Faerie, his essence would have resonated differently. By the look of his soiled and rumpled pants and thin jacket, I'd guess he had been homeless. He could have been anywhere from late thirties to early fifties. It's hard to tell with guys like him, who've had years of living on the street to ravage their features.

The runes on his forehead gave a faint indication of essence. Someone used a spell as they carved them. With yet another jolt of surprise, I realized it had been done by a druid. Essence in and of itself has vague differences based on its source. It's why certain fey were better at manipulating certain essences than others. Druids were attuned to organics, fairies to ambient air, and so on. Sensing who or what species actually used a particular essence was a separate ability, one I didn't normally have. A few species, like trolls, could do it—and I had had recent close contact with a troll. I had thought the residual impact of that encounter had dissipated finally, and made a mental note to have myself checked out.

I stood. "It's a safe bet you're looking for a druid."

Murdock directed his flashlight toward the guy's head. "We're not seeing any obvious trauma. Could those marks have killed him?"

"I don't think so. I'm pretty sure they were done after he was dead."

"What do they mean?"

I shrugged. "Honestly, I don't know. Easy translation is 'The way denied.' It's got a spell wrapped in it, too, so that could change the meaning. I'll have to research it. How long has he been here?"

Murdock inspected the rest of the room with his flashlight. "Probably a few hours. Medical examiner should be here soon. We need a generator, too."

The body had fallen with his right arm beneath him. As I walked around the other side, I noted the fingernails on his left hand were blackened. "Can someone shine a light on his shoes?"

Several someones did. Sure enough, the cheap leather had burnt toes. I lifted one of the victim's eyelids. My stomach did a little flip at the sight of his destroyed eyes. I backed away, wiping my hand on my pants. "He was killed by essence shock. Someone hit him with a major charge and short-circuited his system. He probably died of a heart attack or organ damage."

Murdock directed his flashlight toward the back of the floor. "Looks like his crib's back there."

We walked from the body, the essences of the officers fading away from my senses. The residual essences of the dead man and his druid assailant trailed all the way back to the corner of the room. An old mattress was on the floor under a workbench. Murdock's flashlight revealed the basics of a squat, a meager collection of personal-care products, several books, candles, a few canned goods. Nothing that would be terribly missed if he were robbed while out on the street. It didn't look disturbed.

Another stairwell opened at the rear of the room. We stepped on the landing, Murdock shining the beam down the stairs. Nothing to be seen but years' accumulation of crumbled debris. The druid essence was more distinct. The killer had lingered here, long enough to leave some residual body essence for me to register her gender. Something about it tugged at my awareness, like searching for a word I knew but couldn't place.

I looked back to the body. "The killer was a druidess. She waited here for a while. She either hit him with essence from here when he was coming in the other way, or she spooked him out of his sleep and hit him as he ran off. Who called it in?"

Even in the half-lit dark, the sour twist to Murdock's mouth was evident. "Nine one one. Anonymous."

Anonymous, the most common surname in the Weird. It's the Boston neighborhood where the fey go when they're down-and-out. No one ever saw anything or heard anything in the Weird. I can't blame folks down here, though. When you had no place else to go and ended up in the Weird, you didn't want someone more powerful than you breathing down your neck. You had no place else to run except the grave, and most people avoided that. After I lost everything in my life, I moved into the Weird. The implication that I have nowhere else bothers me sometimes.

Something crunched underfoot. The glow of Murdock's flashlight reflected off a small and shiny object. I picked up a piece of gold worked in a spiral. Sparkles of essence flickered and died on it, leaving me the same vague sense of someone familiar.

Murdock tilted his flashlight toward me. "Find something?"

I rubbed the piece between my thumb and index finger. "Piece of jewelry, I think. I'll play with it and see if it's from our druidess."

Back by the body, a gleam of essence caught my eye. I inhaled sharply. "What the hell?"

"What?" Murdock swung his light as I strode back to the crime scene. A strange flicker of essence neared the body.

"I think he's still alive, Murdock." As I approached, the essence vanished.

I stopped short. Murdock came up beside me. "He's dead, Connor. I don't need your sensing ability to know that."

"I saw something."

Judging by Murdock's expression, I must have looked as confused as I felt. "Are you okay?"

I rubbed my hands over my face and adjusted the knit cap. "Yeah. Maybe I'm just tired."

Murdock nodded. "We'll let the forensic guys take care of the rest. Come on. I'll give you a ride back to your place."

I scanned the body once more but sensed nothing. Maybe I had seen some overlapping essence from the officers around the body. Even with experience, the dual vision of essence and normal sight could be confusing.

We went down the front stairwell. On the ground floor, the medical examiner brushed by, looking none too happy to be roused in the middle of the night for a homeless guy. He didn't bother to acknowledge us.

I opened the passenger door to Murdock's car and dropped myself onto the pile of newspapers on the seat. Murdock pulled a U-turn and drove onto Old Northern Avenue. The main drag of the neighborhood had the calm of late night, only a car or two coasting along. Even the Weird quieted down at night eventually. The streetwalkers and spell dealers gave up and went home. The partiers stumbled into the decrepit backseats of cabs. The only people still out and about were the die-hard and the desperate.

Murdock didn't say anything, and for once I thought he might actually be tired. The man's a machine and puts in more hours than I want to think about. He pulled up in front of my apartment. "I'll let you know if we get an ID."

I let myself out. "I'll look into the runes, see if it's a spell that'll tell us anything."

He leaned across the seat. "Get some sleep first. You look like hell."

As I walked up the four flights to my apartment, I couldn't shake the image of the dead guy. I knew I'd seen his essence before I'd seen his body. I wasn't that tired. It didn't make sense. When someone dies, their life essence vanishes. Period. I'd seen it happen enough times. The old faith said we went on to our afterlife in TirNaNog and didn't come back. Dead is dead.

I entered my apartment, noting the faint odor of old coffee and empty beer bottles doing battle with fresh laundry and Pine-Sol. Home smells. I'm not the best housekeeper and can't afford one. I did my best but let the dust bunnies roam where they will.

I was tired. Too many late nights and too many bars were catching up with me. Maybe Murdock was right. Seeing dead guys walking around dark, empty warehouses might be a sign it was time to get some sleep.

2

I cradled a bottle of wine in the backseat of a cab. Guinness is my preferred drink, but Briallen ab Gwyll has a well-known liking for French wines. A dinner on Beacon Hill was always an opportunity for good food and conversation, whether the invitation came via cell phone or sending. Briallen prefers the intimacy of mental contact. Her cool, feathery touch in my mind was a pleasant surprise after so many months.

The cab pulled up in front of the townhouse on Louisburg Square. In the cool evening air, I admired the old place—five stories of bricks and mullioned windows that dated back to the late 1800s. The gas lamps flanking the entrance made me feel welcome and reminded me of my teenage years when I had been Briallen's student. I broke one of the lamps once swinging on it, and a welder patched it, slightly off center if you looked closely. Briallen wasn't happy and made me memorize an entire land registry in Old Irish as punishment. To this day, I remembered that one Ian macDeare owned all the land from the split oak tree to the ford of a nameless stream by the summer pasture in Ireland's County Clare.

I let myself in. Briallen had keyed the door to my essence long ago with a warding spell on it that told her if I entered. As I set one foot on the stairs leading to the second-floor parlor, noise from the kitchen pulled me to the back of the first floor, where I found the lady of the house busy with a pot at the stove. I placed the wine on the counter and pulled off my knit cap as she gave me a broad smile.

"You look like absolute hell!" She threw her arms around me, tucking her head into the crook of my neck.

"Thanks. You look wonderful." The last time I saw Briallen, her hair and skin were bleached white from the stress of a major spell. Her color on both counts had returned, her skin a warm peach and the healthy glow of chestnut in her hair, the close-cropped length she had preferred for the past few years.

Briallen was a good hugger, but one with ulterior motives. As she released me, her hands came up the back of my head, and she stared into my face. I felt a vague pressure as she used her essence to probe the strange dark mass in my mind. Surprise and intrigue flickered across her face.

"It's changed. It's shaped differently. How do you feel?"

I ran my hand over the scruff of dark hair growing in. "I had a tough time a couple of weeks ago, but I'm okay."

She gave a half smile back. "I heard about Forest Hills."

Of course she did. Everyone had heard about Forest Hills. When a giant dome of essence implodes and people die, news got around. I stopped the disaster from being worse than it was, but I don't remember how I did it.

Briallen waved me to a stool as she stationed herself at the stove. Dinner plates were set on the other end of the kitchen island. For all the room Briallen has in the house, she spends most of her time in the kitchen and the upstairs parlor.

I noticed three place settings. "Is someone joining us?"

She nodded, sipping from a spoon. "My nephew showed up this afternoon. I hope you don't mind."

That was a surprise. I didn't know Briallen had any family. "I don't remember a nephew."

She handed me a corkscrew. "Well, technically he was a fosterling. Long before you showed up."

Amused, I lowered my eyes at her as I poured her a glass

of wine. "I cannot believe all the things I don't know about you."

She handed me a bottle of Guinness and took the stool on the opposite corner. "People a lot older than you still don't know everything about me."

Her eyes danced above the rim of her wineglass. Briallen verch Gwyll ab Gwyll lived a life most people would envy and the rest would find exhausting. When she wasn't teaching at Harvard, she was mentoring at the Druidic College, working behind the scenes at the Fey Guild, or serving as an international ambassador for a variety of people and causes. Sometimes she even took vacations, which supposedly was what a recent trip to Asia had been about. I doubted that, though. Briallen may like Thai food, but she didn't need six months to learn about it on-site.

I tapped her glass with my bottle. "I'm glad you're back."

Before either of us could say more, we heard someone coming down the stairs. Briallen slid from the stool and moved to the kitchen door. "I think our guest is joining us."

I hadn't sensed anyone when I had entered the house. Briallen kept dampening wards everywhere to prevent her essence-infused artifacts from interacting with one another. Plus, she valued her privacy and didn't want anyone walking in and sensing who had been in her home. Even so, moments before the man appeared, I sensed his essence, recognizing first that he was a druid, then, surprisingly, who he was.

Briallen slipped her arm around his waist and pulled him into the room. "Connor, this is Dylan macBain. Dylan, this is—"

He stretched out his hand. "We know each other, Auntie Bree."

From the look on Briallen's face, she hadn't known.

"Good to see you." I shook his hand. He hadn't changed a bit since I had last seen him, still young-looking, dark brown curls snug on his head, dark eyes against pale skin.

Briallen looked from one to the other of us. "How the hell do you two know each other?"

Dylan kissed her temple. "Connor and I used to work together in New York."

Briallen dropped on her stool while Dylan poured himself wine. "I can't believe I didn't know that."

I smirked at her. "I guess we all have things we still don't know about each other."

She threw me a grudging smile. "Touché."

I looked back at Dylan. "What brings you to Boston?"

He helped himself to some bread as he sat down. "Work. I've been asked to fill in as field director at the Guild."

"Keeva macNeve must not be happy about that." Keeva was the Guild's Community Liaison Officer for Community Affairs, which everyone knew was a polite title for Director of Investigations. It was Keeva's job to run field investigations.

Dylan shrugged. "She's on suspension while the hearings are going on."

I helped myself to another beer. The Guild leadership was a mess. A crazy druid had tried to grab Power at Forest Hills Cemetery and almost succeeded in destroying the fey. Maybe even the world. It was the Guild's job to keep stuff like that from happening. Instead, Keeva and a lot of other people who should have realized what was going on fell into his trap. "Keeva almost died. I know for a fact she didn't know what she was doing."

Briallen and Dylan exchanged looks. Briallen pulled an envelope from her pocket and slid it to me across the counter. "I was going to give this to you later, Connor. High Queen Maeve is not happy about what happened here. The Guild wants to talk to you."

I recognized the form letter. I skipped the legal mumbo jumbo and went right to the point:

You are hereby ordered to appear before the inquiry board regarding the events at Forest Hills Cemetery in and around October 1 of this year. Advocacy can be arranged if so desired.

By order of our hand and seal,

Ceridwen, Queen of Faerie
Special Director of Internal Investigations

I let the letter fall to the counter. "Maeve must be pissed if she sent an underQueen."

Briallen tilted her head down and eyed me from under her brow. "It's not a good time to antagonize anyone, Connor."

I splayed my hand against my chest. "Me? I wouldn't think of it."

"You've had problems with the Guild?" Dylan asked.

I laughed. "I guess you can say neither I nor the Guild is each other's biggest fan at the moment."

Briallen rolled her eyes. "Boy, did you just hit a long-running argument, Dylan." She ladled stew for all of us.

I nodded. "I help the Boston P.D. investigate fey issues the Guild ignores. They ignore a lot." Which was true. The Guild was supposed to handle all fey-related crime. Any fey species that manipulated essence—fairies, druids, elves, and anyone else who can trace themselves back to Faerie—was supposed to fall under Guild jurisdiction. In reality, though, the Guild ignored anything that didn't score them political points, especially if it happened in the Weird.

"I remember someone who thought the Guild was the best thing that ever happened to him," said Dylan.

I played with the moisture rings my bottle left on the counter. "A lot has changed since New York."

No one spoke. I refused to look up at Dylan. Dylan and I had some uncomfortable history. We both almost died on a mission, and I handled the aftermath less than nobly, at Dylan's expense. It's one of those things I regret from the time that I thought more about myself than about anyone else. It's been on my list of things to fix someday, but I thought I'd get to decide when. I was wrong. Again.

Briallen looked back and forth between us as she placed

bowls on the counter. She sat back onto her stool and lifted a spoon. "Have either of you ever been to the Orient?"

And with that, the conversation lightened. Gathered around Briallen's table, sharing stories and laughs, felt good. Many people I assumed were friends—real friends—had abandoned me after my accident. It was comforting to enjoy a conversation with people whom I had real history with.

After dessert, Briallen cleared a few dishes, at which point Dylan and I both started doing the same. Apparently when he lived with her, he had been given the same chores I was. Briallen watched us jockeying for position at the sink. "Why don't the two of you go up to the parlor while I clean up?"

Amused, we made our way to the second floor. In the parlor, a small blue fire burned in the grate as it always did. Dylan sat in one of the overstuffed chairs. I went to the window overlooking the backyard. The garden had died off with the cooling weather. The oak tree had dropped most of its leaves, and wind had scattered them to the edges of the small space. The still fountain near the back wall sat cold and uninviting.

"You look good," Dylan said.

I didn't answer right away. I could make out his reflection in the glass in front of me, wavy and blurred. Without looking at him, I crossed to a small table and poured three glasses of tawny port. I handed one to him. As our eyes met, I could see that ten years had not dimmed the issue between us.

I took the chair opposite him, leaving Briallen's favorite seat between us. "You seem to have done well."

Dylan gave me a thin smile. "Nice weather we're having."

I sipped the port. "I'm not sure if there's a storm on the horizon."

He swirled his glass, watching the light reflect flashes of gold. "No. It's clear. Everything's clear."

"You're sure?"

He met my eyes. "Ten years is a long time, Connor. The past is past."

I considered a moment. "I can leave it at that."

He extended his glass. "To friendship, then."

I clinked my glass against his. "Friendship."

"That's a nice sentiment," Briallen said as she came in. She lifted the glass I had poured for her and tapped ours as well. She settled in the chair between us. "Dylan's working on the Met robbery."

Dylan looked at me. "I have never been able to surprise her, have you?"

I shook my head. "I gave up long ago."

He settled back. "Yes, the Met robbery. Someone stole several artifacts from the Celtic Faerie collection."

"Why are you doing footwork for the Met?" I asked.

He stretched his legs out toward the fire. "Someone volunteered the Guild's help because sometimes a pretty trinket is more than a pretty trinket."

"Someone?" I asked.

Dylan shrugged. "I didn't ask, but word did come from above. The Seelie Court's been very nervous about genuine Faerie objects going missing."

I frowned. "I can't imagine something powerful enough to worry the Seelie Court would be lying around in the New York Met."

Briallen shifted more comfortably in her chair. "You'd be amazed at the things that ended up in museums in the early part of last century. Lots of fey had no understanding of where Convergence had brought them, and they sold things off on a promise."

Convergence. Depending on whether you were human or fey, Convergence was a blessing or a curse. When the worlds of Faerie and modern reality converged more than a century ago, the old world order in both places disappeared, and we've been trying to live together ever since.

Dylan yawned and stretched. "I think it has people nervous because Samhain is around the corner. High holidays are always a good time for selling objects originally from Faerie. Some thief is looking to take advantage of the timing to get a good price."

Briallen grinned. "So young and so tired?"

Dylan laughed through another yawn. "No fair, old woman. I've been awake for three days tying up things in New York and reading the current Boston case files."

Briallen narrowed her eyes at him. "Who are you calling old?"

Dylan rose and kissed her cheek. "I have no doubt you continue to run circles around me, Auntie."

I felt a twinge of jealousy at the pleasure on her face.

"I'm going to bed," Dylan said.

He hesitated, and I held out my hand. "It was good to see you."

A look of satisfaction came over him, and he shook my hand. "You, too. Good night, Connor."

He trailed his hand along Briallen's arm as he left the room. We stared into the fire, sipping the port. Briallen broke the silence first. "I'd like to hear your version of what happened at Forest Hills."

I kept my eyes on the fire. "You read the reports. You probably know more about what happened than I do."

"You only gave a statement. You weren't required to file a full report. Tell me the story."

I shrugged. "Murdock and I were working on a case that involved a drug called Float. It turned out that it was made to activate a spell that controlled anyone who touched essence. The full spell activated at Forest Hills Cemetery and got out of control. Essence drained from everything into a huge dome. I apparently figured out a way to diffuse it before it exploded."

"Meryl Dian says you turned yourself into a ward stone," she said.

I looked at her sharply. Meryl told me I had encased myself in granite, that I became a living ward stone and told her I would anchor the control spell. It worked, but I don't know how or why. I asked her not to tell anyone until I thought through the implications. "I don't remember any of it."

"Do you think there's a connection?"

I knew what she was asking. I lost my abilities two years

earlier in a duel with a terrorist, an elf named Bergin Vize. I don't remember what happened then either. I woke up in Avalon Memorial Hospital with no memory of the event, my ability damaged to almost nothing, and a dark mass in my head that no one could diagnose. "Of course, I've been thinking that. But since we don't know what happened to me with Vize, it's just another frustrating question."

Briallen tapped the side of her glass. "Something's come up that has me thinking about essence barriers. The veil is a strong and fragile thing."

With a gentle smile, I poured us more port. "Sounds like Halloween has you feeling nostalgic."

She sipped, gazing into the blue flames in the fire grate. "It was Samhain first, Connor. You know that. The one night of the year that the veil thins between this world and that of the Dead."

I settled back in my chair. " 'Used to thin,' Briallen. At least, that's what they say."

She shifted her eyes at me, mildly annoyed. "It's what *I* say, Connor. I don't speak of Faerie much because so much has been lost. When Convergence happened and this world merged with Faerie, all the Ways between the realms closed. There are things I don't remember, but I do remember the veil thinning. I remember the Dead walking out of TirNaNog."

"Convergence was over a century ago, Briallen. What could it possibly have to do with what happened at Forest Hills?" I asked.

She considered her answer before speaking. "Convergence was a huge essence event, and thousands of fey don't remember their past. An enormous amount of essence was expended at Forest Hills, and you can't remember it. That's too much of a coincidence for me to ignore."

I dropped my head back. "So to understand my injury, we have to solve the biggest mystery in history. What was Convergence, and why did it happen?"

The firelight gleamed in Briallen's eyes. She lowered her head and laughed. "Of course. Finding out what happened to you is the only reason anyone would want to know why Convergence happened."

I frowned, but good-naturedly. "That did sound a little self-involved, didn't it?"

She laughed. "A little. You're not as bad as you used to be."

I stared into the fire, letting my mind slide back a few weeks. All hell broke loose, and a war among the fey almost started. I was in the middle of it, did something to stop it but couldn't remember what. "I'm afraid of what happened at Forest Hills, Briallen. Lots of people died, and there's another blank spot in my memory. I have no idea how many of those deaths are on me. I might even have killed something sacred."

"You either accept that might have happened or let it defeat you, Connor."

I rolled my head toward her. "How can I face something if I don't know what it is?"

"You do know what it is. It's what it always is for everyone. It's you. You have to face yourself. The good and the bad, and, yes, the horrifying. We all have those things within us. You have to remember when to keep it in and when to let it out. Either way, you have to live with the consequences." She spoke softly, staring into the fire, a memory shadowing her eyes.

"How much have you had to live with?"

She hesitated so long, I thought she was going to tell me to mind my own business. "There are things that I can never speak of, things I've needed to do and couldn't explain, but I did them because they had to be done. Some I did out of love and some out of duty, and, yes, even anger and hatred. But I did them, and I live with it. That's what you have to do, Connor. Live with it."

It was my turn to hold my hand out to her. "Will you ever allow me to pity myself?"

She held out her glass. "Wah, wah, wah. Pour some more port."

3

Tawny port has the ability to appear sweet and innocent. I think it's called a fortified wine because it has the tendency to make you think a brisk October evening is refreshing. Which was believable until I found myself more drunk than I thought and lost in my own neighborhood. I wasn't really lost. I wasn't paying attention after I crossed the bridge and missed my street. At least, that was what I tried to convince myself.

I looped the long way around the block past the Nameless Deli. I steadfastly tried not to sway in front of it as I debated whether to get something to eat. The lights were too damned bright, and my hangover was kicking in before the alcohol had burned out of my system. I decided against food. After the huge meal at Briallen's, I couldn't possibly be hungry. I stubbed a toe rounding the corner onto Sleeper Street, hopping and swearing under my breath.

Just when things in my life finally were marching in some semblance of a positive direction, something new had to kick up and throw me offtrack. Of all people the New York Guildhouse could have sent, they sent Dylan macBain. It's as if someone wanted to rub my nose in how much I lost when I lost my abilities. I didn't blame Dylan, of course, though I doubted he had any hesitation about coming to Boston. That didn't make his success feel any better. After everything that happened before I left New York, he seemed to have handled it better than I did. I kicked a water bottle out of my way.

I felt more than saw movement along the curb. This close to the harbor channel that separated the Weird from the financial district, rats strolled at night. They didn't bother me, but I hated when they popped out of nowhere. The gutter was empty. Something flickered, a brief gleam on the edge of my vision. I opened my essence-sensing ability to see where the critter was. Hazy, indistinct essence floated beside me. Pain twinged in my head as the darkness in my mind squeezed. It does that sometimes around essence. It hurt, and I hated it.

The shimmer leaned toward me. Two blades of light faded in and out above it. More lights appeared, dancing motes that gathered into the shape of a hand. A vague sense of unease shivered over my body, and I moved away. The hand receded into a nebulous lump that groped toward me. My body shields activated. I can turn them on and off at will, but these days they react on their own. They were one of the things that were damaged in my duel with Bergin Vize and weren't much help anymore other than as warning signals. Whatever was in front of me, my body didn't like it

I put some more distance between me and the thing. It hovered as though it was considering its next move, then rolled toward me on the air. It worried me as much as it made me curious. I tamped down my sensing ability to reveal an empty street in my normal vision. Not a good sign. Ambient essence that moved with purpose was never a good sign.

A sigh tickled my ears, whispering in from all sides, the sibilant pitch sending shivers down my spine. I shuffled backwards toward my apartment, weighing if I had a fight-or-flight situation. My building vestibule had a warding spell on the main door that could be sealed if I was in trouble. Before I had a chance to consider running for my life, the essence dissipated in a current of air, and the whispering cut off. The pain in my head eased when it was gone.

Another flash of essence, this time radiant pink, pulled me up short. Joe Flit hung upside down above my head, his pink wings keeping him hovering in place. "Where have you been?"

I ducked my head away. "I'll throw up if you stay like that."

"Sorry." He shrugged—disturbing upside down—dropped headfirst, and looped a couple of times in front of me.

I squeezed my eyes shut. "Okay, not helping, Stinkwort."

Joe hated his real name, so I used it to give him a subtle hint that he was being annoying. When I opened my eyes, he was in his more normal position when we go for a walk, a few feet in the air to my side. Normal since Joe is a twelve-inch-tall fairy known as a flit, with bright pink wings he found embarrassing. He's an old friend, which meant we drank together often, laughed at jokes no one else got, and were highly tolerant of each other's less-desirable personality tics except when we weren't.

Joe raised his eyebrows. "Touchy, touchy. Not my fault you're drunk."

"Not drunk." The burr in my words didn't help the denial much.

He opened his mouth to reply, but frowned. He flew over my head and hung in the air, tilting his head from side to side. "I feel something unpleasant. Were you on a date?"

I walked away. "Not funny."

He zipped in front of me. "What's wrong?"

The cracked sidewalk made it difficult to keep from stumbling. "Just remembering stuff I'd prefer to forget."

Joe rolled his eyes. "First you complain you can't remember stuff, then you complain when you do. You're never happy."

I gave my shoulders an exaggerated roll. "So leave if you don't like it."

He didn't. Making a point of not looking at me, he flew ahead, humming to himself. Joe put up with a lot from me. Quid pro quo, though. "Sorry, Joe. Dylan's in Boston."

Joe cocked his head back. "Ah, that. No wonder you're drunk."

"He said he's over it."

Joe snorted. "Yeah, people always get over a knife in the heart. Stay away from him."

"Yeah, I intend to."

Joe stopped abruptly, then grunted with a sour look on his face. A second later, it hit me, too. Two things happened simultaneously: My sensing ability kicked in, and I threw up in the gutter.

Joe wrinkled his nose at the odor. "Port? Ick."

I ignored him. I was always good at sensing essence, but lately my ability had gone into overdrive. On the one hand, it was great that one of my abilities was getting stronger. On the other, it was so strong, I barely saw past it sometimes. Fortunately, this time it came on an empty street between warehouses. Because essence is organic in nature, stone and brick buildings had little essence of their own. They picked it up passively and could even be intentionally infused with it. The buildings around me had the faint haze of white that all buildings in the Weird have. With so many fey living here, ambient essence was everywhere.

Joe hovered in front of me, a concentrated blaze of pink and white. At his side, a faint sliver of blue flickered. He wore a sword at all times, invisible to normal vision. He used a glamour spell to hide it from sight. My ability was so sensitive now, I could see through his sword glamour.

Above us, remnants of the Forest Hills control spell floated, a thin patch of sickly green essence with black mottling shot through it. Even though I had collapsed the main spell at the cemetery, fragments permeated essence everywhere, especially in the Weird, where it had been tested. Anyone with fey ability who touched the essence found their suppressed impulses provoked. The Weird was a cesspool of suppressed impulses, so the spell had ample opportunities to trigger bad behavior. As far as I knew, the only way to get rid of the stuff was a purging spell, and the only person who had been able to do that was Meryl Dian.

Joe shuddered. "That stuff makes me ill."

I wiped my hand across my mouth. "Me, too, apparently."

Joe laughed. "Remind me not to get drunk on port."

I forced my sensing ability off. The haze didn't affect me the way it did everyone else. The dark mass in my head acted like a firewall. I didn't need to see it, though. I could feel it.

"Carmine wants to see you," said Joe.

Carmine. A solitary. Solitary fey fall in two categories: clans of like fey in very small numbers and true solitaries, one of a kind. In Carmine's case, he's one of the latter. In certain places, he's known as a party planner. In less polite places, he's known as a pimp. We had more than a passing acquaintance in my youth. "I haven't seen Carmine in ages," I said.

"He said he needs to talk about a case," said Joe.

"He wants to hire me?"

Joe screwed his face up in exasperation. "I don't know. He wants to talk to you, not me. I'm thirsty again. Let's go find him and grab a drink somewhere," Joe suggested.

We stopped in front of my apartment building. "I've probably drunk enough tonight, Joe."

He looked doubtful. "What's that like?"

I tried to smile. "Maybe tomorrow."

He pouted. "Killjoy."

He vanished in a spark of pink. I inserted the key into the front door of my building. Joe popped back in. "For the record, Connor, you did your best, and Dylan needs to get over it."

I belched. "Thanks."

He waved his hand in front of his nose. "And for the love of everything, stop drinking port." He popped out again.

Between bumping into the corrupted essence and getting sick, I wasn't that drunk anymore. I made coffee and checked my email. Murdock had sent me a copy of his case report on the warehouse murder. The victim had a name: Josef Kaspar. He had a long list of petty crimes—loitering, shoplifting, breach of peace—typical of a homeless man of his age. I wasn't in the mood to review the whole file. The end of a long night wasn't the time to look at someone else's failed life.

My wooden desk chair squealed as I leaned back and gazed out the window. The lights of the financial district glittered across the channel. So many empty offices and yet so much light. Everywhere I've ever been, nobody turned off the lights in offices. It's as though everyone wanted to give the impression they had only stepped out and would be right back. Only, sometimes, through no fault of their own, some don't come back.

All through dinner, I had listened to Dylan's stories—the trials and tribulations of life in the Guild, the puzzle of a complex investigation, the satisfaction of closing a case. Over and over, waves of envy stirred within me. He had the life I used to have. He had the access and the power. The money.

My eyes sought a small piece of worked stone on the bookshelf that ran around the top of the wall of my study. Dylan had made it years ago when he was interested in stone carving. A smooth sphere fit snugly inside a larger sphere cut with Celtic knotwork. The inner sphere moved freely, and the knotwork had affirmations engraved in ogham runes. The one most easily read said *"Life is a series of trust moments."* After our worst case together, he gave it to me. At the time, I thought he was being overly sentimental, but it was one of the few things I kept when I lost almost everything else.

He had seen how a life could be snuffed out in a moment. Even though we hadn't spoken to each other in a decade, he knew what had happened to me. And yet, the ease with which he talked, how he took for granted what he did, gave no hint of anxiety that it could all disappear. No hint he could end up like me or, worse, a dead homeless guy like Josef Kaspar.

Maybe that was why Dylan had shown up. Briallen always said the Wheel of the World works the way It will. Sometimes It's clear, sometimes puzzling, but It's always what It is. Maybe It was showing me that I didn't have that life anymore, but I still have a life. I still do for a living what I did before.

Only I do it differently, without assuming essence abilities will make things right. I had only to engage my mind to figure out how to work with the more mundane tools I had now. But if I could do that and still have enough money to buy the couture sweater Dylan had worn tonight, I'd feel a helluva lot better about it.

4

The Fey Guildhouse loomed over Park Square like an eccentric fortress constructed of New England brownstone. The building occupied an entire city block and rose a full twenty-seven stories above the street, peaking in several towers that in turn sprouted their own little turrets. A series of balconies and ledges staggered up the sides, taking in views of Boston Common to the north, the harbor to the east and south, and the Charles River to the west. The higher up you went, the more important you were. At least that's the theory I used to subscribe to. Now I'm convinced the opposite is true.

Gargoyles crammed every ledge, nook, and cranny of the old place. They clustered in the front portico, clinging to the pillars and the spines of the ceiling vaulting. Essence attracted them, and the Guildhouse vibrated with it. They especially liked the roof, where they basked in the updraft of the building, and the main entrance, where they savored the living essence of people going in and out.

I paused under the dragon head above the main entrance. It's big, intentionally threatening-looking, and not really a gargoyle. Maybe in the old, pre-Convergence sense, when all carvings of fantastic people and animals were called gargoyles. But the dragon had no animated spirit, and that's what counts as a gargoyle these days. After Convergence, some of them, for want of a better word, woke up. No one knew why any more than anyone knew why Convergence happened. The 'goyles talked to people sometimes, strange mental communications that seemed prophetic but frustratingly obscure.

What made me stop, though, was not the gargoyles but the lack of them. Entire sections of the ceiling were bare. No one ever saw a gargoyle move, but they did move somehow. I had a hunch they were checking out the residual essence up at Forest Hills Cemetery. It had to be irresistible to them. More were almost certainly down in the Weird, tasting the strange drafts of twisted essence left over from the control spell.

The Guildhouse's stark entry hall felt chill from lack of sufficient heat. It was the reverse in the summer. It's not that the Guild can't afford to heat and cool the monstrosity. It's that they don't want people feeling too comfortable as they wait for help. And wait they did. More people than ever had problems only the Guild could solve, which meant more people left the Guild with their problems unsolved.

The line for help and relief looped back and forth through a roped queue that was longer than I had ever seen. I hated to admit it, but I used to laugh at those people. Now I'm one of them. Since the duel with Vize, which left me with the dark blot in my head and a monthly disability check in my pocket, my Guildhouse pass privileges had been revoked. But today, I skipped the public queue and used the shorter one to the right reserved for people with temporary passes or appointments.

I flashed my subpoena at the receptionist, a young elf with too much makeup who wore an ill-fitting rust-colored security uniform. The uniform was designed for the brownies who made up the majority of the street-level security guards. It looked good with their tawny skin and sandy blond hair. The elven receptionists, though, wore street clothes until security was tightened, at which point they were made to wear the uniforms. With her pale skin and dark hair, the elven receptionist didn't look happy with her outfit.

Whenever I got into the Guildhouse these days, I took the

opportunity to roam where I could. Certain floors were warded against unauthorized staff, but enough of the building was open that I could have some fun. That usually meant visiting Meryl Dian, druidess and archivist extraordinaire. We had had something going on for a couple of months, though I can't figure out quite what.

When the elevator arrived, a brownie security guard surprised me by acting as an operator. I nodded to him. "Sub-basement three, please."

He held out his hand. "May I see your pass?" I turned it over.

He returned it. "You're cleared for the twenty-third floor only, Mr. macGrey." As he faced the floor panel, I jabbed the SUBBASEMENT button, and we descended. He glared. "I'm sorry, sir, but you are not authorized anywhere but the twenty-third floor."

"I'm visiting a friend," I said.

The doors opened onto a long, vaulted corridor lined with bricks. The brownie held his hand against my chest while he pressed the 23 button. I placed my own hand on him the same way and pressed him against the wall. "I didn't say you could touch me."

I stepped out of the elevator.

"Sir!" the guard yelled. He threw a tangle of essence at me, a binding spell that settled on my shoulders like cold static. Brownies aren't that powerful, so I found myself moving in slow motion instead of stopping. Annoyed, I started to turn back, but the elevator door closed and broke the spell. I shook off the static and walked down the corridor.

Just before her office, I heard Meryl yell, "Muffin!"

Her office was empty. I continued deeper into the underground maze that led to the Guildhouse storerooms. At an open door, I stuck my head in with a smile. "Would you like blueberry or corn?"

Meryl threw a glare over her shoulder that relaxed into a grin. "Rat, actually. I need help."

Holding a malachite orb, she stood in a narrow aisle between wooden cupboards, many of which had gouges in them. Above her, a gold dagger hovered. I leaned against the doorjamb and crossed my arms. "Help. From a rat."

She closed one eye and looked up. "If I recall, Muffin helped you out of a tight spot once."

I smiled because it was true. "Do I want to ask what's going on?"

"C'mere. I'll show you."

She held out the orb. When I took it, my feet rooted to the floor, and the dagger swung toward me. I cocked my head back, but the blade came no closer than a foot. "Nice piece. Breton?"

Meryl leaned over a nearby case and reached her hand behind it. "Fifth century. You do know your weapons."

"Why is it pointed at my head?"

She wedged her whole arm behind the case. "It seeks living essence. It's like Thor's hammer, only I think it works with anyone."

"Thor's hammer," I said, dubious.

She waved her hand behind her. "Next aisle over."

I peered through a shelf to the next aisle, trying to decide if I was being played. I never knew with Meryl. Ever since we became friends—real friends, I think—she had shown me things in the Guild's storerooms I had no idea existed. When I worked at the Guild, I could have come down here anytime I wanted, but back then I didn't have a clue about what was there. Now I saw only what Meryl let me. She loved her job and was fiercely protective of her charges. "You have Thor's hammer?"

She giggled. "No, silly. I do have a sawed-off sledgehammer someone used in a robbery a couple of decades ago. Still has the robber's essence on it."

I examined the malachite orb. The essence charge produced a static spell holding me in place, one like the brownie tried to throw at me, only this one worked. "What exactly are you doing?"

Meryl tried to wedge her head into the gap between two

cabinets to see behind them. "Since the dagger seeks living essence, I had it stabilized with the aspidistra." In the wreck of the odd scene, I hadn't noticed the forlorn plant on the display case. "I used that orb as a ward stone to anchor the plant so no one would move it. Then I put an amplifier ward on the plant because its essence is so weak. I think one of the rats knocked the amplifier behind this case. It looks like the damned dagger has been trying to stab its way out of here for weeks. It almost stabbed me when I came in."

"And it's not stabbing me because . . . ?" I asked.

"Because I modified the orb you're holding to create a buffer. It wasn't a problem with the plant."

She threw off her center of balance so that her feet barely touched the floor. Since she couldn't see me, I made no effort to hide my enjoyment of the view. Meryl may be short, but she's got great legs. She'd probably use them to break my neck if I ever mentioned that out loud. She slid back off the case with a frown. "I can't feel it back there, and this case is too loaded with crap to move. I'm going to get another one."

I looked up. "Why do I get to stay with a crazy dagger?"

She stepped around me. "Because you're spell-stuck until I release it. I won't be long. Maybe."

I glanced around the room. Essence swirled around me in various intensities. The room had a lot of metal in it, the essence warping around it. Meryl apparently stored more than one weapon here. I felt sparks of what people called True essence, the residual signature of something pre-Convergence, direct from Faerie. True essence was rare. And Powerful.

Something rustled. I crouched to see if Meryl's erstwhile helper, Muffin the Rat, had arrived. An odd sigh sounded, and I bolted upright into abrupt silence. A slight vibration trembled in the air, as though something passed overhead. A glance upward showed nothing but shadowed shelves and dark ceiling corners.

"Hello?" No answer. A soft hiss, like the sound of air escaping, tickled on the threshold of my hearing. The thought of snakes flickered in my mind, but the room didn't seem to be holding anything to attract them. Unless poor Muffin wasn't as agile as Meryl thought he was. The hiss became louder. I startled at a flurry of unintelligible voices.

"What the hell . . ." I muttered. I tried to release the orb, but it wouldn't leave my hand. Now I knew what Meryl meant about being stuck. The voices trailed away. The sound of metal sliding on metal pricked my ear. I knew that sound. It's the distinct sound a sword makes when it's pulled from a scabbard. I heard the slight crunch of a footfall on grit.

I opened my sensing abilities and regretted it immediately. The heightened state of my ability picked out every mote of essence in the room. Colors raced in a rainbow of shades, so many overlapping that a touch of nausea hit me as they spun, colliding and separating. I couldn't sort out a damned thing, but I had sensations of movement, people walking the aisles toward me.

Despite the weapons in the room, none was close enough for me to grab. I considered the dagger, but I didn't know the full extent of its properties. It might have conditions I wouldn't like. My skin prickled as cool air wafted over me with a ragged sigh.

A voice yelled behind me. "What are you doing in here?"

The ceiling lights brightened, and my body shields slammed on as I twisted toward the door. The security-guard brownie from the elevator had his hand on the light switch, his eyes bulging in their sockets. Even the calmest brownies turned into a boggarts when prevented from performing their responsibilities. They became maniacal and didn't stop until they completed what they set out to do. This guy was managing to keep himself from going over.

I gave him a sheepish smile. "Hi . . . um . . . Meryl Dian asked me to help with something."

Since even my meager shields dampened my essence, the dagger swung toward the brownie's stronger essence. He stepped closer, one eye whirling up at the dagger as the other stared at me. "I don't believe you. What do you have there?"

I held up the orb. "This? It's a ward stone."

He held out his hand. "Give it to me."

I looked down at the stone and back at the brownie. Restraining a smirk, I held it out. "Okay."

His fingers wrapped around the orb, and the stationary spell slipped off me. I stepped away before he realized he couldn't move his feet. He twisted to face me, his eyes bulging fully. His cheekbones hollowed out, and his body began to elongate. "Get back here!"

"I'm sorry. I have to find Meryl." I closed the door against a shriek of frustration.

Meryl wasn't in her office, so I continued to the next open door. The room inside was well lit and meticulously organized, with shelves holding ward stones of different sizes, herbal jars with tidy labeling, and a wide variety of working tools, both fey and mundane. "I can't believe how neat your workroom is."

Meryl rummaged through a box on a table. "Yeah, I keep it pretty organized. I thought I had another amplifier stone ready, but I can't find it." She placed another box on the table. Flipping it open, she removed several finished bricks of quartz. They were high-end-quality ward stones that could be infused with essence to work or maintain spells. The ones from the box were new, so they had no charge on them.

"Do you ever hear voices in the storerooms?" I asked.

She examined one of the stones and fingered a chip in the veining. "Just the temp on his cell phone when he should be filing."

"No, really."

"Yeah, really. Bob spends more time trying to get a signal down here than he does filing." Meryl stopped shuffling things on the table. "Wait a sec, how did you get out of the storeroom?"

I shrugged. "I came up with a temporary solution."

She gave a sigh that fluttered her bangs. Meryl changed her hair color like other people changed their clothes. This week, the bangs were a rich brown. The rest was pumpkin orange, in honor of Samhain, knowing Meryl. Halloween might have replaced the emphasis of the old harvest ritual, but it kept the color right. "Thanks. I've wasted too much time on this already, and I'm so backlogged."

She pushed the box aside and came around the table. As she passed me, I wrapped my arms around her from behind and kissed the top of her head. She didn't move. Didn't tense, exactly, but didn't do anything comfortable like lean back into me or rip off my clothes in mad passion. She cocked her head to the side, fortunately with a smile, but still didn't say anything. Feeling awkward, I released her and followed her to her office. I dropped in the guest chair while she scooted behind the desk.

"Everything okay?" I asked.

She read something on her computer that made her frown. "Yeah, just busy. You must have heard about the hearing."

"Briallen told me." Her frowned deepened a bit as she continued reading. "Something going on, Meryl?"

She clicked her mouse and shook her head. "No. Briallen and I are having a disagreement about something, that's all."

"What about?" She raised an eyebrow that made me shift in my seat. "Fine. Don't say."

She leaned back in her chair. "How'd you get in this time?"

The various ways I gained official access to the Guildhouse amused Meryl. "The hearing. I'm scheduled to testify."

She dropped her head back and stared at the ceiling. Not amused. "I did yesterday. They want me back tomorrow."

"It didn't go well, I take it."

She rocked her head back and forth. "Ceridwen's a pompous bitch. She said she didn't like my attitude."

I compressed my lips. Meryl didn't take criticism well. Since she was already annoyed, I figured I might as well say what I had been wanting to say for the last couple of weeks. "You're hardly known as Miss Congeniality around here."

She scowled. "It's a job, not a beauty pageant."

"So quit."

She sighed again. "I would, but I like the job. I stupidly

keep thinking one of these days this place will recognize me for what I do and not be so damned political. The last thing I want to hear right now is that I'm cranky to work with."

I picked up a paper clip and tossed it at her. "You have been cranky lately."

She tilted her head forward, a healthy anger storm building in her eyes. "Lately? You mean lately, like since I was possessed by a drys and let it die and thought I watched you die and then thought I was going to die? That kind of lately? Or are we just talking this week?"

I felt a flush of heat. Between her words and the exhaustion in her voice, I didn't know what to say. Nothing bothered Meryl. Actually, everything bothered Meryl, but nothing usually penetrated. We made sarcastic jokes about Forest Hills. I didn't realize what lurked behind the jokes. "Meryl, I'm sorry. I thought you were talking about work. I wasn't considering what you went through."

She shook her head. "You don't remember it, Grey. It sucked. Now I have Briallen bitching at me, and Ceridwen prying into stuff that's none of her business."

A drys was a tree spirit, one druids held sacred, assuming their philosophy went in the way of worship. I wasn't so sure it was a demigoddess, but it was powerful and humbling. I did remember Meryl's being possessed by the drys. She looked amazing. She looked powerful. And scary. Then a cloud descended over my memory. I don't know what happened after that until I woke up with my face in the dirt. "I don't believe you let the drys die. Whatever happened, happened because it needed to."

She shook her head. "You don't remember it."

I leaned forward. "I don't need to. You would never have done anything that drastic if it could have been avoided. You did what needed to be done. I believe that."

The corner of her mouth dimpled. "That's the nicest thing anyone's said to me in a long time."

I smiled. "I didn't say it to be nice. What can I do to help?"

Again with the up-and-down shoulders. "Nothing. I'll figure out something. It's just crap that needs to be ridden out." She gave herself an exaggerated shake. "Okay. Pissy fit over. You look like you haven't slept."

"The dream. It's happening more than once a night," I said. The same dream had plagued me for more than a week. A stone fell through the sky, fell and fell, until it plunged into a dark pool of water. The impact made ripples that grew into waves. The air filled with mist and a sound like thunder. The images became confused, without any clarity, things moving and rushing and calling. The mist vanished, and two figures appeared in the distance, one all black and the other all red. They struggled, then there was a white flash and I woke up with the sound of screaming echoing in my head.

"I still think it's a simple cause-and-effect metaphor. Something happens and causes something else. Your metaphors tend to be pretty simple." Meryl was a Dreamer. She had visions in her sleep that told her things, sometimes things about people, sometimes things about the future. The visions tended to be littered with metaphors that mean something only to the people who have the dreams. Meryl was one of the few people who could consistently interpret her dreams. Mine started after my accident, but I never understood them until too late.

"What about the figures?"

She twisted her lips in thought. "Two many possibilities. You'll have to Dream more to understand if they're your generic symbology or a distinct message. They could be two sides of an argument or two real people or a past memory or a future struggle or . . ."

"Okay, okay, I get it. I have to figure out my own personal metaphors. At least I'm not seeing dead bodies this time," I said.

Meryl looked skeptical. "As far as you know. There is screaming involved."

I slumped in my seat. "You always have a way of looking at the bright side."

She shrugged. "Can't help that. It's my sunny nature. What are you going to say at the hearing?"

I pursed my lips. "Pretty much what I know. I think the part they'll be most interested in is the part that I don't remember."

Meryl leaned back again. "Lots of politics in that room. Briallen and Nigel Martin have a battle of wills going."

Before she became my friend, Briallen was my first mentor on the druidic path. Nigel took over after her. I used to think he and I were friends. Now I'm not so sure. "Briallen and Nigel have been bickering as long as I can remember."

Meryl grinned. "Pretty much everyone is angry with him except, ironically, Eorla Kruge."

"Eorla Kruge's at the hearing?"

Meryl's eyes gleamed with mischievous pleasure. "You didn't know? She got the Guild Director position. It's driving Ceridwen nuts. Eorla refuses to testify or recuse herself from the hearings."

That didn't surprise me. Nigel made some kind of deal with Eorla in exchange for her help at Forest Hills. When Eorla's husband was murdered, she became the most powerful elf in Boston. Even though she was a high-ranking member of the Teutonic Consortium, her politics were nuanced enough to let me like her. She had the deft ability to anger her elven comrades as often as their fairy opponents and still get what she wanted. I respected that.

I glanced at my watch. "Speaking of hearings, I have to go."

Meryl rocked out of her chair. "I'll walk with you. I need to go upstairs and get some supplies before anyone finds out the budget is being cut."

Out in the corridor, I slipped my hand onto Meryl's back and gave it a soothing rub. She didn't pull away. The elevator arrived empty, and she hit the button for the next subbasement up. I hit 23. "How do you always know so much about what goes on around here?"

She eyed me meaningfully. "Because the people upstairs

always treat their assistants like crap, and they tell me stuff while they're waiting for research."

Once upon a time, I was one of those people upstairs. "You are never going to let me live that down, are you?"

The door opened, and Meryl stepped out. "Not yet."

That was when I had my oh-shit moment. "Meryl?" She turned with a smile. "I forgot to mention—I left an angry boggart in your storeroom."

She swept her hands up under her bangs, as anger flooded her face. "I am going to kill you."

The door started closing as she stepped toward me. There was no way I was going to stop it. "Sorry! I owe you one!"

Her sending slammed into my mind. *Oh, you will owe me more than one. Trust me.*

5

The twenty-third floor of the Guildhouse existed in two different towers connected by a sky bridge. One tower held meeting rooms and the main elevator shaft, the other a few private temporary offices with a separate elevator for executives to whisk in and out. When the main elevator opened on the public side, Guild security agents blocked my way. With a queen of Faerie in town, they went for the full security package—Danann fairies in black uniform, chrome helmets, and take-no-crap attitude. I didn't pretend to be oblivious to the process. I flashed my badge and the subpoena without waiting to be asked.

An unusual array of the fey worked the hallway outside the conference rooms. Danann fairies and the lesser clans clustered in groups well away from elves and dwarves. True to their name, solitary fey kept to themselves. Neither the Celts nor the Teuts controlled or cared about them, the outcasts of the fey world. Fey on all sides sported visible injuries from the aborted battle at Forest Hills a few weeks earlier. Every time an elevator opened, all eyes shifted to the newest arrival, seeking a potential ally or noting a potential foe.

I had no time to suss out how the proceedings were going. Within minutes of my arrival, a brownie security guard escorted me to a table outside the door of the hearing room. "Weapons must be left here," he said.

Without my abilities, physical weapons were my only defense. I understood the protocol. Security was security. I pulled a dagger from each boot and placed them on the table. One was a simple steel throwing knife I had owned for years. The other was a druidic blade, laced with charms and spells, that Briallen gave me last spring. "I suggest no one touches these," I said.

The brownie wasn't particularly impressed with the suggestion. Everybody probably told him the same thing. He announced my name and escorted me into the hearing room.

A hearing at the Fey Guild didn't resemble a U.S. courtroom proceeding. The room typically had seats in the back for spectators, a lone chair in the middle for whoever was being questioned, and a raised dais in the front for hearing officials. If the person questioned had an advocate, the advocate stood. Fey folk seeking help subjected themselves to the will and word of High Queen Maeve at Tara. Maeve's law could be cold and nasty. Sometimes that was good. When it wasn't, it wasn't good at all.

The first clue that my hearing wasn't ordinary was the absence of spectators. The only people present sat on the dais and were among the most-high-powered fey in Boston. Since I wasn't being charged with anything as far as I knew, no advocates were present. I hadn't requested one, figuring it would look like I had nothing to worry about. For now.

Ceridwen was, in a word, a babe. Most people found Danann fairies irresistibly attractive. Part of that was glamour, spell-masking that enhanced their best features. Part of that was their Power. The Dananns considered themselves the elite of the Celtic fairies. Without a doubt, they ruled with that attitude. They were a damned attractive bunch with the firepower to cinch it, and Ceridwen was no exception.

She sat tall in the center of the platform, her diaphanous wings undulating on currents of ambient essence, points of light flickering gold and silver in the faint veining. Auburn hair burnished with gold highlights fell in waves down her back. Her eyes glowed amber with an intensity and depth that would humble anyone. Those eyes sent a shiver of awe through me. In a many-ringed hand, she held an ornate spear, intricately carved applewood worn white with age, tipped with a sharply honed claw. A silver filigree depicting leaves and apples wrapped the whole of it. On the shaft near Ceridwen's hand, ogham runes glowed and formed the words *Way Seeker.*

On her right sat Ryan macGoren, enjoying his status on the Guild board. We had had run-ins in the past that left me with a less-than-ideal opinion of him. Even other Dananns considered him ambitious, including Guildmaster Manus ap Eagan, who sat on the other side of Ceridwen. Manus looked in rough shape. He had contracted some kind of wasting disease that baffled the best healers known to the fey. Manus's suspicions of Ryan had drawn me into the investigation that had exposed the coup plot at Forest Hills. Accident, to be sure, but a damned good one. Given that he was suffering from accusations of failure, I had no idea if Manus blamed me or not.

To the left of the Dananns, Nigel Martin and Briallen studiously ignored each other. I suppressed a smile. Those that follow the druidic path by their nature were prone to debate. Briallen and Nigel epitomized those debates. They had been sticking me in the middle of their arguments as long as I could remember. I considered myself lucky to have had them as mentors, but I would be hard put to explain which of them influenced me more.

On the right of the Dananns sat Eorla Kruge, the new elven director. Eorla made eye contact with me and nodded slightly before returning her attention to the papers in her hand. I admired Eorla's intentions but doubted she believed she'd have much success at the Guild. It was and remained Maeve's creature, and no elf ever truly influenced the course of Guild policies in their favor.

Last, on the end of the table next to Eorla, was Melusina

Blanc, the solitary fey director. Melusina had a strange look, skin unnaturally pale with shades of gray, hair a tangle of silver tinted almost blue, and eyes so light the irises appeared white. Where Ceridwen's gaze made one look away from amazement, Melusina's did from discomfort.

If elves had little pull on the board, the solitaries had even less. At best, Melusina was a token nod to the existence of solitaries. The irony was that since neither the Seelie Court nor the Teutonic Consortium thought of solitaries as allies, Melusina's vote ended up being particularly powerful in close calls. No fool, she used it to gain help and privileges so often denied to her kind.

As usual, the dwarven director was absent. For complicated political reasons I never understood, they refused to attend meetings but did not give up their rights and titles.

Ceridwen stamped the base of the spear on the floor. "We are Ceridwen, Queen. We speak for Her Majesty, High Queen Maeve at Tara. Connor macGrey, Druid, you are hereby sworn to speak truth in matters addressed here. You may sit."

I took the forlorn chair facing their table. "Just Grey. I don't use the patronymic."

She gave no indication that she heard. "We have read your statement of the events of Forest Hills. Can you elaborate on what is not in the report?"

I tried to look innocent so I wouldn't appear uncooperative. Get in and get out was a good hearing strategy. "Could you be more specific?"

Ceridwen lowered her eyelids and softened her face with a thin smile. "We are Ceridwen, *Queen*."

I paused in confusion, then realized the subtle emphasis on her title. "My apologies. I'm not used to using royal protocol. Could you be more specific, Your Highness?"

Ceridwen's smile flexed slightly higher. "No. Proceed."

Cute. Ceridwen was on a fishing expedition. I decided to keep to the details of my original statement. "The blood of a living tree spirit called a drys was used to make a drug. The drug activated a control spell that would bind all essence—all of it, everywhere—to one person. That amount of essence couldn't be contained, and the spell fed on everything around it and grew. I somehow short-circuited it. I have memory loss from the event and do not know how I did it."

Ceridwen remained for a long moment with her head tilted to the side. "Tell us again of this tree spirit, the drys."

I shrugged. "There's little to tell, ma'am. Her name was Hala. She was the physical incarnation of the oak."

Ceridwen leaned forward. "And how do you know this?"

My eyes shifted momentarily to Briallen and Nigel. "I am a druid, ma'am. Sensing essence is one of the abilities the Wheel of the World grants us."

Her eyes narrowed. "Are we to assume that you believe this tree spirit can govern the use of essence?"

I saw where she was going. Ceridwen—and probably Maeve and the rest of the Dananns at Seelie Court—were spooked that druids could use a drys to gain controlling power over essence. If druids did, they could trump the power of the Seelie Court and risk the Danann's perceived superior status. "No, ma'am. I do not believe that. In fact, before she died, the drys Hala was horrified by what had happened. It was the spell that affected essence, not the drys. The drys's blood was merely the catalyst of the spell."

She nodded. "Explain."

I felt a flicker of essence from Briallen, as though she momentarily had activated her body shield. Then I realized what was annoying Meryl. Dananns were fey of the air. Ceridwen was looking for druid lore, which focused on organic matter. Even as a powerful Danann, she wouldn't understand the use of tree essence personified by the drys. I suppressed the urge to roll my eyes. The hearing was an excuse for another political fencing game. I answered her honestly. "I cannot, ma'am. I only felt the results of the spell, not how it was created."

Twin spots of rose appeared on her cheeks. "I see. Then can you tell us why the effects of the spell remain?"

I shook my head. "No, ma'am. The remnants of the spell

haven't dissipated yet. Others more knowledgeable than I might understand that."

Ceridwen stood abruptly, her eyebrows drawing together. "Druid macGrey, come before us."

I glanced at Briallen, but she did not meet my eyes. I did what Ceridwen asked. She positioned the spear between us. "This is the spear Way Seeker, the Finder of Truth. Place your hand upon the spear and answer us."

I stared into Ceridwen's fathomless golden eyes. I could refuse. Since I was born in the States and had never sworn fealty to Maeve, I was not a subject of the Seelie Court. I wasn't even a Guild agent anymore, which would have obligated me to follow her request. I brought a slow hand up to the spear. I didn't think I had anything to lose.

My hand closed around the spear. The silver plating and heartwood beneath pulsed cold. When I wrapped my fingers around it above Ceridwen's hand, more ogham runes flared into view below the first set. *Way Maker*. Another moment later, yet a third set of runes appeared. *Way Keeper*.

A subtle touch in my mind warned me I was about to receive a sending. From experience, I recognized Nigel Martin's deft touch. *I see the runes. Say nothing of them.* I had trained with Nigel a long time. No one in the room would know by looking at me that he had spoken in my mind.

Ceridwen cocked her head first to one side, then the other. She might not know Nigel had spoken to me, but she had enough ability to know something had passed through the air. "There is no private communication in our presence." She didn't take her gaze off me. "Tell us again, Druid macGrey. What do you know of the taint that infects the essence of this place?"

The spear glowed with a harsh golden light as essence shot up my arm. Sensing the surge, the dark mass in my head convulsed and deflected it. The essence shot back down my arm, and the spear flared. With a concussive force, the spear jolted itself out of Ceridwen's hand and threw her back in her chair.

Her eyes blazed with light as she leaped to her feet. "You dare!"

Baffled, I held the spear between us. "I don't know what . . ." I didn't get to finish. Ceridwen raised a clenched fist that glowed with white power. She brought her arm back to cast the essence at me. Briallen and Nigel jumped to their feet. With a shout, Briallen threw a protection barrier between us while Nigel held his own hand out with essence forming in it.

"This man's essence is damaged, Your Highness. I do not believe he intended anything," Nigel said.

Anger suffused Ceridwen's face. "Leave us. All of you but macGrey."

The other directors filed out with a mixture of sentiments on their faces. Eorla Kruge looked curious, while amusement spread on Melusina's face. Ryan macGoren had paled. Manus hesitated. As Guildmaster, I would guess he could insist on staying, but he bowed to Ceridwen instead. Nigel and Ceridwen locked gazes. She let the power ebb out of her hand. Only then did he do the same and leave.

Briallen moved closer to me. "Are you all right?" I nodded. She gave my arm a squeeze and walked to the door.

"Remove this protection spell," Ceridwen said to her.

Briallen lifted her chin. Yellow light danced in her eyes. "Remember to whom you speak, *under*Queen. You have no authority over me, Ceridwen." With an angry flick of her hand, the protection barrier rolled over and surrounded me completely rather than dissipating. Briallen slammed the door behind her.

Ceridwen stood in a cloud of essence, a barely contained flame. She held her hand out and said, *"Ithbar."* The spear jerked out of my hand and back to hers. "We are bonded to this spear. How did you take it from us?"

I held my hands out to either side. "I don't know."

She placed the butt of the spear on the floor between us. "Grasp the spear and answer us."

The angry demand rubbed me the wrong way. "I'm telling you the truth. I don't need to be compelled."

She took a step forward. "We are not asking, druid."

"I noticed. The answer is still 'no.' "

She took another step, and Briallen's protection barrier glistened between us. My body shields kicked in as essence built up in Ceridwen's eyes. Without Briallen in the room, I didn't know if the protection spell would hold up against whatever Ceridwen was about to do. I decided not to find out. I held my hand up and took a gamble. *"Ithbar."*

Ceridwen's jaw dropped as the spear wrenched out of her hand and flew into mine. It was almost as tall as I was, with a balance to it that felt like it was carved for me. I pointed it at her. "I may not know how to use this, but I'm willing to bet this nice, sharp point can pierce your body shield before you have a chance to throw that essence at me. Shall we test that theory?"

Ceridwen went white with rage. "This is treason."

I threw the spear to the floor. "I'm not your subject. Threaten me again, Ceridwen, and I'll give you more than your little toothpick to worry about."

I stalked from the room, leaving the door open behind me. Sweeping up my daggers, I secured them in their boot sheaths without pausing. People loitering outside the room tilted stunned faces in at Ceridwen. They drew away from me as I passed. Not the Guild security agents. Five of them blocked my way at the elevator. "Her Highness demands your attendance immediately," one of them said from behind his featureless chrome helmet.

"Tell Ceridwen she can call me and make an appointment at my convenience," I said. His body stiffened at my casual use of her given name. Nothing insults royals more than treating them as equals. I moved to step around the agents, but they shifted in front of me again. I glared at the agent who had spoken. "I am not going to say this again. I do not answer to Tara. Now move."

Manus pushed his way through the gathering onlookers, with Nigel at his side. "Let me speak to the queen," he said. He closed his eyes and frowned. If doing a sending over such a short distance caused him that much pain, he really was in bad shape. He opened his eyes. The security agents nodded and moved to one side.

I inclined my head toward Manus. "Thank you, sir."

He held my shoulder. "A small favor at most, Grey."

Nigel joined me in the elevator. When the doors closed, I glared at him. "What the hell happened in there, Nigel?"

He raised a calm eyebrow. "Technically, you insulted the High Queen Maeve via her proxy."

I frowned. "I *know* that."

Nigel smiled. "Yes, but this time she might actually hear about it." He extended a long, thin finger and pressed the elevator STOP button. "Now, you tell me what happened."

I leaned against the wall of the car. Nigel was healthier-looking than he had been a few weeks earlier, though more gray hair mixed in with the brown. The way he wore it swept straight back and falling to the back of his neck gave him an academic air. Academic he certainly was. He was also a powerful druid. He had been pushed to the limit at Forest Hills and almost died. "It's the thing in my head, Nigel. It rejected the compulsion spell from the spear, just like it resisted the control spell at Forest Hills."

He nodded. "Yes, well, you were difficult to compel even before you had that problem. But why did you knock Ceridwen off her feet? Not very polite."

"I didn't. At least, I don't think I did. I think the spear was reacting to what it perceived as my desire."

Nigel slipped his hands in his pockets and looked down at the floor. "Hmm. The spear. I think this spear is more than it appears to the Seelie Court."

"The runes."

He pursed his lips. "Yes. I could feel that they were made for druid eyes only. Those runes invest whoever holds the spear with the authority of law."

"Me? I'm not at that level." I had left my druidic studies long before I completed a mastery of law.

Nigel's eyes shifted back and forth as he considered the implications. "I agree. It's curious that it responded to you. It means you have the right to use the spear just as Ceridwen does, maybe more so because of the second runes."

I nodded. "She said it was bonded to her. When I called it, it came to my hand."

His eyebrows shot up. "It came to you? How did you know how to call it?"

I shrugged. "Ceridwen used the command in front of me. When I used it, the spear jumped to my hand."

Nigel's eyes wandered again as a slight smile came to his face. I'd seen the look before. He liked nothing better than a puzzle. "That means it's now bonded to you, too. If we can figure out the command for the second line of runes, the spear will surrender itself to you alone. She won't like that."

I sighed. "Why me?"

I meant it only rhetorically, but Nigel answered anyway. "These things follow a pattern of circumstance. The right conditions at the right time and the right person." Then he dropped a slight sarcasm into his voice. "Of course, Briallen would probably tell you it's the Wheel of the World, but you know I don't subscribe to such notions."

I shrugged. "Either way, I didn't ask for it. What about the other runes?"

"When the bonded holder of the spear holds it, everyone can see the *Way Seeker* set. Many spears like it were made for court purposes. They're not that rare among the fey. Maeve probably gave it to Ceridwen not realizing it was something more. When you touched the spear, I felt druidic resonance from the *Way Maker* runes. I'd wager that no one in that room but you, Briallen, and I could see them."

He stopped speaking, lost in thought. When he didn't continue, a suspicion came to my mind. I didn't think he knew about the third set of runes. "Successive sets take precedence over the last?"

He shrugged. "Of course. That's the way these things work. The spear responds to need. Ceridwen came on a truth-seeking mission, and the spear bonded with her on that level. If your need were only truth, the druid runes would not have activated, and you and Ceridwen would simply share ownership. For some reason, the spear is responding to your need for the rule of law. Full ownership will pass to you if we can learn the command word for the second set. If another druid has the need and knows the command, you would then share ownership with him. What doesn't make sense is you're not trained in the law. It's curious."

Again Nigel stopped speaking and confirmed my suspicion. He had not seen the blaze of essence that read *Way Keeper*. I pushed it one more time but in a way that I hoped wouldn't arouse his suspicions. "What about a third set?"

He looked up and smiled. "That would be extremely rare, especially on a spear of truth and law. Very little takes precedence over those two. A third set is feasible, but usually for a unique purpose."

Great. There was no way the spear reacted to my legal abilities. I always wanted to be the guy who hired lawyers, not the guy who had to take someone else's call. My gut told me the spear was responding to me for the third set of runes, which the spear or whoever made it decided I was the only one to see them. "I don't want it."

Nigel released the STOP button on the elevator, and the car descended again. "Just because it's yours doesn't mean you have to use it. It will come if you command, no matter where it is. What you do with it from that point on is your choice."

The doors opened on the main lobby, and I stepped out while Nigel remained. He held the door. "Do me a favor, Connor? I know you don't have enormous respect for the monarchy, but could you keep it reined in until Ceridwen leaves? She'll understand why I called up that essence, but she won't be pleased with me. I have much to do, and keeping her calm is difficult enough as it is."

A favor. Nigel Martin, my old, domineering mentor, was

asking me for a favor. Not too long ago, he would have told me to do as he said and expected me to do it. I guess the ass-chewing I had given him a few weeks ago had had its effect. "Not a problem, Nigel. The last thing I want to do is talk to Ceridwen again."

He sighed and pushed the elevator button. "That's what I'm afraid of. After what just happened, I'm sure she's going to want to talk to you." The doors closed.

Out in the afternoon sun, Briallen waited on the sidewalk. Two Guild security agents and a few brownie security guards made a not-so-subtle perimeter around her. Other pedestrians gave them a wide berth. She looked relieved when she saw me. "Walk me home?"

"Of course," I said.

Tension flowed off her as we made our way toward Boston Common. The brownie security unit stopped following when we moved through the tingle of the invisible shield surrounding the Guildhouse. The Danann security agents remained a few paces behind us. Briallen didn't speak. We crossed the street and entered the broad lawn of Boston Common. About halfway across the open green space, Briallen wheeled around to face the agents. "I told Manus I don't need security."

One of the agents inclined his chrome helmet toward her. "We have our orders, ma'am."

She set her face in annoyance. "I don't care what your orders are. I don't want . . . oh, dammit, I don't have time for this crap." She muttered something Gaelic and waved her hand at the agents. In the cool air, a puff of steam wafted over them. They both startled, then looked around in confusion. They turned and went back toward the Guildhouse. Briallen slipped her arm through mine, and we resumed walking. "That's better."

At the base of the fairy hill in the center of the Common, we threaded our way through a number of gargoyles in the grass. "That's odd," I said.

Briallen hummed agreement. "Yes, I find it very interesting. Gargoyles are sensitive to essence. I think they're sensing something about the fairy ring at the top of the hill. There are indications that a veil may form for the first time since Convergence."

Every year, a circle of flat-top mushrooms grew near the grassy summit of the hill. How the ring appeared was a mystery, one of those places that had been unnoticed, yet known for years. Who used it first and whether it sprang organically from the ground or was seeded, no one knows. There was a Power in the ring even human normals could feel. I've been seen a lot of fairy rings, and the Boston ring was one of the strongest. "That's wishful thinking, Briallen. It's just Samhain. They could be attracted to the increase in fey people performing seasonal rituals up there."

She stopped again. "Maybe."

She placed her hands on either side of my head and sent warm lines of essence into my head. "That's a relief. I was worried that damned spear did something to the darkness in your mind."

"I've bonded with it."

She shook her head. "I hate those stupid things. Nigel loves them, but in my experience, artifacts like that have a way of screwing up things."

I tilted my head down at her. "I seem to recall someone giving me a charmed dagger."

She gave me a friendly poke. "That's different. I *gave* it to you. Things like the spear work of their own accord. Some idiot puts a bonding criterion on it, and who the hell knows where the thing will end up."

After what Nigel said, I couldn't resist. "Maybe the Wheel of the World influences where it ends up."

"Yes, well, the Wheel of the World functions quite fine on Its own, thank you. It doesn't need some old druid making weapons that can muck things around."

We reached Beacon Street and crossed into the Beacon Hill neighborhood. Cheerful pumpkins and cats decorated doors and windows as we strolled past the old townhouses. Samhain was one of those holidays that everybody celebrated in some form. It had different levels of meaning depending on the culture. For the Teutonic fey, it was a celebration of the continuity of life. For the Celts, it was a more mournful affair of remembrance for those who had died. For both sides of the fey divide, it was the start of the new year. Of course, for human normals, it was all about candy. Given a choice, I preferred the candy.

On the sidewalk in front of Briallen's townhouse, she took both my hands in hers. "Listen to me, Connor. The Guildhouse is in absolute turmoil. I actually like Ceridwen, but I'm worried she's going after Manus. My suspicion is that she wants to replace him with Ryan macGoren because he'll be more obedient to Maeve. If that happens, I'm afraid it will fracture the board even more."

I cocked my head. "And I care about this because . . ."

She tugged my hands. "Because the Dananns are terrified of this taint on the essence here, and they don't want it to spread. You accidentally got in the middle of all this, and you know macGoren is not your friend. I have influence, but at a certain point, I may not be able to keep them from bothering you. They think you might be lying about what you know of the Taint. It was made by a druid and stopped by a druid. All the Seelie Court sees is a threat to its power, and when that stuff starts happening, people get hurt."

I brought her hands up to my lips and kissed them. "I promise not to poke or tease the Faerie queen, okay?"

She chuckled. "Don't make promises we know you can't keep. If I could make you go on a vacation right now, I would."

I swung her hands playfully. "No, really. I have an odd little murder case I much prefer dealing with. I will avoid Ceridwen completely if I can."

She nodded. "Okay, that I can believe."

I gave her a wicked smile. "Am I mistaken, but did you imply back in that room that you are peer to a Faerie queen?"

She laughed again. "Oh, I'm not implying. I am. Years ago, I was made an honorary underQueen for services rendered to the Seelie Court. Since Convergence, none of the underQueens and underKings have physical realms anymore, so I ended up on equal footing. See what I mean about criteria? You never know what the results will be."

I shook my head. "The more I learn about you . . ."

She kissed my cheek. "The less you know. Go solve your murder, sweetie. I have a political crisis to manage."

6

I waited for Murdock in what had to be the most run-down doughnut franchise in the city. I liked doughnut shops. They're one of the few places that cross all social lines. Everyone likes doughnuts. If they say they don't, they're lying. At a doughnut shop, you can get a sense of a neighborhood in ten minutes. And, of course, the coffee kept me alive. Murdock wouldn't be caught dead in one, but I didn't have a public image to maintain.

Murdock pulled up in front, and I left the shop. I tossed a tattered magazine off the passenger seat and handed him a cup of coffee as I dropped into the squalor of his car.

"That's going to cost you," he said, as I shoved the last bite of a glazed doughnut in my mouth.

I smacked my lips. "There's no other reason to go to the gym."

Murdock turned off the Avenue and down D Street. "Got a call down on Boston Street in Dorchester."

"That's out of your jurisdiction."

Murdock tapped the steering wheel as we waited at a red light. "Yep. Someone thought I might be interested. Even mentioned your name."

Boston had absorbed the town of Dorchester years ago, but it retained its name and its smaller neighborhoods. Some were nice, and some had pockets as bad as the Weird, only guns were the threat instead of spellcasters. Boston Street off Dot Ave was one of the nicer places, young professionals, decent restaurants nearby, and working streetlights.

We pulled up to a typical triple-decker—a three-level wooden building with bay windows that looked like it came from a Monopoly game. The usual assortment of police vehicles clogged the street. The front door of the building stood open, crime-scene tape flanking the steps. Uniformed officers kept the human normal crowd back. A plainclothes officer dressed in dark brown pants and a Red Sox jacket nodded at Murdock when she saw him get out. "Hey, Murdock, long time, no see."

Murdock gave her a wide grin. "Hey, Liz." There was a subtle shifting of eye contact between them that told me all I needed to know about at least one part of their past. Murdock has a knack for loving and leaving without trailing broken hearts in his wake.

Murdock jogged the short flight of steps. "This is Connor Grey. Connor, Liz DeJesus."

She shook with a firm grip I liked in anyone, man or woman. "Good to meet you. One of my guys was talking to one of yours, Murdock, and gave me a heads-up. I'd appreciate anything you can tell me on this."

As I joined them on the top step, the essence hit me immediately. Druidess, definitely, and a personal essence I recognized in particular. I looked over Liz's shoulder.

The open door revealed a small landing with a crooked area rug. To the left stood a narrow mail table, knocked askew, a vase of dried flowers on its side. To the right, a staircase went up to the second floor. Next to it, a hallway led back to an open apartment door. In front of the apartment door, the victim lay on her back like a discarded doll.

Liz led us in. "Olivia Merced, sixty-seven years old, single. An upstairs neighbor found her like this. He remembers hearing a door buzzer about seven A.M."

Olivia Merced looked fit and young for her age. By her

outfit, I guessed she had been dressing for the day when the door buzzer went off. She wore black dress slacks with a light blue T-shirt and a pair of fleece bedroom slippers. My stomach fluttered at the sight of scorch marks at the toes of her slippers. "Did she work?"

Liz shook her head. "No. According to the neighbor, she did mostly volunteer work. Check out her face."

Her head had turned to the side when she fell. I had to press myself against the staircase to lean over her without touching her body. Slashed across her forehead were six ogham runes. "Same as our guy the other night, Murdock."

I pulled back and rejoined them at the threshold, trying not to think about the pain the woman must have felt. "Same killer, too. The essence matches what I felt at the warehouse."

Murdock's eyebrows were drawn down. "What could a homeless man in the Weird have in common with a retired woman in Dorchester?"

My eyes scanned the hall. "As victims, they're too random to be random. No one kills like this without a reason. For one thing, you have to store up essence to do this. For another, it's exhausting. The murderer had a real motive to connect them. That makes them calculated executions."

Liz stared at me with a classic yeah-right look. Lots of cops did when I talked about essence or the fey or Faerie. It was easier to believe it was all something called magic, that there were no rules or process or limits.

Liz shook her head. "You know what the media's going to do with this."

I felt a little flash of anger. "You mean now that a nice old-lady charity volunteer bought it instead of just a homeless guy in the Weird?"

Murdock cleared his throat. "We're all on the same side here, Connor. Liz is only stating the obvious."

Liz gave me a tight smile. "Everyone's tense right now. Let's look at the bright side. With all the resources the mayor's pulling for security, maybe a little media attention might remind him there's still real crime out here."

I glanced at her with an embarrassed smile. "Sorry. Some people think I have a hard time not getting personally involved in my cases." With all the street fighting going on in the Weird the last couple of nights, the Josef Kaspar murder scored one sentence on the evening news. The one mention in the local section of the newspaper I found was an inside item. It's hard not to get aggravated about it.

Whenever a crime involves the fey, a report goes to the Guild. They're the best equipped to handle them. In reality, they picked and chose what they wanted and left the rest to the Boston P.D., which usually didn't know what to do with them. More often than not, most of the cases got filed and ignored. Especially if they involved the Weird. It's bad enough too many poor people don't ever see justice done. It's worse when officials claimed it was someone else's problem to solve. If it weren't for people like Murdock, people who didn't care where you lived or what you were or how much money you made, the Weird would have had no hope at all.

Murdock stretched his neck and sighed. "Okay then, we should start cross-referencing the victims, see if we can find a connection."

I wandered down the steps as he and Liz hashed through procedures. A large telephone switching unit stood on the curb across the street. It would make an inconspicuous place to stand with a straight-shot view of Merced's building. I kept my body language casual so that the scene gawkers wouldn't follow me. Sure enough, as soon as I neared the big silver box, I felt the essence. The killer had lingered there, using the box to hide behind. From the strength of the essence she had left, I'd guess she waited an hour or two. Again, I felt the strange layer of an essence signature that I could almost recognize. Familiar, but off somehow.

Olivia Merced lived on the first floor. The neighbor had said he heard a buzzer around 7 A.M., which would have been around dawn. The killer would have watched her lights come on and waited until she was sure Merced would be dressed to come to the door. That made twice the killer had shown up early and waited. Whoever she was, she was patient.

The metal surface registered several patches of the same druidess essence. She must have touched the box or leaned on it. I waved over one of the patrol officers and asked him to secure the area. It was a long shot, but they might be able to lift a fingerprint.

Murdock came down the stairs, and I joined him at the car. As I slid into the passenger seat, I gave Liz a wave, and she returned it. I took it as a sign she wasn't angry. "Old friend?"

Murdock didn't react as he pulled a U-turn. "Yep."

"That's all I get?"

"Yep." Murdock kept his social life close to the vest. I couldn't complain, though. I hadn't told him much about what was going on with me and Meryl.

We rode back to the Weird in bumper-to-bumper traffic, watching the neighborhood change from a livable stretch in Dorchester, to a desolate stretch under the Southeast Express-way and elevated subway tracks, and into the residential sec-tion of South Boston. Home once. Long ago, my brother Callin and I played stickball on those streets. Cars were fewer then, and more families raised their kids in town.

Murdock knew those streets, too. His own family lived down on K Street. His sisters had an apartment together nearby, but he and his brothers still lived with their father, who was the police commissioner. They had all joined the force, except Kevin, the youngest, who was a fireman. Public service had become genetic.

With a few turns through side streets, Murdock avoided the lights and ran a straight shot up D Street. As we neared the Weird, the streets got dirtier, the sidewalks more crum-bled, and the houses more run-down. Late-October weather made it all worse, with the vestigial front yards dried and patchy, and the few surviving trees bare. We slipped into the warehouse alleys and left South Boston.

Everyone who grew up in Southie and left says they want to move back there. But I had nothing to draw me back. My parents sold years ago and moved to Ireland, and my brother Callin lived who knows where. No, for me, Southie was just a memory. A good one, mostly, but not a place I could go back to.

Murdock pulled up in front of my building. "I'll send you the file when I get it from Liz."

I hopped out. "Trust me. We're going to find an obvious connection on this one."

Murdock gave me a crooked smile. "Yeah. It always works that way."

7

As I waited for Carmine to arrive, the cold wind off the harbor couldn't hide the odor of rot wafting up from the Fish Pier. No matter how often the loading docks were washed down, the parking lots swept, and the dumpsters sealed, the accumulation of years of dead fish permeated the concrete and asphalt. It was enough to put me off tuna. Only almost. If I knew how most of the food I ate had gotten on my plate, I'd probably be vegan. Clams might look like something hacked up from a watery hell, but, damn, they tasted fine with beer.

While you could find someone to pay for sex almost anywhere in the Weird, the Fish Pier was ground zero for it. That's what people came down here for. Only steamy windows kept the place from becoming an orgy late at night. If people could see what was going on in the car next to them, I had no doubt they'd join in. Car after car circled in and out, cruising the loading docks to survey the merchandise huddling against the closed doors of the truck bays. Someone would see something he liked, point his car at the bay, and flash his lights. If more than one worker stood in the bay, the regular johns had a system for flashing their blinker lights to indicate whom they were interested in. The seller would respond with a sending giving a menu and prices. If the john was interested, he flashed again, and they closed the deal somewhere else in the lot. The city could do little to stop it. There was no verbal solicitation to record, and no fey who could lure a john with a sending worked on the force. The entire situation drove the Boston P.D. crazy.

Because of the cold, Murdock offered to drive me to the meeting so I wouldn't freeze standing out in the frigid air. He slumped in the driver's seat, not wrinkling his clothes by some miracle. From outside the car, someone might think he was asleep, but up close, no one could mistake his alert eyes. I leaned against the door, trying to keep awake against the onslaught of heat from the vents. The temperature control in Murdock's car was nonexistent. Joe fluttered around in the backseat, singing dirty bar songs and making us chuckle.

"He knows you're here, right?" Murdock asked.

I nodded. "He'll be here."

Joe fluttered up and hooked his knees around the rearview mirror. He seemed to be into hanging upside down lately. "He'll be here. I had lunch with Carmine this morning."

"You had lunch in the morning?" I asked.

When Joe nodded, it amused me that it works the same upside down but wasn't nearly as nauseating to see when I was sober. "Well . . . wait . . . or was it breakfast last night? What do you call it when you eat at dawn and then go to bed?"

"Drunk pizza," said Murdock.

Joe laughed so hard, he slipped off the mirror and hit his head on the police radio. The whiff of alcohol on his way down told me there was pizza in his future. He crawled in the back, muttering about unstable car accessories.

"I got a subpoena from the Guild today," Murdock said.

Last spring, Murdock was hit with a stray bolt of essence during a fight with a crazed fey guy. He went into a brief coma, and when he woke up, his body essence had increased. Since then, he seemed to be some kind of living dynamo. He's not fey, though. His body essence still reads human, but what a human from Faerie might feel like. I don't know for sure. The humans in Faerie didn't come through during Convergence, so I don't know precisely what their essence would be like.

Murdock had been at Forest Hills. His strange essence had kicked in, and he plowed through the fighting like a bull-dozer. The last thing I remembered about Murdock that night was hiding in a grave with him hoping no one would kill us. According to Meryl, he was out cold when the big stuff hit the fan. "Don't let Ceridwen rattle you. She's only a mouth-piece."

Joe hooted. "Ha! Don't let her hear you say that. The underQueens all want to be High Queen, only Maeve knows how to keep everyone arguing with each other long enough to leave her alone."

"What the hell is an underQueen?" asked Murdock.

"It's a queen who hasn't figured out how to kill the High Queen without anyone realizing she did it so that she can get elected the new High Queen," said Joe.

I threw Joe an amused look. He threw his hands in the air. "What? You think I don't pay attention?"

A black stretch limo pulled in and parked not far away from us. Carmine liked to be careful when he met someone in private. If he's feeling safe, the limo will be in sight. If he's not, strange people start telling you you're trespassing. He's been elf-shot and stabbed more times than I can remember, so he makes sure he knows who's coming at him.

The lights on the limo flashed. "I'll be right back," I said.

I left Murdock in his overheated car and approached the limo with my hands out to the side, not so wide as to draw attention from the customers nearby but wide enough to show I didn't have a knife or gun. Carmine knows I lost my abili-ties, so while I've never given him a reason to fear me, he still prefers to know I'm not holding steel in my hand. People like him live longer that way.

The rear door popped open, thumping R&B rhythms into the night air. I slid inside. Two young fairies, a male and fe-male, slept cuddled next to Carmine while a solitary fey with green, scaly skin sat saucer-eyed, staring out the side window. Up front, beyond the closed privacy window, two dwarves watched the action on the docks.

Carmine lounged in the middle of the side seat wearing a gold lamé suit that matched his hair color and enhanced his crimson complexion. Even though he was a solitary fairy, he had no fear of any other fey. That told me Power lurked within him that he was willing to show. He flashed his row of tiny triangular teeth. "Connor, Connor, Connor, long time, no see. Are you looking to party?"

Once upon a time, I traveled in certain circles that enjoyed a good bacchanal, and Carmine often supplied entertainment. The fey have different notions about sex and drugs than humans do. We're not restricted by Judeo-Christian ethics for one thing. Most fey don't breed well for another. Recreational sex was much more recreational than human normals were comfortable with. As long as everyone has fun and no one gets hurt, pretty much anything goes, and when Carmine planned a party, the emphasis would be on the "anything."

"My budget's a little thin at the moment."

He laughed, a soft, high-pitched giggle. "Ah, when you lost your abilities, my friend, I lost a good customer. Welcome to my humble carriage."

Carmine's charm is so transparently insincere, it's hard not to be amused. "Thanks."

He sipped champagne from a glass flute, his eyes thin slits above hard, brick-colored cheekbones. "I understand you're looking into the death of Josef Kaspar."

It dawned on me that the warehouse where Josef Kaspar was found was near the Fish Pier, and the Fish Pier, of course, was Carmine's territory. Anything that happened in a radius of a few blocks, Carmine heard about it. "He turned up dead in a warehouse around the corner from here. Do you know something about it?" I asked.

Carmine hummed, rustling his hair with a few shakes. "Kaspar, poor thing. He dreamed his old despair would end in love, but his love ended in a dream of despair."

"You knew him, then?"

Carmine shrugged. "Not really. Like all of us, he was in love once. Like some of us, he let it defeat him when it wasn't returned. He did occasional errands for me in exchange for a little company from my girls."

"He died of essence shock," I said.

The ridge of skin above Carmine's eyes rippled. "Did he now? That's nasty. He didn't bother anyone I'm aware of."

"I think he may have been stalked by a druidess," I said.

A mischievous smile crossed his face. "We've all been there, haven't we?" He leaned forward and poured himself more champagne. He gestured at me with the bottle, but I shook my head. With Carmine, I couldn't be sure that alcohol was the only stimulant in the bottle. I wasn't in the mood for anything unexpected.

Joe took that moment to appear. *"De da, fear dearg!"*

Carmine flashed his tiny sharp teeth. "Ah, Master Flit, and how is your head this evening?"

Joe did a tight loop around the green solitary, who had not budged an inch. "Couldn't tell you. I'm keeping myself inebrilated."

Carmine chuckled. "Indeed, Master Flit. If we could all enjoy the world as much as you, it would be a finer place and I would be a richer man."

Carmine settled against the seat, sliding his bare feet onto the legs of one of the sleeping fairies. "A woman came around a couple of weeks ago looking for Kaspar. A druidess. Rather shady if you ask me."

Carmine's calling someone "shady" bordered on hilarious. "Shady?"

A corner of his mouth twitched in wry amusement. "She was slumming and thought she was getting away with it. Thought if she tarted herself up with secondhand clothes and a spacey voice, I wouldn't notice that her essence lit up like a lighthouse in a dead calm."

Joe wandered aimlessly around the floor of the limo. He was half-drunk when he showed up in Murdock's car, and the faint haze in the limo was making him stagger. He tripped and fell at the feet of the sleeping fairies and decided to lie there.

"Did you tell her where to find Kaspar?" I asked Carmine.

He shook his head. "No. I know she hung around for some time afterward. Either she found Kaspar on her own or found someone willing to talk."

"Why didn't you tell her?"

He took a long sip of his champagne. "That's why I wanted to talk to you. Strangers have been asking questions about people in the Weird. This woman was seen associating with these people. When I received word she wanted to talk to me about someone, I was immediately suspicious."

I shifted in my seat. "What do you mean by 'strangers'?"

Carmine licked his lips as if deciding whether to keep talking. "People of a distinct Teutonic persuasion, shall we say? They are asking for information about the Red Man. You can guess why that might give me pause."

He did pause, as if I needed time to notice his rich red skin tone. I thought of my dream of the red and black figures. "What was the druidess wearing?" I asked.

I couldn't blame Carmine for the surprised look on his face. "A ridiculous clown outfit of secondhand clothes. Why ask?"

A man wearing a gold lamé suit insulted by poor fashion sense can only amuse. "Just curious. Were these people maybe, um, unhappy with your services?"

Carmine shook his head with exaggerated slowness. "On occasion I have a dissatisfied customer, but not groups of them. Too many for it to be a coincidence and too many pretending to need my services. Naturally, it made me a bit cautious. They're not local, so it's either the Guild or the Teutonic Consortium. I only spoke to the druidess because I thought I might find out what was going on. Instead, I seem to have picked the one person who had her own agenda. I don't like hidden agendas that aren't mine."

I chuckled. "How do you know I don't have a hidden agenda?"

He stared at me with hooded eyes, so long that I thought he might be more drugged than I imagined. He broke into a startling smile. "Don't take this wrong, Connor, dear friend, but your motives are often transparent to me. One of my talents is to sense desires. When you wanted to make money, you made money and didn't care who knew it. When you wanted to get laid, you practically wrote 'one-night stand' on your forehead. And when you wanted to catch someone, only a blind fool would stand in your way. You always have your reasons, but you're not very good at hiding them."

I reminded myself not to ask questions I didn't want to hear the answers to. I was about to protest, in what I'm sure would have sounded a pathetic, self-defensive way, when a shiver of pain made me wince. The essence inside the limo became visible as my ability came alive. Carmine gleamed a shade of gold, while the fairies glowed pale white. The other solitary shone with dim blue light so faint, I wondered if she were dying. Joe looked his normal pink self.

"Did you see her alone?" I asked.

His eye ridge flexed. "I consider you a friend, Connor. Are *we* alone?"

"Then maybe you caught her off guard, and she bluffed about having an interest in Kaspar," I said.

Carmine showed his row of fine, sharp teeth. "And then killed poor Kaspar to cover herself? That's a level of deceit even I find impressive."

He had a point. "What would you like me to do, Carmine?"

He tilted his glass again in a toast to me. "Bear in mind, our druidess may have friends. Dig a little deeper, and I won't have to."

He drained his glass and stared, a hard glint in his eye. Carmine might have a party-man reputation, but he knew how to take care of himself and his business. I had no doubt that included eliminating distractions and threats to either. "I'll keep it in mind."

The dwarves in the front seat sprang into motion and hustled out of the car. Carmine leaned forward and stared out the windshield. "We have a little problem."

I peered out the driver's side of the car. Near the loading docks, the green and black of tainted essence wavered between two parked cars. An essence-bolt flashed in one of the cars. Carmine leaned back again. "Damned Taint. It's upsetting my staff terribly. We try to keep the trouble to a minimum, but business has been off."

Before I could say anything, Murdock ran across the parking lot. "Damn. Gotta go, Carmine. Thanks for the talk."

I jumped out. The green-black Taint danced on an eddy of wind that trapped it between the cars and the loading dock. The dwarves pounded on the windows of one car, while Murdock tried to see inside the other. Once I was away from Carmine's music, I could hear screaming.

An explosion of essence from the first car blew the passenger door off. It struck one of the dwarves full on the chest and knocked him to the ground. An angry fairy wearing only a short skirt emerged from the car. Bright flashes popped in her agitated wings as her eyes blazed a neon yellow. She shot into the air and fired down at the car. The driver inside ducked as the windshield shattered and a rain of glass showered in on him.

The fairy rose higher in the cold night air. She hesitated with her hands out. Confused, she faltered in flight as she flew out of the Taint. Her hands fluttered to her face at the scene below her. With a horrified cry, she descended to the loading dock, where her fellow workers gathered around her.

Screams grew louder from the other car. Murdock yelled to someone inside to open the door. Essence began to shimmer around him in a shade of deep red as he banged on the window.

"Murdock, be careful." I could see the Taint flickering around him, but it didn't interact with his essence the way it did with the fey. Or me. The Taint actually withdrew from me as I approached.

Murdock ignored me and kicked at the door. I rushed to the opposite side of the car. Inside, an elf straddled a human male. With methodical repetition, the elf swung his fists at the man's head and chest. I beat on the window, but the elf seemed in a trance. Joe appeared inside, a little unsteady on the wing, and buzzed the elf's head. If the elf hadn't inflicted so much damage on his client, it would have been comical.

Murdock let out a roar of frustration, and his essence blossomed crimson. He smashed the driver's side window with his fists, grabbed the door, and yanked it off its hinges. It skittered across the pavement in a shower of sparks. Murdock reached into the car and pulled the elf out. He tossed him away as if he were weightless. The elf screamed as he hit the ground and tumbled across the pavement.

Murdock leaned into the car. "Can you hear me?"

The bloodied man did not respond. Murdock stepped back, and he called on his radio for an ambulance. The poor guy inside the car was going to have to do some explaining to someone. Murdock pensively examined his hand as he listened to the garbled radio response.

I jogged over to the elf. He lay on his side, wearing only a T-shirt, an unnatural bend in his arm. He was unconscious, but breathing. I started to take my jacket off to cover him when Carmine's limo pulled up. The rear window descended, and I heard the trunk pop.

Carmine leaned out. "There are blankets in the back, if you would do the honors. Is he all right?"

I collected the blanket and spread it over the elf. "Looks like a broken arm, but he's alive."

Carmine put a cell phone to his ear. "I'll have my staff healer take care of it."

I had to shake my head in surprise. "You provide health care?"

The ridge above his eyes went up. "Of course. I have good people, Connor. It wouldn't do to have them out of commission for long."

Smiling at the absurdity, I walked back to Murdock. "Are you okay?"

He still had the thoughtful look. "Yeah. I feel like I've just gone on a five-mile run."

I eyeballed the missing car door. "Your essence surged. You get an adrenaline boost when that happens."

He didn't respond. "Murdock . . ."

He shook his head. "Not now, Connor."

I compressed my lips. All summer he had been in and out of Avalon Memorial as one fey healer after another examined him. No one could find any obvious signs that the strange change to his body essence was hurting him. But no one could figure out what had happened to him either. I found it intriguing because I couldn't tap essence anymore. If we could figure out what happened to Murdock, it might help figure out how to fix me. Not that I was being self-involved. I was worried about Murdock. The whole thing wouldn't have happened to him if it hadn't been for me. Briallen thinks I blame myself too much. Sometimes, she's right. Sometimes, I don't think I blame myself enough.

The few remaining cars pulled out of the lot as the sound of sirens drew near. Before any official vehicles arrived, a plain black sedan turned in. A dwarf hopped out of the passenger side, while a tall, elderly druid eased himself out of the driver's seat. They huddled over the elf. The druid's hands glowed white as he trailed them over the comatose elf. The essence winked off. The two conferred. The dwarf nodded, picked up the elf, and eased him into the backseat of the car while the druid returned to the driver's seat. They departed as an ambulance and a squad car arrived.

Murdock waved them over. He looked over at me. "Don't say anything to them about . . . you know. I don't want this getting back to my father until I've had a chance to talk to him."

I could live with a little omission of facts. Happens all the time in law enforcement. Commissioner Scott Murdock was riding the current anxiety against the fey in the city for all it was worth. Politically, he had managed to constrain the less-well-off fey in the Weird, leaving the more powerful ones alone. With the city on high alert, he was more than willing to let the Weird burn a little if it meant the rest of the city felt safer. The fact that his own son insisted on patrolling that same neighborhood galled him no end. If he knew about Murdock's newly acquired body shields, he'd go ballistic and convince himself that the fey were a contagious infection. He's the type.

As EMTs unloaded the guy in the first car onto a gurney, I left Murdock to handle the situation the way he wanted. I waited in his car while Joe snored in the backseat.

More emergency vehicles arrived. Carmine had to have someone on the police department payroll for this amount of attention. Help in the Weird tended to happen a helluva lot slower otherwise. Secrets were the true currency of the Weird, and, knowing Carmine, he had a long list of secrets that various people didn't want revealed. It wouldn't be the first time someone did favors to keep someone else quiet. But, like all secrets, eventually they would be revealed. Then all good hell would break loose, and it would be fun to watch the reputations fall. As long as one wasn't yours.

8

The Book Spine was a slice of bookstore on Congress Street. When I say slice, I mean slice. The place was an alley fill-in between two larger buildings, no more than a dozen feet wide. Inside, a checkout counter sat to the right and cubbies for bags and knapsacks rose to the left. You needed the cubbies if you wanted to move around without getting wedged between the stacks or getting a swift kick for bonking someone with a knapsack. There were only three stacks: the right wall, the left wall, and one down the center. The trick was there were five levels. Steep, narrow stairs at the back of the long floor let you up to the first three. The last two were open air. If you couldn't fly or levitate, you had to rely on the kindness of other browsers or an overworked staff person to lift you.

The symbols carved into Kaspar's and Merced's foreheads remained a mystery. I had exhausted my own library, and the Internet had offered little more than amateur sites. It's impossible to search for a rune if you don't have a name for it. The symbol had to be a sigil of some kind, either cultic or gang-related. Murdock was looking into the latter, but I jogged around the Weird enough to recognize most of the gang signs and didn't think that would go anywhere.

I picked up a small dictionary of symbols bound in red

leather. The copy was old, handcrafted inside and out. The cramped script flared here and there with essence. Sometimes, when a sufficiently powerful fey writes down a rune, one that needs to exist only as a sigil to activate its purpose, the rune activates. Whoever had written the dictionary had made a classic error by inscribing symbols. Nothing dangerous as far as I could tell, but not the smartest thing to do.

I tucked a larger tome under my arm, a cross-cultural reference on symbols in ancient religions. Depending on one's view, essence manipulation was either a science or a religion. I had come down on the science side for years, but that was before I met the drys. Druids considered the drys as the incarnate essence of the oak, and therefore sacred. They were something—some*one*—I had taken for a myth. The old tales from Faerie told of gods and goddesses, minor deities and sacred rites. For most of my life, I assumed they were glorifications of real people lost in the mists of time. Fey people, to be sure, but no more godlike than anyone else who could manipulate essence. After feeling the power of the essence of the drys, I had to wonder if I had been wrong all this time. I still wasn't sure.

A cell phone rang. It took me a moment to realize it was mine. After breaking my old one at the Kaspar murder scene, I had replaced it and forgotten I changed the ringtone, too. Before losing the call to voice mail, I juggled the books under one arm while avoiding knocking into a small fairy browsing next to me. I didn't recognize the caller from the ID, which was surprising since I don't give my cell number out to many people. I answered it, expecting a wrong number.

"I'll be damned. It is you," Dylan said.

The fairy next to me returned my courtesy by slapping my face with his wings as he reached for a book on an upper shelf. "Dylan. How'd you get this number?"

"Should I be concerned that a dealer in stolen goods has your private phone number?"

The undercurrent of teasing was so typical of Dylan. "I assume you are talking about Belgor?"

"Is that a guess? Or do you know more than one?"

I eased my way down to the narrow stairs. "Now, now, Dyl. I have my secrets."

"Mmm. I wouldn't have guessed. Yes, it's Belgor. There's been an incident at his store, and he says he will speak only with you."

I slid the books onto the counter and smiled an apology at the cashier. I hate when people talk on their cells when they interact with other people. "Sounds like Belgor. Has he been raided again?"

"No. He's been assaulted. At least, that's what it looks like."

The cashier rang up the books, and I handed him three crumpled twenties. The budget gets depleted this way all too often. "Is he hurt?"

"Banged up and angry. I'd appreciate it if you came down here and helped sort it out."

I gathered my change and purchases and walked outside into the dull light of the late afternoon. "I'm around the corner. I'll be right there."

I disconnected. Belgor was a snitch. A big, smelly snitch, but a good snitch. He had owned his store on Calvin Place for as long as anyone could remember. It masqueraded as a convenience store and curiosity shop. At some point, it probably was a legitimate business, but these days his profits all come from the back room. He knew how to play the legal game and cover his tracks, but that didn't make his wares any less stolen. He did a fair amount of buying and selling that could be considered aboveboard, but he wasn't particular about asking where things came from.

I walked the short distance up Stillings to Calvin Place, a one-lane stretch that ended one block away on Pittsburgh Street. It was best to keep your arm in the car when you drove through, or you risked catching it on a wall.

I stopped short on the corner. On the cold, shadowed side of the street, several people stood in front of Belgor's Notions, Potions, and Theurgic Devices. The shattered windows of the shop did not look out of place on the dilapidated storefront. Shards of glass littered the ground, but the biggest surprise was Belgor himself. The old elf stood on the sidewalk, his meaty arms crossed over a stained skintight sweatshirt that barely covered his swollen stomach. I had never seen him in daylight. Having done so, I wanted to scrub the memory from my brain. As I recovered from the surreality of his presence outside, his heavily jowled face swayed in my direction. I was surprised yet again by a streak of blood smeared beneath his greasy hairline.

Dylan stood a few feet away talking with a Boston police officer as well as another druid and a fairy who both had the look of the Guild about them. He wore a long maroon coat over one of his signature red-colored shirts, the current one a striped crimson. He gave me a broad smile. "Please ask him what happened. He's being obtuse and noxious."

I glanced over at Belgor as he flexed his long, hairy, pointed ears. "He can hear you, you know."

Dylan rolled his eyes. "Oh, I know. I've already told him to bathe if he wants courtesy. If he doesn't start talking, I'm yanking him in no matter what he says."

"First tell me why you're here," I said. I didn't want to make any promises to Belgor without knowing the circumstances. With the Guild involved, even if it was Dylan, there would be circumstances.

Dylan gave Belgor a sideways glance as he shot a sending to me. His voice slipped smoothly into my head, ten years' separation failing to erase the partnership groove we had. *The New York robbery. Our information pointed to this location as the likely spot for the transfer of the Met jewelry. We had the place under surveillance. Our agents were distracted by something and didn't see anyone go in. About an hour ago, the windows exploded and a woman ran out with Belgor hot on her heels. We're waiting for a warrant, so stall him some more to keep him outside.*

Since I can't do sendings anymore, I looked at Belgor as I chose my words. "Distracted?"

Dylan frowned. *I'll tell you later. Not pertinent, I think. I'd like to hear what you think, though.*

I grinned as I walked past him. "I'll have to bill for consulting."

Belgor blocked the door to his shop. He appeared wider than the door, so I half wondered whether he had come out through the missing window. The stink of onions wafted off him, competing with his usual bitter body odor. He had swiped at his forehead, smearing the blood and revealing a short gouge above the bridge of his nose.

I didn't like Belgor. He played games, played loose with the law, and played me for a fool at times. But he knew when to play for me instead of against me. He didn't like associating with me any more than I did with him. The fact that he told Dylan to call me meant he had information he would trade to make whatever had happened vanish. "Did you have an EMT look at that?"

He rolled his large lower lip downward. "Please, Mr. Grey. I've had worse cold sores."

I tried not to think about that. "What happened?"

Belgor's eyes shifted within their folds of fat. He looked at Dylan first, then the other Guild agents. "I had an unruly customer. Nothing more." At the same time, he did a sending. *I must have a guarantee of discretion.*

Though I'd never told him, Belgor knew I couldn't do sendings anymore. How he knew, like so much else he knew, I wouldn't venture to guess. "I'll do what I can to help you, but I need more than that."

He pumped his lips before speaking. "A woman came in and asked to purchase lottery tickets" . . . *It was an appointment* . . . "She seemed agitated" . . . *I was facilitating a transaction* . . . "I gave her what she asked for and she attacked me" . . . *I have something that the Guild may misconstrue.*

Now I saw his problem. Belgor dealt in stolen goods. It was what made him an excellent information source on occasion. He had years of practice and kept his crimes petty enough not to attract attention. But every once in a while, he moved something bigger. Back when I was an agent, I'd caught him a couple of times but didn't turn him in. Instead, I turned him. In exchange for information, I'd let the stolen-goods transactions slide as long as he moved the items back to their rightful owners. I wasn't with the Guild anymore, so I couldn't make him any promises. On the other hand, I owed him a little at this point, and if I could swing it, it would put him back in my debt.

"Have you ever seen her before?" I asked.

He shook his head. "Not that I recall, Mr. Grey" . . . *Perhaps a long time ago. There was something familiar about her.*

I peered over Belgor's shoulder into the shop. The setting sun illuminated shelves that hadn't seen real light in decades. I half expected plant life to spring from the thick dust. "Can I see where she attacked you?"

"I have asked these gentlemen to leave as I do not wish to file a complaint, but they refuse" . . . *Just you, Mr. Grey* . . . "I know my rights and wish to forget the incident."

I nodded. "I understand. But you know I'm not with the Guild anymore. I'm only a concerned friend."

Belgor checked the dubious smile that had begun to form on his lips. "In that case, I will allow you to pass, but no others."

I glanced at Dylan. He didn't say anything, trusting me. Belgor followed me over the threshold into the store. He waved a finger across the open doorway, then pointed it across the gaping holes of the windows. A thin streak of essence followed the hand. Dylan would recognize it as a trip-wire alarm if anyone tried to pass inside.

"At the counter," Belgor said.

He was too large to pass me, so I walked ahead of him down the main aisle. The faint hint of an ozonelike odor filled my nose. Essence-fire left it behind. As I came around the end of the aisle near the back, Belgor didn't need to tell me where the action had been. The next aisle had a long scorch mark across the floor to the front of the store and the missing windows.

The shelves to either side still smoldered from the heat of the elf-shot.

"She attacked you with no warning?"

Now that he had room, Belgor moved behind the counter, where he rested his thick hands. Except for the trashed aisle, that arrangement was how we usually dealt with each other. "She said, 'Die, betrayer,' then lunged at me with an essence-charged knife. I returned the courtesy with elf-shot that sent her through the window."

" 'Betrayer'? That's an odd word, don't you think? Do any betraying lately, Belgor?"

The sides of his mouth pulled downward. "I am in the business of trust, Mr. Grey. I would not knowingly betray a confidence."

I had my doubts about that but let it slide. "Let's cut to the chase. What do you have that you don't want the boys outside to see?"

Belgor didn't move, still considering how much to trust me. "Follow me."

He pulled aside a curtain behind the counter and entered the back room. I had been in there before. The ten-foot-square room was packed with junk and saturated with the charred-cinnamon stench of Belgor's body odor. It also hummed with essence. This was where he hid his more esoteric goods for a select clientele. A stained, sagging love seat sat to the left, facing a huge wide-screen television showing C-SPAN. DVDs of a different kind of sport littered the top of the TV. Belgor worked a strong market for porn that barely skirted below what even the fey would consider obscene. I remained at the door.

He lifted a shirt box from the side of the love seat. Looking at me briefly, he tilted the lid of the box open. A gold neck-ring known as a torc nestled in a pile of tissue. Torcs are neck jewelry favored by the fey, C-shaped and worn by sliding the open gap around the neck. The age and gold content of this one made it worth a pretty penny. The essence wafting off it—pure Faerie—made it more rare and doubled its value.

Any kind of original material from Faerie demanded high prices. Fey abilities worked better with it.

"Why didn't she wait until you handed it over before she tried to kill you?"

Belgor closed the box. "She wasn't here for the torc. She came for some jewelry. The torc was my . . . processing payment, shall we say?"

It didn't make sense to me. The torc was worth a fortune. "How much jewelry are we talking about?"

"Three fibulae, pre-Convergence, very nice quality, made of gold and silver, and a lovely ring, from Saxony, I would say, by its craftsmanship."

It was a decent list. Fibulae were old brooches used to clip clothing together. Old, as in the previous millennium. Still, the torc looked priceless. It had to outvalue the sum of the other items. "How did the deal came about, Belgor?"

His eyes shifted for several moments as he decided what to tell me. His risk. If he didn't tell me enough and got screwed by the Guild, his fault. If he told me too much and I could hold it over him, my gain. "A courier I occasionally work with told me he had an opportunity. His client did not want to conclude the transaction with him directly for personal reasons, but asked that I hold the material until she arrived. In exchange, I could retain the torc."

"You were directly asked for?"

"Apparently."

"And the torc was specifically offered as payment?"

He sighed. "Yes."

I shook my head. "You were baited, Belgor. You let your greed overwhelm your usual caution."

Nodding, he frowned. "So it would seem, Mr. Grey. I have not erred like this in many years. The question now is what we do about it."

I chuckled. " 'We'? I'm not seeing a 'we' here, Belgor."

Annoyance flickered in his eyes. "I believe I know the source of this material. It would be of particular interest to the Guild. I will pledge to you that I will find the name of the purchaser in exchange for helping my role in this unfortunate affair be overlooked."

Given Dylan's stakeout, I knew what particular Guild interest he might be talking about. "You know I'm not Guild anymore."

He smiled. "Yes, but you are not held in high esteem at the moment. Providing this information would go far to ingratiate you with your former masters."

I let slide the crack about former masters. "That would benefit me with the Guild. Why should I do this for you?"

The shrewd look from years of dealing came over Belgor. "I am sure we will both know that moment when it arrives, Mr. Grey."

We stared at each other in the gathering gloom of the store. The sun had gone down, leaving the sallow, dirty bulbs as the only source of light. The scene could have been any one of several Belgor and I had acted our way through over the years. This part of our interaction infuriated Murdock. While he understood the game of looking the other way to further the greater goal, Murdock thought Belgor crossed the line too often without consequence.

"Is there anything else in here you have to worry about?"

Belgor shook his head. "As I've always told you, Mr. Grey, I am a legitimate business owner."

I sighed. "Take it out of the box and mask it with a dampening glamour. Make it strong enough to last at least until tomorrow morning."

He didn't smile or gloat but got down to business. He flipped the box lid onto the love seat and gathered the torc in its tissue wrapping. As he muttered under his breath, little flashes of green slid off his fingers and wrapped themselves around the packaging. I opened my essence-sensing ability but could no longer feel the torc. A fey who could sense essence—and, more importantly, Dylan—would pick up nothing but the ambient essence of the Weird. Belgor handed me the package, and I slipped it inside my jacket.

I flexed a thin smile. "Let's invite them in, shall we?"

9

Murdock had arrived while I was inside with Belgor. He and Dylan eyed each other in front of the store with wary professional courtesy. The Guild and the Boston P.D. didn't have the greatest rapport in the best of times. With the Guild alternating between ignoring minor essence fights in the Weird and coming down hard on major ones, and consulting the police or the city on neither, these were decidedly not the best of times. They both looked relieved when I stepped into the street. "I see you've met each other."

Dylan extended his hand to Murdock. "I didn't realize you were that Murdock. I've read interesting things about you."

Murdock didn't smile back, but he did shake. Dylan didn't let it faze him. "You're in homicide, aren't you? What brings you down here?"

Murdock shrugged. "I work the Weird. I heard the words 'Belgor' and 'Guild' and figured something interesting might be up."

Dylan glanced at the Boston patrol officer who stood to the side. "I couldn't guess where you might have heard the words."

If there's one thing policing organizations hate, it's jurisdictional disputes. If there's one thing policing organizations love, it's irritating each other over jurisdictional disputes. The

Boston patrol officer had probably called Murdock a fraction of a second after arriving on the scene and seeing Guild operatives. Murdock looked at the missing window. "Belgor bite off more than he could chew this time?"

I leaned against the building opposite the shop. "Hard to tell. He claims a nutcase attacked him."

Dylan frowned. *You were in there a long time.*

I gestured to the store. "We can go in. He's just shy."

Dylan and Murdock exchanged glances. The problem with working with partners is they knew how you operated. They knew the kinds of corners you liked to cut. They knew what your sarcasm meant. And they knew when you were up to something. The look they exchanged said as much. It also said neither was sure how much the other understood me.

Murdock, I knew, would cut me some slack. He wouldn't push it in front of Dylan without knowing who he was and where things stood between the two of us. Dylan would be thinking the same thing. He would wonder how far Murdock had gone to cover my back, as he himself had covered for me in New York. Those were things I knew because I'd been partners with both of them and knew them just as well.

Dylan strode into Belgor's shop with an air of command. He kept a professional detachment that reminded me of someone observing a museum exhibit, *Late-Twentieth-Century Commercial Pigsty, with Elf.*

Murdock and I stayed out of the way by the counter. I had no official capacity to help, and Belgor wasn't dead enough to motivate Murdock to flash his badge.

While he examined the scorched aisle, Dylan let his underlings run the routine questions by Belgor. He scanned the space with an investigator's eye, stopping here and there to examine merchandise as if he were shopping. About three-quarters of the way down the aisle, he crouched. "Mr. Belgor, could you join me, please?"

Hearing that, I realized I had no idea if Belgor was his first name or last or only. Belgor moved up behind Dylan, blocking my view, so Murdock and I walked up the main aisle to the front and came around the other way.

Dylan pointed. "Is this yours?"

Belgor stretched his fleshy neck to see the item in question. In the kick space below a bottom shelf lay an old gold dagger with a black hilt. Dylan's question was moot. The dagger had elf blood on the tip and, given its freshness, Dylan and I had no problem sensing the blood was Belgor's.

Belgor's hand fluttered to his chest in mock-surprise. "Most assuredly not. You flatter a humble shopkeeper, Guildsman, to imply I could afford such a thing." He liked to pour it on thick.

Dylan gazed at me from under his brow. Despite the interference I had run for Belgor on occasion, the Guild had a hefty file on his history. Dylan wasn't naïve enough to think Belgor was anywhere near that humble. I didn't need to look at Murdock to know what he was thinking.

Dylan spread his fingers above the dagger. It rocked a bit, then left the floor. As Dylan stood, the dagger rose higher until it hovered above his hand. The light in the room gave it a soft glisten except near the tip, where Belgor's blood dulled the shine.

"Breton," Dylan and I said at the same time. We shared a comradely smile.

"I've seen its mate in the Guildhouse storerooms," I said.

Dylan let the dagger drop lower. "Can you sense the druid essence?"

I suppressed a small flutter of annoyance. I couldn't tell if he was asking out of curiosity or condescension. "It's druidess, if you want to be precise."

He let the dagger settle back to the floor. "You're ability is more fine-tuned than mine. I've never been able to sense gender."

I smirked. "No comment."

He met my eyes, and we both grinned like schoolkids. He

turned to Belgor. "I'm sorry, Mr. Belgor, but we'll need to search your shop."

Belgor backed toward the counter. "Sincerely, Guildsman, there is no need. She was a troubled soul to be sure. I have no desire to press charges."

Dylan slid his hands into his coat pockets. "Very kind of you. Unfortunately, we have to follow procedure. If you do not wish to cooperate with the investigation, you can discuss that later with an advocate. In the meantime, we should collect evidence in case you change your mind."

Belgor rubbed his lips and looked at me. "As you wish, Guildsman. I want no trouble."

Dylan smiled. "Good. Please let me know if you have any questions."

I didn't look at Belgor as we left the shop. Dylan stared at the slice of night sky above the small lane and tugged his collar up. "Getting nippy. Do either of you want to go for dinner?"

"I'm on duty for another hour, thanks," Murdock said.

I hesitated. "Sure."

Dylan extended his hand to Murdock. "It was a pleasure to meet you."

"Same here. I'll catch up with you later, Connor." Murdock shook and walked back to his car without another word. He's not big on the hello and good-bye. Dylan watched him leave without comment, not amused so much as curious.

A black car with Guild diplomatic plates pulled into the lane. Dylan opened the back door and slid inside, while I got in on the opposite side. A brownie in plain Guild security uniform manned the driver's seat. Dylan leaned his head back against the seat. "I'm starving. Do you like No. 9 Park?"

I snorted. No. 9 Park Street was one of the best restaurants in the city. Not liking the place was like not liking air. "Who doesn't?"

"You heard the man, Loddie. No. 9 Park."

The brownie pulled away from Belgor's shop.

"Interesting guy, that Murdock. Have you worked with him long?" Dylan asked.

I gave him a knowing smile. "Like you haven't read the files to know."

He smiled with warmth. "You were always better than me at asking a question you already knew the answer to."

I made myself more comfortable as Loddie pulled onto Old Northern Avenue. "So what do you want to know? He's a good guy, a good cop. He cares about what he does and doesn't like bullshit. He started asking me to take on consulting jobs when we met at the gym. That's about it."

"The gym? So you're friends as well?"

That was what he really had wanted to ask the first time. "Yeah, I'd say we're friends. We work out together and occasionally have dinner. We don't really socialize beyond that."

Dylan nodded. "And this Belgor. Do you work out with him, too?"

Dylan goes for a clueless dry humor that always made me chuckle. Especially because with him, more often than not, Dylan's faux cluelessness is not so far from the real thing. "The only reason Belgor would be in a gym is if someone wanted to try lifting him. He's an institution in the Weird. He could find out what you had for breakfast, and you'd never figure out how. Murdock hates him because he usually covers his tracks too well to get arrested. I tolerate him mostly. One of these days he'll go too far, and he'll end up spending time behind bars."

Dylan pursed his lips. "Fencing stolen antiquities might be too far."

I looked out the window. "Yeah, well, you'll have to catch him doing something like that. You never know, though, you might surprise you and help your investigation."

Out of the corner of my eye, I saw Dylan glance at me. "I don't think I'd be surprised at all." His tone was amused and matter-of-fact and confirmed he knew damn well something was up at the shop. I would have been disappointed if he didn't.

I didn't respond. The city glittered by, deep red and amber streaks of light on the other side of the glass. The soundproofing of the car kept noise from intruding. The seat—the luscious leather seat—gave comfortably beneath me. It smelled new. Every Guild car I'd ever been in smelled like new leather, always. I could smell the faint cologne Dylan wore—he still liked sandalwood apparently—and the almost dusty scent of the brownie in the front seat. I closed my eyes for a moment, and, for that moment, I felt like it was ten years ago, cruising around New York with my best bud, in the soothing comfort of a chauffeured car on the way to a party.

"We're here," Dylan said.

No. 9 Park is housed in an old townhouse on Beacon Hill. Its high-end design makes what would be cramped under normal circumstances feel cozy. The black-clad staff moves with polished smoothness, trained to glide in and out of service without startling the diners. Crisp white tablecloths glow against the muted taupe walls, soft candlelight warming the blemishes away from patrons' faces. Even though Dylan had been in town only a couple of weeks, it didn't surprise me in the least that the host knew him. When she offered to take my jacket—which in a place like that is more a subtle directive than a suggestion—I was relieved Dylan had his back to me so he couldn't see my face. He'd be suspicious if I insisted on keeping my battered leather with me. Left with no opportunity to slip it out unseen, I let the torc go with it. I doubted coat-check theft was a problem at such a place, but such things do cross your mind when you're smuggling stolen goods.

Dylan ordered wine and leaned back against the banquette. "I love this place. It reminds me of the city."

I chuckled. "Check the stats, Dyl. Boston is a city."

He twisted his lips in an exaggerated smile. "You know what I mean. New York misses you, you know."

I rolled my eyes. "New York misses nothing, and, before you ask, no, I don't miss it. You're doing well by it, though."

A waiter appeared with the wine. "It's been good," Dylan said. "The Guildhouse is a challenge, but I've managed to make my way."

I sipped the wine. There was a time when I would never

consider how much something that good cost. "Something tells me this assignment is a stepping-stone."

The edge of his lips twitched. "Of course. I get to use a visit to Auntie Bree as an excuse to further my career."

That made my eyebrows go up. "I can't imagine Briallen would be pleased to hear you phrase it like that."

He snickered. "She'd laugh and call me a naughty boy. She'd be hard-pressed to claim innocence as to where I learned to lie honestly."

I laughed, too. If Briallen had taught me anything, it was always to appear innocent to further my own ends. Of course, I had taken that too far and confused innocent with oblivious. People hadn't called me arrogant for nothing. Some still did. "So what's next? Department Director?"

Dylan lounged back. "Oh, I'm already that. I'm looking to move to a more elite position."

He was too young to mean Guildmaster. "Black Ops?"

He looked around the restaurant. "You know Black Ops are mythical, Con. It would be an exciting thing to do. If it existed, I mean."

I poked my cheek out with my tongue. "Of course. What was I thinking?"

The waiter placed a small collection of breads on the table. Dylan ran through several questions with him about the menu, convinced he was missing something, before making a final selection. The waiter topped off our glasses as he left.

Dylan's eyes shifted back and forth as he looked down. It was a behavioral tic that meant he was sorting through his thoughts. I remembered it well. He glanced up at me. "You know the Weird pretty well, don't you?"

"Sure. I live there."

"Have you . . . have you noticed anything . . . different lately?"

I exhaled sharply through my nose. "In the Weird? How about every day? Ask me what you want to know, Dylan."

"What do you know about the Taint, and have you noticed any particular people connected with it?" he asked.

I eyed him for a long moment. "This sounds like Cerid-wen's hearing."

He gave an indifferent shrug. "The Seelie Court is very worried about the Taint."

"Everybody is."

"Come on, Connor. You asked me to be up-front. Return the courtesy."

I sighed. "What we've been calling the Taint is the remnants of the essence from an out-of-control spell. It provokes hidden impulses and desires, usually violently. The only person who had any control over it is dead."

"Have you noticed anyone trying to control it?"

I knew my smile had an annoyed curl to it. "Only the Guild."

Dylan ignored the gibe. "What about the Teutonic Consortium?"

I rubbed my hands over my face before answering. "No, I haven't. Now, can I ask you something? I know you're loyal to both the Guild and the Seelie Court. If you're trying to understand the Taint, can you please not assume it has some nefarious Teutonic plot behind it? You sound like Nigel, and he let that assumption blind him to the truth."

He pursed his lips. "I'll let you in on a secret, Con. Part of the reason I am here is to track Teutonic spies. That part of my job led me to the Taint, not the other way around. I'm seeing a correlation. I'm not making any assumptions yet."

"Fair enough."

Dylan twirled his glass, watching the light reflect in the deep ruby wine. "You've had a rough time here."

I gave an embarrassed shrug. "It's been a roller coaster. I was pretty bitter about losing my abilities, but I think I'm getting over it."

Dylan's eyebrows gathered. "You keep saying you've lost your abilities, but you seem to end up pulling off some heavy-duty spells. You either have abilities you never knew you had or you sure as hell have some new ones."

I hunched forward, cupping my wineglass. "That's the big

question. Most of what's happened this past year seems lucky, but lately I've been starting to wonder. I know I'm blocked from doing lots of things I used to do. At the same time, I can do things I never could before."

"Like sensing gender in essence," he said.

I nodded. "Yeah. It goes deeper than that, though. Sometimes I can sense what species initiated a spell even if personal essence isn't left behind . . ." Dylan looked surprise. ". . . yes, exactly like a troll. I had a run-in with a troll not so long ago, and I seem to have gained a faint duplication of his ability."

"So, the question is, did you always have the ability to sense like that and never knew it, or do you have a new ability to absorb others' abilities," he said.

"That's what I'm trying to understand."

Our meals arrived, and the conversation drifted to reminiscing. We laughed over shared history as I ate quail with figs and steak au poivre. A decadent chocolate thing appeared for dessert. I relished every bite, marveling that I had forgotten how much I loved high-end food. Now that I knew about Dylan's relationship with Briallen, I understood where he had developed his taste for expensive port.

"Do you have many solitary fey here?" he asked, as I finished telling him about the odd essence I had encountered on my way home from Briallen's the other night.

I scraped little lines with my fork in the remains of the chocolate sauce on my plate. "Sure. More than most people realize. I certainly didn't until I started living in the Weird."

"Maybe a solitary you've never encountered before produced the presence."

I shook my head doubtfully. "It wasn't corporeal, though. With my essence sensing off the scale, I think I would have felt a body present, but it was more vague, like an afterthought. It was like fairy essence, but the whole thing felt random."

Dylan leaned on his hand. "This is the type of thing I was talking about earlier. Do you think it could have been someone using the Taint to create a spell?"

"No, it wasn't the Taint. I know what the Taint feels like. This thing felt odd and somehow directed at me."

Dylan took on a serious look. "You know, you're right. If I wanted to attack you, I'd send a blobby thing to point at you."

I leaned back and shook my head. "You're hopeless. How anyone promoted you is beyond me."

He wore the patented Dylan macBain rogue smile as he met my eyes. "Good luck and charm."

I smirked. "You're half-right."

Still smiling, he sipped his port. "Really? Which?"

I chuckled. "I lied. Neither."

When the bill arrived, Dylan didn't mention it as he slid a credit card into the check folder. There was no question who would be paying in that restaurant. Loddie waited at the curb when we came out. "Take the car, Con. I'm going to walk back to Auntie Bree's."

The sleek black town car idled in the chill night air that surrounded us. "I'm not going to object," I said.

Dylan laughed, then became serious. "Come to New York, Connor. Name what you want, and I'll make it happen."

I searched the sidewalk as though an answer might be there. "The Guild tossed me, Dylan. You'd have to expend a lot of political capital to do that."

He shrugged. "No, I wouldn't. I've looked at your file, Connor. Your expulsion is on a pretty technical point. The Boston Guild may claim they're afraid of the liability because of your loss, but they make exceptions to that all the time. Someone wanted you out. There's a smoking gun lying on a mantel somewhere. Come to New York. We don't have to abide by Boston's decisions."

I gave him a sheepish grin. "I'll have to think about it. Can I take a rain check on the offer?"

He gave my arm a squeeze. "Of course. Take as long as you need." He pointed at the car as he walked away. "Enjoy the ride, buddy."

His maroon coat swayed as he strode up toward the state-

house and turned the corner. Briallen lived a couple of blocks
farther. I slid into the passenger seat of the car. "Mind if I sit
up front, Loddie?"

His neutral expression didn't change. "Whatever sir prefers."

I snorted. No one had deferred to me like that in a long
time. As he drove me back to the Weird, I resisted the urge to
play with the stereo system. I slumped in the seat and let the
heat lull me into a doze.

Dylan could do what he said. He always came through on
a promise. I wouldn't be a full field agent, though. The Boston
Guild was right about one thing—my lack of ability would be
a liability in the field. I could leave Boston, set myself up as a
prime researcher. I would be willing to work for Dylan like I
never would work for Keeva macNeve. I'd be able to pay my
bills again. Have a nice apartment again. I let myself imagine
living that life again, racing around the streets of New York
in black cars and taking calls from power brokers. I could
have more tales to tell like the ones Dylan and I had spent the
evening reliving.

As the car pulled up in front of my building, a depression
settled over me. I could do all that, but it would leave too
many questions behind me. I had lost my abilities in Boston. I
had lost my memory here. I had lost a way of life I enjoyed. If
I went to New York, I would always wonder if I'd walked
away from finding the answer to what had happened. Maybe
I'd even be giving up the chance to figure out why it happened. It was tempting, yet . . .

But then there would be Dylan. I left New York because of
things that happened involving him, and he knew that. Despite
the evening and the ease in which we fell into our old familiarity, I didn't know if either of us could work with the other again.
And if I felt that, he had to be wondering the same thing. We
hadn't been partners for nothing. We had the same concerns
and drives. Well, up to a point. And that was the point I left.

"Sir? Would you like me to take you elsewhere?" said
Loddie.

I had been woolgathering while the car waited at the curb. I looked up at the crumbling facade of my building. "No thanks, Loddie. I think I'll stay home for now."

I let myself out, and he drove away. I felt rooted to the sidewalk as I stared at my desolate street. I pulled out my cell phone and hit speed dial. It picked up on the second ring.

"Hi. I really need to see you right now," I said.

"I'll be right there," Meryl said.

10

Sunlight crept into the living room, spreading across me as I sprawled on the futon. Meryl unconsciously moved into shadow. As a die-hard moon daughter, she preferred to revitalize her essence at night.

She looked at me intently, curling sideways. "So, you've told me what you loved about New York. You've told me what you love about Boston. But you've avoided what happened with Dylan. I think we've come to the point where you let it out."

I stretched and rolled off the futon. I turned away from her, knowing full well physically turning away was more evasion. I refilled our coffee mugs without speaking, putting sugar and cream in mine. Meryl took hers black. I handed her the mug and sat in the chair opposite the one she had occupied most of the night.

I sipped the coffee. "This isn't quite the way I pictured you in my apartment first thing in the morning."

She grinned. "Really? It's exactly what I pictured."

I shook my head, smiling, and sipped the coffee again. "Coffee's good, huh?"

Meryl propped her feet on the edge of the futon, her big, chunky thigh-high boots scuffing the sheets. "And the weather's lovely. Get on with it, Avoidance Boy."

I sighed. "Have you ever seen a Staten Island Ferry?"

She cocked her head at me. "Nope."

"They go back and forth from Staten Island to the Battery in lower Manhattan twenty-four hours a day. They're huge. The larger boats can carry six thousand passengers. The *Pride Wind* was one of the smaller ones, only about three thousand five hundred capacity. Still big."

Meryl dropped her feet to the floor and straightened in her chair. "You were there that day?"

I nodded. Everyone knew the *Pride Wind* and what happened. It was a major disaster averted, but still a disaster. "Dylan and I were on Governor's Island that morning running security for the diplomatic reception that never happened. We were checking the perimeter of the island when we saw the first explosion on the ferry. A Danann fairy from the Washington Guildhouse was with us, and he flew us out."

Meryl's jaw fell open. "Wait! You were *on* the ferry?"

I let my head fall back against the chair. "Yep. The records were sealed because of national security. I'm not supposed to talk about it. Anyway, the Danann dropped us on the stern, then went back to get help. We never saw him again.

"At first, we didn't know what had happened. Remember, this was ten years ago. No one really thought 'terrorists' then. It was in the backs of our minds, though, because of our security job for the diplomatic reception. We didn't know the reception and the attack were connected until later. The terrorists intended to blow up the ferry in view of the reception because they knew news crews would be filming. The reception was supposed to be outside, and the attack was supposed to happen as the ferry passed, but the terrorists screwed up their communications.

"After the initial explosion, the captain stopped the ferry. Dylan and I guessed something had blown in the hold. People panicked, pushing their way to the port side to get away from the smoke. We tried to keep things calm. We did sendings among the passengers to find more fey to help, but very few were on board that morning. Dylan decided to go to the bridge to find out what was going on. I stayed behind to keep the passengers away from the smoke coming from the starboard side. Then the second explosion went off on the port side.

"Chaos broke out. No one knew where to run, so people were running everywhere. I managed to get the crowd to go to the stern. That's when the bridge blew. The whole boat shuddered and began to list to port. It was hard to see through all the smoke. People were screaming and crying and fighting over life jackets.

"The next thing I knew, I heard essence-fire. I pushed my way through the crowd midships and found Dylan. Two fairies were attacking him, which confused me. I thought they were panicked or something, or that maybe Dylan had tried to press them into service, and they'd refused. Then they started firing into the crowd, and my instincts took over. I deflected what I could of that first barrage, then flanked Dylan and struck back at them. I was the more aggressive offense fighter, so Dylan let me coordinate our defense."

I paused, realizing where my need to talk about this had come from. Talking to Dylan, who was on the *Pride Wind* with me that day, and telling him about the strange attack in the alley had dredged everything up again. Maybe that was why I had gotten so down last night, given how it all ended in New York.

Meryl waited while I gathered my thoughts. "In the middle of all this, Dylan managed to tell me what had happened. The fairies had blocked his access to the upper decks and the bridge. They were lookouts, protecting three druids who were detonating the bombs. Unfortunately for them, preventing Dylan from going up to the bridge saved his life and sealed their own fate.

"When the fight started, anyone who could get away did. We had a large span of the middeck to ourselves. The fight with the fairies was at a stalemate until the druids showed up. They had good coordination and pushed us back toward the stern, where the passengers were."

I stopped talking but didn't look at Meryl. She kept silent

and let me have the moment. It was at that point in the fight that I'd made my first hard decision. I took a deep breath and continued.

"We were already outgunned, and still another fairy turned up. Six against two with no help coming yet. A couple of low-powered druids and solitaries among the passengers took occasional shots at the attackers, but they weren't enough. They were civilians. Office workers and families. They'd probably never used their abilities to fight like that in their entire lives.

"I knew Dylan and I couldn't protect the passengers much longer, so I told him to build an *airbe druad* behind us. I figured a druid hedge would at least buy us some time and stop the essence strikes from hitting anyone. Dylan couldn't split his essence to form the hedge and continue the fight. I couldn't let up my defense to do it myself. I had the command, so I ordered him to use the passengers' essence. That was hard. I had never drained the essence from bystanders to power my abilities. I had never needed to. It was the lesser of two evils at that point, drain them and hope they didn't die, or not drain them and watch them die.

"Dylan didn't hesitate. He trusted my decision and acted on it. He has an amazing command of essence control. Not a single person he tapped that day died from the spell. The entire time, he shot back at the attackers whenever he could. He was incredible.

"I kept firing. I deflected their shots, wove nets of essence out of them and threw it all back at them. They didn't give me a chance to rest, and I did the best I could to return the favor. We reached another stalemate. I lost all sense of time. I remember wondering why no one came from shore to help. When I saw the case report later, I couldn't believe that the entire event transpired over twenty minutes from the time the first bomb went off to when . . . to when it all stopped.

"When I thought it couldn't get worse, the strangest thing happened. Human normals showed up with guns. They weren't there to help us. They were with the fairies and the druids.

They fired at the *airbe druad*, trying to kill passengers. But Dylan . . . Dylan held the hedge. The fey passengers still standing did their best to help him.

"But we were losing. I couldn't stand much longer by myself. I had been forced all the way back to the hedge. Dylan blazed with essence, keeping the barrier up with one hand and firing at the terrorists with the other. He was burning out. The essence channeling through him was tearing him apart. But he didn't stop.

"Another bomb went off, the last one, but we didn't know that then. We both fell to the ground. The druids and the human attackers fell, too. The fairies were airborne and continued firing, pinning us to the floor. I managed to get to my knees.

"Something flew through the air toward me. I thought it was debris. I couldn't do anything about it without taking my attention off the fairies. Dylan shouted and pushed me out of the way. A second later, I heard this sound, this wrenching groan, come out of him. I knew something was wrong. He was sprawled on his back. It wasn't debris that had flown by me. It was a knife. A cheap, stupid knife. It had struck him in the chest, right in the heart."

I stopped speaking again. My face felt warm, my heart pounding in my chest as I remembered the moment. I closed my eyes, steeling myself to finish. I had told the whole thing only once and never said a word about it again, but I needed to finish it for Meryl. And for myself.

"I don't remember what the terrorists were doing at that moment. I just don't remember. I wasn't looking at them anymore. All I saw was this dark red stain pouring across Dylan's shirt, this dark red stain against a red shirt. The look of horror on his face is etched in my mind forever. I leaned over him. He reached up for me, his hands shaking uncontrollably. I will never forget the shock and fear in his eyes.

"Everything seemed to stand still. Everything seemed to fall away from me, nothing but me and Dylan on a blank white canvas. To this day, I don't understand how I knew to do what I did, but I must have released a huge pulse of essence into him. The next thing I knew, Dylan gave a strangled gasp. I had stopped his heart, frozen it in place, and shut his whole body down into a deep trance state. My own essence wrapped into his. I felt the pain of the knife, felt what he felt as he lost consciousness."

I was breathing faster, avoiding looking at Meryl. Heat rushed into my face, and I knew I wasn't going to be the stoic, emotionless man telling a story. I opened my mouth to speak, but closed it again. After another long pause, Meryl shifted in her seat. "It's okay, Connor. Finish it."

I met her eyes. They brimmed with tears.

"I killed them, Meryl. With a single, searing thought, I killed three fairies, three druids, and three humans. They were mind-linked to others, and I killed them, too. I killed fourteen people in an instant with my mind, burned them to empty husks. I saved over two thousand people that day, but I did something I can't ever take back."

Meryl didn't hesitate. She got up from the chair and curled in my lap. Wrapping her arms around me, she buried her face into the side of my neck. I felt tears on my cheeks, felt her tears on my neck.

I held her tightly against my chest. "For a few hours with Dylan last night, I really wanted it all back. But then what happened came back in a rush, and I didn't know what to think. I thought of you. I don't know exactly what happened to you that night at Forest Hills, Meryl. But when I saw you standing there, blazing with essence, I knew what you had to be going through. I knew and was horrified for you. Don't think for one moment I don't understand something of what you gave up that night."

Her body shuddered against mine as she sobbed. We held each other, and I rocked her, wanting to hold her against everything, keep out everything out that might hurt her. She brought her face up, vibrant red blush against her white skin, tears clinging to her eyelashes.

I closed my eyes. Our lips met and parted, and she didn't pull away, but held me tighter. Her hands gripped my head as we kissed, my arms encircling her as our mouths met, no more words, but a sharing of what we couldn't express. I stood, lifting her in my arms as she wrapped her legs around me. Refusing to let go, I lowered us both onto the open futon, tangling into each other, kissing and kissing until it was no longer a kiss but a hunger, an urgent need for connection.

She began to glow, essence coiling off her slick skin and surrounding us both in an aura of white light. My skin burned with electric intensity. The thing in my head shifted, a firm pressure against the back of my eyes, not pain, not pleasure. My body shields activated, but they didn't repel Meryl. They reacted to her essence and what I was feeling, trying, but not quite merging. I heard a high whining sound and it was me and it was Meryl and it was the power of our joining. The light filled my vision, urging me on, urging both of us, deep rasping breaths as we surrendered to the rush of emotion.

We sprawled away from each other. Chests heaving, we stared at the ceiling. My jeans were twisted around my ankles, and my sodden shirt had ridden up to my chest. Meryl lay with her boots planted on the bed, her skirt flipped up onto her naked torso.

"This isn't how I pictured it," I said.

She laughed. "Me either."

I laughed, too, like I hadn't in a long time. I rolled toward her and traced a spiral in the moisture of her cleavage.

She trailed her fingers through the thick stubble on my head. Neither of us spoke for the longest time, spooned together and lost in thought.

Meryl cleared her throat. "You never said why you left New York."

"I couldn't bear to hurt Dylan after saving him like that."

She rolled her head toward me. "Why would you hurt him?"

I looked into her eyes. "When I bonded my essence to him, I felt what he felt. I didn't realize Dylan was in love with me."

She propped herself on one elbow and leaned her face over mine, her crazy orange hair tickling my cheeks as she gave me a lopsided smile. "Gods, you're freakin' clueless sometimes."

I kissed her again.

11

After some clothing adjustments, Meryl and I dozed off a couple of times. The final time I woke up, I was alone. No note. She didn't return the messages I left on her cell. The lack of response was making me anxious.

I hadn't expected what had happened with her to happen. Sure, I wanted it. Her. But when Meryl wasn't dismissing my attempts at seduction, she was laughing at them. I was beginning to think her lack of interest was more than teasing. And yet, last night, when it was the farthest thing from my mind, when I felt so alone on the sidewalk in front of my building, she was the first person I thought of, and she responded. Never in my life had I had sex with someone out of grief. I didn't know what to think about it. It didn't give me pleasure or pain. Release. It felt like release, but from what I couldn't quite figure.

Maybe she was upset with me. Maybe she thought the whole evening had been a ploy to get her into bed finally or that I had taken advantage of her at an emotionally vulnerable moment. Maybe I was a bad lay, and she was in shell shock. I threw the last one in to amuse myself. I hoped.

Beyond all the anxiety of what the sex meant in terms of our relationship, I needed to talk to her about my dream again. It had changed. I still saw the stone and the rippling waves, but the two red and black figures at the end appeared to tangle and merge as they fought. In the dream, they were too distant to recognize any features that would identify them as real people. I couldn't tell if they were related to the stone or the ripples or even each other.

The next day, the door buzzer jolted me out of my chair like an electric shock. Unannounced visitors to my apartment were rare. I didn't live in a drop-in part of town. No one I knew who would visit me lived in the Weird, except maybe my brother Callin. He wasn't likely to ring my bell without calling. Given that, my anxiety spiked whenever someone knocked on my door. I was supposed to be living in a secure building, which was kind of a joke since my neighbors were art students and dwarves with crazy schedules. When the door buzzer went off, at least that meant the front door was closed for a change. I pressed the intercom button. "Yes?"

The old speaker crackled with a male voice. "Connor macGrey, Her Highness, Ceridwen, Queen, requests your presence."

When someone uses the "mac" in my name, it's a sign they don't know me at all. "When?"

"Now, sir."

I leaned on my shoulder against the wall. The hearing wasn't going to go away. The Seelie Court could drag it out for as along as they wanted, or at least until they were sure that I—or any druid—posed no threat to its power. The fact that Maeve had sent an underQueen to investigate showed how seriously she took the matter. A lesser queen to be sure, but still a queen. I pressed the intercom. "I'll be down in a minute."

My sweatpants and T-shirt were not much of a royal audience outfit. I swapped into black jeans and threw a black button-down shirt on and my usual boots, the ones that have one occupied knife sheath each. It wasn't formal, but I'd be damned if I was going to make myself any more presentable than that on such short notice.

The liveried driver waited outside my building. He opened the rear door of a limo for me.

"I prefer to ride up front," I said.

He inclined his head and closed the door. "As you prefer then, sir."

Even though I was basically telling him I was giving up the privilege of being pampered, he walked with me to the opposite side of the car to hold the passenger door for me. He guided the limo back to Old Northern and turned toward the channel bridge. A police squad car sat at the end of the bridge. The lone officer waved as we passed him.

Boston hates limos. The old streets are short and narrow and don't afford much turning space. People still want their luxuries, though. Two days ago, I had been in a black town car with Dylan. Now, I was in my second limo in as many nights. One could argue I was moving up. I knew better, though. Even when the ride is free, there's a price to be paid. Besides, I didn't think Carmine's pimp limo counted as moving up.

We didn't travel far but pulled up to the Boston Harbor Hotel. If I'd thrown a rock out the window of my study, I'd have hit the place. Before I could get out, another liveried brownie opened the rear door on the driver's side. I couldn't help smiling at the confused look on her face when she saw the empty backseat. I thanked the driver and let myself out.

The second brownie rushed to my side. "I'm sorry, Druid macGrey. The driver should have let you sit in back."

She hurried to keep pace with me into the lobby. "I insisted on the front. Are you my escort?"

"Yes, sir. This way, sir." Two more liveried servants flanked an elevator. I stepped inside with my anxious escort, and she pressed the floor panel for the Presidential Suite, the best rooms in the place. Despite its name, more royalty than democratically elected officials stayed in the suite.

The elevator escort turned me over to yet another servant in the suite's foyer. He was in what might be called uniform casual since he didn't have a cap or epaulets. If I'd been dealing with anyone else but a royal member of the Seelie Court, I'd have suspected someone was trying to either impress or intimidate me. But I knew the Seelie Court. They took this level of servitude for granted and didn't care what I thought.

The house servant bowed and left me in the living room. I supposed the room made some people feel at home, but it looked nothing like my place. The room was decorated in soft shades of blue and beige, with vaguely Asian accents. It had three sofas in a space larger than my entire apartment. The lamps had been lowered to let the harbor lights twinkle in the windows. Quiet music played, a traditional harp-and-flute melody that I assumed was meant to be soothing.

Ceridwen stepped into the room, stopping in front of the windows to face me with a soft expression that grew into a small smile. She wore casual clothing, a flowing tunic in rust with loose pants. She had gathered her hair in a loose knot at the middle of her back. "I'm glad you came."

I strolled to the center of the room, still taking in the surroundings. "I wasn't sure I had a choice."

She laughed, not loud but too long, as she turned to the wet bar and filled two small glasses with whiskey. She handed one to me, held hers up, and we tapped.

"*Sláinte,*" she said.

"And yours," I responded.

We sipped. She didn't say anything but stood with a slight glimmer of the whiskey on her deep maroon lips before gesturing to the sofas. "Let's sit."

She draped herself along the end of a couch, pulling her bare feet up off the floor and toying with her glass. "We seem to have gotten off to a bad start."

I leaned back into one of the other sofas. "Are we at the start of something?"

She smiled through another sip. "We offended . . . *I* offended you. I apologize."

I chuckled. "You must really want something if you're willing to apologize."

Ceridwen stared at her glass, perhaps deciding how to respond. "I am here for the truth of what happened at Forest Hills. No one here has been cooperative."

"Maybe you should try a little less emphasis on commanding presence and a little more on diplomacy."

She laughed again, this time honestly. "Yes, well, there is that. I'm not used to having my motives questioned. At Tara, the knowledge that I desire an answer is sufficient to produce results."

"This country has a problem with that attitude. We had a little revolution over it."

She nodded, continuing to affect a bemused smile. "Yes. I noticed you said 'we.' You consider yourself a citizen here?"

I leaned my elbows on my knees, rolling the glass between my palms. "I've never sworn fealty to Maeve, if that's what you're asking. Have you?"

She slid from the couch and retrieved the decanter. She topped off my glass before sitting again. "Of course. All the underKings and -Queens did after Convergence. It was necessary."

I eyed her over my glass. "Necessary, but not sincere?"

She pursed her lips in amusement. "Oh, I don't think you know me well enough to dare that question. The events of Forest Hills were felt at Tara. There was a dimming of essence. Do you really not remember anything else from Forest Hills?"

I shook my head. "No."

"What if I said I don't believe you?"

I shrugged. "What if I said I don't care?"

The appearance of amusement finally slipped from her. "You don't know what you're dealing with, Connor macGrey. A druid with no abilities means nothing to the players involved."

I smiled broadly to annoy her. "And yet here is a queen of Faerie serving me drinks."

She gave me a measured look, then turned on her bemused smile again. "So it would seem."

She rose from the couch and went to the windows. The music played as she stared off to the harbor. One of the ways

I can distinguish the difference between the fey and human normals is by the strength of their body essence. The fey have a more pronounced aura around them and, as Ceridwen stood looking out the window, I felt her withdraw hers into herself as much as she could. "Call the spear."

I stood. "Why?"

She didn't face me, but her eyes shifted to my reflection in the glass. "I want to see if you were able to take it from me because you were in a place of concentrated power. It's at the Guildhouse now. If it responds to your call from there, it's bonded to you."

I debated whether she was leading me into a trap. I couldn't see how it would be any more of a risk than walking into her suite. She didn't need the spear if she were going to overpower me. I lifted my hand. *"Ithbar."*

I felt the coolness of activated essence, and the spear appeared, cold and slick in my hand. The faint odor of ozone tickled my nostrils.

Ceridwen did not turn but lowered her chin. She held a hand out. *"Ithbar."*

The spear shivered out of my hand and into hers. I clenched my stomach as she turned and planted the butt of the spear on the ground. "We are not pleased by this. The spear is ours, Connor macGrey. It would be foolish of you to forget that."

"If you own it, tell it to ignore me," I said.

"This spear is key to the defense of Tara, Grey. Maeve is under threat; perhaps the entire Seelie Court is. If you interfere with our security, you could doom yourself as well."

"What threat?" I asked.

She compressed her lips, annoyance flaring in her eyes. "Bergin Vize. That is all you need to know. That should be enough to tell you the danger of Maeve's situation. I am appealing to your honor as a druid of our people. You must tell me how to control the Taint."

I wondered if the mere mention of Vize's name was expected to throw me into a panicked rage. Maybe a few weeks earlier it might have worked, but at the moment, Ceridwen's motives were too suspect for me to buy into it. "That's a pretty clumsy attempt to get me to cooperate. I've already told you everything I know. I know nothing more about the Taint and even less about the spear. You brought the spear into this, not me. I have no idea why it bonded to me, but obviously you don't have the control over it you thought you did. Don't blame me, and don't threaten me."

Her eyes went cold, the fathomless cold of an ancient fey. "We make a better ally than enemy."

As unsettling as her stare was, I wouldn't let it cow me. "So do I, Ceridwen."

I sensed her essence surge, but she held it within instead of releasing it on me. It ebbed away. It probably had occurred to her that a dead body in such a nice hotel would wreck the carpet.

A faint bitterness crept into her face. "You wouldn't last long at Court."

I gave her my back and walked toward the foyer. "Maybe Court wouldn't last long around me." ·

I let myself out. The liveried servant startled when I appeared at the elevator. He must have been expecting a sending to tell him we had finished. The elevator opened on the same anxious woman who had ridden up with me. "Sir," she said.

We didn't speak until we hit the lobby. I held my hand up and said, *"Ithbar."* The spear materialized in my hand. I handed it to the brownie. "Please delivery this to Ceridwen. Tell her to be careful; the point can be sharp."

I hated when royalty acted like royalty. It was why I never considered the diplomatic corps. Briallen might have felt comfortable playing their annoying games of privilege, but they made me want to hit the players. If I hadn't gotten the point across to Ceridwen that she couldn't intimidate me, she sure as hell would get it when her servant got back upstairs.

One of the lobby servants started to lead me across the thick carpeting toward the front doors. "This way, sir."

At the back end of the lobby, doors led out to the harbor. "No, thanks. I'll walk."

I strolled the dock overlooking the channel. Luxury yachts rested at the pier behind the hotel. In nice weather, the plaza hosted everything from movie nights to concerts to weddings. I could see and hear them from my apartment. Across the mouth of the channel, the Weird shimmered with a rainbow light of essence. I picked out the faint blue glow of my computer in the upper window of my dilapidated warehouse apartment. No boats docked beneath it, but a fair amount of sea wrack clung to the pilings.

I glanced up at the hotel. Either Ceridwen didn't have essence-masking security, or she didn't feel she needed it. I found her suite with no trouble. Her tall figure blazed as she stood at the window, the spear in her hand. I couldn't make out the details of her face, but I had no doubt she was staring at me. I continued along the dock.

A cold wind came up the channel as I turned onto the Old Northern Avenue bridge. It's a swing bridge that pivots to allow boat traffic. Rusted steel beams form trusses in a complex pattern that, depending on your aesthetic, is picturesque or an eyesore. Either way, it makes crossing the channel on foot convenient.

Someone walked in the roadway about midway across. As he came toward me, I noticed he wore a collared shirt and long pants, a little underdressed for the cold weather. He glared at me, like someone in a bad mood looking for an excuse to get into it with someone on the ass-end of town.

A gust of wind rushed from the harbor, stirring up sand and debris. Grit flew in my face, and I shielded my eyes against it. The wind moaned across the bridge, the many gaps and crossbeams in the trussing acting like a pipe organ. When the eddies of sand settled, I crossed the bridge. The guy was gone. I checked for essence nearby in case he was a drunk lurking in the shadows, waiting to jump me. Nothing. I chalked it up to his thinking better of it.

On the Weird end of the bridge, a police car blocked the road leading back into the financial district. A lone patrol officer wearing official outdoor gear stood by the car. We nodded as I passed. A car pulled up, and the officer signaled it to turn back into the neighborhood. Behind his patrol car, a police barrier had been set up with a sign that said BRIDGE CLOSED TO INBOUND TRAFFIC. I looked back along the bridge. I'd come across on the outbound lane and hadn't noticed anything unusual except the walker. My curiosity piqued, I retraced my steps.

"Bridge closed, sir," the officer said.

"I just walked over it. It's not blocked on the other end. Is it safe?" I said.

The officer kept a professional look on his face. "It's safe to walk on."

I cocked my head. "Are you saying I can't use it from this direction?"

He gave a curt nod. "No one can use the bridge to enter the financial district without clearance. Order of the police commissioner."

I exhaled sharply. "You're kidding."

A subtle change came over him, a hardening of features that cops get when they think they're about to have trouble with someone. He stared at me, not speaking. I smiled and nodded again. "Thank you."

I wasn't going to argue with him. The guy was only doing his job. If Commissioner Scott Murdock thought barricading the fey in the Weird was going to help, *he* was the idiot, not the poor patrol officer who had to enforce it. I shook my head. It was window-dressing security. Blocking the bridge might stop foot traffic, but plenty of fey flew and swam. The police would have their hands full trying to stop them.

I stepped around the police car, glancing back at the officer, the bridge stretching long and empty behind him. I paused again and looked back. The bridge was empty. The officer stared. "Move along, sir," he said.

"Did you see anyone else on the bridge?"

"Sir?"

"A guy on the bridge, walking out of the Weird. He didn't pass me on the bridge. Did he come back this way?"

The officer's hand nonchalantly dropped near his weapon. "You're the only person to come through, sir. Please move along. That's a direct police order to clear the area."

I held my hands out and down. "No problem, Officer. Thank you again."

I made for my apartment on Sleeper Street. Something about the guy on the bridge felt familiar. I have a good memory for essence signatures of people I know, but he had been too far away for me to sense him. By the time I reached my apartment building, I had convinced myself that the look he gave me meant he knew me, knew me and didn't particularly like seeing me. I didn't particularly like not seeing him then, not knowing where he went and why the cop hadn't seen him. I kept a sharp ear and eye out all the way down Sleeper, but no one followed me.

No fancy yachts or doormen or limos waited outside my building. The Boston Harbor Hotel glowed with yellow light across the channel. I didn't bother trying to see if Ceridwen was still watching. She had likely gotten bored by now and moved on to some other power scheme. I hadn't helped myself by irritating her, but at this point, there wasn't anything she could do to me.

If Ceridwen continued hassling me, I'd have to figure out a game plan to get her off my back. And if Commissioner Scott Murdock thought he could keep people from the Weird out of the city, he was in for a surprise. I didn't know what I would do, but I wasn't going to sit back and take it. I thought I'd let the two of them play it out, then cross that bridge when I came to it. And no police officer or Faerie queen was going to stop me.

12

Murdock lay on his back, sweat glistening on his forehead as he breathed with exertion. As I looked down at him, he gave me that smirk, the one that says, "Yeah, I can do this." His arms came up, his chest expanding with a last burst of energy, and he dropped the bar on the rack. Rolling up from the bench, he shot his elbows out and gave his body a twist first in one direction, then the other.

I slipped a couple of plates off each end of the bar and took his place on the bench press. He came around to spot me. Again with the smirk, he held one hand above the bar to make the point that he wouldn't need two hands to lift it off me if I lost it. I finished the set and sat up, running a towel over my face. "Are we going to talk about this?"

He grabbed the chin-up bar, lifted himself in the air, and talked without missing a beat in his set. "Why does everyone feel the need to 'talk about this'?"

I shook my head. "Aren't you the least bit concerned?"

He dropped to the floor. "You have one more set."

I lay back. The last two reps threatened to fail, but I would be damned if I let him get the satisfaction of pulling the bar off me. Again. I stood and stretched.

Murdock and I worked out together. It was how we met. Jim's Gym is low-key, on the edge of the financial district, just over the bridge from the Weird. It wasn't so far that I talked myself out of going and not so near that I obsessed about working out. Murdock didn't care where it was because he drives. He parks in front and puts his little "I'm a police officer and can park wherever I want" card on the dashboard. Once we started on a case together, we didn't discuss it during workouts. It kept some normalcy in our friendship.

We worked our routine at the empty end of the gym. Late afternoons tended to be quiet, and the only other people exercising were out of earshot.

"Murdock, you're bench-pressing twice your weight."

He stood at the dumbbell rack re-sorting the weights by size. "I know."

I leaned against the rack and crossed my arms. "I'm just saying, I think you're awfully accepting of it."

He gave me a lopsided grin and picked up a dumbbell set. "What do you want me to do? Go to bed and pull the covers over my head? I got zapped with an essence-bolt that should have killed me and instead made me stronger. What does it mean? Beats me. I can either accept it unless it becomes a real problem, or I can freak out. I'm accepting it."

He curled the dumbbells with little effort, as if he were only doing toning exercises. With fifty-pound weights. He replaced the dumbbells. "Want to see something?"

I gave him a noncommittal shrug. He faced a wall about fifteen feet away. One moment he stood still; the next he ran full tilt at the wall. Just before he hit, essence flared around him in a full-fledged body shield, stronger than most I had seen. My jaw dropped. He rammed the wall with a crunch, but the crunch came from the cinder blocks cracking. He wasn't even breathing heavy.

"How the hell did you learn to do that?"

He smiled. "Nigel Martin. He reached inside my mind and somehow switched on the body shield when he needed me to run point for him at Forest Hills. I sort of saw how he did it in my head and figured out how to do it myself. Cool, huh?"

I chuckled. "You know what you just did? When they figure out how to work their body shields, probably every fey runs into a wall to prove it. Usually they're about twelve years old, though."

He grinned. "I feel like a kid."

He pointed at the dumbbells, and I picked up much—much—lighter weights than he had. "Does your father know?"

Murdock scowled. "Now who's acting twelve? No, my father doesn't know. You know he doesn't like the fey. I'm willing to accept what's happened. He *would* freak out."

I let it drop. Murdock kept an open mind until he came to a conclusion. It took an act of Congress to change it after that.

Murdock had dinner plans, so I slipped on my running shoes and waited outside while he hit the showers. An inland breeze took the bite out of the air temperature. When everyone else starts wondering when the weather's going to change, it's already changed two weeks earlier in the Weird. Between the channel and the ocean, it's the first place in the city to get cold or muggy.

Murdock exited the gym smelling like a date. He wore his hair gelled, a department-store cologne, and his camel-hair overcoat. His eyes shifted left and right, taking in the immediate vicinity. I don't think the cop thing ever turns off for him. We jumped in his car. I tossed his gym bag into the backseat. "Where are you off to?"

He tilted his head to the side to watch the red traffic light he had stopped under. "No place special."

"Uh-huh."

He didn't change his expression. "Uh-huh."

One of these days, Murdock will tell me about his social life, and it will be a revelation. I can't complain too much. I hadn't said a word about what had happened with Meryl. As soon as I could figure it out myself, maybe I'd say something. He drove over the Old Northern Avenue bridge, waving to the cop on duty as we passed the checkpoint. We stopped dead in our tracks behind a traffic jam.

"How ridiculous is it that you had to escort me to the gym?" I asked.

He nodded. "I know."

"Can't you say something to your father?"

"I did. Didn't make a difference."

People gathered in the street a few car lengths ahead. Two elves, a fairy, and dwarf had tumbled into the street, blocking traffic and drawing a crowd. They were going at one another with fists and the occasional essence-bolt.

"What did he say?"

Murdock drummed his fingers on the steering wheel. "He said the Weird is a threat to the city. Pass the carrots, please."

"That's it?"

"That's it."

The brawlers looked awkward, as if they had never been in a fight before. I guessed that was possible, but not for four different people in the Weird. Murdock leaned on his car horn. "Two more minutes and my siren's going on."

"I feel like we should be eating popcorn."

He sighed. "We're seeing this almost every day."

My essence-sensing ability confirmed my suspicion. Green essence with black mottling wafted around the fighters. "They're in a cloud of Taint."

The two fairies hit the dwarf with a white bolt of essence, and he barreled down the street. The blow knocked him out of the Taint's field. He got to his feet in confusion. Taking a step back toward the fight, he shook his head, then walked away.

Murdock nodded. "We've been given orders to stand down if fights involve the fey. When the Taint hits, they lose control. A couple of patrol guys have ended up in the hospital."

"Your father must be fuming."

The corner of his mouth twitched. "Yeah, I'm kinda torn about that. On the one hand, I agree with his frustration. On the other, it's nice when he's in a froth about something that has nothing to do with me."

At least I could count on Murdock for some indignation about the situation. Even if it was the dry, sarcastic kind.

One of the fairies drifted out of the green haze and seemed to come to her senses because she didn't rejoin the fight. Her companion flew up beside her. They hovered in the air arguing. They must have both realized what had happened and flew off. The elf looked ready to take on someone else, but at that point the traffic began moving again, and we drove around him.

Murdock pulled to the corner of Sleeper Street. He stretched his right arm behind my seat and retrieved a folder. "Liz DeJesus found this in Olivia Merced's apartment."

The file held document photocopies of an old case dating back at least twelve years. I glanced at the first few pages, then at Murdock. "Merced filed for divorce because her husband was a con artist?"

Murdock nodded. "It gets better."

I flipped through more pages, but didn't see anything more than an exhaustive list of contempt charges detailing the case against Liddell Viten, Merced's husband. The last page held the "gets better" part. The Boston P.D. investigation had been suspended and the case turned over to the Guild. "The husband was fey?"

Murdock made the turn onto Sleeper Street. "Yep. He had everyone fooled with a glamour that made him appear human. His real appearance was anything but."

I raised an eyebrow. "A solitary?"

Murdock pulled up at my building. "Right again. Something called a kobold. There's nothing else in the archives because that's what happens when something gets booted to the Guild. I did some digging in the newspaper morgue. The Guild found Viten. He died in detention. Guess who was the Guild agent in charge of the case?" I shook my head. Murdock flashed me a self-satisfied smile. "Keeva macNeve."

I dropped my head against the seat. "Great."

"Now, I could go through channels and request the Guild file, which might take weeks . . ."

I looked at him. ". . . or I can ask Keeva."

He gave me an innocent look. "Not that I'm asking."

I laughed. "Oh, no, not that you're asking. Fine. I'll ask her. Just don't expect her to be all that forthcoming. Given her suspension, two dead human normals related to an old case she had a prisoner die on won't be high on her priority list right now."

"Guess you'll have to charm her." He pulled away.

I jogged up the stairs to my apartment, dropped my gym bag and the file, and ran down again. As tempted as I was to read the case, if I started, I wouldn't do my run. I needed to do my run. I used a telephone pole to do some warm-up stretches.

Running at night in the Weird was more common than one would think. Most of the time, though, healthy exercise was not the reason unless you counted running for your life. If someone is moving fast down here, they're either running from someone or after someone. It attracted attention, if only from spectators waiting to see if a fight would break out. Lately, that's becoming more the case. If the Boston P.D. was avoiding the essence battles, the Guild still had security agents patrolling the skies. They interfered only when large groups gathered, but other than that, they were more for show.

I decided on a short route, taking the straight shot up Old Northern Avenue. "Oh No," as the locals called it, was in its commuter mode. It didn't have the rush-hour jams of other parts of the city because the Weird isn't a shortcut to anywhere except maybe Southie. Office workers wandered down after to work for an esoteric errand. The few restaurants that the mainstream knew about had their Samhain specials running. Early Halloween parties would rev up later in the evening, and the neighborhood would do brisk business.

I made it to Harbor Street without incident. I passed the boarded-up offices of Unity, a neighborhood help center that had closed with the murder of its founder, Alvud Kruge. After his widow, Eorla, joined the Guild board as his replacement, the help center had closed. This Samhain would be tough going for her. I didn't know her well, but I knew she loved her husband and missed him. Between that and her recent travails with the Guild, she had a lot to put behind her.

To shake up the run, I chose an alley route back. The alleys were the most unsafe parts of the Weird—but they made a fun run if you were vigilant and kept out of them too late at night. Lanes weaved in and out and appeared to go nowhere, only to open up into more twists and turns. It was early enough that I wasn't likely to run into anything nefarious.

The back sides of warehouses sported a riot of graffiti. All of the Weird was gang territory to some extent, and gang members tagged the walls with their sigils to warn off rivals. Lately, the gangs had been in transition. Lots of strife from recent deaths and retaliations. New symbols had cropped up in the past few weeks, blotting out the old, challenging the existing rulers of the streets. The Taint wasn't helping. New gangs formed, old ones merged, but the rivalries were still the same old petty posturing and grievances.

The alleys represented what people feared about the Weird, the signs of decay that threaten an entire city. Politicians claimed that the poverty and danger down here made the well-meaning citizens of the city vulnerable, which was why they did stupid things like put up police checkpoints. In reality, poverty and danger were filling the void left when prosperity and hope receded. The battered warehouses stood as forlorn reminders of better times. Shattered glass littered the ground, the evidence of windows no one cared to maintain or replace. It was all part of the life-and-death cycle of a neighborhood. What had once been vibrant and alive was now dark and still. Someday it will change course, but not today and not soon. And as with all cycles of change, pain would feed the process.

I heard the first whisper about a quarter mile from home. When you're running, and you hear a whisper, you know it's not natural. I reached a desolate stretch of alley paralleling Stillings Street, a dumpster-lined gauntlet behind bars that catered to the down-market crowd. At first, I thought it was the wind. Then it became louder, words on the edge of hearing. My skin prickled, and I slowed to a light jog.

The alley angled in such a way that I couldn't see far in either direction. A limp breeze moved, barely enough to rustle the papers and garbage that lined the building foundations. The whispers rose, a run-on of voices tripping over one another almost rhythmically, like they had that morning in the Guild-house storeroom. I turned in place, trying to locate the source of the essence. Nothing registered. The whispers faded.

I started running again. My skin prickled, and I had the sensation of someone coming up behind me. I dodged to the right and flattened myself against a wall between piles of trash. Empty alley. Not a sign of anyone. In my peripheral vision, flickers of essence moved, but whenever I looked toward them, they vanished.

I felt foolish, jumping at shadows among shadows. The whispers resumed, rising and falling in a pained cadence. Twice I jogged backwards a few feet, and still saw no one. The strange sensation faded. I relaxed, chalking it up to the general atmosphere. The Weird has a history and sometimes it likes to remind people. On the corner of the last block before my apartment, I skidded to a halt.

A fairy hovered in the air in front of me, his face suffused with anger. He blazed with an indigo essence, so intense he looked translucent. It took me a moment to realize he was an Inverni, a powerful clan the Dananns had conquered when they took over the Seelie Court.

The temperature dropped as the field of his essence swirled near. He folded his sharp wings back and dove at me. I threw myself to the ground as he swept over. My body shields flickered on, small patches of hardened essence softening my impact with the asphalt, but not by much.

I scrambled to my feet. My body shields were no defense against an Inverni. I ran, knowing it was pointless. I couldn't outrun him, but I didn't want to be another dead body in an alley in the Weird. The main avenue was less than a block away. My lungs burned with cold air as I sprinted, hoping he would leave me alone in front of witnesses.

He came up behind me, his essence preceding him like a

fog. At the end of the alley, he hit me between the shoulder blades. Pain lanced through my torso as something pierced my spine, burning with cold fire. I stumbled against a wall, unable to draw breath. The pain intensified, and I watched in shock as the Inverni emerged from my chest. His forward momentum carried him into the air. He looked back at me with hatred and faded from view.

Clutching at the sore spot in my chest, I staggered the last few feet to Old Northern Avenue. Reality reasserted itself in a blare of traffic noise. People walked by as if nothing were amiss. I gulped for air, easing the tension in my lungs. My sweat-damp face felt cold as I made my way on unsteady feet to Sleeper Street. Leaning against a light pole, I glanced back. No one took an interest in me, no furtive looks or unnatural nonchalance. I had been attacked, and no one had seen it.

Baffled, I walked the last stretch of sidewalk to my apartment. Inverni fairies couldn't make themselves intangible. And they didn't teleport like flits. I had no idea what to make of it. Whatever mess the Taint was creating with essence was getting worse if stuff like this was happening.

I scanned the empty street one more time. Whoever it was had vanished. The security ward snapped into place as I closed the vestibule door behind me. It didn't make me feel any more secure. If someone could literally slip through my body, I had my doubts a warding spell would keep anything out of my building.

13

The only thing more surprising than getting an appointment with Keeva macNeve on short notice was getting an appointment that did not require me to get up before noon. I wasn't a morning person, and I didn't apologize for it. Keeva, on the other hand, played the corporate game and was at her desk before most people got out of bed. She liked rules. That didn't mean she always followed them. She's more subtle about getting around them. Me, I break them if they're in the way.

As I crossed the central lobby, the line for help looked like it hadn't moved since the day of the hearing. But that was cynical. The line had moved at least twenty feet.

In the two years since my accident with Bergen Vize, I had regained minor essence abilities. For most of that time, I'd moped and whined about not being a top Guild investigator. I was over that part. I couldn't go back. Not with Keeva in charge of my old department. I was bitter and angry with the way the Guild booted me out and kept me out. That part I wasn't over. If I knew myself as well as I thought I did, I never would be.

A surprisingly long line led to the appointment desk. The elf receptionist had managed to personalize her security uniform by adding a bright yellow scarf. She probably wouldn't get away with it for long. While I didn't care for the style, I had to give her points for simultaneously matching her eye shadow and sticking it to the Man.

A motley group going to the hearing waited at the elevators. A surprising number of solitary fey mixed in with fairies and elves. Solitaries usually avoided the Guild. Even though a bunch of them had tried to kill me, I felt bad about the number of bruises and bandages I saw. Like everyone else, they had been provoked by a spell to do what they did. Most people aren't at their best when they're on a murderous rampage.

When the elevator arrived, a brownie security guard waited inside again. Before anyone else could board, four brownie security guards hustled me into the elevator and the doors closed. One of the guards grabbed my arm. "Connor Grey, you are ordered held for questioning."

Despite my inclination to clock the guy, I simply pulled my arm away. I hate being manhandled. The four brownies positioned themselves around me.

"Ceridwen can't just grab anyone she pleases," I said.

The lead brownie glanced at me and away.

"What am I being held for?" I asked.

They stared straight ahead. Even the lead guy didn't bother looking at me. "You are on Guild property and are being detained for questioning."

I glared at him. "That's not what I asked."

The elevator doors opened. The lead brownie waved off someone trying to board.

"I'm not putting up with this." I pushed forward. The two brownies behind me grabbed my arms. The doors closed.

"Fine. You're just making this worse. I'm going to sue Ceridwen for unlawful detention, and I'm going to name all of you." They did a good job of being unimpressed. Whatever Ceridwen was up to, she wasn't going to get any cooperation from me if she thought this was the way to get what she wanted. Especially after her little game in the hotel.

The elevator opened on a quiet lower floor. The brownies escorted me down an empty corridor. The Guildhouse had entire unused sections. The lead brownie opened a door and stuck his head inside. He motioned for me to enter. I pushed open the door. The small, spartan conference room held a table with four chairs around it. Two of them were occupied. On one sat the brownie I had left in the basement storeroom. On another, Meryl sat with her face in a cool, neutral pose. She folded her hands on the tabletop. "Have a seat, Mr. Grey."

I dropped in the seat and crossed my arms. "Very funny," I said.

Meryl looked at the brownie. "Did I say something funny? I don't think I said something funny." The brownie had a hangdog expression.

Meryl turned back to me. "Let me introduce you, Grey. This is Tobbin Korrel. Tobbin has been a security guard at the Guildhouse for three years. He has an excellent employment record and is well liked by his coworkers. Not two weeks ago he managed to prevent a mentally ill selkie from drowning a receptionist in the lobby without anyone getting hurt. He has a wife and three kids. He gets up every day, comes to work, goes home, pays his bills, and maybe occasionally takes the family out for ice cream. When he is asked to do something at work, despite whatever utter stupidity it may involve from his superiors, he complies as long as he isn't asked to do something illegal. In short, Grey, he's a nice guy who does his job. What do you have to say to that?"

I frowned at her. "Hi, Tobbin."

She arched an eyebrow at me. "Is that really all you have to say to Mr. Korrel?"

I sighed impatiently. "Look, I'm sorry, Korrel. I have a problem with rules that make no sense, in this place in particular. I shouldn't have taken it out on you." I glared at Meryl. "Satisfied?"

She pursed her lips. "That covers your behavior in the elevator. There's the little matter of the storeroom."

I closed my eyes for a moment, trying not to be angry. "I'm sorry I trapped you in the storeroom."

"And?" said Meryl.

I couldn't think of anything else I had done. "And what?"

"And if there's anything you can do for Mr. Korrel to make up for it, you will be glad to, right?"

I gave in. "Yes. I really am sorry, Mr. Korrel. I was a jerk. Call me anytime."

Meryl slid paper and pen toward me. "Now give him your number."

My face felt hot as I wrote it down. Meryl intercepted the paper as I handed it to Korrel. "It's the right phone number, Meryl."

She smiled as she passed it to the brownie. "Just checking. Is that satisfactory, Tobs?"

He nodded. "Really, this wasn't necessary."

Meryl tapped his arm. "You have no idea how necessary this was. I apologize for wasting your break time."

"Thank you." He nodded with a nervous smile and left.

Meryl and I stared at each other. I counted to ten before I trusted myself to speak. "That was a nasty thing to do."

Her blank expression vanished behind an angry frown. "How's it feel?"

I stood, the chair skittering back a little more dramatically than I intended. "I got your point. I'm not a child, Meryl."

She shrugged, indifferent to my anger. "You think? Then don't act like one. Here's the thing, Grey. You knew I wouldn't leave you in that storeroom. You knew I'd be right back. He didn't. He also knew those rooms are warded, and no one would hear him. He had to take a sick day to recover from the boggart mania. I have no sympathy for you right now."

I bit back what I was going to snap at her. I hadn't considered that. I sat again. "Okay, now I really feel like crap."

She compressed her lips. "Good. Karma's a bitch."

I rubbed my fingertips across my scalp. "Okay, okay, I hear you."

She lifted a huge black pocketbook onto her shoulder. "Good."

As she came around the table, I took her arm as gently as possible. "Will you have drinks with me later?"

She checked her watch. "We both have meetings. Call me, and I'll let you know if I'm free."

I smiled. "It's a date."

She rolled her eyes. "Here we go with that again. I'll call you."

She outpaced me down the hall. When I reached the elevator lobby, the stairwell door was closing. I didn't know what to think. First we have sex. Then we have a disciplinary meeting. If that was Meryl's idea of hot, I sure as hell was baffled.

I took the elevator without further incident to the Community Liaison Department. The user-friendly name implied it was some kind of fey boosterism group. In reality, it's a crime unit, pure and simple. It used to be the center of my world, but not anymore. I could probably get a research position with the unit. In fact, Keeva macNeve had even offered me one. I turned it down. I didn't want to define myself by my job anymore. Not after I realized that it could all be taken away without any say from me. Besides, with Keeva in charge, I'd go insane answering to her.

The department buzzed with activity. A few people acknowledged me, but no one made the step of engaging in conversation. When I worked there, I tended to socialize only with other high-level agents, the ones who had the option of not being nailed to their desks. It was an elitist division that I had no problem with. Of course, the payback is that people I considered underlings no longer have to give me the time of day.

The Guildhouse had dampening wards everywhere to keep the ambient essence levels down. The side effect was that you couldn't always sense who was coming your way. Dylan didn't realize I was standing at the door, watching him work. He had been moved into an office that last I knew was being used as a storeroom. The storage boxes were cleared out, and the original office furniture was rearranged so the desk angled in the corner, facing both the window and the door. I knocked.

He looked up as though rising from a deep pool of concentration. When his gaze reached me, he smiled broadly and started to stand. "Hey! I didn't know you were here today."

I waved him back down. "I just stopped by to say hello."

He gestured at a guest chair. "Sit. Sit."

The chair was not as comfortable as I thought it would be. Dylan rocked back in an oxblood leather chair that coordinated perfectly with the expensive mahogany credenza behind him. "What are you up to?"

"I stopped by to ask Keeva some questions about a case."

He gave me curious look. "I didn't know you were working together."

I shook my head. "It's an old case that's related to the thing I'm working on with the Boston P.D. You look like you've settled in."

"They gave me a great space. Check out the view."

I didn't need to look out the window. "I like how you can see the fairy hill on Boston Common and the dome of the statehouse at the same time, sort of a metaphor of the city."

Dylan started to say something, but stopped as sudden realization came over his face. "Danu's blood, this is your old office."

I laughed. "Yeah. How do you like the chair?"

Grinning, he swiveled in it. "I should have known. Extremely comfortable and expensive."

I nodded. "I tried to take it with me when I left, but they wouldn't let me. It's probably for the best. I would have sold it by now to pay bills."

I glanced down. Dylan had several open files and a number of photographs scattered about the desk. "Are these the missing museum pieces?"

He picked up a stack of photos. "I'm trying to figure out why these particular pieces were taken."

He pushed a photo toward me, a shot of a torc. The one Belgor had given me. The one hidden in my kitchen cabinet. I hate lying to Dylan, especially when he knows I'm doing it. He knew something was up at Belgor's. I didn't want to linger on the topic. "That's pretty."

Dylan nodded. "Expensive. Probably from an old Irish king."

He examined another photograph. "This one's odd. It's a Saxon ring. It was in the Celtic collection because an old fairy donated it."

He handed it to me. The gold ring was a classic design of the ouroboros, a scaled snake biting its own tail. The snake eyes were set with small rubies. It was as nice as Belgor said it was.

The remaining photos were of three fibulae, antique brooches for holding clothing together: a horned serpent in gold, a tree made of silver with tiny gold apples, and another gold one that looked like mistletoe. "The fibulae all have druidic symbols. That could be a connection."

Dylan nodded. "Arguably, it's all druidic. I think the motive is most likely profit. Boston's Samhain draws a lot of people, so the market's here."

I slid the fibulae photos to the bottom of the stack. "Which is why you were staking out Belgor. You mentioned your agents were distracted when he was attacked."

He looked out the window in thought. "They didn't see the attacker enter the store. A distraction spell must have been used on them to lull them into inattention."

"They were spotted," I said.

"They're very good agents. I'd be surprised if both of them were seen," he said.

"Then I'd say whoever the attacker was knew Guild operations, either through experience or a leak."

He sighed loudly. "Yes, well, the organization here is lax, if you ask me."

It's funny. I had issues with the Boston Guild, but hearing Dylan criticize it made me bristle. "Guildmaster ap Eagan has been sick for a long time," I said.

"Yes, well, I don't get why Maeve hasn't stepped in sooner."

"Maeve doesn't do a lot of things she should," I said.

He smiled to soften the tone of the conversation. "Okay,

buddy, calm down. I was only making an observation. Auntie Bree said you have issues with the Guild, and obviously I don't know them all."

"Sorry. Bad habit. How's the rest of the show going?"

Dylan rocked his head. "Busy. Incredible number of assault and batteries in the last few weeks. The Boston P.D. is staying out of it, which is and isn't helping. The police are much more cooperative in New York."

"We have Commissioner Murdock to thank for that. He would like nothing better than for the Weird to break off and float out to sea," I said.

Dylan chuckled. "Yes, I've talked to him. Walks the line a hairbreadth from insulting."

I saw an opening to take Meryl's advice and spread a little more good karma. "Keeva can help you with him."

He arched an eyebrow. "Really? I didn't think diplomacy was one of her skills."

I had to laugh at that one. Obviously, he had been on the receiving end of one of Keeva's barbed comments. "She and the commissioner are two sides of the same coin. She can help you."

He pursed his lips. "You know she's on suspension."

"She'll be cleared. She's good at what she does, Dylan. Let her do it."

The sly smile came back. "Why the support? I don't get the sense she likes you."

I shrugged. "I owe her a couple of favors. Putting in a good word for her is a no-brainer."

His smile became a little more genuine. "I'll take your word for it, then. I'll cut her as much as slack I can."

I stood. "Thanks. I should let you get back to work."

From another folder, he took out more pictures, grainy shots of a building interior, and slid them across the desk. "I shouldn't show you these. Security photos from the Met."

It took me a moment to realize the same person appeared in them, a small, blond-haired woman with a rather plain face. He spun the photos back toward himself to examine them. "We haven't identified her yet. I was hoping you might recognize her. She entered the U.S. three weeks ago and visited the museum twice before the robbery. We know she met with Bergin Vize at least once in the month before she left Germany."

In addition to being the thug who either accidentally or intentionally destroyed my fey abilities, Vize was an international terrorist, part of a group of people intent on bringing down the Seelie Court. He'd helped plan a major attack in Boston the previous spring and manipulated a mentally unstable fey man into nearly causing a cataclysm. I killed the plan, and High Queen Maeve apparently executed the perpetrator. "Why didn't you arrest her?"

"We wanted to track her movements. We lost her in New York, but we believe she came to Boston. She's the reason I'm here. I thought you should know," Dylan said.

I don't have proof, but the fact that Vize had been involved in two terrorist plots that also almost killed me was no coincidence. "Do you think she could be behind the odd attacks against me?"

He shook his head. "I don't see any connection to you at all other than Bergin Vize, and he's connected to a lot of stuff. I've never heard of spells that work the way you've been describing. But there's more going on than just that. We suspect a major terrorist operation is in the works. Her friends in Europe have gone into hiding," he said.

"You mean the Guild has lost Bergin Vize again," I said.

"You're not supposed to know that," he said.

I didn't know what to think. First Ceridwen dangled Vize in front of me, then Dylan. Ceridwen I didn't trust. Dylan I wanted to. He surveyed the piles of paper on his desk. "You can be part of this again."

I shook my head. "Freelancing suits me for now."

He looked at the photos, then back at me, slight disappointment on his face. "Okay—for now. If you hear anything related to this, let me know?"

I don't know why he trusted me. "Sure thing."

I walked the corridor on the opposite end of the floor until I reached Keeva's office. She had two nameplates outside her door. The top one had most of her full name with its old country spelling, CAOIMHE AP LAOIRE MAC NIAMH AES SIDHE. Fairy commoners often ended their names with their clan affiliation, like Danann Sidhe. The monarchy, though, used the simple Aes Sidhe. Everybody knew they were Dananns. Americans had a hard time with the old spellings and diphthongs, so like a lot of fey, Keeva anglicized her name for easier pronunciation by the local folks. Hence, the bottom plate read a simple KEEVA MACNEVE.

Her door was ajar. I pushed it open with my foot and found Keeva staring out the window. She had a great view of South Boston and the harbor beyond it. When I knocked, she pivoted her chair slowly toward me, an annoyance on her face that did not change much when she saw me. "How do you do it?"

Without waiting for an invitation, I took the guest chair. "Do what?"

She pulled her chair up and leaned across her desk blotter. "How do you not work here and still manage to make my life miserable?"

I tried an apologetic smile. "It's a knack?"

She glared. "I'm not amused."

"Why don't you clue me in to the problem?"

Her eyes flicked to the door for a fraction of a second. "Dylan macBain."

I shrugged. "I'm not responsible for him."

She rubbed her neck in frustration. "If I have to hear one more story about what great fun it was working with you 'back in the city,' which I assume he means that slab of concrete and garbage on the Hudson River, I will not be responsible for the removal of his tongue."

I exaggerated looking up in pleasant memory. "Yeah, it *was* fun working with me back then."

She growled. "You must have used up all the fun part before you came here."

"So, I'm guessing you're not happy with the current job share?"

She huffed and turned back to the window. "It's only procedural. It'll be cleared up in another day or two, and Mr. Wonderful will be on his way back to the city." She used her fingers to make air quotation marks when she said "the city."

I leaned back. "He's just doing his job, Keev. He's good at it. Like you said, he'll be gone soon."

She didn't move. "How'd you like me to sign off on that visa request?"

I had been banned from entering Germany. For more than six months, I had been trying to persuade Keeva to let me have a diplomatic visa from the Guild to go there and hunt down Bergin Vize. The Germans weren't pursuing him, and I wanted to see him face justice. Besides being responsible for my loss of abilities, he had a litany of terrorist crimes to his name. Keeva had denied my request every time I asked, so I decided not to sound enthusiastic. "Sure."

Keeva whirled back to her desk with a sarcastic smile. "Sorry, my signing privileges have been revoked."

I disappointed her by chuckling. "At least you made me laugh this time. I thought you were going to bribe me to do something."

She narrowed her eyes and pursed her lips. "Hmm. Interesting. Let me get back to you on that."

"Come on, Keeva. It can't be that bad."

She sighed. "Not only does he talk about you incessantly; he shadows me on everything I do, which is very little."

I had sympathy pangs for her. I knew what it was like to be sidelined by the Guild for reasons beyond my control. "For what it's worth, I don't think it's fair you're on suspension. It wasn't your fault."

"I know that. I don't understand why Ceridwen's being such an ass about it."

Keeva is always careful about appearances and her political gamesmanship. "Oh, my, my! Did I just hear you insult a queen?"

She gave me a smug smile. "Even if you do tell her I said that, I doubt she'd listen. She's not exactly on your list of admirers at the moment."

"Word travels fast."

"All joking aside, Connor. You should be careful. She *is* a queen. If you must annoy her, please leave me out of it."

That was the Keeva I knew, always watching her own back. "I'll keep that in mind. Anyway, I have something you can do without permission. I need a copy of a Guild file."

Keeva's expression brushed up against a sneer. "Why don't you ask your little friend in the basement?"

Meryl wasn't one of Keeva's favorite people, precisely because Keeva didn't impress her. I didn't rise to her bait on that. "Because I thought you could give me a little insight on the case. The Boston P.D. file says you were the agent in charge." Appealing to Keeva's vanity tended to work like a charm, and Murdock did say I should charm her.

"Which one?"

"Olivia Merced."

Keeva considered, then nodded as she remembered. "I know the name. She was part of the Ardman case. Liddell Viten."

Typical of the Guild to name the case after the fey victim and not the human one. "Merced is dead. So is a guy named Josef Kaspar."

She arched an eyebrow. "Murder-suicide?"

I frowned. "No. Why would you say that?"

"He was her fiancé before Viten showed up. Never got over it. I think he was homeless. In fact, he figured out Viten was fey and turned him in to the Guild hoping Merced would go back to him. That woman annoyed the heck out of me with her constant calls about him. I told her to call Boston P.D."

Once again, the Guild took a case only to screw over the human-normal element. Merced never got her justice. I ran down the basic details of the current case. "They were ritually murdered the same way. You probably have the report from Murdock here somewhere."

"If that's an ogham curse, I've never heard it."

"Well, you've connected the two murders. We definitely should look at the file."

She sighed. "I'll send the report to Murdock. I'm so depressed, it wouldn't be any fun to say no."

Keeva glanced out the window. "Boston wasn't the only place Liddell Viten scammed women. He had a partner in New York named Rhonda Powell. He killed her for some reason. When we were transferring him there for a court hearing, he overpowered his guards and escaped into the storerooms. He seriously injured three people before he was taken down."

"You took him out?"

She shook her head, a curious and smug gleam in her eye. "She didn't tell you? Meryl Dian killed him."

14

Meryl wasn't in her office. Given our conversation in my apartment, I was surprised she hadn't mentioned Viten. I searched the subbasement, but the storerooms were all closed. I called her cell. She still wasn't answering. I kept pulling my cell phone out to check the ringer volume, but it was fine. She wasn't calling. Yet. I hoped "yet." No one I ran into at the Guildhouse had seen her. I tried searching the building, but security spotted me and showed me the door.

I wondered why Meryl hadn't told me about Viten. Everybody has at least one thing they don't share. Briallen hinted about dark things in her own past, things she didn't want to talk about. I kept repeating that to myself. There were things in my own past I hadn't told Meryl. But I did tell her the worst thing I ever did. She had to know that. I had to shake off the feeling she didn't trust me. Maybe after Forest Hills, she didn't think anything else needed to be said.

Which brought me to huddling in the Guildhouse garage bay to see if I could catch her leaving the building. The security guards down on the ramp checked on me at irregular intervals. At some point, they decided I wasn't a threat, but they still kept tabs on my movements around the garage door. The weather had turned cold, enough to threaten frost in some places around the city. The wind made it feel colder, so I used the building to protect myself as much as I could, which wasn't much. I was cold.

The evening exodus of Guild employees had passed by at least an hour. Car after car had driven up from the deep basement garage. Drivers eyed me like the security guards had, probably wondering who was the nut with the too-thin leather coat who was bouncing on his heels. Someone handed me a dollar, which was nice.

A high-pitched engine whine echoed up from the garage, and Meryl's black MINI Cooper appeared. I stepped in the travel lane when the car hit the bottom of the ramp. Meryl's orange hair was hard to miss in the lurid glare of vapor lights. The car engine revved, then the car surged upward. Meryl's face was expressionless as she sped toward me. Instinctively, my pointless body shields flashed on as the car neared the top. Meryl slammed on the brakes and stopped within inches of my knees. She waved.

I ignored my racing heart as I walked around to her window. "If I pay, will you go for a drink?"

She grinned. "Get in."

Meryl kept her car immaculate. She didn't say anything, but I knew she checked out my shoes as I got in to make sure I wasn't tracking in dirt. She turned into traffic through Park Square, tore around the monument in the center, and parked in the loading zone in front of the Craic House, an old pub that attracted a lot of Guild employees. We got out of the car, and Meryl tossed her keys to a guy who looked like a bouncer.

"This place has valet service now?" I asked.

Meryl looked at me like I was insane. "No."

She didn't elaborate, leaving me to conclude she had a private arrangement with the guy. No surprise. At almost every bar and pub I'd been to with Meryl, she knew either a bouncer or a bartender.

The after-work crowd had thinned, so we landed a table easily. Within moments, the waitress delivered two pints of Guinness. The Craic House, then, was one of those places where she knew the bouncer *and* the bartender. Meryl could put it away with the best of them, but she never got drunk that I could see.

"We haven't gone out for a drink in weeks."

Meryl sipped her beer. "Ceridwen's pulled me into the hearing four times."

I smiled down at the table. "It's not like you don't enjoy irritating her."

She made a funny snarl face. "I hate it. I come in to work every day not knowing whether I'm going to be filing or defending myself."

"That's a lie. I've seen your office. You never file."

"You sound like Nigel," she said.

Meryl and Nigel Martin had recently become friends, or at least friendly. I found the situation a little suspicious on both sides. For all her denials about playing Guild politics, she was good at wiggling into the power structure without looking like she was up to anything. Nigel, on the other hand, had motives for everything he did. His sudden interest in Meryl could have been coincidence. It could also be about the fact that he and I were not on the best terms and that Meryl was an available resource for an old mentor to keep tabs on his wayward protégé.

"He must be loving all this court intrigue," I said.

She snickered. "Gods, yes. Ceridwen's spear is like catnip for him. He calls me constantly."

I gulped some beer. "Any clues why it likes me?"

"The spear?" She shrugged. "It's a pretty powerful artifact. From what I can tell, its original purpose was that of a silver branch."

"A key to the Magic Kingdom?"

She nodded. "Yeah, you can use it to get into Faerie. Well, maybe once upon a time you could. Since Convergence, there hasn't been any opportunity to use a true silver branch, so the Seelie Court has been using it for its other capabilities.

"It has properties independent of the holder—like the truth detection. Ceridwen made me touch it when she was

interrogating me. When I told the truth, the spear was react-
ing, not Ceridwen. She just watches for the reaction signs.
Nigel's worried about its being in the hands of the Seelie
Court."

"Are you saying it has a mind of its own?" I asked.

She pinched her lips. "I wouldn't go that far, no. But it reacts to things on a level I don't think we're capable of understanding. Whoever made it was either a genius or a madman,
and whoever tinkered with it was just plain stupid."

"Tinkered?"

She nodded. "Nigel's been very intrigued, so he asked me
to research it. The spearhead was either changed or added
later. The silver filigree was bonded even later, and it also has
silver-branch properties on its own. It fades in and out of history. You wouldn't believe where it's been. It was probably
with the elves in Alfheim at one point. The elven armies do
love their spears. I think they were the ones who changed the
spearhead."

I leaned back, impressed. "How do you find this stuff?"

She flipped her hands up at the wrists and batted her eyelashes. "I'm just a girl with a computer."

"Yeah, right. With more stealthware than the Pentagon."

She checked to see if anyone around us could listen in. "I
almost got caught in Austria. I hacked a museum server, and
the next thing I knew, I was chased across the Web. It was
cool. They were good."

I knew that wasn't the end of the story. "But not good
enough."

She shook her head, clearly proud. "Nope. Before I lost the
connection, I was able to confirm the filigree was done in Brit-
ain after the spear disappeared from Germany. The spear has
its own silver-branch properties, but someone decided to en-
hance them with the silver filigree. If I had to guess, it was for
a spell that allows multiuser interface functionality with a primary dimensional portal via a single active administrator."

I laughed out loud. "You so just overgeeked yourself."

She made this cute I'm-so-embarrassed face. "Um . . . I

meant to say that there was probably a spell that allowed whoever used the spear for a silver branch to take as many people
as they wanted across a veil between the realms."

"Much better, thank you."

She scrunched up her nose. "So, how's *your* case going,
Mr. Smart Guy?"

I swirled the dregs of my beer. "Strange. Unlike you, the
most exciting thing that's happened in my search is bumping
into a crabby fairy in a bookstore. I have a rune spell I can't
figure out. I was wondering if you could look into it for me. It
might distract you from Ceridwen."

She rolled her eyes. "Oh, golly, Mr. Grey, really? I'd love
to do your consulting work for you. When can I start?"

I pouted playfully. "Hey, I'm paying for the beer, aren't I?"

She pursed her lips. "It'll take more than a round to convince me."

I doodled the rune spell on a bar napkin, breaking the
runes across two lines to keep them from accidentally activating something. Like Meryl said, even though I didn't have my
abilities anymore, sometimes tools simply react to their envi-
ronment. "Two dead bodies with the same ogham runes. They
read like 'grave denied' or 'the way to death denied.' Considering the dead bodies, I don't get what they're supposed to
accomplish."

Meryl circled three runes. "You're probably being too lit-
eral, which is how the modern mind works. You're translating
those runes as 'death-home,' which logically means grave or
graveyard. But the word used here for death is not a definite
form—it's more like 'not mortal living,' which could be an
invocation to a god or goddess."

I turned the napkin toward me. "I hadn't thought about
that."

Meryl nudged her glass. "Ask me about kennings."

I signaled the waitress for another round. "I know what
kennings are."

Meryl hummed and bobbed her head as if she were listening to music. When the waitress delivered the Guinness, she

stopped humming and leaned forward. "And we're back from our commercial break. Every dru-kid knows kennings are poetic metaphors, but that's different from figuring out whether you're looking at a kenning and what it could mean. There's intuition and cultural context to take into account. This is the part where you say, 'That's bloody brilliant, Meryl. You should have some hot, spicy chicken tenders.' "

To prove I'm not dense, I waved the waitress back. "That's bloody brilliant, Meryl. You should have some hot, spicy chicken tenders. In fact, let me order and pay for them."

She winked and lifted her glass. "Excellent. I don't usually like ad-libbing, but that's good. Anyway, given what I know of the cultural context of the Old Irish, and this ogham spell looks Old Irish in form, I'd say death-place is a kenning for Mag Mell."

She downed the remainder of her beer as the waitress arrived. "Another round, please, and I believe the gentleman is adding onion rings to his order."

I added onion rings to my order. "Why Mag Mell?"

She shrugged. "It's a place-name kenning from the text position, and given that you found it at a painful murder scene, the type of otherworld would be the opposite of pain. Mag Mell—the plain of joy—where the dead living is easy. Plus, it's Samhain. Murderers aren't very creative about their timing."

Impressed, I shook my head and smiled. "You really are brilliant."

She stood. "Yes, well, now I have to pee. When I come back, remind me to tell you about the time I killed Liddell Viten."

She walked off into the crowd. My entire body felt like it was sinking into the chair. I couldn't speak when the waitress served our order, but stared at the food and wondered what to say when Meryl came back.

Meryl returned, took an onion ring, and chewed it with a caustic smile.

I licked my lips. "You talked to Keeva."

She shook her head and gazed up at the ceiling. "No, I didn't. I got several messages from you and a request from macNeve to send the Ardman file to Murdock. Whatever could have occurred in the complex mind of Connor Grey for him to be calling me so frantically?"

"Why are you acting so offended?"

She narrowed her eyes. "Are you going to tell me you weren't going to ask me about it?"

I felt like a schoolkid caught skipping out. "No, but I don't know why you're making me feel guilty about it."

She piled some chicken on her plate. "You're right. You shouldn't feel guilty about asking. You should feel guilty about being passive-aggressive. You could have left a message about it or asked me when we first sat down. Instead, you do this 'please, please, call me' crap and 'aren't these interesting runes' crap when I know damned well all you really want to do is ask about how I killed someone."

I reached across and grabbed her arm as she was stabbing a chicken tender. Someone might call me brave. "Hey! Knock it off! You are being so out of line right now. First off, I've been calling you since *before* I knew about Viten. And second off, excuse me for respecting the fact that you know a helluva lot more about runes than I do."

She tried to pull her arm away. I made her work at it before releasing her. "You don't know anything, Grey. All I've ever done is my job, and I don't think it includes watching coworkers injured, or killing an escaped prisoner, or getting attacked by flying knives, or feeling like I did something wrong because I happened to be in the wrong place at the right time and helped stop a major interdimensional meltdown."

I stabbed my finger at the table. "You work for the Guild, Meryl. It's in your job description under 'other duties as necessary.'"

She threw herself back against her chair. "That's not even funny."

I still had my fingertip jammed against the tabletop. I took a deep breath and let my hand fall flat. "Why are we arguing?"

Meryl rubbed her hands up under her bangs. "You're right. It's not your fault. It's the Guild's. I'm just tired that after all these years, I'm still looking for recognition. That place owes me, big-time."

I put a sickly-sweet smile on my face. "I can't fault them. Your attraction for me started because of our mutual disgust at the Guild."

She leaned her head on her hand and popped a piece of chicken in her mouth. "Now that's funny."

"Tell me about Viten so we can drop it," I said.

She toyed with a water ring on the table before looking up at me. "There's not much to tell. I was in my office alone. It was just after I had been promoted, actually."

"That's recognition," I said.

She shrugged. "Sure, if getting the job only because the chief archivist left is considered recognition."

"Anyway . . ."

She smiled grudgingly, which faded. "Anyway, I heard a scream, then I heard essence-fire. When I reached the door, I saw a body in the elevator and two more down in the hallway. I didn't know if they were alive or dead. Coming toward me was Viten. I didn't know his name then. In fact, I didn't think he was the attacker. He seemed so calm, I actually thought he was some kind of security guard coming to evacuate me. He acted like he didn't see me. I asked him what was going on. All of sudden he grabbed me by the neck. My body shields came on, and he started to lose his grip. I could feel him charging essence into his hands."

She took a deep breath. "I grabbed him by the head and let loose with everything I had."

She frowned, playing with the water rings.

"You essence shocked him," I said.

She met my eyes. I saw no doubt, no trauma. Just the direct stare of someone who had done something to survive. "If I had to do it again, Grey, I would do it exactly the same."

I nodded once in agreement. I had been there, too. You did what you had to do to get through. "I'm sorry. It's not just morbid curiosity, you know. I have a murder investigation, and I need to cover all the bases."

"I get it. You need to work on your delivery," she said.

I fussed with an onion ring to avoid making eye contact. "So, I was worried you weren't returning my phone calls."

"Yeah, sorry about that, too. It really has been crazy."

I played my index finger across the back of her hand. "Yeah. Yeah, sure. I thought, you know, after . . ."

A slow smile cut across her face. "Oh, shit. It was a day-after call, wasn't it?"

I hoped I wasn't blushing. She'd never let me forget it. "Yeah."

She leaned across the table and kissed my cheek. "Thank you. That was sweet." She settled back and began eating again.

"That's it?" I asked.

Her eyebrows went up. "What?"

"Meryl, we had sex."

She nodded. "I was there, remember? I'm not going to turn into some kind of call-me, call-me chick, if that's what you're worried about. I'm not holding you to anything for it."

I took a deep breath. "What if I want to be held to something?"

Her face became unreadable. "We had a moment, Grey. We needed each other. It was good for both of us, but I don't want it to get blown out of proportion."

I nodded, knowing I was nodding too much and feeling stupid. "Sure, sure. Fine."

She took my hand in hers. "Will you stop? Geez, we're not virgins here. Lighten up."

I forced myself to smile. "Okay. I don't want to play games."

She lifted her beer, and a vicious curl came to her lip. "I wouldn't think of it."

I had no idea why I wanted to be with this woman.

15

The Boston Police Area B station house down on West Broadway had the look of a grizzled survivor. Even though the Boston P.D. paid my bills more often than they knew, I never felt welcome at the station house. I worked on cases because they didn't. I helped close cases they couldn't. They tolerated me because of Murdock, but I was under no delusion they liked me.

As if to demonstrate the point, everyone in the detective bullpen managed to be on the phone as I waited at the counter. A full fifteen minutes passed before someone offered to track down Murdock. He appeared in the hallway and motioned me to follow him. He opened the door to a dingy conference room with a table, a few scarred wooden chairs, an empty watercooler, and peeling paint. An open file box sat on the table.

"MacNeve sent the Ardman file," he said

"She must really be bored to move this quickly." I tilted the box and removed the files. Folder after thick manila folder slid onto the table, and Murdock tried hard not to look panicked that I was making a mess. Except for his car, he's tidy. We each grabbed a stack and began reading.

The Merced investigation had been referred to the Guild when the fey connection had been made. Given Viten's history and the Guild's usual interests, he must have scammed an important fey or two. Otherwise, the Guild wouldn't have taken that kind of case for a human normal.

Murdock slid an old file photo across the table. "Rosavear Ardman. She's still in Boston."

The woman in the picture looked petite, but strong. She had a pleasant enough face, not particularly beautiful. Part of a wing was visible behind her, the sharp and narrow profile of the Inverni fairies. The Inverni clan had a power struggle with the Dananns eons ago, literally, and they lost the rule of Faerie. Ardman had looks, money, and, most importantly, royal connections. It's no wonder the Guild grabbed the case.

Murdock straightened the folders. "Viten scammed Ardman. He lived with her at the same time he was married to Merced. Neither knew about the other. Josef Kaspar apparently put the two con jobs together and went to the Guild."

"Why would he go to the Guild and not the police?"

Murdock shrugged. "It happens all the time. The Guild may not take the bait on a human case often, but when it does, it bites hard. If someone thinks they're getting nowhere with us, they try the Guild."

I shook my head. "I had no idea."

Murdock gave a small smile. "You didn't think just because the Guild is manipulative that it couldn't be manipulated, did you?"

I hadn't thought about it, but it made sense. Bureaucracy was bureaucracy, no matter what species was involved. I whistled and slid a financial summary sheet to him. "Viten had millions."

Murdock didn't look. "He scammed over a dozen women. Most of the money disappeared. His typical con involved marrying money, getting his name on the assets, then moving them before the women found out. He would vanish before that, take a new name, and select a new target."

Viten was a fraud, all right. The Olivia Merced divorce file documented a trail of financial gymnastics that Wall Street wished were legal. Merced caught on to him earlier than the others. Still, he managed to seduce a fair amount of money from her. He must have suspected he was caught, because his assets started disappearing before Merced filed papers on him. The money was never recovered.

"Keeva told me he had a partner," I said.

Murdock sorted through the files and handed me one. "A druidess named Rhonda Powell. Unconnected as far as I can tell. They ran different scams together. Powell usually posed as an heiress, and Viten would act as some kind of father figure looking out to protect her money."

I flipped through the file. Powell had been as bad as Viten, bilking lonely widowers out of millions as well. A New York City police report deep in the file caught my attention. I showed it to Murdock. "He killed her."

Murdock nodded. "Things apparently went sour between them. If I had to guess, she wanted money. Viten handled the cash. As far as I can see, she needed his access to get it. When Viten died, the case was assigned to the fraud unit."

He frowned and flipped back and forth between several pages. "He shot Powell at Rockefeller Center, in full view of several witnesses. It was an execution."

I nodded in understanding. "Her abilities would have been a match for him, but her shields couldn't stop a bullet. He probably had enough ability to keep the bullet path from warping."

Murdock shook his head. "Still, why so public? If they were partners, he must have had ample opportunity to kill her and not be seen."

I leaned back in my chair. "Maybe he wanted to send a message to someone. Maybe she threatened him, and he didn't have time for anything else."

He moved the file pages aside. "I'm putting this on the odd list. The only murder. The only partner. Public. It doesn't fit what else we know about Viten."

"Did the victims get their money back?" I asked.

Murdock shrugged. "Some of the cases were years old.

They targeted elderly people who were..." He paused, searching for words.

"... not fey," I finished. The Guild always lost interest when the essence level plunged. Murdock didn't respond. He knew the story.

The New York angle surfaced when Viten was arrested in Boston. Once his glamour had been stripped, it was evident he was a Teutonic kobold—thin lips, hooded eyes, and a small, flat nose. The skin tone tends to a pale tan, the hair a drab, wispy white. They're cousins in a way to the Celtic brownies, only their manic sides are more integrated into their personalities. Sometimes that's a good thing, sometimes not. All kobolds bear an uncanny resemblance to one another. With such subtle features, they were expert glamourers. It doesn't take much to hide their true selves under an illusion. Viten played on that when he was arrested, claiming mistaken identity.

Murdock handed me another set of papers. "Do you know how Viten died?"

I pulled out investigation reports with Meryl's name all over them. "I just found out yesterday."

Murdock kept his eyes on his file. "Do you want to talk about it?"

I glanced at him. "Meryl told me what happened. It was a legit takedown."

He let it drop. I found an evidence receipt. "What's in this?"

Murdock opened a file. "Personal effects. There's a list here somewhere."

I sat back and folded my arms. "You've read this entire file already, haven't you?"

"Not the whole thing. You sleep late, remember?"

I looked out the window. "I had a busy night."

"Everyone's dead," said Murdock.

"What?"

"Everyone's dead. The only living person related to the Ardman case is Ardman. She was a victim. Other than Viten,

I don't see a connection to Merced and Kaspar. I don't see a motive."

I shrugged. "Maybe Ardman needs an interview."

Murdock gave me a thin smile. I closed my eyes. "You're going to ask me, aren't you?" I opened my eyes. Murdock hadn't changed his expression. "She might not agree to do it."

He shrugged. "Hey, not my fault the fey avoid the police."

I crossed my arms. "Hey, not my fault the police avoid the fey."

He did not lose the smile. I sighed. "Fine. I'll ask Keeva to set up a meeting with Ardman. I hate you, by the way."

16

After much fawning and charming on my part, Keeva agreed to arrange an interview with Rosavear Ardman. I understood Murdock's desire to talk to the only living person related to the old Viten case, but I didn't see any connection to the current murders. Murdock was meticulous, though, and liked to worry his way down every side street of an investigation if the main road was going nowhere.

The late-October sun warmed my face as I waited for Keeva on the lower end of Boston Common. From my bench, I had a straight-shot view of the tall trees that surrounded the fairy ring next to the Civil War monument. This year an enormous mushroom crop had sprouted. The local news broadcast pictures, and the ring had been inundated with visitors ever since. Schools made field trips to see it; shoppers from Downtown Crossing made a side trip to check it out; office workers ate their lunch on the hill to watch the activity. Once word spread, anyone who knew the least bit of essence manipulation wanted mushrooms for spells and potions.

A few dozen feet away from me, midday traffic raced down Charles Street after being freed from the congestion in front of the Guildhouse on the next block. Security barriers narrowed the road there to one lane, annoying everyone who drove and pleasing politicians who thought it made them look tough on terror. Fairies flew above the Guildhouse, mostly Danann security agents in their black uniforms with the chrome helmets. So typical of the powerful to worry about themselves. Granted, the Guild board directors had been attacked, but the Guildhouse was an impenetrable fortress. A small nuke might penetrate all the bound-up essence. Might. But human normals can't see a fey essence shield. A concrete Jersey barrier, on the other hand, apparently was a comforting sight.

Keeva shot into view about the Guildhouse, her slender form and voluminous head of red hair easy to recognize. You get used to seeing fairies fly. What you never get used to is the allure of their wings in motion. The gossamer-thin membranes moved on unseen currents of essence, mesmerizing pinpoints of light in delicate veinings winking on and off. The wings looked so fragile, yet they had an incredible power to shift and shunt enough essence to lift a body in the air. Keeva landed lightly in front of me.

I nodded at the hill. "When was the last time you danced in a ring?"

She gazed up and smiled. "Not since I was very young."

We walked toward Beacon Hill. "Did you ever make it through the veil?" I teased.

She chuckled. "I thought I did. I spent a few summers at Tara with friends when I was young. The ring there is very powerful, but even it doesn't open to the other side anymore. We used to pretend, though. A weird fog formed if we did the dances right, but no one could ever see through it."

"That's more than I ever saw."

She shrugged. "It was only fog in the night. When you're a kid, you can turn that into the veil between the living and dead if you have your best friends spooking you into it."

Charles Street wound around the western base of Beacon Hill, an area known as the Flat. It was the retail shopping district for the well-heeled, not so impressive an address as Briallen's on Louisburg Square, but most Bostonians would have a hard time making the rent there, never mind owning an apartment.

"Thanks for arranging the interview. I'm surprised you wanted to come," I said.

Keeva paused at the window of an antique store. "I was getting stir-crazy. I made macBain let me go."

"Made him? I wasn't aware anyone could make Dylan do anything."

She smiled at me. "I discovered your Number One Fan hates memos. I've been burying him in them. I think he wanted a break."

For a moment, it felt like old times, Keeva and I actually relaxing around each other. We did that back when we were partners. Which was not to say we let down our guards, but we could be social on occasion. On Pinckney Street, Murdock pulled up in front of the Ardman townhouse and met us at the door.

"I thought I was going to be late," he said.

Keeva gave him a curt nod. Their polite animosity reflected the reality of their competing agencies. "Let me take it from here, gentlemen. Rosavear knows me."

A young human-normal woman answered the doorbell. Most fey preferred other fey clans to act as servants, old habits from the days when servant was a code phrase for conquered slave. "Guild Director Keeva macNeve and guests. Lady Ardman should be expecting us," Keeva said.

She grasped Keeva's hand. "Sophie Wells, pleased to meet you, Director macNeve. These are the gentlemen from the police department?"

Keeva introduced us, and Wells shook hands with sincere attention before stepping back to let us in. The Ardman house was grand yet small-scale. Old movies shot on soundstages gave people the impression Boston brownstones were enormous. Most were smaller inside than the run-of-the-mill McMansions in the suburbs these days. A small foyer paved in black-and-white stone tiles opened onto a comfortable, tasteful parlor decorated in ochre and maroon.

Wells gestured to the room. "Please have a seat. I'll let Lady Ardman know you're here."

Keeva and I sat on opposite ends of the couch while Murdock wandered to the window. Despite my typical experience with fey royalty, Lady Ardman appeared without the usual cooling-our-heels waiting time. She was a small woman, strongly built with a blunt attractiveness. Her long, narrow wings glowed a faint indigo, darkening to almost black at their sharp tips. Keeva had dropped the glamour hiding her wings when we entered the house, and they undulated behind her in soft gold-and-white folds. Inverni fairies tended to be smaller than their Danann cousins, but they still packed a punch in the essence department. They made no bones about reminding each other.

Keeva and I stood. I didn't know many Inverni, so I took the opportunity to get a decent imprint of the species essence, especially after my strange experience in the alley during my run. As I shook her hand, her essence felt odd, not at all Danann but powerful in its own right. Species essence resonated similarly from person to person. She didn't feel like my alley attacker. My attacker's essence was a shadow of Ardman's.

"I'm sorry to bother you, Rose, but these detectives were hoping you might help them with a case," Keeva said as the three of us took seats. Murdock remained attentive beside an armchair.

"You're no trouble, Keeva," Ardman said, her smile a bright flash of white.

"It's about the Viten case."

And the smile disappeared. "I see. What could possibly have happened after all these years?"

I took that as my cue. "Lady Ardman, two people have been found murdered recently. They had a history with each other and the Viten case. We're concerned their deaths might be related to it. My first question is have you noticed anything out of the ordinary lately that might concern you?"

Ardman straightened in her seat as her wings darkened. "Murder? Am I in danger?"

Keeva shot me an annoyed look. "Mr. Grey is asking as a precaution, Rose."

She didn't seem to believe her. "I haven't noticed anything. Is there something I should be looking for?"

I softened my apparently insensitive tone. "I was hoping you could tell us. Our files do not show any living associates for Viten. We were wondering if your memory was different."

"Lionel didn't have any friends that I knew of, if that's what you're asking," she said.

"Lionel?" Murdock asked.

Ardman looked at him as if she were only now realizing he was in the room. "That's the name he used with me. I never knew him by his other names." She paused, looking at Murdock with an uncomfortable expression. She approached him and lifted her hand to his face. "May I?"

Murdock looked down at the hand and nodded. Ardman touched his cheek. After a moment, she regained her composure and withdrew to her chair. "Have you walked the Ways, Mr. Murdock?"

Murdock glanced sharply at me. "She wants to know if you are fey," I said.

He gave a tentative smile. "No, ma'am."

Ardman considered him. "Are you sure? Perhaps you don't remember. Your essence reminds me of the fey friends of old."

Keeva cleared her throat. "Detective Murdock is human normal, Rose. He was involved in a fey event that disrupted his essence."

Ardman looked about to say more but remained silent.

"Did you ever meet a woman named Rhonda Powell?" asked Murdock. A little out of left field, but the Powell murder obviously still bothered him.

Ardman stiffened. "It is rude to mention her to me, Detective Murdock. That affair was a private pain to me for years that I never wanted revealed. But to answer your question, no, I never met her. Lionel kept her in New York as far as I know."

"You don't know anyone else who might have an interest in your old case?" Murdock asked.

"Are you doubting my word, sir?" Ardman asked.

Keeva glared. "I think that's enough, Detective Murdock. Lady Ardman has answered your question. Other than ensuring she feels safe, I believe we are finished, don't you?"

Murdock didn't react to her. "That's fine. I just have one more question: Where were you last Thursday and the Tuesday before?"

The surprise on Keeva's face made my day. Ardman laughed. "I supposed that is a polite way of asking me if I have an alibi on the days of these murders. I was here, Mr. Murdock. Both days. My staff's loyalty does not extend to lying if you would like to verify that."

Murdock nodded. "Thank you."

"Thank you for your time, Rose," said Keeva. Sophie Wells reappeared to let us out. As soon as the door closed behind us, Keeva whirled on Murdock. "That was way out of line, Detective."

Murdock's eyebrows went up. "What?"

"You don't accuse royalty of murder, even if she is an Inverni," she said.

I frowned. "Lay off, Keeva. He didn't accuse her of anything. He was doing his job—even if she's 'an Inverni.' What makes you think the Boston P.D. care whether she's royalty or not?"

She narrowed her eyes at me. "You're welcome for the help." She launched herself into the sky with an angry buzz and disappeared over the roofline.

I shook my head as I watched her go. "It never lasts."

17

I sat on a concrete block overlooking the fairy ring, waiting for Dylan. The trees on the hill had dropped their leaves in a thick carpet around the mushrooms. The air felt damp, cool, not cold. The fairy ring gave off its own warmth, a residual effect of its power. Gargoyles crouched among the trees, humming to themselves as they enjoyed the concentration of essence. They gathered around the fairy ring like an odd bunch of people watching the grass grow. I was curious why Dylan had asked me to meet him there instead of at a bar.

Despite the late hour, people milled outside the ring. Two Danann security agents roamed the perimeter, not actively preventing anyone from going near the ring but sending the message to behave. They ensured the mushrooms didn't get damaged. Every year the city asked the Guild for security backup since it was better equipped to deal with drunk fey people who might, for instance, accidentally set things on fire with their minds. The Guild beefed up security on Samhain especially. Fey groups arrived with competing claims to the spot, fought over space, and trampled the ring as they attempted to perform their ceremonial rituals. The veil between worlds wouldn't open, just as it had never opened since Convergence; people would be disappointed; everyone would go home grumpy. Except the here-born like me.

The here-born were fey who never knew Faerie or the ability to travel the Ways across realms. The Samhain celebrations have the odor of nostalgia for something we don't remember or believe. Older generations may talk of speaking with the dead and seeing long-lost loved ones, but to the here-born, they're all just stories like those of Santa Claus. Nice to know growing up, hard to swallow as an adult. We went through the prayers and the ceremonial fire-lightings, then hightailed it out on the town for Halloween parties with the human normals.

"Woolgathering?" Dylan asked as he came up behind me. He swung his long legs over the concrete bench.

I shrugged. "A little. I was just wondering if rituals mean anything to me."

Dylan gazed across the fairy ring. "Everyone has rituals that mean something to them. You're asking a larger question."

I eyeballed him. "Do tell, O, psychic one."

He kept his gaze ahead, but smiled. "You're wondering if anything means enough to you to have a ritual for it."

Dylan always seemed to understand what I was thinking before I did. Apparently, he still had the knack. "True enough. I've been ripped down to the point where everything I thought I wanted is kinda meaningless."

Dylan swayed his feet in small arcs. "We used to want the same things. You're not as sure of yourself as you used to be."

I smiled ruefully. "Maybe not all the same things. Lots of things have changed about me. I'm going to go with 'that's a good thing' for now."

He seemed about to say something, but changed his mind and chuckled. "Yeah. I guess you have to. We have to. Everyone has to get through the day."

I glanced at him. That sounded a little world-weary for Dylan, but I didn't detect any hint of melancholy about him. He was happy with where and who he was. It showed in the set of his jaw and the relaxed way he held his shoulders. He may recognize flaws in himself, maybe even admit to them, but they didn't bother him. They never had, for as long as I could remember. He was comfortable in his own skin in a way I didn't know if I could be anymore.

We sat in companionable silence. "Why did you leave like that, Connor? After everything that happened, you up and moved to Boston without even discussing it."

The question was ten years in the making. I tried to brave it out, so I didn't look at him and tried to sound indifferent. "It was my career, my decision."

He snorted. "I didn't say you needed my permission. We were a team. A good one. After the *Pride Wind*, we could have written our own orders. I thought you'd at least ask my advice. Danu's blood, you left a message on my answering machine and didn't take my calls for a year before I gave up."

I rubbed my face. "I didn't want the responsibility."

He frowned. "For what?"

I couldn't look at him. I didn't want to see the hurt. "You. I didn't want to be responsible for you. That day on the ferry, when our essences merged, I felt what you felt. I didn't want the responsibility of not hurting you. So I left."

He shook his head. "Uh . . . thanks?"

My chest tightened with anger. I never wanted to have this conversation. Whether I was angry at myself for causing the situation or Dylan for pressing it, it meant facing up to yet another example of my bad behavior. I knew I had to if I wanted to get on with my life. I didn't have to like it.

"What did you want to happen, Dylan? Have me tell you I didn't feel the same way? Did you want to hear that? Could we have worked together after that? What would have happened if you took too many risks for me and died because of it? What kind of position is that to put me in?"

He shrugged and smiled. "The same one you'd be in anyway. When our essences merged, I felt what you felt, too, you know. The difference between us was that it confirmed what I already knew. I'm not stupid, Connor. I knew the score. The one thing I knew was that regardless, we would still do the right thing at the right time. That's why we worked so well together. When that knife hit my chest, you threw yourself in front of that essence-bolt to protect me, and it had nothing to do with how you felt about me personally and everything to do with the man you are. Above everything else, I knew I could always respect and trust you. I thought you would do the same."

I frowned. "What essence-bolt?"

He looked at me in disbelief. "The essence-bolt on the *Pride Wind* that hit you in the head. I thought it killed you."

"Dylan, I don't remember getting hit with an essence-bolt."

His face turned pensive. "I'll never forget it. You fell next to me. Everything but you faded to white. All I could see was you. The next thing I knew, you merged our essences and saved my life."

I stared at my feet. I didn't remember. My stomach felt sick. All this time, and Bergin Vize wasn't the first time I'd lost my memory. Maybe the *Pride Wind* wasn't the first time either. How the hell was I supposed to figure out the first time I didn't remember something?

"Con?"

I shook myself out of my reverie. "I'm sorry, Dyl. That's all I think I can say, and it doesn't cover it. I should have trusted that you would have been okay about it."

"You did, but, maybe not in the right way. I got over it. You. I would have either way. But, thanks. I needed to hear that," he said.

"I'm an idiot. We could have been friends all this time."

He shrugged. "We're druids. Ten years is nothing."

I didn't want to get into my mortality fears, so I tried to lighten the mood. "Now that that's out of the way, want to go get a beer?"

He hesitated, and I felt a smidge of guilt that he was thinking I was trampling on his feelings again. "Actually, I asked you here for your input on my current job." He nodded to the fairy ring. "I was hoping with that hopped-up ability of yours, you could tell me what's there."

It wasn't an unreasonable request. My essence-sensing ability focused on the surrounding essence, and an alternate vision of the landscape materialized. For those who can see, essence manifested as light in an infinite array of colors and intensities. Why it did that was anyone's guess, but the effects of the various kinds and levels defined what it meant to be fey. Some of us could see it acutely, while others had a vague sense that it was there. Some fey had the ability to manipulate it with fine precision, and some did it with blunt force. Human normals can't see or use it at all, one of the many reasons they fear the fey. I can't say I blamed them.

The fairy ring emitted a spectrum of yellow hues, the ring of mushrooms a deep gold, the ground within and without it a deeper bronze. Above the ring, the air shimmered a faint yellow-white in an inverted cone that twisted off into the night sky. The Taint surrounded the cone in a mottled green-and-black vapor. It made my stomach queasy when I looked.

"Except for the Taint, it looks how a fairy ring looks around Samhain—a bright spot of focused air essence, the kind fairies love. They don't call them fairy rings for nothing."

Dylan squinted. By the way he focused, he was using his own ability to look at the ring. "Exactly the same?"

The colors were unusually bright considering Samhain was still a few days away. "Stronger. I think. I've never been this sensitive to essence before, but it looks stronger than it usually does this early. The Taint amplifies essence, Dyl. That's what we're seeing—the natural increase of essence during Samhain, enhanced by the Taint."

He considered before responding. "I think it's more than that. Essence has been building for days, especially here in Boston. Fey portals are glowing more intensely everywhere, but nowhere as strongly as here. A lot of smart people think the veil between worlds may finally be thinning again."

I stared at the thickening yellow essence. Convergence closed all the realms—Faerie, TirNaNog, Valhalla, Avalon, Caer Wydyr, Asgard—all sealed off from this land where I was born and raised in Boston. Some people thought the realms weren't sealed but were simply gone, destroyed by a cataclysm no one remembers. What we saw every year, when the so-called veil thinned, was a residual memory on this side of the veil, the only side that existed anymore. Every Samhain, the fey gathered about their fairy rings and hoped that maybe this time they'd find a way back to Faerie. "It's an illusion, Dylan. The Taint is raising false hope."

"Bergin Vize is certainly curious about it," he said.

I narrowed my eyes at him. "Spill it."

"He's been spotted around Externsteine."

If Tara was the Irish heartland of the Celtic fey, Externsteine in Germany served the same purpose for the Teutonic fey. Ancient rock formations formed a line of spires that the Teutonic Consortium claimed they had inhabited eons ago. It was outside the Teutonic Consortium's homeland, but Donor Elfenkonig, the Elven King, was granted sovereign status over it.

"Celts haven't been there in centuries. There's no fairy ring at Externsteine," I said.

Dylan leaned back on his hands. "I said fey portals are flaring—fairy rings, stone circles, standing stones—anything positioned at traditional sacred sites."

My memory clicked. The ancient German tribes used stone pillars carved like trees to commune with the realms of their gods. The most famous, some say the only true one, was near Externsteine. It vanished in the Middle Ages. My Middle Ages. Who knows whether it still existed in the Teutonic regions of Faerie. Almost the first thing the Teutonic fey did after Convergence was restore the pillar at Externsteine and give it the original's name. "The Irminsul," I said.

Dylan nodded. "Reports say it's alive with essence like this fairy ring. We know most every associate of Bergin Vize has gone deep underground. The pattern to their last sightings indicated they're moving to join him at Externsteine."

"Then the Elven King is supporting him?" I asked. It would explain why the Teutonic Consortium was no help with arresting him.

"If he is, he's covering his tracks. We can't make a connection," said Dylan.

I stared at the fairy ring. "So Vize gets into TirNaNog. He'll get the safe fey world he wants and stop trying to blow up this one. We'd be rid of him."

Dylan perched one foot on the wall and rested his chin on his knee. "I'm not sure. If he wanted to get to TirNaNog, he could have someone kill him. He'd die and wake up there."

"Not if he wasn't sure it existed. Maybe he wants proof."

He sighed, more in thought than exasperation. "According to the legends, the portals connect this world to the other realms. There's no rule that says when you enter through one portal you can't exit through another."

"You think he's going to go in through the Irminsul to come here? Is that why you're worried about the Taint?"

Dylan let out a low chuckle. "Not here, Con. There've been Teutonic spies at Tara. I told you, we're seeing evidence that a major assault is being planned. Three major portals are showing signs of opening to TirNaNog—here, the Irminsul, and the fairy ring at Tara. The Seelie Court wants to shut the portals down as a defense measure."

I tried to wrap my head around that. "Shut them down? After all these years of trying to find a way back to Faerie, they want to shut down a possible way in?"

Dylan leaned back. "TirNaNog is only part of Faerie. If—and it's a big if—TirNaNog opens, it doesn't mean that it will lead to all of Faerie. If TirNaNog opens in Germany and here, it will probably open in Tara. Vize could use it as a path to attack the Seelie Court. If the Elven King is supporting Bergin Vize, Maeve could fall and the Celts with her."

I shrugged. "Maeve has an army, Dylan. She won't roll over for them."

He nodded. "And her army is spread all over Europe. She can't afford to pull troops back to Ireland on a 'maybe.' If Tara is attacked, Maeve will never be able to gather reinforcements in time. It's a win-win situation for Donor Elfenkonig. By letting Vize do his dirty work, he either finds a way back to Faerie through TirNaNog and decimates the Celtic fey on his way or he stands aside while Vize attacks Tara through TirNaNog and ends up the dominant fey leader here. Either way, Maeve loses."

Things shifted into place—the hearings, the pressure on me and Meryl, Ceridwen's anger about the spear. "That's why Ceridwen wants to know what happened at Forest Hills. They want to use the Taint."

Dylan looked at me speculatively. "Boston is the wild card because it's not an ancient fey site. Whatever's happening in that fairy ring must be related to the Taint. If the Seelie Court can understand what happened that opened the portals, they might be able to control access to all of them. They need you and Meryl to cooperate."

I hopped off the stone. "What the hell, Dylan? Is that why you asked me here? Make me feel all guilty about the past and get me to spill my guts about Forest Hills?"

"No. You're misinterpreting my intention," he said.

"Really? The Guild didn't figure Connor Grey's old pal would persuade him to help Maeve find a weapon she can use against the Elven King?"

He rocked forward and grabbed the edge of the seat. "Back off, Connor. I'm trying to manage a mess you helped create."

I threw my hands out. "I didn't create any mess. I didn't make that control spell. Meryl and I told you guys everything. She almost died, and I can't remember a damned thing."

He shook his head. "That's not good enough. You have to remember something. I'm not supposed to tell you all this, you know. Ceridwen would blow a fit if she knew the secrecy I'm breaching here. She's been speculating that you are involved. Your feelings about the Seelie Court are hardly a secret. There are bigger issues here than you and me."

I wanted to hit him. "That's what Ceridwen said to me. You're not helping your case."

He set his jaw. "We need to know what you and Meryl know."

An angry surge of adrenaline reached out to my abilities.

The black mass in my mind was having none of it. Daggers of pain blocked the connection before it could form. "Go to hell, Dylan."

I stalked away. In my anger, I didn't pay attention to where I was walking. I stepped through the circle of mushrooms and entered the fairy ring. Red pain flashed across my eyes as the darkness in my mind convulsed. The essence of the ring resonated with a strange sensation of otherness, something slick and clinging as it touched my skin. My vision blurred, and the ground shifted beneath my feet. Everything went dark, and I had the impression of huge towering stones. In a flash, the familiar Victorian buildings around the Common reasserted themselves as I stumbled out of the ring. People lingering nearby stared at me like I was some kind of ghost.

Dylan stood to my left, far from the stone block I had left him sitting on. Panicked, he rushed to my side. "Are you all right?"

I shook my head to clear it. "I saw . . ." I stopped. I wasn't sure what it was.

He held my arm. "What happened? You froze and then fell forward."

I pushed him away. "Nothing. Get away from me."

He reached for me again. "Con, let's go somewhere and talk . . ."

I didn't answer. I made my way down the hill toward the Downtown Crossing retail district. Dylan called my name a few times but didn't follow me. I mingled in among shoppers, envious of their obliviousness. No one paid me any attention. People went about their business, catching a store still open or rushing home late from work. They didn't look like they knew or cared about fairy rings or Faerie queens or strange essence portals. Good for them. They didn't know how lucky they were.

I was tired. Tired of the unknown. Tired of the suspicions. Tired of getting sucked into Guild politics. I didn't care about the fairy ring or Maeve or Donor Elfenkonig. I just wanted my life back. But every day it seemed the more I tried to heal myself, the more things changed for the worse. My mind was damaged. My abilities gone, my memory screwed. The constant pain in my head. I didn't know if my memories were buried or just not there at all. And now I was hearing strange whispering voices and seeing people no one else saw. It was starting to scare me. After everything that had happened, maybe I was losing it. The worst part was trying to figure out if I would know I was losing it or if I would become too demented to know the difference.

Dylan was right about one thing. I might not like the Teutonic Consortium, but that didn't mean I was willing to hand Maeve the means to stomp all over Europe through mysterious fairy portals, even if I could. As far as I was concerned, the Seelie Court was only slightly less dangerous. Playing mind games with me by using my friends was a strange way to treat someone Maeve wanted for an ally. She had never done anything to make me think she cared about me, or even that she knew I existed. Why should I care about her? If that was how they all wanted to play, they deserved whatever Bergin Vize and Donor Elfenkonig threw at them, and it wasn't my problem. I had my own hell to deal with.

18

Someone was singing in my apartment. I stood to the side as I opened the door, in case it wasn't who I thought it was. You can never be too sure of anything in my line of work. My building had security wards everywhere. Still, it had taken a year for me not to freak out when I heard noise when there should be no noise. I had keyed the wards to allow certain people past them without setting them off. It's a short list.

Joe sat on the counter. He was on my list because otherwise he would keep setting the wards off whenever he had an urge to eat whatever I had handy in the cabinets. With his cheeks engorged, he waved half an Oreo at me. "Milk."

I took a shot glass out of the cabinet, poured the milk, and placed it next to him. He put the cookie down and gulped from the glass. And belched. "I can't believe you still haven't bought a nice flit-size glass for me."

I crossed my arms. "I can't believe you steal my food."

He feigned innocence. "Steal? It's still here. Sort of."

Popping the remains of the Oreo in his mouth, he swigged some milk and made a face. "You don't happen to have a bit of the whiskey to go with this?"

I pulled a pint of Jameson's from the cabinet. He held the shot glass up as I topped it off. "This is disgusting," I said.

He sipped and sighed. "Ah, but it reminds me of my child-hood. Any mother will tell you, whiskey is the best way to wean a wee one off milk."

"Flit mothers work it a bit differently." I resisted the urge to use a patronizing tone. Who was I to criticize what makes sense for a flit mother?

He toasted me and finished the glass. "Ah. You are a most excellent host."

I leaned against the back of the armchair facing the kitchen counter. "Joe, let me ask you something. You've killed people, right?"

He fluttered up from the counter. "Only the ones I've wanted dead."

"How many?"

He swayed in the air, humming. I think someone had had a little Jameson's before he got to my place. "I'm not sure. Enough to make the complaints annoying."

Having a conversation with Joe was an art form. I was used to his out-of-the-blue comments, but this was a new one. I've known him all my life, but he sometimes forgot that I haven't known him all *his* life. He makes strange references and non sequiturs that assume I know what the hell he's talk-ing about. "Complaints?"

He screwed up his face. " 'Course. I'm not mind-deaf like *some* people."

Not the direction I wanted the conversation to go, but with an opening like that, I had to ask. "Who complains, Joe?"

With a loop in the air, he flew to the window and did a handstand on the sill. I wasn't impressed. He cheated by using his wings to hold steady. "The ones I've killed with their sing-ing all the time. Can you see the queen naked from here?"

I joined him at the window. "No, she pulls the blinds. What singing people did you kill?"

He huffed and looked at me with concern. "Are you daft? Why would I kill singing people? You're acting strange. Are you okay?"

Said the drunk flit.

"I'm fine, Joe. I've had a lot on my mind lately," I said.

He swooped back to the kitchen for another cookie. "You think too much. Think, think, think, all the time, thinking."

He flew back to the window. Actually, he flew into the window, banged his head, and fell on his back. "You have a crack in your ceiling," he said.

"You made it when you flew into it last month."

"Is that a crack?" he asked.

"Drink, drink, drink, all the time, drinking," I said.

He rolled with laughter. Laughing myself, I went to the kitchen counter to get a beer. When I turned back to the living room, I froze. Joe lay on the floor chuckling. Above him, the view outside the window was filled with Guild security agents in flight, sweeping across the harbor. "What the hell?" I said.

Joe sat up, his laughter fading when he saw the agents. Without a word, he vanished. I grabbed my coat and ran down to the street. Sirens wailed as I hit the sidewalk. At the corner of Old Northern, at least a dozen police cars swept by. The officer at the security barricade near the bridge pointed at me. "Inside! That's an order!" he shouted.

I didn't argue. It wasn't worth the delay, and he had the badge. When you're on your own turf, you don't need to use the main streets. I backtracked around my building to the dockside, across the rotting loading dock to the next street, and cut through an empty warehouse. Two blocks farther, and I was back on Old Northern. Several more blocks down, flashing police lights joined flares of essence-fire.

Joe popped in next to me. "It's a fight. Dylan's tearing it up with some gang, and Keeva's got tin-heads with her."

Sudden winds buffeted me from every side as I ran toward the commotion. Empty police cars clogged the street. The officers were not in the fight. They stationed themselves in secure positions on the side streets and alleys to keep pedestrians away. The dark mass in my head vibrated, like it was trying to decide whether to stab me in the brain. My essence-sensing ability kicked in on its own. A cloud of Taint filled the sky, tendrils of it dangling into a cluster of people in the street, mostly dwarves and elves, facing outward in a circle. The dwarves were shielding the elves, who were taking shots at the airborne Guild agents.

Calmly facing them, Dylan was wrapped in a dense body shield, white bolts of essence leaping from his hands. He moved forward, his fire intercepting his attacker's shots, the two streams of essence sparking and dissipating as they tangled. What he missed warped around his shield.

The mass of Taint moved like a balloon made from mist, shuddering and bouncing in the wind as it floated above the fight, the tendrils hanging down fluttering and swaying, leaping from one person to the next. The elves and dwarves were trapped, but not going down without a fight. The Taint would goad them to fight as long as it remained stabilized. Keeva held her agents above the fray to avoid losing control of them to the Taint. She had learned her lessen at Forest Hills. Dylan could hold his own, but the Taint made it all a stalemate.

"Joe, can you get in there and avoid the Taint?" I asked.

He hovered higher, his eyes shifting as he scanned the street. "I think so. Want me to go kill them all?"

I whipped my head around. *"What?"*

He snickered. "I know they're not singing, but I'll kill them if you want. I still don't know why you hate singing people."

I shook my head. "No, Joe. No killing unless you have to. I need you to do two sendings. Tell Keeva to circle around behind Dylan and do some weathering to blow the Taint off. Tell Dylan to be ready to hit the fighters. Tell them both to do it the moment you distract them."

"Me? What am I supposed to do?"

"Give those guys an essence flash in the face and jump out as fast as possible," I said.

"Ohhhh. Tricksy," he said. The tickle of a sending brushed against my senses as Joe leaned forward, then frowned. "Ha! Keeva called me a little pest, which is really quite rude, isn't it?"

"She's called you worse." Regardless of what she thought,

Keeva complied. She circled down and landed next to Dylan. The air around her vibrated with particles of blue and white as she prepared her spell-casting. I gave her time to build up a charge.

"Now, Joe! Get in and get out!"

He vanished. A fraction of a second later, he appeared in a tangle of Tainted essence strands in front of the fighters, and a fraction after that, released a bright burst of pink essence that spotted my vision. The frontline fighters swung their faces away, disoriented by the flare. Keeva released her spell. A blast of cold air rushed down the street, and the Taint collapsed into itself, then shredded off. A tightly focused bolt of essence shot from Dylan's hand and knocked the line of fighters off their feet. The elves and dwarves scattered in confusion as Guild agents moved in. I lost sense of what was happening as everyone rushed forward.

Police shouted at me as I ran through the scattered cars. In the aftermath, Guild agents and police officers chased down the fighters who had run off while the rest were immobilized in spellbindings. I joined Keeva and Dylan standing over several inert bodies that agents were binding in cocoons of white essence.

"You've still got your fight coordination down. Good work," Dylan said when he saw me. Nice words, but he didn't look at me.

Keeva scowled, but the tension between me and Dylan seemed to lighten her mood. "Yeah, thanks," she said.

Dylan watched Keeva escort her agents to a nearby van as they carried several elves away. "Your friend Carmine was attacked. The primary attacker got away. These were her support team."

"You were protecting Carmine?"

Dylan kept a professional detachment. Still didn't look at me. "Not really. Some people were taking an odd interest in him. When you showed up to talk to him at the Fish Pier, Ceridwen was convinced you were part of some conspiracy, so she increased surveillance on him. Lucky for him."

"Is he okay?" I asked.

Dylan nodded. "Pretty banged up, but he probably wouldn't have lasted much longer if we weren't there. I can't figure what it's about."

"Carmine told me some Teutonic guys were looking for a Red Man. What was the attacker wearing?"

By his expression, Dylan thought the question was weird. "Mismatched clothes. She looked like a homeless woman. Why?"

"That sounds like the druidess who visited Carmine a few days ago. She said she was looking for one of the victims in the murder case I'm working on with Murdock, but Carmine said he saw her with these guys and was worried about himself."

"Why didn't you tell me?" he asked.

I shrugged. "I just did. How was I supposed to know you were tracking these guys?" I hesitated, uncertain whether to continue. I hadn't told anyone but Meryl about my dreams. Given what Carmine told me—and what he looked like—I decided to put my personal feelings aside and act like a professional. "I dreamed of a red figure fighting a black figure. It looks like someone took out the Red Man."

Dylan gave me a considering look. "But who is the man in black?"

I was wearing my jeans and leather jacket, both black. "I helped stop the fight. Maybe it's me."

Forgetting we were angry with each other, Dylan laughed. "Danu's blood, Con. Now you're a Dreamer? Is there no end to this supposed loss of abilities you have?"

I didn't respond. If I knew the answer to that question, well, I'd know the answer to that question. He watched the rest of the street fighters being led to a police van. "Our cases have crossed. I guess this means we're working together," he said.

Dylan's offer to go to New York was sincere. I knew it was. If I could make being at the Guild again work, going to New York could be the way to make that happen. Maybe this was a sign I was wrong, that maybe everything that had happened to me in Boston didn't need to be resolved in Boston. Maybe I needed to put everything that had happened at the Boston Guild behind me and stop being so angry. Move on instead of eking out a bare existence. Maybe I needed to trust Dylan's motives, too. Playing out the case together, seeing how we worked together, might answer some of those questions for me.

We made a good team. We always had. As long as I knew I could trust him. After our argument at the fairy ring, I didn't know what to think, but not trusting him didn't sit well.

"Yeah, I guess we need to work together," I said.

Dylan stretched his arm out. "Damn, you don't happen to know a good reweaver in town, do you?"

His coat sleeve had caught some essence flashback. A slash of blackened material marred the rich maroon fabric. As we stood there, me in my black jacket and Dylan in his deep red coat, the imagery in my dream floated through my mind again. A cold feeling crept into my gut that had nothing to do with the wind off the harbor.

19

Like all hospitals, Avalon Memorial had an odor that told you immediately where you were. In addition to physical ailments, it specialized in fey-related illness and issues. As you walked the corridors, the usual antiseptic odors mingled with mists and vapors that were uniquely fey. It smelled like an herbalist shop set up in an operating room. Dylan had left a message that Keeva had been admitted. He thought I would want to know. That was it. No mention of why. No mention of our argument.

Two voices drifted up the hallway before I reached the room at the end of the fifth floor. Over the years, I had gotten more than familiar with both voices in their raised, annoyed versions.

"Dammit, Gillen, enough's enough," I heard Keeva say.

"Shut up and stick your wings out," he replied. My eyes met those of a nurse at the station desk, and she gave me a little conspiratorial smile. Gillen Yor was High Healer of Avalon Memorial. Irrascible was his middle name, sometimes his first. Usually a workforce despised his type, but Gillen was refreshingly equal-opportunity impatient and rarely arbitrary. It meant a lot to a nurse when he tore a new one into a famous fey regardless of who was around.

The door to Keeva's room was open. She faced the hallway, arms crossed tightly across her chest. Her wings were, in fact, flexed out as far as they could go. Through the gossamer membranes, Gillen's silhouette moved as he sent short pulses of yellow essence into her wings. Keeva glared. "You have to leave now, Gillen. I have Guild business."

Gillen didn't even bother looking up. "Sit down, Grey, and if I hear one word out of you, I'll give you a headache."

I shot a sympathetic shrug at Keeva and sat in the chair by the bed. It would be an exaggeration to call Gillen my personal healer. Since my accident, he had taken my case more for the challenge than out of empathy. Patients did not pick Gillen; he picked them. I kept quiet as he finished examining her, barking questions at Keeva while she barked answers back.

He moved in front of her. I pulled my feet back before he had a chance to give me a hint by stomping on them. I suppressed a smile at the juxtaposition of him and Keeva. Even with her seated, he had to look up at her. He must have been having a frustrating day since the ring of hair around his bald spot was pulled in several directions. By the way he peered at her, he was assessing Keeva with his druid sensing-ability. While the two of them stared at each other, I took a look myself.

Keeva was a Danann fairy related to an old royal line. Dananns have potent levels of essence. It was part of the reason they won the Seelie Court. Any history book will tell you, people and families who lead—rule—did so because some kind of physical advantage lurked in their past. The Dananns may keep their dominance through money and politics these days, but it was founded with a conquering army.

Even someone with weak ability could read Keeva's body essence. She glowed with Power. To her credit, something I always hated to give, she used the threat of that Power more than its expression. The threat was enough. Only a crazy person would go after her using essence as a weapon. Keeva would not hesitate to respond in kind.

And yet, someone had been crazy enough to go after her.

In the midst of all her flaring white-and-golden essence swirls, her head and her chest glimmered with faint orange light. That's essence damage. A larger anomaly glowed deeper within her essence but resisted the damage. She was healing, but the injury was considerable.

"You need rest and healing. Two weeks in bed, no work," Gillen said.

Her essence flared bright with emotion. "First I'm confined to my desk; now I'm confined to bed? What is this, a conspiracy?"

"A conspiracy? At the Guild? What is the world coming to?" I said. I couldn't help myself. Keeva liked to pretend the Guild was an office with management glitches. I preferred to think of it as a fetid swamp of intrigue and backstabbing.

They frowned at me. Gillen's long eyebrows moved like cat's whiskers as I became the subject of his scrutiny. "Your essence gets odder all the time," he said.

Without asking, he grabbed my hand and examined it like it wasn't attached to the rest of me. Bedside manner was not Gillen's strong point. He hummed and grunted a few times, but whether he was chanting or thinking was hard to tell. He dropped my hand. "The troll essence has bonded. You're not reading pure druid."

I flexed my fingers. A troll had saved my life by infusing me with his essence. Most of it had dissipated, but somehow I had retained the ability to manipulate inorganic matter. I couldn't burrow through rock like a troll, but inorganic particles clung to me if I touched them too long. "Is that bad?"

Gillen shrugged. "Can't tell. Maybe if someone would make time in his busy unemployment schedule, I could run some decent tests."

He pointed a bony finger at Keeva. "Bed!" he said and left.

"You look like you've had better days," I said.

Keeva slid off the bed and rummaged in her designer leather handbag. "I've had worse."

"What happened?"

She pulled makeup out of the bag. Leaning toward the

mirror on the wall next to the bed, she applied eye shadow. When a woman puts on makeup in front of a man, she's not putting it on for him. "I was attacked in my bedroom."

"Oh? How is Ryan, by the way?" Ryan macGoren was Keeva's current lover. The stomach-churning rumor had it that the feelings were real and mutual.

She didn't bat an eyelash. "Funny man. Funny, funny man."

"Seriously, what happened?"

She sorted through lipsticks and picked one. "I was asleep. Someone entered my suite and set off the proximity wards."

"Suite? You weren't home?"

Her eyes flicked toward me in the mirror and back to her lips. "In case you haven't noticed, Connor, it's been a little busy since the fey no-go zones went up. I was working late, so I stayed at the Four Seasons."

"How long have you been doing that?"

She brushed her hair. "A week or so."

"That sounds like a lot of work," I said.

She paused, then turned toward me. "I've been getting threats. I killed a few people at Forest Hills, Connor. There are people who aren't happy about that."

Keeva had been manipulated into attacking people—poisoned, actually. Joe had stopped her with a head shock of essence. He didn't want her to know he did it. "I was there, Keeva. You didn't know what you were doing."

She resumed fixing her hair. "But it happened, and I have to deal with it. Including dodging angry people on the street."

"So, someone could have been following you for days," I said.

She gathered her cosmetics and tossed them in her bag. "Right. Probably a thousand people saw me go back and forth from the Guild to the hotel."

"So give me details. What happened?"

She let out an exasperated sigh. "I woke up. The alarms were going off. Someone rushed in firing essence-bolts at me.

I was already on the move. We exchanged fire. He got a lucky shot in. By the time I got up, security had arrived, and he was gone."

"He?"

Keeva considered. "Actually, it could have been a woman. It was dark. I don't even know what kind of fey it was."

I thought about it for a moment. "You were definitely followed. It sounds like security and escape routes were scoped out. The timing was off for the kill."

Her face relaxed with a smile as something occurred to her. "The wards. With all the threats, I set up extra wards. Whoever knew my routine wasn't expecting that."

I nodded. "You were lucky. Whoever it was knew how to get past your basic security. You should probably have a security detail for a while."

She arched an eyebrow. "I *am* security detail, remember?" She gathered her bag and slung it over her shoulder. "And speaking of which, I have to get back to work."

I followed her to the elevator. "Gillen said rest, Keeva. He's right. Between the head shock at Forest Hills and whatever happened to you last night, you need to rest."

She punched the DOWN button. "I think I can handle myself, thank you."

We rode the elevator down. "Fine. Then who knows enough about your security warding to get all the way into your bedroom?"

Keeva didn't slow down as we walked through the main lobby. "Whoever it was got lucky, Connor. Leave mc alone."

I grabbed her arm. "Okay, then what about me? You set up the security in my apartment. Are you confident I'm protected?"

A sneer curled on her lips as she looked at my hand. "Is the great Connor Grey afraid?"

I let her go and threw my hand in the air. "Play it your way, Keeva. You get overconfident, you get killed. Sorry I was concerned for both of us."

"This isn't your problem," she said. She pushed through

the revolving door and jumped in a cab. By the time I hit the curb, the yellow car had pulled away. Murdock's car rolled up from the fire lane, where he had been waiting for me. I slouched in the passenger seat without bothering to toss the newspapers. He edged into traffic.

"She didn't look bad. I'm glad I didn't bring flowers," he said.

I snorted. "She's in denial. All the damage is on the inside."

"How'd it go down?"

I briefed him on her attack.

"We should put protection on Ardman and Meryl," he said.

"You think it's related to Viten?" I asked.

He shrugged. "Just covering the bases. That's four attacks related to the case."

"I count only three, assuming Keeva's is related."

He gave me his oh-so-patient look. "Did you read the Guild file on Ardman?"

"Of course," I said. He looked doubtful. "Okay, I read most of it." He gave me the look again. "Okay, okay, I skimmed. I was bored. It was financial crap."

He sighed. "Josef Kaspar needed independent verification that Viten was fey; otherwise, the Guild would have dismissed his complaint. He tracked Viten for a few days and made a connection. Your buddy Belgor."

My mouth dropped open. "Belgor ratted Viten out to the Guild?"

"Hard to believe from such a paragon of virtue," he said.

I let the comment go. Murdock used snitches as much as I did, but Belgor annoyed him. Since the elf didn't traffic in the kind of stolen goods the human-normal judicial system cares about, it was a waste of time for Murdock to charge him with anything, assuming he had something. Belgor knew it and didn't deal him any dirt. "He's been working on something for me. This sounds like a good time for a visit."

Murdock made the quick turn onto the elevated highway

that would loop us back to the Weird. We pulled onto Calvin Place. The plate-glass windows of Belgor's shopfront had been replaced. Fingerprints and streaks covered them and would probably never be cleaned if Belgor kept his usual standards. I was surprised he didn't spray dust on them to fit the rest of the décor.

The little bell above the door rang when we entered. To all outward appearances, the shop seemed the same room full of oddities. While a certain amount of ambient essence filled the space—the echoes of times past in used wands or ward stones, the vibrant hint from a sealed jar of strange herbs used in potions—none approached the level of potency that normally lurked in Belgor's merchandise.

The old elf stood behind the counter at the rear, leaning meaty hands palm down on the countertop. He didn't look happy to see me. He never did. The feeling was mutual. We weren't friends and never would be. Despite helping each other on occasion, our entire interaction was based on friendly opposition.

"You've cleaned out the place," I said.

He worried his thick lips. "I cleaned *up*, Mr. Grey." So his recent slip-up with the museum goods was forcing Belgor to be careful. He was immortal. He could afford to lose money for a while. That should mollify Murdock.

He hit me with a sending. *They are listening.* His eyes shifted to the curtained door to the back room. My sensing ability got an immediate hit of a Danann fairy signature, a Guild security agent judging by the strength. I caught Murdock's eye and nodded toward the door.

I leaned against the counter. "We thought we'd stop by and see if you remembered anything more about your attacker."

His neck wattles gave a little shimmy as he shook his head. "Unfortunately, no, Mr. Grey. My mind has been quite occupied with repairing the damage."

I have learned that the gentleman who acquired the museum merchandise and the courier who brought it here were both paid by an Inverni fairy.

I trailed my finger through the dust on the counter. "Maybe you screwed her out of a deal?"

Belgor glowered. "Occasionally, my needs do not coincide with my clients' needs, Mr. Grey. But I do not believe I've ever done anything to provoke anyone to kill me."

Murdock snorted at that. If he hadn't been a cop, he probably would have taken a shot at Belgor himself. I wrote "Viten" in the dust. "Maybe you ratted on someone, and a little revenge came into play?"

His ears flexed down, long, pointy hairs sticking out the ends. He looked at the name for a long moment before wiping it away. "A much more likely scenario, though I prefer to use the term 'information-sharing.' "

Interesting. I did not find a name, but perhaps you have, he sent.

There weren't many Inverni fairies in Boston, and Rosavear Ardman was the only one related to the Viten case. The idea that she was involved in attacking a slovenly stolen goods dealer in the Weird made my head whirl. "Maybe I have."

I realized I had responded to his sending by Belgor's nervous glance at the curtained doorway. I mouthed, "Sorry." "I assure you, Mr. Grey, as soon as I remember anything more, I will contact you or the Guild."

I dropped a five-dollar bill on the counter. "Thanks, Belgor. Sorry to bother you. We only stopped in because Detective Murdock wanted a lottery ticket."

Belgor waved a hand toward the thick roll of scratch tickets for the state lottery. "What would you like, Detective?"

Murdock shot me an annoyed look. He's not a fan of gambling, even if it is state-sponsored. He pointed at one of the numbered rolls. Belgor tore off a ticket and slid it across the counter. "Good luck, sir."

We returned to Murdock's car. He tossed the ticket at me. "The Guild's got a babysitter on him?"

"Danann security agent," I said. "Belgor came through with some interesting information, though. He said an Inverni fairy paid for the museum heist."

Murdock pushed his lower lip out. "Ha. I knew something was up with that Ardman woman. After we interviewed her, I double-checked the Viten files. Viten used a different alias and glamour to hide his identity in New York. The Guild made the connection through financial records."

I thumbnail-scratched at the silver patches on the ticket. "So?"

A sly look came over him, the one he gets when something clicks. "According to the file, Ardman didn't know about the affair with Powell, but the other day she said she did. I thought it was odd but didn't have a reason to follow it up."

"Huh. I'm still not seeing a motive for the murders. What's Ardman get out of it?"

"Maybe we need another visit with her, too."

"I hope we have better luck with her," I said. I held the scratch ticket up. We didn't win the lottery.

20

A surprised Sophie Wells answered the door when we rang the bell on Pinckney Street. "Is Lady Ardman expecting you?"

"She should be," said Murdock.

Wells looked like she was trying to decide whether that answered her question, but she did let us in. She led us into the parlor, then knocked on one of the pocket doors at the back. At a muffled reply, she slid a door open and leaned her head into the next room. I couldn't hear the exchange, but Wells turned to us with a professional smile and pulled the door open all the way. In the next room, Lady Ardman rose from her desk.

"Is something wrong?" she asked.

I kept my tone neutral. "We've received some new information we'd like to talk to you about."

Ardman glanced at the secretary, who nodded and left the room. "What can I do to help, gentlemen?"

"It concerns the Met robbery in New York. We were hoping you might be able to shed some light on the situation," I said.

The pleasant cooperative expression slipped off her face. "I thought you were here about Lionel. What would I know about a robbery in New York?"

I slid my hands into my pockets to look relaxed. Keeva was right about one thing when it came to dealing with fairy royalty—an aggressive stance rarely worked well. "The two seem to be connected. Some of the stolen items turned up here. The information we have is that the thieves were working for someone else. That someone paid a large sum of money for the job, and we have a strong lead on the source."

Ardman sat on the couch. Turning away and not meeting the eyes is always a good sign I'm on the right track. "I don't see how this involves me, Mr. Grey."

I pursed my lips a moment. "Lady Ardman, two people are dead. A murder attempt was made last night on Keeva macNeve. You don't seem the type to let people die who are only trying to help you. If you know something, you have to tell us."

She closed her eyes and rubbed her forehead. "I don't know anything."

Murdock stepped closer. "Why didn't you mention you knew about Viten's affair with Rhonda Powell?"

Ardman looked at him in surprise. "What are you talking about?"

"Last time we spoke, you said the affair was a private pain for years," he said. "According to the case file, the Guild uncovered the affair through financial records. You told the Guild back then you didn't know about the affair until after Viten was arrested."

Ardman's hesitation confirmed that Murdock had hit on something. The Inverni woman stared at her hands. "This is extremely embarrassing, but I suppose it doesn't matter anymore. I discovered the affair and confronted him. He told me he would break it off. I never met that woman, but I knew her name."

She didn't look embarrassed. She looked nervous.

"Why didn't you say anything?" I asked.

Tears welled up in her eyes. "Fear, Mr. Grey. I suspected

Lionel was having an affair. I'm embarrassed to say I went through his things. I found a soul stone that wasn't mine. Lionel had a protection charm on it, because he knew I touched it. We argued, and his lies poured out. He told me he would take care of the situation. That's how he put it. 'Take care of the situation.' I didn't think anything about it at the time. But that phrase came back to me when I read that Rhonda Powell had been murdered. I feared for my life if I were to say anything after that."

I could buy that. Finding out a husband's mistress was shot dead right after an affair was discovered would spook anyone. "Do you know if he had accomplices other than Powell?"

She paled. "I didn't think so. Lionel trusted no one. Not even his mistress as it turns out."

Her voice was soft. I crouched in front of her. "Lady Ardman, who did you pay for the Met robbery?"

The tears began to fall. "I don't know what you're talking about."

I put my hand on hers. "Lady Ardman, financial transactions can be tracked. If you tell us what happened, we may be able to stop more murders. Please tell us before it's too late."

She sobbed and fumbled with a handkerchief. "I don't know who she is, Mr. Grey, but she knows everything about me. She has my soul stone and would give it to me if I gave her money. She said if I didn't give her the money, she would destroy the stone."

"Did she give it back?"

Ardman shook her head. "She said she's not ready yet."

"Ready for what?"

"I don't know! All I wanted was the stone. I didn't know anything about murders," said Ardman.

"Why is this stone so important?" Murdock asked.

I shook my head at him to let it go for now. I dropped my voice. Meryl told me once that I lose sight of the human emotion of a situation when I'm investigating. "Rosavear, she's killing people connected to Viten. You're more connected than any of them. I don't think she's going to give your stone back."

She hit her knee with a clenched fist. "I knew it. I knew it wasn't over."

"We need you to help us catch whoever this is. Can you do that?"

She nodded vigorously. I gestured for Murdock to join me in the foyer.

"We have to bring the Guild into this," I said, when we were out of earshot.

"I'm not going to argue," he said. "What the hell is a soul stone?"

"It's an old custom between fey lovers. They give their souls to each other. It takes a lot of ability. You branch off the soul and infuse a ward stone with it."

Disbelief swept Murdock's face. "The fey have detachable *souls*?"

I kept my eye on Ardman. "I doubt it. If I understand the theory behind the spell, it's not really a soul like you think. It's more their basic life spark, the core of their essence."

"And Viten made one for Powell and Ardman," he said.

I nodded. "Right. Only lovers do it because it's an enormous trust issue. If you crush a soul stone, it's like physically crushing someone's heart. The person dies."

If anything, Murdock looked even more stunned. "Are you kidding me?"

I held my hands up. "That's what I've heard. It may or not be the soul, but it's one helluva powerful spell."

He shook his head with an odd look of anger. "That's bullshit. Souls don't work that way."

I was about to say something flip but stopped. Murdock's Catholic. Talk of using a soul in a spell was treading way too hard on his theology. "Think of it as essence, then. Here's the key part, though. Whether it's the soul or essence or whatever, if you fatally injure the body of someone who has a soul stone, the soul stone can revive the body."

Murdock shook his head several times before speaking. "God, I can't believe this."

I nodded. "Viten shot Rhonda Powell in New York while her soul stone was in Boston. She's not dead."

21

Things moved quickly once Ardman agreed to cooperate. Given her history with the case, the Guild allowed Keeva's participation in the investigation. I suspected it was to keep her out of the way with a crime the Guild thought was unimportant. Ceridwen had bigger issues to worry about.

Sitting in Keeva's office and planning a Guild surveillance operation after so much time was surreal, yet oddly comfortable. Keeva had been surprisingly compassionate in debriefing Ardman. Caring on her part made red flags go up for me, but then the cynic in me found a reason for her kindly attitude. When all else fails, royalty closes ranks, even if they're not of the same line.

"It's a huge leap to think it's Rhonda Powell," Keeva said.

"It fits," I said. "No one else is alive. No one else knows what she knows."

"Correction. No one is alive. Powell is dead," she said.

"I guess we'll have to see who's right," I said.

She smiled. "I guess we will."

Ardman had a prearranged signal with her blackmailer for setting up meetings. We had her send the signal. The idea was to stage a meeting, keep Ardman protected, and trap Powell—or as Keeva would have it, whoever—before she had a chance to escape. After going over the security plan for the umpteenth time, I stretched in my chair and exhaled loudly. "You still haven't told me where you are going to be in all this."

She compressed her thin lips into an even thinner smile. "Monitoring everything. That's all you need to know."

I shrugged. "Be that way. Just remember what Gillen Yor told you."

"I can take care of myself, Connor."

Dylan stuck his head in the doorway. "Can I steal Connor for a minute?"

Keeva shooed me out the door with a flutter of her hands. If anything confirmed why I'd rather jump off a bridge than work for her, that gesture did. I joined Dylan in the corridor.

"Follow me," he said. He kept his head down as we made our way across the department. When we reached his office, he checked the hallway, then closed the door and leaned against it. "Meryl's been arrested."

I pinned him against the door. "What are you pulling, Dylan?"

He tried to push me off, activating his body shield, but I clung to his jacket. I shook him. "What did you do?"

He released his shield and raised his hands to the sides. "We're not going to get in a fistfight, Connor. I didn't do anything."

We stared at each other. I knew him like I knew few people, the way he looked when he lied, when he was afraid, and when he was telling the truth. I dropped my hands. "What the hell is going on?"

He straightened his jacket. "I'm not sure. Remember that knife we found at Belgor's?"

"The Breton dagger?"

He nodded. "It wasn't the mate to one here like you thought. It *was* the one here."

I frowned. "I don't understand."

He held his hand up to silence me as he tilted his head to the door. He waited a moment, then continued. "I asked Meryl to bring me the other dagger you saw in the storeroom. When she released the essence field on it, we discovered it was a counterfeit. The dagger from Belgor's was the original."

"So why is Meryl under arrest?"

Guilt crept over his face. "She says someone else switched the daggers. I had the logs checked, but Meryl is the only one who entered that storeroom. When Keeva and I were called down to the Weird because of Carmine's attack, someone entered my office and took the knife."

"And what has any of that got to do with Meryl?"

He compressed his lips a moment. "Meryl's the only person who had high enough clearance for the storeroom and access to the department floor. She was seen on the floor that afternoon. I was debating what to do when Ceridwen caught wind of what was going on. She's charging Meryl with theft, tampering with evidence, and assaulting Belgor."

Hot anger gripped my chest. "This is bull, Dylan. Meryl comes up here for work all the time, and you know it. You and Ceridwen want her to answer questions about Forest Hills that she doesn't know the answers to."

Dylan shook his head. "Don't throw me in that pile, Connor. You know this is Ceridwen."

Frustrated, I spun away to keep from hitting him. It would have been dumb. It would have been striking out at the nearest thing, and he just happened to be it. Besides, Dylan could hold his own against me, even without his shields. "I want to talk to Meryl."

His worried look was genuine. "I'm not sure that's a good idea. You're on Ceridwen's list, too."

I rubbed my hands across the stubble on my head. "I don't answer to Ceridwen. I want to talk to Meryl, Dylan, and I want to do it now."

We didn't speak as he tried to decide what to do. Finally, he opened the door. "Let's go."

We took the elevator to a subbasement deeper than Meryl's office. I knew the place. It didn't get used much. Not unless the Guild wanted someone to disappear. The doors opened on a dim hallway, burning torches casting sooty light against walls of granite blocks. It should have had a sign that said: HINT: DUNGEON.

Halfway down in the gloom, two Danann security agents guarded an oaken door with a cast-iron dead bolt. They didn't move when we reached them. I felt sendings passing between them and Dylan. One of the agents opened the door.

"Make it quick," said Dylan.

I squinted against the harsh light from the small room. A cot and commode took up opposite corners. A plain wooden table stood in the middle. In the lone chair, Meryl relaxed with her hands behind her head and her feet up on the table. The door closed. I listened for a lock to slide into place, but none did.

Meryl dropped her feet to the floor. "I hope you brought some C-4. I really want to blow something up."

Just seeing her made my anxiety ease. As I came around the table, she stood, and I wrapped my arms around her. That meant I lifted her off the floor since I have a least a foot in height on her.

"Are you okay?" I said into her ear.

She giggled. "This is so lame, Grey."

I released her and kissed her on the top of the head. She hates that. I love that she hates that. "Meryl, Ceridwen can ruin you."

She waved her hand dismissively. "Blah, blah, blah."

I scanned the room and tapped my ear. "Can we talk?" I mouthed to her.

She pointed to a broken cup on the sink. "Yeah, we're fine. They left a listening ward. If that's the level of sophistication I'm dealing with, I'll be out of here tomorrow."

"What happened?"

She dropped back in the chair and jabbed her finger at the table. "Winny ap Hwyl happened. When I find that bitch, I'm going to kill her."

"Who the hell is she?"

"Rhonwen ap Hwyl. An old friend. *Former* old friend. She used to be chief archivist here. I hadn't seen her in years. She asked me to lunch and oh-gee-can-I-see-the-old-place. She stole the dagger the day she came to visit three weeks ago. I really am going to kill her," she said.

"Why didn't you just tell them that?"

She had the good grace to look embarrassed. "I didn't sign her in."

"The receptionists have been warning you about that for years."

She slumped in her chair. "It wouldn't matter anyway. I didn't steal the damned dagger, and I sure as hell didn't attack Belgor. Ceridwen isn't going to let a little thing like the truth stop her."

A thrill of realization went through me. "Your friend attacked Belgor. Anglicize the name Rhonwen ap Hwyl."

She let out an impressed whistle. "Rhonda Powell. Winny ap Hwyl was Viten's girlfriend. But how the hell did she survive a bullet to the head?"

"He made her a soul stone."

"I'll be damned. I didn't think those really worked." She paced behind the table, her face flush with excitement. "Holy crap! That's why Viten was down here. I never understood why he didn't just go to the lobby and run out the front door when he escaped his guards. Now I do. He came down to the archives to get his personal effects. He was going after Winny's soul stone."

The evidence tag from the Ardman file floated up from my memory. I rummaged in my jacket and found an ATM receipt with a pathetically low balance. I drew the ogham runes from the Viten evidence tag from memory. "This is where Viten's personal effects were stored. Is it the same room where the Breton dagger was?"

Meryl shook her head. "No, that's the one next to it. Now that I think of it, Winny asked to see the dagger's storeroom specifically. Maybe she had the wrong location."

"Could she have gotten in when you were distracted?"

She shook her head firmly. "The doors are keyed to my essence. Best security I know."

I tapped the receipt. "How do I get into that storeroom?"

"No problem." She placed her palm flat on the paper and chanted. Little shots of blue light dripped off her fingertips and faded into the paper. When she handed me the receipt, the paper was infused with her body essence. "Put this flat against the door and push."

I stood. "I'll get you out of here, Meryl."

She glanced at the door and winked. "I mapped this place, Grey. Don't be surprised if I send you a postcard from the Caribbean."

22

Dylan looked relieved when I left the cell alone, like he half expected Meryl and me to come out with guns blazing to make a getaway. We didn't speak until we were in the elevator, out of earshot of the guards. "I need to know whose side you're on," I said.

He met my eyes, straightforward with no hesitation. "Connor, I know you've been through a lot, so I'm not going to be insulted by that question. I wouldn't have told you anything if I wasn't on your side."

I hit the button for Meryl's office floor. "I need to check something. I don't want to ask you to lie if someone asks you about it. Do you want to wait here?"

He shook his head. "Before I answer that, I have to ask you something. If Meryl's really involved in something, will you do the right thing?"

I clenched my jaw. "I am doing the right thing. She's not involved."

He glanced up at the elevator lights. "Then let's go."

I led the way past Meryl's office to the maze of corridors where the storerooms were. Months ago, Meryl showed me the elegance of her ogham filing system since I never bothered to learn it when I was on staff. Because of the potent stuff in the archives, she had layers of security that ranged from baseline electronics to full-spell locks that only senior staff knew. She's explained it to me several times, but I still don't get it. A few wrong turns finally brought us to the room where the dagger had been stored. The first symbol on the ATM receipt matched the one above the next storeroom down. I pressed the receipt against the door, and Meryl's essence seeped into the wood. The lock clicked open.

Inside, file cabinets and storage boxes spread out in orderly ranks in an uncluttered room. We found the proper aisle and cabinet. I placed my hand on the handle of a drawer, looked at Dylan, and pulled. I closed my eyes in disappointment. The drawer was empty.

I leaned against the opposite filing cabinet. Dylan withdrew a slip of paper from the drawer. "Evidence from the Ardman case?"

I took the paper. "The woman who stole the dagger is named Rhonwen ap Hwyl, a.k.a. Rhonda Powell. There's no record she was here. To make it more fun, she's a former Guild employee."

Dylan pursed his lips. "And now you're going to tell me that this drawer shouldn't be empty."

I gave him a half smile. "Now do you wish you had waited by the elevator?"

He shook his head. "Nothing is ever simple."

I closed the drawer. "I want to see the entry log. Meryl says they never came in here."

We wound our way to Meryl's office. The Guild's logging systems were open to inspection by security staff, and you couldn't get a higher-level security staff than Dylan was. I rebooted Meryl's computer and slid the keyboard to Dylan. "You have access to the log."

He logged in, and the main Guildhouse menus came up. I accessed the archives' logs. The dagger's storeroom hadn't been entered except the past week when I found Meryl replacing the missing essence amplifier. I spotted the likely date of her friend's visit listed a few weeks earlier. Cross-checking it against the storeroom where the Ardman evidence was stored, the log showed the room had been accessed the same day. Meryl's security signature had activated the lock.

Dylan pointed out the access-code identifier. "That's a problem."

I rested my fingers on the keys without typing. "If it wasn't Meryl, how did she get in?"

Dylan walked to the opposite of the desk. "Powell must have somehow replicated Meryl's essence to gain access. A glamour could work, but I doubt a security lock could be fooled by it like people are."

We heard the metallic slide of the elevator, then voices in the hall. Dylan leaned out to look, and a professional smile sprang across his face. "Your Highness, I'm surprised to see you down here."

Ceridwen. Not the person I needed to see. The hallway had a straight view from the elevator. I couldn't slip into the storeroom area without her seeing me. The ATM receipt still had some of Meryl's essence on it. I pressed the slip of paper against the space between a credenza and a filing cabinet. A barrier spell feathered like cobwebs against my face as I walked through the wall.

On the other side of the illusion, a tunnel led to the subway. Meryl had let me use it once. She hadn't keyed it for me. I wouldn't have made it through without her essence on the ATM receipt. The light from the office cast a bare illumination into the hidden space. Dylan's voice trickled through the spell, but I couldn't make out what was being said. He glanced into the office and indicated no surprise when he didn't see me.

The dark mass in my head fluttered with a burst of pain at the same time a mental image of Ceridwen's spear popped into my head. It shone like a bright sliver of essence in my mind. Dylan backed into the office, with Ceridwen following him. She had the spear.

"I'm sorry you had to look for me, Your Highness," he said.

Ceridwen spoke to someone in the outer hall before closing the office door. With a confident smile, she tilted the

spear toward Dylan, rolling the tip across his cheek in a caress. "The truth this spear seeks takes many forms, Druid
macBain. We had only to ask it to guide us to you."

Dylan looked uncomfortable. Ceridwen cradled the spear
in the crook of one arm and glanced down at the desk. "Have
you found anything?"

He shifted some papers. "Nothing out of the ordinary. I've
only begun looking."

Ceridwen scanned the routine chaos of Meryl's desk. She
nudged a stack of books and picked up something small. As
she toyed with it between her thumb and index finger, it caught
the light with a metallic sheen. She dropped it back on the
desk. "We want to know if you find anything remotely interesting."

Dylan kept smiling. "These are the archives, Your Highness. Much of it is interesting. Can you offer me some guid-
ance?"

Ceridwen considered him with a measuring look. "Neither
of us is from here, Druid macBain. We were sent in the best
interests of the Seelie Court. We trust you have no conflicts in
your loyalties."

"None," Dylan said.

Ceridwen nodded once. "Good. We need to keep Meryl
Dian confined until we acquire the answers the High Queen
seeks. Find us the means to keep her so or the answers we
need, and we shall be very appreciative."

Dylan bowed. "I will do my best to serve the needs of the
Guild and Court, Your Highness."

She leaned forward, half-closing her eyes and smiling se-
ductively. "I want you to know that I shall personally be
very"—the smile widened—"appreciative."

Dylan blushed from his neck to his hairline. "Thank you,
Your Highness."

Ceridwen straightened and became businesslike again.
"You may call us at any time."

She left. Dylan picked up a sheet of paper and wandered to
the door as he read. Pausing at the threshold, his eyes shifted

down the hallway for a fraction of a second. He dropped the paper on the desk and faced the wall I hid behind.

I suppressed a chuckle as he peered at me from inches away. He pressed his hand against the wall. From my side of the spell, the hand flattened as he encountered what he perceived as a hard surface. "I can sense the residue of your essence here, Connor. Are you there?"

I stepped forward, letting my chest replace the wall beneath his hand. "I see you can still blush on cue."

He dropped his hand. "I don't think she suspected you were here, do you?"

I shrugged. "You know Dananns are not very good at sensing essence, and there's a lot of it in here."

He nodded at the wall. "Care to explain that?"

"It's a hidey-hole Meryl showed me. She uses it when she doesn't want to talk to people. She keyed it to my essence." If I revealed it was actually a full-blown exit, Meryl would be less understanding than Dylan would be if he knew I didn't tell him the whole truth. I felt guilty not telling him, but he would appreciate the nature of confidences.

A small earring lay on the desk where Ceridwen had dropped it. Something felt naggingly familiar about it. Ceridwen's brief contact with it had left her essence, but beneath it was Meryl's.

Dylan leaned against the desk. "Con, I know there are things you're not telling me, and I'm letting you. At some point, I expect you to tell me. Am I fooling myself by thinking that?"

That stung. He had every reason to say it, but coming from Dylan, it was tough to hear. I pretended to be interested in a pile of reports on Meryl's desk. "I hope not."

He bowed his head in thought. "Good. Because I would question my instincts if you walked away without a better explanation. I don't want that to happen again."

I lowered my head, too. "I know. I'll say I'm sorry now, but I promise this time we'll talk."

He lifted his head. "I'll take your word for it. Now, give

me five minutes to settle in my office, then get out of here without attracting attention."

He pushed away from the desk. I waited to make sure he left the floor. I picked up the earring again. It was a triskele, the druidic symbol of three spirals made with one continuous line. The symbol was generic, but something about the earring felt familiar. I stared at it and stared at it. I shivered as I recalled where I had seen it, or rather, its mate. It was bent and broken, but the piece of metal I found at the Kaspar murder scene was the mate to the one I held.

I stared and stared. The druidess essence I felt at the murder scenes was familiar. Familiar like Meryl. It wasn't the same, but close. She was angry with the Guild, angry with the way she was being treated. Maybe something happened to her at Forest Hills, something I didn't know about or understand. I was worried about myself. Maybe I should be worried about both of us.

I shook my head. Something was wrong. I was missing something. I refused to believe Meryl would kill two people for revenge of some kind. I put the earring back on the desk. She didn't do it. I trusted my instincts.

I walked back through the wall. The spell resisted a little this time. I groped my way down the dark passage until I came to a staircase. Keeping my hands on the walls, I climbed the long flight of stairs. At the top, pushing hard against the spell blocking the exit felt like sliding through molasses. The receipt essence was almost drained.

I exhaled when I made it through. The dim lighting of the subway tunnel blinded me after the total darkness of the stairs. The wall behind me appeared to be a solid concrete slab when I pressed it. I pulled out the receipt. Meryl's essence had faded to nothing. I would have stuck in the wall like a fly in amber if it had dissipated any sooner.

The platform at Boylston Street Station sat level with the train tracks. An old wire security fence prevented passengers from wandering into the tunnel. It worked more as a visual deterrent since you could walk around it. If you didn't want to be seen doing that, a gap near a wall worked just as well. I mingled with passengers coming down the stairs on the inbound side.

Concrete arches separated the two halves of the station with wrought-iron fencing preventing anyone from crossing the tracks. An outbound train must have just come through because the opposite platform was empty. A lone man walked down the outbound side. He stared at me. I hate when people stare for no reason, playing their dominance games with strangers.

I stared back. The guy moved to the edge of the tracks, not taking his eyes from me. He seemed angry or annoyed. Three more steps, and he stopped on the tracks. I don't know if anyone else had noticed him because I didn't want to lose the staring game. The echoing station picked up the rumble of an approaching train. I moved closer to the iron fencing. He broke our gaze and looked up the tunnel. Headlights appeared in the tunnel on his side. He turned back to me.

"Train's coming," I said.

Light illuminated the tracks, throwing his solemn face into a white relief.

"Buddy, step back," I said.

He didn't move. I shouted as the train pulled in, my voice lost in the screaming of its wheels against the steel tracks. I rushed to the fence. The train stopped with a set of windowed doors opposite me. The man was inside the train. Almost. The floor of the car was several feet higher than the ground, cutting through him at the waist. He hadn't changed his expression. *You're going to die soon,* he sent.

The train pulled away in a rush of color, leaving behind an empty track. I backed away as several people cast anxious looks at me. They probably thought I was nuts. I would have. I was already thinking maybe I was. Really. As in, hallucinating and losing it.

My mind reeled as I rode the next train to Park Street Station. Maybe I couldn't handle stress anymore. Maybe the thing in my head was causing brain damage. Maybe I was letting everything get to me like I never did before. Keeva was pushing herself beyond her limits; Meryl became more entangled in murder the more I tried to prove otherwise; Dylan was playing both friend and foe. And Joe had been too drunk lately to have a coherent conversation. Murdock might be a good sounding board, but he didn't appreciate what it was like to deal with Guild messes, never mind the possibility that I was losing my mind. I hit a speed dial on my cell.

"It's about time you called. Come on up," Briallen answered. She hung up before I could whine like a scared child.

23

The door to Briallen's house was always unlocked to me, allowing me to pass through her protective wards. I did a lot of growing up in her house, spent years learning things I never imagined possible when I was just a little kid. I trusted her with my life.

As I stood in the foyer, I sensed Briallen's essence trailing upstairs. I found her in the parlor by the fire. She stared into the flames, unmoving, though I knew she had sensed me the moment I'd entered the house.

"Ceridwen had Meryl arrested," I said.

Briallen didn't respond immediately. "Sooner than I thought."

I slumped into the opposite chair. "You knew?"

She pulled her legs up on the seat and adjusted her robes around them. "It was only a matter of time. Ceridwen is afraid of failing. High Queen Maeve doesn't take disappointment well."

"But Meryl doesn't know anything."

Briallen smiled as she sipped from a large mug. "I'm sure she would dispute that."

"You know what I mean. She's told them everything. We both have."

She leaned her head back in the nook of the chair, her eyes half-closed. "Have you?"

Her tone made me blush, caught out like a ten-year-old telling a fib. It's the tone she uses on me when she knows something that I think she doesn't know. "Okay, everything they need to know."

Briallen tweaked an eyebrow. "Deciding who needs to know what and who gets to decide that is the seed of most arguments in the world."

I sighed. "I hear what you're saying, but I don't remember anything but what I've told them. Ceridwen essentially threatened me to get me to talk, and even Dylan doesn't seem to believe me."

"He mentioned you argued," she said.

A little anger flared up. "You see? Ceridwen thinks arresting Meryl will put pressure on me to talk, and now Dylan thinks running to you will do it."

She let out an exasperated sigh. "I think it's only fair to point out that you're doing a little running to me right now."

"That's not true."

She scoffed at me. "Sure you are. You think Meryl's been arrested to put pressure on you, and you want me to confirm it. Did it ever occur to you that after you spoke to Dylan, he believed you? Has it occurred to you that Meryl doesn't exactly make any attempt to inspire confidence in her veracity?"

"She's telling the truth," I said.

Briallen thrust her index finger at me. "*You* believe that. *You* do. Not the Guild. Just like you don't want the Guild telling you what to do, the Guild doesn't want you telling it what to think. Meryl's a big girl. She'll decide what to do."

"If there is something she's hiding—and I don't think there is—she won't say it, just to spite Ceridwen for treating her like this. She's stubborn," I said.

Briallen shrugged. "Then she'll have to live with the consequences. Connor, you know Meryl well enough to know she won't do anything she doesn't want to. She's a druidess. She takes that seriously. Let her decide how to respond. Sometimes the Grove and the Guild do not have the same agenda."

"Don't let Ceridwen hear you say that, or you might end up in a cell yourself." I couldn't help the dig.

Briallen grinned. "I'd like to see her try. At the bottom of all this, she knows the Grove and the Guild want essentially the same things. It's just a matter of whose means to the end get used. Now, can we put this aside and discuss why you came to see me?"

Getting slapped down by Briallen didn't exactly put me in the mood to make myself vulnerable. I feigned innocence. "I came about Meryl."

Briallen laughed. "Oh, bull. You know I knew Meryl was under arrest ten minutes after she did. Something else is bothering you."

I bit my lower lip. "Okay, you're right. I came to ask you about something odd. Lately, I've been . . ." I didn't realize until that moment how strange and embarrassing this was going to sound. ". . . well, I guess you can say I've been hearing things. Like, things no one else does. And I'm seeing people who aren't there."

She didn't laugh or look at me like I was crazy. "What are they saying?"

I slid deeper in the chair. "I'm not sure. It started a little over a week ago. I kept hearing whispering. Then the whispers got louder, and I began to see people, too. At first, I thought it was some kind of spell, but it's happened too many times in too many places. They're angry. One of them attacked me, and, just now, on the subway, one of them told me I'm going to die."

Briallen leaned forward. "You're a druid. You'll live a long time, Connor."

"Yeah, as long as nobody kills me first. And we don't know how long a life I have anymore, Briallen. Whatever Bergin Vize did to destroy my abilities might have wrecked my chances for a long lifetime, too," I said.

Her eyes shifted to me. "I used to worry that you weren't going to live long. Do you know I never see you in my visions? The only way I know you're involved in something I see is because of reactions around you."

I exhaled sharply. "A dwarf said that to me not too long ago. You can't see my future, and I can't see my past."

"It's all connected, Connor. We are all connected. You know I believe that. Maybe whatever you are hearing and seeing is sending you a message that you haven't figured out yet. Maybe the Wheel of the World is trying to teach you something about yourself," she said.

I frowned. "By making me feel crazy?"

She smiled. "Maybe, Connor, maybe you're supposed to do things based on who you are and not what you know."

"But if I don't know anything, who does that make me?"

She shrugged. "A child who sees ghosts and runs to an adult for help."

I closed my eyes. "I hope you mean that metaphorically."

She giggled. Briallen giggles sometimes. It annoys the hell out of me. "Connor, I'm not going to say you're not hallucinating. You are a druid with damaged abilities. Things are happening to you that never happened to you before your accident. But what you just told me is exactly what's been plaguing you for two years: You can't remember, and you're afraid of the future. Maybe you're manifesting your own fears."

"What if my fears are real enough to kill me?"

She sighed. "All fears are real. It's what you do about them that matters."

I stared into the fire, letting the flickering light mesmerize me, the warmth soothe my skin. "You're saying I should let go of the past."

She shook her head. "If you think that will help, then do it and see what happens. I can't give you answers to questions only you can answer."

I dropped my head back against the chair. "You kick me in the balls every time I come here, and I still come back for more."

She laughed. That laugh, that lovely Briallen laugh. "And then you leave with tougher balls."

24

From our parking spot on Charles Street, Murdock and I had a good view of the Ardman townhouse. At least four Danann security agents monitored the area, two along the roofline across the street from the townhouse and two more nearby posing as shopkeepers. The Flat had enough fey living in it that Powell wasn't likely to notice anything unusual. As a concession to me and Murdock, Keeva agreed to use wireless headsets instead of sendings. As security agents cycled through a check-in every fifteen minutes, I heard at least one voice I didn't recognize. If I knew Keeva, she had more agents squirreled away along the street than she had told me about.

Murdock sipped his coffee. "She hasn't shown in two days."

"She'll show. Ardman is on her hit list," I said.

"Maybe Ardman signaled her it's a trap," he said.

I rocked my head against the headrest. "I doubt it. She's too scared Powell will crush the soul stone."

"So why doesn't Powell just do it?"

I crooked my neck toward him. "You know, that's an interesting question. She got the money and museum stuff, too. What's the delay?"

"The whole soul-stone thing bothers me," he said.

"Let it go, Murdock. Just because tradition says it's the soul doesn't mean it is. It's just a powerful spell," I said.

He sipped his coffee again. "Said the man who didn't believe in a drys until he met one."

He had a point. Meeting an actual incarnation of essence gave me pause on the whole faith issue. "I said it was possible the drys was a demigoddess. She could just as easily have been a powerful species of fey I'd never met before."

"Meryl believes in them."

I cocked an eyebrow at him. "When did you talk to Meryl?"

He kept his eyes on the townhouse. "I ran into her on Oh No the night you had dinner with Dylan. She was shopping for something I couldn't pronounce."

The night I had dinner with Dylan. The same night Belgor was attacked. Meryl was in the Weird. I pushed the thought away. I was not going to go there. "And you talked about the drys," I said.

"Just briefly. She was asking about my body shield. She said she had a dream about me. Said I was riding a flying horse on fire."

Meryl has a geasa on her about her dreaming. It's an obligation—deeper than a command, really—to do a certain thing or suffer dire consequences. Meryl's geasa is that if she has a dream and knows someone in it, she has a duty to tell that person. "Stay away from carousels. Her dreams come true," I said.

He took another sip of coffee. "Will do."

Something rustled within the pile of discarded fast-food bags in the backseat. I knew the cause because I sensed the essence. Murdock didn't react, which I thought was kind of curious. People hear something mucking around in their car, they tend to react a little. Then again, Murdock's car is such a sty, he's probably used to all kinds of critters roaming around in it. The rustling sound came again.

"There's no food back there, Joe," Murdock said nonchalantly.

"Who says I'm looking for food?" Joe's muffled voice came from beneath several layers of paper.

I chuckled. "How'd you know?" I said to Murdock.

Murdock kept his eyes on the street, but amusement played on his lips. "The first time I thought it was a rat. I whomped him with the billy club."

Joe crawled out of the paper wreckage. "And I gave him a nice zap back."

Murdock shifted his coffee to the side away from Joe. "It didn't hurt."

"Did, too," said Joe.

Murdock sipped his coffee. "Did not."

"Liar."

"You're lying."

"Am I hearing this?" I asked. Murdock laughed silently. Since we'd first met, I had been teaching him about the fey and how to react to them like a fey person would. Flits were a hurdle because he had a hard time not acting surprised when they teleported. Not flinching at Joe's arrival was a definite improvement. Engaging in Joe's penchant for squabbling wasn't. It was bad enough I did it.

Joe poked a finger in his ear, then scratched his head vigorously. "Still hearing singing?" I asked.

"At least a week now," Joe said.

Murdock kept his eyes on the street. "What singing?"

Joe made a face at me that implied Murdock was clueless. "Dead folks. It's Samhain, Murdock. You hear things."

I whipped my head around. "What did you say?"

Joe started to say something, then snapped his mouth closed. His eyes opened wide and broke open a huge grin. "I hear dead people!"

"Oh. That clears things up," said Murdock.

Joe wobbled in the air and poked him in the shoulder. "Yes! Yes! Yes! The veil's thinning! I haven't heard the voices since home."

I twisted in my seat. "Wait, wait, wait. Back up, Joe. Dead people? Is that what you meant by singing the other night? You hear dead people?"

Joe fluttered back. "Of course. It's just the haunts trying to make me regret what I did to them, soften me up for when they come calling on Samhain and try and scare me to death. That never works."

I slumped back in my seat in relief, too stunned to say anything. I wasn't going mad. I wasn't hearing voices that weren't there. I was hearing voices that were there. I wasn't going mad, if not going mad meant I was perfectly willing to believe that instead of having brain damage, I was being haunted by dead people. Not mad at all. "Can they attack you?"

He stopped looping. "Nah. Maybe on Samhain itself. The really angry ones can make you think they're doing it before that, though. I hate those kind. Stupid mind tricks. This is great. I haven't heard anyone in Anwwn since I was in Faerie."

"What's Anwwn?" Murdock asked.

"It's an hour after eleven," Joe and I said simultaneously. Joe screamed a laugh and slapped me on the shoulder. It was a favorite bad pun when I was a kid. Apparently, it still worked for Joe.

"Anwwn is what the Welsh folk called TirNaNog," I said.

Joe fluttered to the dashboard and faced the street. "The Wheel of the World turns, and the realms align. I hope I can get through. It'll be great to see some old friends," he said.

"Can you sit somewhere else, Joe? We're trying to be inconspicuous here," said Murdock. Joe stuck his tongue out and hopped down to the console between the seats.

"Fairies can come and go to . . ." Murdock paused. ". . . to the afterlife anytime they want?" The thought that the Celts didn't have a separate heaven and hell wasn't sitting well with Murdock.

Joe puffed his chest out. "No, just flits. We can get in anywhere."

"The traditional stories don't quite say that," I said.

He shrugged. "Well, of course they don't. They're about the kings and queens, aren't they? They always do what they want. That's why they're kings and queens, bringing people in and out with their branch charms and such. But the flits can come and go 'cause we're flits."

He jumped up and down. I hadn't seen him so excited in a long time. "This is the greatest! I have to go check the Ways and see if it's true."

He vanished. Murdock didn't react. He was getting better at it.

"I can't tell you how relieved I am right now," I said.

"Yeah, he's a bit much when he's drunk," said Murdock.

"No, I mean I'm not crazy. I thought I was hallucinating and going crazy. All this time, I've just been hearing people I killed," I said.

Murdock slowly turned his head and stared at me. "Uh-huh," he said.

"No, well, what I mean is . . . Wait a sec, there goes the secretary again," I said.

I was watching Ardman's secretary, Sophie Wells, but my mind was reeling with the idea of the dead haunting me. After so many days of anxiety, the things that had been happening to me had a rational explanation. Rational, of course, being a relative thing in my life.

Wells stepped off the threshold of the Ardman house, her movement snapping me back to attention. I'd told her twice to stop that because it made her look suspicious and might tip Powell. At least she had varied the time of her coffee run. She adjusted her scarf against the cold. The scarf was the all-clear signal that Powell had set up with Ardman, and she had worn it every day at the same time. Wells passed the car without looking at us this time, another thing I had had to explain to her. She wasn't stupid, just inexperienced.

Less than a minute later, she quick-stepped across the street from the opposite direction. I knew I didn't see her pass us and loop around. She turned the corner onto Pinckney, and her coat fluttered open to reveal her white blouse. No scarf. Suspicious, I did a flash sensing on her and grabbed the door handle. "It's her."

Murdock didn't waste time debating and followed. Wells had entered the Ardman townhouse by the time we reached the front door. I tapped on my earpiece. "Keeva, Wells is the target. She's glamoured."

Keeva's voice spoke calmly in my ear. "We've got Ardman in her office."

I nodded to Murdock. "The office off the parlor. You first, then me."

Murdock pulled his gun and opened the door. He led with his gun, and we strode through the foyer. Both pocket doors were open to the back office. Wells stood in the arch. Lady Ardman rose from her desk as Wells turned toward us with a confused look.

"Police. Hands out," Murdock said.

"What . . ." said Wells. She raised her hands in front of her.

Murdock rushed her and pointed the gun to the side of her head. "I said hands out, not up."

Panicked, Wells froze. "I don't understand, Officer."

Murdock pressed the gun against her temple. "Hands out or I put a bullet through your head. You know what that feels like, don't you, Powell?"

The fear slipped from Wells's face and became anger. "Lady Ardman, please! What's going on?"

Ardman smiled. "Let's all drop the masquerade, shall we?"

She slid her hands behind her neck and removed her necklace. Her face rippled, the colors blurring and shifting, and a glamour fell away. Impressed, I nodded as Keeva dropped the necklace on the desk. "Rhonwen ap Hwyl, a.k.a. Rhonda Powell, you are under arrest."

Wells moved nothing but her eyes, looking first at Keeva, then Murdock, then me. With a shrug, she stretched her hands out to the side as essence rippled over her. There have been moments in my life when I've seen things I couldn't believe, times when my eyes denied the reality in front of them. None of those times prepared me for the woman who stood in front of us. She shrank a few inches in height, her blond hair darkening to a pumpkin orange. I was wrong. I had been wrong. I was wrong, and I couldn't believe I was wrong.

"I can explain everything," Meryl said.

Keeva didn't miss a beat. "We can talk about that at the Guildhouse."

With a stricken look, Murdock relaxed his stance.

I struggled to find my voice. "Meryl, I don't understand."

A sad smile softened her face. "You will, honey."

Essence surged around her. Murdock's body shield flashed behind Meryl, filling the room with an angry red glow. In a blur of motion, he coldcocked her with his fist. She crumpled to the floor as Keeva deflected a ball of white essence that shot across the desk. It arced over her head and shattered a window.

Security agents rushed in, their hands primed with white light. Keeva came around the desk and stood over Meryl's body. "You're a little rough on the ladies, Detective," she said.

Speechless, I sank to my knees and checked for a pulse. Relieved, I found it strong and regular. I pulled her against my chest. Even though she seemed fine physically, her essence wavered in my vision in an odd cycle of white and blue. Something was wrong.

Looking deeper, Meryl's essence shone with a green haze but with an unnatural geometric shape burning blue in the middle of it, as if she had two different body signatures. I opened her coat. Something heavy shifted in the fabric. I slipped my hand into the inside pocket and found a brick of granite shot through with yellow crystal. Exactly like the ward stones Meryl used at the Guildhouse to amplify essence.

Without the ward stone, the woman in my arms blurred and changed shape. Her hair lightened to an ashen blond, and her features relaxed into the blunt face of someone I didn't know. Repulsed, I pushed her away.

"Rhonda Powell. You were right, Connor," said Keeva.

I looked up at Murdock. "How the hell did you know?"

He shrugged. "She called you honey. Meryl never calls you honey."

I shot to my feet. "Are you kidding me?"

He backed away as he holstered his gun. "I'd be lying if I said I knew it wasn't her, Connor. You were looking at her face. I keep my eyes on hands until they're in cuffs. Hers turned white. I've seen that enough around you guys to know what comes next. I hit her when I saw that essence shot about to release. I'd do it again even if I was sure it was Meryl."

Two responses warred within me. I wanted to thank him. I did. With Keeva's physical condition weakened, he'd probably saved her life. Without her, Murdock would have his body shield, but I would have had no protection. But hearing the truth of the matter, that at the right moment, he put his personal feelings aside and hurt someone he thought a friend, struck a very deep chord. It was exactly what I feared I would do to Dylan. No matter how justified, it didn't make me feel any better.

Keeva saved me from speaking. "Impressive reflexes, Murdock. I guess I owe you my thanks."

He inclined his head to her. "You're welcome."

Keeva gestured to the Danann agents. "Make sure she's properly secured. If she tries to escape, you are authorized to use any means necessary to take her down." The agents wove a binding spell around Powell's inert body, strands of fierce light winding about her body like rope. With practiced ease, they chanted a levitation spell to carry her out of the room.

"You could have told us you were here," I said.

Keeva gathered up her necklace glamour. "I don't believe in using civilians as bait."

Murdock and I exchanged glances. It was a dig at us. We had used a young human as bait not too long ago. It hadn't ended well.

"She should be in police custody," said Murdock.

Keeva sighed. "You're never happy, Murdock. You complain about the Guild not taking cases, and now you're complaining that we are."

"You're not taking the murder cases. You're taking a blackmail case," he said.

Keeva walked to the front door. "Have your father call me. I'm sure the commissioner and I can work something out."

Murdock's strange essence surged again, a crimson flickering that enveloped him like a shroud. "Let it go, Murdock. She's baiting you."

He nodded without speaking, and his essence settled. "I want to be there for the interrogation."

I hefted the ward stone Powell had used to create the Meryl glamour. "I think we're all going to enjoy this one."

25

Another day, another visit to the Guildhouse holding cells. Keeva had locked Rhonda Powell in the deepest subbasement the Guild had to offer. The only furniture in the granite-block cell room was the chair that Powell occupied. Five-foot-high quartz obelisks tipped with silver surrounded her to form a triangular essence barrier—standard protection wards. They suppressed most fey abilities. Protocol called for an added calming spell in case the suspect became agitated and tried to use essence anyway. Not that Powell needed it. For someone in as much trouble as she was, she acted like she was bored waiting for a doctor's appointment.

Against the chill in the room, Powell wore the brown plaid coat that matched Wells's. Glamours can change clothing, but it makes them harder to maintain over time. Without the glamour, Powell had the kind of bland, round face that's easily overlooked in a crowd. Like her lover Viten, that plainness was an advantage when using glamours. It's a heckuva lot easier to maintain strong facial features over slight ones than vice versa.

Keeva leaned against the wall near the door with her hands in the pockets of her black jumpsuit. To anyone who didn't know her well, she maintained an air of calm. I knew her, though. The set of her jaw and the steady stare meant she was in no mood for games. I couldn't blame her. The downside of being one of the good guys was you didn't get to kill someone who tried to kill you. At least not so you would get caught.

Dylan stood with his hands clasped behind his back. He glanced at Murdock and me when we walked in. "We know you arranged the Met robbery with money you extorted from Ardman. We have video surveillance of you at the Met," he said.

She shrugged. "Lots of people go to the Met."

"Dead people?" Murdock said.

She sneered at him. "Obviously you've mistaken me for someone else. I demand to be released."

Keeva cleared her throat. "I've heard that before. A little over ten years ago, someone else sat in that chair. Someone you know."

Scorn filled Powell's face. "I don't know what you're talking about."

Keeva strolled closer to the barrier. "We know you were Liddell Viten's partner, Powell. Viten shot you in the head, yet here you are. I'm wondering if Viten's not dead either."

Powell's gaze fell away. "He's dead."

"Then why kill people who could identify him?" I asked.

She looked at me with an impatient arrogance. "I killed no one."

"I can identify your essence at the murder scenes," I said.

A crooked smile broke across her face. "I doubt it. You would have to testify to what you truly sensed, and what you truly sensed was not me. I believe you already have the murderer in custody."

I kept my voice even. I didn't want her to have the satisfaction of knowing how angry I was. "Meryl Dian killed no one. You had the means and motive."

Powell feigned surprise. "Meryl Dian? I never mentioned her. But now that you bring her up, I had lunch with poor Meryl not too long ago. She's very troubled, you know. Something terrible happened to her a few weeks ago, and it wouldn't surprise me if she's become unbalanced. And bitter. Very bitter. She intimated that she would get what was coming to her from the Guild. In fact, she hinted about an old case she knew about with lots of money lying dormant. I have to wonder if there's some improprieties in her financial situation. Poor thing probably thought she didn't get enough recognition and decided to take matters into her own hands. I'd look into that if I were you."

I didn't exactly count to ten, but I did stop myself from saying anything. Powell was a con artist and, like all con artists, knew how to push people's buttons. I didn't let her. Instead, I looked at Murdock. "Meryl's going to love this story."

Keeva moved from the barrier and leaned against the wall again. "Nice theory, but it doesn't quite explain why you showed up at Rosavear Ardman's disguised as Meryl Dian. That, my friend, will throw more than enough doubt on your story."

Powell pursed her lips. "Did Lady Ardman ever mention her love of antique jewelry to you? She asked Meryl to arrange something for her, a purchase I believe. Meryl told me she was overworked and feared she wouldn't have time to complete the transaction with Ardman, so when we had lunch, she asked me to help her. She told me Ardman was a little paranoid so it would be better to glamour myself. I was under the impression it was a legitimate transaction. An old friend involved me in murder and robbery. I feel used."

Keeva withdrew a dull stone from her pocket. She held high it enough for Powell to see. "This stone was found in your possession. You threatened to crush Ardman's soul stone unless she cooperated."

Powell emitted a small surge of essence, the kind that reflects a change in emotion. She shook her head, but her eyes were riveted to the stone. "Soul stones are a myth. Meryl gave me that ward stone for safekeeping."

Keeva withdrew another stone from a different pocket and looked at it reflectively as she rolled it around in the palm of her hand. "Do you recognize this stone?"

Powell affected boredom.

"It's an interesting story how I came into possession of this particular stone," said Keeva. "A long time ago, I had a small case that turned into something much bigger. A con artist was implicated in a murder in New York. I handled the extradition, packed up the evidence we had collected, and sent it to the Guildhouse down there. Things didn't work out as planned, though, and the murderer ended up dead before trial. Months later, the unopened evidence was returned to me. I sent everything to the archives but kept this stone in my office as a reminder that I should be more vigilant in the future."

Keeva lifted her gaze to Powell. "It occurred to me recently that it could be a soul stone. Why else would Liddell Viten risk going down to the archives instead of escaping? But, you know what, Powell? I agree with you. The idea is absurd."

Keeva's hand glowed white with essence. She clenched her fist, and the stone crumbled. Powell blanched, clutching her chest in panic. Keeva brushed dust from her hands as Powell regained her composure. Keeva took yet another stone out of her pocket. "What an interesting reaction, Powell. That stone was a fake. Lady Ardman told me that you asked her for your soul stone, and you didn't believe her when she said she gave it to the Guild. Lady Ardman identified it for me. This one's yours, Powell, the very one you tried to steal out of the archives a couple of weeks ago and were sorely disappointed to find missing."

Powell finally showed a break in her demeanor. She struggled to remain unimpressed, but real fear crept into her eyes. Keeva placed a hand on the obelisk nearest her and shot a bolt of essence into it. The essence barrier collapsed. She stepped up to Powell. "I'm no fan of Meryl Dian, but I know a setup when I see one. Where are the artifacts you stole from the museum?"

"I told you I didn't . . ." Powell didn't get to finish. Keeva's essence pulsed to life, her wings flaring huge and white. With one hand, she grabbed Powell by the throat, lifted her from the chair, and thrust her against the back wall.

Dylan moved forward. "Director macNeve . . ." he said.

I grabbed his arm, and he stopped. I had never seen her lose her control when she was angry. Her methods could be aggressive sometimes, but she never crossed the line too far. Besides, I liked the look of terror in Powell's face. She was getting a taste of what her victims must have felt.

Keeva's eyes blazed white-hot as she leaned in toward Powell's terrified face. "Listen to me, Powell. You're legally dead. Know what that means? If I kill you, there's no crime. If you don't start answering questions, I'll keep killing you until I get them."

Powell's eyes bulged as she clutched at the hand at her throat. Keeva let out a burst of essence that made the druidess convulse. Powell dropped to the floor. "Start talking," Keeva said.

Tears poured down Powell's face as she coughed. "I demand an advocate," she said.

Keeva tangled her fingers in Powell's hair. Dylan pulled away from me with enough force to send the message he wasn't going to be stopped this time. "Enough," he said.

Keeva ignored him. She yanked Powell's head up. "I'll see if we have to allow an advocate in for a dead person. In the meantime, think about your soul stone."

She released Powell's hair, turned on her heel, and tossed the ward stone to Dylan. He caught it one-handed.

"You're welcome," she said to him as she walked out.

26

"I demand the return of my soul stone," Powell said.

Dylan reactivated the protection barrier around Powell. "You're not in a position to demand anything."

She stared for so long, I could almost see her evaluating her options. "I have information to trade that the Guild will want to know."

Dylan held the soul stone between his thumb and index finger. Its pale blue surface had an intricate series of depressions that looked like ripples in the sand on a beach. "So talk," he said.

"I want a promise in writing to turn over the stone before I will say anything," she said.

Dylan shrugged. "I'll need more than that before I agree, assuming I do. Make it worth it."

Powell adjusted her clothing and resumed her seat. "A terrorist attack on the Seelie Court is imminent. Is that enough for you?"

Dylan twitched a small smile at me. "I already know that. I also know the sun rises every day, the sky is blue, and you're not telling me anything. The Seelie Court is under constant threat of attack."

Powell kept her expression calm, but she couldn't hide her

annoyance. "Bergin Vize is going to launch an assault against High Queen Maeve."

Dylan moved toward the door. "Bergin Vize, Powell? Are you sure? Next you'll be telling me the Elven King hates Maeve and fairies have wings. You don't have anything to trade."

He gestured for Murdock and me to leave.

"He's found a way into TirNaNog," Powell said.

Dylan opened the door. "And now we move into fantasy."

Powell jumped to her feet. "You have less than hours before it happens. Give me the stone, and I will give you the names of all the Boston operatives I know that you didn't arrest when the pimp was attacked."

Dylan paused. "Now that's out of left field. Why should I care about them?"

Powell let a little confidence slide into her posture when she saw Dylan's hesitation. "Because they're part of it. Get me that signed promise. Now. And I will tell you what you need to know."

"How do you know this?" he asked.

She smiled. "You will get what I know in exchange for the written guarantee and the stone. How I know the information will be a point of discussion if you bring charges against me."

Smooth and confident. She was already negotiating the next phase before we had even agreed to the first. If Viten was her mentor, lovelorn widows didn't have a chance against him. Dylan appeared to consider what she said. He left the room without another word, and we followed.

Keeva was nowhere in sight outside the holding cell. If I had to guess, she was talking to the legal department about a hypothetical situation of an officially dead person's rights. The legal guys would smile, not ask real questions, and try to come up with a convoluted strategy to justify what Keeva wanted. Hypothetically, of course. I would win a bet that Rhonda Powell was not officially in the building. Yet. I knew how it worked. I had played that game myself when I was an agent. It didn't occur to me at the time that it was a bit fascist. I guess it never does when you're in charge of it.

Dylan raked his hand through his hair. "She's good. And she does know something. She connected the attack on the pimp with Vize's operatives. That's not public knowledge."

Murdock stared at him. "What about the murder charges?"

Dylan shrugged. "One thing at a time, Detective."

Murdock breathed out sharply through his nose. "If you have time, right? After the Guild takes care of its robbery and extortion charges, and some story about a terrorist attack, then maybe you'll look at making her accountable for non-fey murders."

Dylan threw me an irritated look. Like I was responsible for Murdock's annoyance and not the Guild status quo. "Some people would at least be satisfied that she's in custody," he said.

Murdock shook his head. "It's not the first time I've heard that one. I'm not some people. Some people would consider that two humans wouldn't be dead today if the Guild had focused first on Viten's fraud charges against a human woman ten years ago instead of his fey murder charges in New York. I'll send our files over. Nice working with you."

He gave me a twisted smile and walked to the elevator.

"Someone's annoyed," Dylan said.

"Just because he knows how things work doesn't mean he has to be happy about it."

"Like it's my fault," Dylan said.

"If you're not part of the solution . . ." I left the rest of it hanging. I didn't want to get into it with him. Dylan had a Guild mind-set, one I knew well. We'd argue about it at some point, but right then I had only one thing on my mind. "When are you going to release Meryl?"

"You shouldn't be here without Detective Murdock. Let me show you out." By the tone of his voice, he was talking for the guards' benefit. Which meant he didn't trust them.

He pulled me away from the agents. "I need to play that

carefully, Con. It's going to take us a while to discredit Powell's story about Meryl. Ceridwen won't let her go easily."

A wave of anger made me feel hot. "You have an innocent person locked up, Dyl, and you want me to wait while you play politics?"

He squeezed my arm. "Don't be dense, Connor. If we don't clear Meryl the right way, Ceridwen will find another excuse to hold her."

I steadied my breathing to calm myself. "What can you do, then?"

He dropped his hand. "We're missing something. I think it's time we went back to square one."

"The Met robbery," I said.

"It happened before both the murders and the Guild robbery. It was the start of whatever her plan is. Let's look at the file again."

The elevator doors opened on an empty Community Liaisons floor. Sundown was the traditional time for Samhain dinner, so the staff left early. Even so, Dylan closed the door to his office.

Files and evidence bags covered the desk. Dylan flipped open a folder and removed the insurance photos of the stolen Met items: the three fibulae, the torc, and the ring. With his usual tidiness, he lined them up by age of item. "They span centuries. The ring is fourth-century Saxon, and the torc is sixth-century Norse. The three brooches are all fairy circa fifth century, but from three different clans."

I leaned over the desk for a closer look. "There's no connection over that time period. They could be purposely random to hide the one item she really wanted."

Dylan slid the ring photo out of the line. "Okay, let's pull the Saxon ring. Its value is in its antiquity. The Teutonic Consortium would never let a true ring of power sit in a museum without making some claim to it."

I had already dismissed the torc and ring as irrelevant. They were used to entice Belgor, which Dylan didn't know. Powell was smart. She wouldn't have risked losing them if her plans went wrong. The fact that she did lose the torc and hadn't tried to retrieve it was proof enough. I wondered about the ring, though. Belgor mentioned it was part of his payment yet not where it ended up the night he was attacked. He probably still had it, a nice antique that would be easier to off-load than the torc. Of course, I couldn't tell Dylan all that. Not yet. Old partner and former Guild agent I may be, but at the moment I had the torc in my kitchen. Ceridwen would relish charging me with obstructing a Guild investigation and possession of stolen property.

I pushed the photo aside. "Let's pull the torc for the same reason."

That left the three fibulae—an apple tree, a mistletoe branch, and a horned serpent. Mystic symbols of life and the afterlife. A thrill of realization swept over me. "Put them back, Dylan. Put all of them back."

He lined up the photos again.

I tapped each photo in turn as I talked. "They *are* all connected. The ring is an ouroboros—a guardian of eternal life—and it matches up with the horned-serpent brooch, which is a symbol of Cernunnos, the lord of the life cycle. The torc is another Cernunnos symbol—the sign of rule over the life cycle. The mistletoe and the apple tree are talismans to the land of the dead, which is also the land of the ever-living. It's all circular. She's trying to make some connection between life and death."

I crossed my arms in triumph. "I don't believe a word she says, but I think she was telling the truth about Viten. She misses her boyfriend. She was trying to get into TirNaNog through any means she could except killing herself."

Dylan nodded slowly and pointed. "The apple-tree brooch. It must be a real silver branch that will grant her passage if the veil thins."

"That's the obvious one. The mistletoe and the serpent could be genuine, too."

Dylan leaned back in his chair. "What about the dagger from the Guild storeroom? She stole it—twice."

"That, my friend, she specifically wanted for some reason. It's not connected to the museum pieces in any way I know. Powell knows something about it we don't."

He looked skeptical. "She's not going to tell us."

Dylan was using the ward stone from Powell's jacket as a paperweight on a pile of notes. I hefted it in my hand and put as much evil in my grin as I could. "I know someone who knows more about ancient artifacts than the two of us combined. You have her locked up."

Dylan closed his eyes melodramatically. "Why do I have the feeling this is going to be trouble?"

Amused, I shrugged. "Trouble's Meryl's other main forte."

27

The door to the cell room opened with a groan. On the bed, Meryl lounged, reading a book propped against her knees. Without looking up, she held out her index finger and continued reading. Dylan and I waited until she closed the book and dropped it on the bed. "Hey, guys, what's up?"

"It's a breakout," I said.

She swung her feet to the floor. "Can we wait until after dinner? I ordered the lobster."

Dylan shook his head. "You are an odd person."

She grinned at him. "That never gets old."

I showed her the quartz warding stone. "Look familiar?"

She grabbed it. "My amplifier! Where the hell did you find it?"

"Rhonda Powell. She was using it to impersonate you."

Meryl passed the stone back and forth between her hands. "I can't believe I bought that bitch lunch."

"It has your essence all over it. Powell used it to get into the Viten evidence room. That's why it looked like you opened the door."

"We have her in custody," Dylan said.

Meryl scrunched up her face and closed one eye. "Does this mean I can't have the lobster?"

I took the chair nearest the bed. "The Guild insists on it.

Dylan thinks he should wait to release you until Powell's discredited."

She pursed her lips, then blinked a few times. "Okay."

That threw me. "Okay? Meryl, it's ridiculous."

Indifferent, she stretched back on the bed. "I'm getting paid while I sit here and read, Grey. It's even better than jury duty because they feed me and the food is good. Did I mention I ordered lobster for dinner?"

"Odd, odd person," Dylan muttered

While Dylan spread the museum photos on the table, I explained the setup at the Ardman townhouse that had led to Powell's capture.

"I hate to say it, but Keeva does know her shit," said Meryl.

I laughed. "You should have seen Powell's face when Keeva crushed the fake soul stone."

Despite his discomfort with the way Keeva handled Powell, amusement crept onto Dylan's face. "I did get a little satisfaction at that. But it was more satisfying seeing the look on Ardman's face when I gave her soul back."

Meryl looked impressed. "You know how soul stones work?"

He shrugged modestly. "It's an old interest."

I pulled a chair to the table. "Anyway, Meryl, since you are being paid as you say, maybe you can earn some of it and get yourself out of here."

I ran down my theory regarding the Met items. Meryl examined each photograph and played with their layout. She likes to pretend she doesn't care, but a good puzzle is red meat to her. Finally, she nodded. "I think you're right about her getting into TirNaNog. If the veil opens, it's an opportunity she wouldn't want to miss. But she's not going for a visit."

She slid on the bed to lean against the wall. "You're missing the obvious question: Why kill everyone related to the Viten case if Viten is dead?"

"Revenge," said Dylan.

Unconvinced, Meryl rocked her head from side to side. "Think it through. She's had ten years to do that, but she didn't. Now she has a chance to visit her dead lover. Why risk getting caught by taking revenge on the people who brought him down? The only reason that makes sense is if Viten is alive."

"It's Samhain," I said. "If the veil opens, he can come here."

"Right. But he would only be able to stay for the night until sunrise. That's when the veil closes," she said. "Why not use a soul dagger and accomplish something bigger?"

Dylan arched an eyebrow at her. "The Breton knife is a soul dagger?"

Meryl grinned. "It seeks living essence. That's why I had it warded the way I did—to keep it from stabbing anyone who walked in the room."

I looked from Dylan to Meryl. "I'm lost."

Dylan shook his head in amazement. "It works like a ward stone. It absorbs essence—life essence especially. I didn't make the connection because the knife is so old. I had no idea those kinds of blades were used that long ago. Powell captured the life essence of her victims."

Meryl stretched out on her side. "She essence-shocked them, then trapped their life essence in the Breton dagger."

"I get it. I don't get why," I said.

Meryl leaned forward with an avid look. "Winny wasn't going to visit Viten. She was mounting a rescue. She was going to try to pull him out of TirNaNog. With everyone involved in the case dead, they could live happily ever after."

Dylan gathered the photos and put them back in the folder. "The living can enter TirNaNog with a silver branch, but the dead can leave if they acquire enough soul essence. All Viten had to do was kill a living person with the dagger. The feedback from the souls in the blade would revitalize his own soul enough to win release from TirNaNog."

My head bopped between them like a Ping-Pong ball. "Okay, I guess I'm the class dunce. I never heard of any of this."

Dylan stood by the door. "Some people actually read a book or two after training, Con, and not just when they have a specific need of the moment."

Meryl cocked her head. "Really? He did things in the need of a moment? No long-term investment?"

Dylan shifted his eyes back and forth between us. "Uh . . . I don't think I'm touching that one. I'm going downstairs to talk to Powell again."

Meryl pulled herself to the edge of the bed. "Downstairs? You have her downstairs? Where downstairs?"

Dylan paused in thought. "This side, fourth cell down."

Meryl leaped to her feet. "Idiots!"

She knocked Dylan aside, tore open the door, and ran past the startled guard. The guard hesitated, uncertain whether to pursue her.

"We got it," I said. Meryl was already down the hall and going through the stairwell door. Dylan and I jostled each other chasing after her. "She's going to beat the hell out of her, you know," I said.

"Wouldn't be the first time that happened today, would it?" he asked.

We hit the lower level in time to catch Meryl struggling with the guards outside Powell's cell. The two Dananns had her arms pinned to her sides. I knew that determined look on her face. She glowed with a rich green light and released a burst of essence. The guards fell, stunned. Meryl kicked open the door and rushed inside. We reached the cell. Hands on her hips, Meryl stared at the empty space within the essence barrier. Powell was gone.

"How did she get out?" Dylan said.

Meryl pointed down. "Trapdoor in the floor."

Dylan gaped. "How the hell would she know that? How did you?"

Meryl rolled her eyes. "She was chief archivist before me. Winny showed me half the secret doors in this place."

Dylan released the barrier. Meryl crouched and pressed five floor pavers in sequence. Essence flared around the edges and vanished. A dark hole appeared. She sat down and swung her feet into the opening.

Dylan grabbed her shoulder. "Whoa! Where do you think you're going?"

The glare Meryl threw at his hand could have shriveled it. He judiciously removed it. "After her," she said.

"We'll go. You're under house detention," he said.

Meryl glowered at him. I've seen that look, too. "I know these tunnels. You don't. You either come with me, and I let you pretend I'm still in your custody, or get the hell out of my way."

Dylan stared at her dumbstruck. It's not every day that a high-ranking Guild department director has it thrown in his face that his rank doesn't matter one bit to the person in front of him. Of course, most directors don't work with Meryl either. She waited a good five seconds before she jumped.

28

I tried not to laugh at Dylan's dazed expression. "Make a decision, partner. She moves pretty fast."

He jumped. There was no question whether I would follow. The drop wasn't long, but I flubbed the landing in the dark. Meryl lit a small ball of blue light above her palm. "Took you long enough. She went this way."

Dylan and I followed as she jogged into the darkness. The tunnel was like the one off Meryl's office, a low and narrow corridor of granite. We moved without speaking, passing openings that breathed air over us, sometimes cool, sometimes warm. I opened my sensing ability, the dark mass in my head not objecting. Not long ago, I would get headaches and nosebleeds when I did a trail scenting. Ever since Forest Hills, the ability had expanded, and the dark mass left me alone. Which was great, but it left me anxious, like waiting for a hammer to fall on my brain.

Powell's essence permeated the tunnel. By the strength of the trail, she didn't have much of a head start. After we left, she must have waited in the cell only long enough to make sure we weren't coming back in immediately. "Where's this lead?" I asked.

Meryl didn't pause when she answered. "A nexus. From

there she can go into the subway, the sewer, or a couple of other places."

Within minutes, we reached the nexus. Our corridor fanned open, and the path split left and right. Directly ahead, stairs led up and another flight went down. Powell's essence went to both side directions and down the stairs. Meryl cursed under her breath.

"How the hell did she do that?" I asked.

She tilted her head, trying to gauge the right direction. "This nexus loops back on itself several times. She ran in a few circles to confuse us."

"Her essence trail has been getting thicker. We're getting closer," I said.

Meryl nodded. "I hate to say this, but we either split up or flip a coin."

"We have more than two choices," said Dylan.

Meryl couldn't help twisting the corner of her mouth. "Yeah, well, I didn't bring my poly-dice. I'll go left; Dylan goes right. You stay here, Grey, and watch the stairs. I don't want her coming up behind us."

"I'm not going to stand here and wait. I'll check down the stairs," I said.

In the blue glow of her light, Meryl looked spectral. "And if she's down there, what are you going to do, annoy her to a standstill?"

"Ouch," I said.

Meryl muttered, and a point of yellow light danced in the air above her other hand. She flicked her fingers, and the light sailed down the stairs. "That'll pop if she passes it. If it pops, I suggest you run like hell and call us, in that order. Winny is no slouch in the essence department."

"Fine," I said, annoyed and embarrassed. Dylan sparked his own light, and the two of them moved in opposite directions. My regular vision faded as their lights receded. My ability showed three ghostly essence signatures. Nothing lived in these tunnels to give off a sign of life. The darkness was so complete, I felt an overwhelming sensation of dizziness. I closed my eyes to stave off vertigo.

The sound of their footsteps died away. Time dragged as I listened for the faintest popping sound from the stairs. I focused on the essence around me, alert for the slightest change.

A gleeful sending from Meryl burst in my head. *Got her!*

I moved in an instant, chasing after Meryl's essence down the left-hand corridor. In the dark, I misjudged the floor and hit the wall when the path curved away, rounding upward.

Watch it. She set binding traps, Meryl sent. The essence signatures appeared to end ahead. I slowed my pace and ran into a wall again. The corridor bent sharply to the left. I swore loudly and kept going.

I can see her.

"We're here," I shouted. My voice rang hollow in the dark. The floor dipped abruptly, and I grabbed the granite wall to keep my balance. A burst of light ahead blinded me. I squeezed my eyes shut, using only my sensing ability to see where I was going. Another flash made my eyelids glow red, and essence-fire crackled loudly in the stone passage.

My body shields triggered against a binding spell that slithered from the ceiling. A streamer of hot light grabbed me. The shields stopped the binding from burrowing into my neck. Bindings come in two flavors: whole field, which feel like a numbing blanket thrown over your head, or ribbons, which feel like burning rope. Powell favored the latter. The binding looped on my neck pulled me against the wall. More ribbons snaked out of the wall, wrapping my arms and legs. I fought the urge to struggle. Resistance signals the ribbons to send fiery pain through the nerve endings.

I need . . . Meryl's sending broke off so quickly it stung.

"Meryl!" I yelled. The binding against my neck burned. I ignored it and yelled again. "Meryl!"

No answer. "Dylan!" I didn't think I was that far ahead of him.

I was close enough to hear fighting. Sendings don't take

long to make or send, unless you're me. The dark mass in my head clawed at my brain whenever I tried. I didn't care. Taking a deep breath, I wrapped my memory of Meryl's essence with the desire to talk to her. I pushed the thought out, one word calling Meryl's name. I gasped at the finger of pain that hit the bridge of my nose. The sending drifted away, a lazy tendril with none of the speed and power it should have had. This close, it should have reached her instantly. She didn't respond. I didn't know if it meant she didn't receive it or couldn't.

"Dammit, Meryl! Answer me!" Nothing.

A cool breeze fluttered across my face, cloying and unnatural. Dull green phosphorescence oozed out of the wall opposite me. It dripped down and pooled on the floor. Another glob appeared next to it, and another farther down. A moan quivered on the breeze, low and steady, then a sibilant whisper began to build. Another spot blossomed, then two more. More bubbled up from the floor and one on the ceiling. The whispering grew louder, breaking into voices tripping over one another.

The phosphorescence bulged from the walls. The ceiling spot sagged, grew thick and bulbous, and dropped to the floor in a gelatinous ball. The whispering became ragged and gasping as the sour green essence took on more substance. Blunt appendages sprouted from them, stretching out to test the air like the night of my alley run.

The essence emitted a strange vibration. The various masses gathered, spun, and swirled, shaping themselves into bodies. A face appeared in one, long and haughty, pressing toward me. It shook and sharp wings swept up out of the gelatinous mass. More coalesced, bodies shaping into human form, druid and human and fairy.

This was no time to be helplessly bound to a wall. "Dylan! I could use your help here!"

More than a dozen figures ranged around me, laughing at the feeble sound of my voice. I had met some of them before—the Inverni from the night of my alley run, the druid from the subway tracks, and the vanished man on the bridge on the night of my meeting with Ceridwen.

"Are you remembering?" a Danann fairy said, his voice echoing among the others. A woman stepped closer, blond, angry, white sparks in her eyes. Her hand burned on my cheek. "Do you remember the pain you've given?"

A druid pressed an index finger into my side, sending a shock through me. "Do you fear it?"

They moved in, their faces livid, eyes malevolent. Their essences electrified my skin. My heart raced, the binding spell tightening as I tried to pull away. Hands thrust forward, plunging into my body, and I screamed.

"Do you repent?" said the Inverni. He pushed his hand into my face. It seared pain into my skin. I knew him then, his essence familiar as it violated mine. He was from the ferry. They all were. I knew them all, remembered them, their body signatures stamped on my memory. The attack on the *Pride Wind*, the group that almost killed me and Dylan. My dead had come calling.

"I regret nothing," I shouted through the pain. "Nothing!"

"Then suffer our pain through the night," a druid said.

The Inverni pressed harder. I screamed as his hand sank into my head. They closed around him, all of them, hands clawing at my flesh, burrowing into muscle and bone and sending my body into convulsions. The dark mass in my mind spiked and somehow I screamed louder than I already was doing. Their expressions changed, became perplexed, then fearful.

The Inverni screamed, too. The others tried to pull away, but something dark trailed out of my skin, like a thick, curling mist. They screamed, all of them at once, a howling of rage and horror. The binding spell seared my flesh, but darkness wrapped the ribbons, and they sloughed off like char. Darkness filled my vision, blotting out everything.

I slumped to my knees, hearing screams, feeling essence pour into me as the mist snared the remaining figures. They died again. But this time, they didn't just die. This time their essences disintegrated, the dark mist tearing them to shreds, rending them to shards of light that had no integrity, no hope of incorporating into whoever they were. The mist absorbed it, sucking in the light, pulling the essence into my body.

I fell forward, gagging, chaotic images flooding my brain, places and faces I knew I'd never seen. I blacked out. At least I think I did. My body hung suspended in a nothingness, not the dark mist, but a blackness, silent and deep. Dying screams echoed in the nothingness, ringing hollowly in my ears.

Someone called my name from far off. The screams faded away. I drifted in the blackness, numb with the silence. I heard my name again, louder. White light filled my mind, flooding me in a wash of soothing essence. I opened my eyes. Dylan knelt over me, his face frightened even as he radiated healing essence over me. "Connor? Can you hear me?"

The mist dissipated. I found my voice. "I'm okay."

He gave a ragged sigh as he pulled me to his chest. "Danu, you don't look okay. What the hell happened? Where's Meryl?"

His warmth enveloped me, his essence wrapping me in a cocoon of relief. The fog lifted from my mind. I sat forward, breaking his embrace. "We have to find her."

Blood rushed to my head as Dylan helped me up. I leaned against the wall to steady myself, feeling the stone flow onto my fingers. My skin felt alive, every nerve ending firing. I breathed deeply.

"You were screaming," he said.

Dylan's essence illuminated the corridor. No evidence of my attackers remained. "I killed them again, Dylan. The ones from that day. They came for me, and I killed them again."

He brought his hand to my chin, tilting my face from side to side. "You had smoke coming out of your eyes. Dark smoke like nothing I've ever seen. It had no essence, like it wasn't even there."

My face felt the memory of it, something I recognized but didn't understand. "The thing in my head came out. It's still in me, though. I can feel it more than ever. It feels bigger. I think it's growing."

He wrapped an arm around my shoulders and guided me back the way we had come. "We have to get you to Gillen Yor."

I pulled away. "No! Powell's going to kill her, Dylan. I can't let that happen."

He looked about to argue, then nodded with a sad smile. "I know. Whatever's happening to you, Con, you're still who you are. Let's go."

We passed a section of hallway with high concentrations of essence. Burn marks scorched the walls. An intricate web of binding spells hung in tatters, already fading. "They fought here."

Anxiety settled over me as I sensed the essence trail. They moved together, but Meryl's signature was faint while Powell's blazed.

"This was part of her plan somehow," Dylan said behind me. "There are too many binding spells. She must have set them a while ago."

The hallway ended at a spiral staircase of stone. "Powell waited ten years for this. She's a contingency planner. She saved Meryl for last so Viten could kill his killer," I said over my shoulder.

I took out my cell phone. No signal. We were too deep underground. The stair wound about its central axis, turning over and over, progress that felt like a standstill. A signal bar flickered into view on my screen. I called Murdock, but the connection broke. The steps vibrated under our feet with the dull rumble of a subway train. We reached the top, an incongruous metal door with a modern spring bar. It popped open into the decrepit remains of an ancient bathroom.

A glamour spell snapped in place behind us as we left the room, hiding the door behind a wall of dirty tiles. I recognized the narrow platform of Arlington Street Station, two blocks away from the Guildhouse. My cell signal stabilized, and I called Murdock again.

"Where are you?" I asked.

"I'm on the Common. The place is a zoo," he said.

"Powell's escaped. She's got Meryl, and I think they're headed for the fairy ring. Can you get up there?"

"I'm not far. We have a command post at the monument."

"Meet you there." I disconnected.

A train arrived as we reached the stairs. A throng of fey disembarked, pushing to the exits with the excitement of children. Dylan and I shoved our way up the steps, fighting elbows and wings and nasty glares. We exited to the corner of Arlington and Boylston.

Police guarded the entrance gates of the Public Garden, blocking everyone from entering. The streets were mobbed. We joined the crowd heading for the Common, hundreds of people of every conceivable species of fey imaginable.

At the end of the block, the Common glowed with more radiant essence. The light burned brightest through the bare limbs of the trees where the land sloped up to the towering Civil War monument and the fairy hill beyond it. Fairies of all kinds filled the sky, their wings flaming with essence as they swooped and swirled in dance. As we ran down the lane that passed the bandstand, the crowd swelled, slowing down as more people flooded into the park. Everyone wanted to be on the hill.

I stopped, amazed. An inverted funnel of misty gray light twisted into the sky, long wisps of the Taint revolving around it.

Dylan spoke in my ear with awe and wonder in his voice. "It's really opening, Connor. The veil is opening."

I pushed ahead. "That thing better be exit only."

29

Thousands of laughing and shouting people packed the blocked-off streets around the Common. Groups gathered and merged with a confusion of harps and lutes, drums, horns, and electric guitars on portable amps. Anything that could make a noise, someone banged, blew, or strummed—elven death dirges clashing with Irish bands playing tympani punk, dwarven horns blasting against Gaelic windpipes against police whistles and megaphones—even a mariachi band on the baseball diamond. Fey and human alike danced and cheered, humans in Halloween costumes, fey in the traditional garb of their clans.

On the lower end of the Common, police manned barricades separating the open field from the rise of the hill where the Civil War monument and fairy ring stood. Dylan showed his Guild badge to an officer to get us into a cordoned-off emergency path that wound its way through the crowds. Another security perimeter was set up around the monument at the top of the hill. Police, fire, and EMT communications units ranged in the rough circle, creating an island of relative calm in a sea of chaos. Marble statues representing war and peace stared down from the war monument's pedestal in mute testament to the fact that things hardly ever truly change.

The essence within the fairy ring churned, a concentration

more dense than the night Dylan and I argued. It was so intense, the unaided eye could see it. I didn't need a sensing ability to see it. No one did.

Murdock waited near a temporary fence that was yet another barricade to the fairy ring. His body shield shimmered over his long camel-hair overcoat, the hardened crimson essence providing a level of safety I could only dream about. With all the colliding essence on the hill, any fey who noticed a body shield on a human probably dismissed it as a trick of the light. I didn't like the grim look on his face. "They went in about ten minutes ago," he said without waiting to be asked.

My chest tightened at the word "they." I gripped the metal fencing and stared into the fairy ring. "Was Meryl all right?"

He cocked his head to listen to something on his radio before answering. "I didn't see her myself. I'm told she was mobile but dazed-looking. Powell had a doctored Guild badge that got them into the inner perimeter. With all the Guild types in there, no one thought anything was wrong. They were last seen near the edge of that column of light. There was a bright flash, and they vanished."

"I want to get in there," I said. Murdock didn't hesitate. Dylan and I followed him to a break in the barricade, and between their two official passes, no one tried to stop us.

Researchers and politicians roamed the restricted area around the fairy ring. The politicians were there for the photo op and the privilege of saying they could get in because someone thought they were someone important. The researchers were primarily fey, primarily from the Guild. Briallen and Nigel worked in separate groups, which was no surprise. Any other time, I would have loved to hear them argue back and forth about what was happening.

Flits flew around the thick essence like multicolored moths to a flame. Higher up in the air, fairies from the larger clans pressed closer. Fairies were air folk. Airborne essence attracted them and fed their essence-manipulating abilities. Drawn by the concentration of essence, the Taint had gravitated to the funnel, ambient wisps of the control spell that deepened in color as they collided and weaved together. A pressure headache sprang up behind my eyes. If the dark mass in my head didn't like concentrated essence or the Taint, it definitely didn't like the two of them together.

Murdock pointed to a spot that looked no different from the rest of the funnel. "This is where they went in."

Shapes moved within the fog, faint impressions of bodies and faces. The funnel essence radiated a distinctive resonance unlike any I knew. I touched it and found not a misty vapor but a slightly repulsive texture like cool, pliant skin. I pushed, and it dimpled in under the pressure, not separating or tearing.

Briallen broke away from her group. She wore a wireless headset, an incongruity for her that I could not stop staring at. Briallen rejected most technotoys. She could. Lots of technology replicates what she can do with her own innate abilities. "It's happening, Connor. The veil between worlds is thinning. Tara is secure, but there's rioting at Stonehenge and Carnac."

"There's always rioting at Stonehenge," Dylan muttered. He trailed along the ring, sparking little cantrips into the mist, fascination gleaming in his eyes.

"Did you see what happened with Meryl?" I asked.

Briallen stared up at the mist. "She had a binding spell on her. I was too far away to do anything. What I want to know is how the hell they went through."

"A silver branch," I said. "At least one of the items from the Met robbery was the real deal."

Briallen had a bemused expression. "Before Convergence, we used to take things like that for granted. If the conditions were right, you could even pass through a portal into Faerie or TirNaNog or the Glass Isle without a silver branch. Part of me is thrilled the veil has thinned, and part of me is terrified."

Dozens of flits popped into view, chattering excitedly as they swarmed around the fog. Briallen pause to listen in on her headset. "Word has spread. We'll probably see more flits."

Dylan returned from his circuit of the ring. "The Taint's amplifying the veil."

Briallen nodded. "That's what I thought. What I don't know is if people go through the veil, what effect the Taint will have on them. In the old days, people with unfinished business came back from TirNaNog, and they weren't very nice about it."

Something high up within the veil pressed outward and formed a dull gray lump on the swirling surface. The swelling receded, bulged again, and took on shape. The veil stretched as someone pushed against from the other side, the surface lightening from expansion until it was transparent enough to see a Danann fairy in an old-style court tunic. He struggled against the gray essence, pushing farther out, tendrils of mist elongating until they snapped with a silent flicker of light. He tumbled and caught air on long, translucent wings, hovering in confusion above our upturned faces. Shock registered on his face at the sight of the surrounding buildings. If the datedness of his clothes meant anything, he had never seen structures so tall. He muttered something in Old Irish that translated roughly as "Where the hell am I?"

He flew toward downtown.

"That was a dead guy?" Murdock asked.

"It depends on your definition of dead," Dylan said.

I reached for the spot where the fairy had exited, but the surface closed before I could touch it. Another bulge formed and dissipated near my head, and I imagined someone on the other side trying the same thing I was. A hand rested on my shoulder. Briallen looking at me with shared concern. "She knows how to handle herself."

"This is my fault," I said.

"Don't start that again." Briallen brushed her hand along the side of my head.

I jerked away. "Stop that."

Annoyance flickered across her face, but she didn't remove her hand. "I was only going to check if you were all right."

"Don't change the subject to the thing in my head," I said.

"I will if you stop ignoring that something's not right. I can feel it."

I met her gaze. "Something happened, Briallen, and it changed. I don't need you to tell me it's growing."

She dropped the hand. "You're right. And you shouldn't be here. Between the Taint and this veil opening, I'm worried."

I stepped away from her. "I'm sorry, Briallen. I got Meryl into this. I can't leave."

"I don't know whether to be proud to hear you say that or throw you over my knee," she said. Her expression changed abruptly, and she held a hand against her earpiece. She glanced up at me as she listened intently. "A mist has formed at the grove."

She didn't have to tell me what grove. Boston druids and druidesses met in an oak grove on Telegraph Hill down in Southie. "I'm not surprised, I guess. There's a lot of residual Taint down there."

She peered into the distance as if she were looking through the surrounding city to the ring of oak trees. "We stationed people there, in case, but . . ." Her voice trailed away.

"No one very powerful, right?"

She surveyed the remaining fey. "Promise me you won't do anything stupid?"

I grinned. "Do you really have to ask?"

Her hand found my cheek again, only this time in a warm caress. "She'll be fine. If there's one thing Meryl does, it's the unexpected."

Without another word, she hurried down the hill to a nearby black car.

Dylan's gaze went up over my shoulder. "We've got company."

"Looks more like incoming," Murdock said.

Above the crowd on the Common, airborne fey scattered from a growing cloud of light. The light resolved into rank upon rank of Danann security agents, several hundred, all in black, their chrome helmets reflecting their innate essence. Front and center, a figure burned with hot golden essence.

"That's Ceridwen," I said. She was the last person I wanted

to see. If she hadn't been so paranoid, Meryl would have been at her desk and made sure Powell was in a secure room. As if to draw even more attention to herself, she had the spear with her. I had a lightbulb moment. "Dylan, give me Powell's soul stone."

He hesitated. "Why?"

I didn't want to tell him. If he didn't like the idea, it wouldn't work without the stone. "I need it for leverage."

He looked suspicious. "Leverage with whom?"

Ceridwen would arrive in a moment. I didn't have time to argue. "Dylan, you wanted me to trust you. I'm asking you to do the same. If you don't want Ceridwen to know you gave it to me, you need to give me Powell's soul stone right now."

Dylan pulled the stone from his coat pocket, rolled it between his fingers, then tossed it to me. "Whatever you're going to do, make it good."

Ceridwen landed at the communications area near the monument. Several security agents swept in after her, but the rest remained in the air. She ordered the park cleared, her voice amplified by a spell. Angry murmurs ran through the crowd, but stopped as soon as the security agents spread out. They didn't fire on anyone, but their reputation for hair-trigger tempers prompted people to head for the streets.

Ceridwen carried the spear like a scepter as a contingent of agents escorted her to the fairy ring. She played the role of command leader for all it was worth.

"What's with the getup?" Murdock said.

Ceridwen wore classic fey warrior armor, a torso-fitting corselet of stamped red leather and a matching helm with a short nose guard. The fey used as little metal as possible in their fighting gear because it had a tendency to warp essence. The Dananns didn't mind adding some for effect to send the message that they were powerful enough to overcome the warping.

"Let's just say she's not subtle when it comes to asserting her authority."

She stopped a dozen feet away. "Move away from the ring."

Dylan bowed and did as he was told like a good Guildsman. From a cautious point of view, I didn't have a problem with it. Even if he had never sworn fealty to the High Queen, he was her employee. It wouldn't look good at his performance review if he had "defied an order from an underQueen" in his file. Murdock, true to form, did not move, which I liked even more.

Ceridwen stepped closer. "We said move away from the ring. You are interfering with Guild business."

Murdock didn't flinch. "We're investigating an abduction, ma'am."

With a gleam of gold, she let some essence show in her eyes. "We are declaring this area under our jurisdiction. Move or face the consequences."

Murdock frowned. "With all due respect, ma'am, I don't believe you have any authority over me."

She gestured with the spear to her bodyguards. "Take them into custody."

As they moved, Murdock muttered into his radio and stepped in front of me. He pulled out his gun. "I am giving you a lawful order to lay down your weapon."

The shock on Ceridwen's face was priceless. She raised her spear. "I said take them into custody!"

The lead agents raised their hands, essence sparking in electric arcs as they powered up. Murdock's body shield bloomed like a ruby flame. Whether he planned it or not, it had the nice effect of covering me in its field. Dozens of police officers materialized around us, guns drawn and pointed at Ceridwen. That's what happens when you give orders without coordinating with the local force. The agents hesitated, their urgent sendings tickling at my mind as they refrained from firing. At least they hesitated. Left to her own devices, Ceridwen looked ready to beat anyone who came near her.

I felt Nigel Martin coming before I saw him. The Taint accentuated everyone's essence, but I would have sensed my old mentor without it. He pressed between two agents and stopped between Murdock and Ceridwen. He looked at Murdock, but he addressed Ceridwen. "What is the meaning of this, Your Highness?"

Ceridwen lowered the spear. "Druid Martin, you know the peril here. These people must be removed."

Ever calm, Nigel clasped his hands behind his back and tried to stare me down.

I shrugged. "I'm deferring to the local authorities, Nigel. Talk to the guy with the gun."

Nigel glanced at Murdock. "Detective, you are risking an international incident."

"I don't take orders from the Guild," said Murdock. "Unless I get orders from someone I do report to, this woman is going to be arrested for threatening a police officer."

"We have diplomatic immunity," Ceridwen said, barely containing her outrage.

"You'll get a phone call," said Murdock. How he kept a straight face when he said that, I'll never know. His brothers in blue didn't even try. I heard more than a few chuckles.

"Get her to back off, Nigel," I said.

He glared. "Connor, you continue on this pointless course of defiance. Lives are at stake here. Move aside, or I will move you personally."

"The only life at stake here is Meryl Dian's. I don't answer to you, and I sure as hell don't answer to Ceridwen," I said.

She pushed forward and raised the spear like a club. "I will not stand for any more insolence from you and that traitorous bitch!"

That did it. She went a word too far. "I've had it," I snapped. My mind opened to the spot where the spear burned so brightly, tasted the essence that lay there, felt the power that called to me even as I called to it. *"Ithbar."*

The spear jerked in Ceridwen's grip. Her eyes widened, but she refused to let go. Amazingly, it dragged her toward me. She turned golden bright as she called up essence to resist my command.

"Stop!" Nigel shouted.

Nigel thrust his hand forward and a ball of white light shot out of his palm. I ducked as it broke into a tangled net shooting right for me. Murdock's body shield flared and absorbed the hit. I couldn't believe it. The bastard had really tried to hit me with it.

Ceridwen gripped the spear with both hands, but she could not restrain it. Inexorably, it pulled away from her. When it came within reach, I grabbed it. A fierce cold Power raced up my arm. Inches away from each other, Ceridwen and I locked gazes. Her eyes vanished within featureless orbs of gold as she fought for control, trying to batter my mind into submission. The spear shuddered between us, our arms jerking with its struggle. I refused to relent, demanding it come to me. The silver filigree on the spear reacted to the sudden influx of so many different energies around it. It rippled on the shaft of the spear, coming alive like dancing drops of mercury. Icy strands of it oozed around my fingers and raced up my forearm.

An angry, animal growl came from deep within Ceridwen's throat as she called more essence to bear. The dark mass in my head surged through me. Darkness flowed out of my hand and touched the spear. Essence exploded between us. Ceridwen screamed in rage and frustration as the power of the spear flung her into her bodyguards.

Meryl had told me the spear was a true silver branch. I had to hope she was right and see if it would grant passage into another realm. I spun toward the fairy ring and thrust the spearhead into the veil. A tear ripped the haze, liquid yellow light bursting out and sluicing down on me. My head blistered as the dark mass jumped. The spear responded to my will again, and the hole wrenched wider at my thought. Tainted essence slithered and flapped around the opening. It dove for the white line of power in my hand, the darkness mass and the spear both convulsing at its touch. I threw myself into the rip, and my head exploded in a thousand knives of pain. A raging torrent of ebony and emerald, white and gold smeared across my mind.

I fell into the veil between worlds.

30

I staggered under an assault of searing pain. Essence whipped around me in a kaleidoscope of burning colored light. Wind raged through the air, a high-pitched wailing that tore at my mind. I propelled myself blindly through the radiant bands of power, desperate to get away. The darkness in my head and the brightness in my hand warred with each other and the air, flinging me in one direction after another. The maelstrom stripped me down to impulse and instinct until the desire to escape the pain ripping through me was all I knew.

The onslaught receded, slowly, grudgingly. The ground stabilized, and I stumbled into an empty space, an eye of calm within the storm. Around me, a dense, smoky haze rustled and shifted, a barrier that flashed with sparks of essence. Exhausted, I leaned on the spear. All the joints in my body ached like they had been pulled apart and snapped back together. A constricting pressure throbbed along my left arm. I pulled off my jacket. The silver filigree from the spear had replicated itself around my forearm.

The wind died. In a milky gray sky, bands of darker gray essence scudded like ragged clouds after a storm. Light flashed, visible light, not the colored manifestations of essence. A booming sounded in the haze, vibrating the ground in a rhythm that grew stronger with each increase in volume.

The dark mass in my head shifted one way, then another, as if trying to avoid a trap. Something moved through the mist, something huge, with an essence signature more intense than any I knew.

The presence drew nearer, becoming brighter and brighter in the vision of my sensing ability. A dark shadow figure formed within the shadows of the haze, the shape of a man wrapped in a vast aura of light. The haze drew away from him like the parting of curtains. Shards of essence encircled his head like a crown. Over a long red tunic, he wore a cloak that shifted through hues of yellow. He had the look of the Danann about him, if it were possible for the Danann to look more radiant than they did. He furrowed his brow when he saw me. "Such a small dark thing ripples the Ways."

He had an enormous intensity, more than the tree spirit I had met, more than anything I had ever met. I didn't have much experience with kobolds, but he didn't feel like one or any other fey I knew. I held the spear defensively. "Viten?"

Surprise etched across his face when he saw the spear, and a shudder ran through him. His cloak came alive with motion and melted into his body. He grew larger, and sank cross-legged to the ground, his hair turning dark, his eyes showing the threat of a wild animal. Essence flowed from his temples and branched from his head with a burnished light. "Do you come to mend the Ways or to bend them?"

His voice sent shivers through me, resonant and deep. "I'm looking for someone," I said.

The giant swelled, his color fading, then he settled back. "A woman."

"Her name is Meryl Dian."

He shuddered as he flowed into a standing position. Thick hair sprouted from his head into long tangles above deep-set eyes that glittered in hues of storm and shadow. A blue robe flared out of his back and across his shoulders. I stepped back.

"What is this?" I asked.

His entire body spasmed. "Naming is a deep matter."

"Dammit, where am I?" I asked.

Yellow essence swirled, and the first incarnation reappeared, wrapping his golden cloak about him with a smug smile. "You've danced on my borders many times, but never crossed. How come you now with a sliver of the Wheel?"

"What borders? What do you mean?"

The figure moved nearer, essence rising like a shadow. "You warp the Ways. You are not worthy to wield such Power. Surrender it to me."

I held the spear across my chest. "No."

He shivered, his body fragmented, then pulled back together. He extended a jeweled hand. "Surrender it."

The gesture felt oddly indifferent, as if he had merely asked me for some small token. He didn't look happy. I sought his eyes, but their shifting colors made it difficult. He made no move to take the spear. Despite his enormous essence, whatever he was, he seemed unable to act. Feeling more confident, I hefted the spear. "You can't take it from me, can you? You'd have done that by now."

The unsettling eyes remained fixed on me as his skin blurred and shifted, swelling as he fleshed into the burly giant. He sat before me again, looking down at me with a feral gleam. "What value has this woman that you dare the Ways?"

Talking about the value of anything would be a dangerous question from a normal fey. I had no doubt a mistaken answer could be dangerous. "What value should be placed on a life?"

The giant grunted, as if confirming something in his own mind. "You would wager your life for something that you cannot assign value?"

"It's not my place to wager."

The giant laughed, a deep rumble that I felt in my own chest. He swept into the form of the blue-robed man. The spear tugged at my hand, and I tightened my grip. "Sorry. I'm keeping it."

His body undulated and the roar of crashing waves broke through the mist. "You do not know what you risk."

I had to crane my neck to see his face. "I never do, buddy. Are we done? Because I don't have time for this."

His enormous hand reached for me. I instinctively held up the spear. He paused, shuddered, and the wild man was back. "You dare much. The living disturb this place to no good end."

I tilted the tip of the spear away from him. He was enormous. No need to provoke him any more than I had. "I'm here to take the living back with me."

Again, the disconcerting shudder, and the blue-robed man reappeared. "In this, then, we are aligned. I will be obliged to you if you succeed."

"Can you point me in the right direction?" I asked.

The golden-cloaked king shuddered into view. "The Wheel of the World turns as It will. It is not mine to lead even a sliver of It."

The wild man returned. "The wielder wheels and is wheeled but chooses his own path. We are the Wheel and Its instrument."

The robed man towered up. "The Ways seal and unseal. A needle binds even as it pierces."

A great wind rose. The figure pulsated as its forms sought to dominate each other, then spun outward in a flash of white. It vanished. He vanished. They. Whatever the hell it was. The mist wall wavered and dissipated.

The dagger in my right boot twisted in its sheath, digging into my ankle. A spell maintained it as a short fighting knife most of the time, but it changed shape through some means I didn't understand. Heat emanated from the hilt as I withdrew it. It squirmed in my hand and stretched into the full length of a sword. The last time it did that, I was in a fight for my life.

I faced an opening in a wall of standing stones. A brief glimpse of Nigel leaning over Ceridwen flashed by. The scene slid to a vision of the Civil War monument on the Common, then another of the townhouses on Beacon Hill. The perspective never remained for long, as if the opening itself was in constant motion. My stomach did a little flip. I was looking at Boston through the perspective of the fairy ring. I was in the hazy column of essence, really and truly beyond the veil. I had entered TirNaNog.

31

An enormous circle of standing stones surrounded me, enclosing several acres of beaten grass. Granite lintels ran along the tops of the standing stones except for a single break in the circle opposite my position. In the center, nine trilithons stood, arches formed of two standing stones with a lintel across their tops. They made a crescent around a towering pillar stone tapering to a height of several meters. I had seen paintings of such places, fantasies I thought, of what an active stone circle would look like. It was Stonehenge on steroids.

A woman in an ancient druidic robe brushed past me and approached the portal to Boston. When she stepped between the standing stones, gray spots of essence materialized like a barrier. She pressed forward, muttering, and melted through to the other side. A perplexed look came over her face as she stared at a Boston police officer, and her body shield activated as the scene swept away from me. However she made it through, it looked a lot less painful than when I had done it.

Around the circle, the other portals between the standing stones showed a steep grass embankment outside the circle. A few standing stones framed an opalescent haze of essence that resonated the same way as the fairy ring back on Boston Common. Across the inner field, the Dead of TirNaNog moved from portal to portal, attempting to walk through, but except for a few with powerful body essences, they met the same resistance I had earlier. Two portals framed visions of rioting on the other side, and another showed a huge bonfire. Around me, fey of all kinds gravitated to the portals, pushing at them like the druidess had done.

I paused by a trilithon in the center. The lone breach in the outer circle of lintel stones aligned with the back of the crescent-shaped arrangement of center stones. A long line of standing stones marched off into the wide field beyond the stone circle. Stone circles have a causeway approach and an entry portal, and this one was no different. Bigger by a factor of ten, but classic.

The place resonated essence in a pale shadow of what I knew, except for two things. The pillar stone at the center shone stark blue-white, an intense concentration of Power. And a trailing streak of two body signatures—Powell's and Meryl's. Their trail led from the Boston portal, around the center of the henge, and out the entrance portal. Powell had come to find one of the Dead and taken Meryl with her outside the circle. I followed them to the gap in the circle.

Beyond the two large stones that flanked the entrance, an earthen embankment surrounded the entire stone circle, rising higher than my head. A ditch lay beyond that, then another embankment, not as high as the first, but still taller than I was. And another ditch beyond it, and another embankment, and on and on with each embankment becoming progressively smaller, while each ditch became shallower. The causeway itself ran straight and flat, lined with paired standing stones for nearly a quarter mile. As the embankments to either side became low enough to see over, a green field came into view and spread for miles outside the standing stones of the avenue. A breeze danced over the grass, sending flowing waves over the surface that caught afternoon sunlight and tossed it back.

At the end of the causeway, the hope that I would find Meryl and leave quickly faded. A few scattered people roamed the field. They had essence signatures with the distinct edge of TirNaNog about them like the Dead within the circle. On the edge of sight, a forest line crouched in several places, dark and motionless. Except for the Dead moving toward me, the only other movement was a dark smudge on the horizon. It was too far off to make out details, but the essence within it shone brighter than everything around it. Whoever was out there was alive.

I hesitated. It would take me hours to reach them. If it was Powell, I could wait until she returned to the circle. One of the few things I knew about the land of the Dead was that time moved at a different pace, sometimes slower, sometimes faster. I had no idea how much time had passed there between Meryl and Powell going in and my arrival. In Boston, it was late evening and still was when scenes from the Common flashed by the portal. In TirNaNog, it felt like late afternoon. Maybe Meryl didn't have hours. Maybe she didn't have minutes. My chest hurt at the thought that I might be too late.

The spear flickered with essence. The landscape blurred, and I had a strange falling sensation. The feeling passed as quickly as it came. I didn't know what caused it, unless the mass in my head had started causing physical damage to my brain. A faint sound of thunder rolled toward me. I didn't have time to worry about it. I started jogging, keeping my eyes on the movement along the horizon.

Essence lit up the spear again, and the landscape blurred roughly. I stumbled, uncertain where my feet were landing, feeling light-headed. Recovering my balance, I started running again. I wasn't going to let the thing in my head stop me, even if it meant hurting myself more. The dark line on the horizon became a distant group of riders on horseback. I stopped. They were impossibly closer. Behind me, the stone circle was farther away than I could have run in so short a time.

Somehow I was jumping through the landscape. I froze. Disappearing from one spot and appearing in another wasn't just jumping. It was teleporting. I was teleporting. The spear vibrated in my hand as I stared down at it.

Joe once told me that when he teleported, he looked for the

thing he wanted until he found it, thought about going to it, then he just went. It was a typical Joe explanation. It sounded too simple, so I dismissed it as pointless. When I was standing at the end of the entrance avenue, the spear had flashed when I thought of reaching the horizon. When it did, I was closer to my destination.

Taking a deep breath, I pointed the spear and concentrated on the dark line of travelers. The spear spiked with essence. My sensing ability opened like it never had, my inner vision telescoping to the horizon. The body essences of the riders shimmered like candle flames as clearly as if they were next to me. They materialized in my mind with an incredible clarity—elves and dwarves and solitaries. They all resonated as living beings, not the odd essence of the Dead.

The spear bucked in my hand. Like that first time it had come to me in the hearing room, it reacted to my thoughts, responding to what I was thinking and feeling. Essence channeled up my arm, electrifying the silver mesh with cold pain. The dark mass in my head seethed, as if angry or threatened. I wasn't calling the essence; the spear was. It touched me, felt my desire. It was the same process as doing a sending, only instead of sending my thoughts, I sent myself. The spear's essence leaped into my head, forcing its way in. The dark mass stabbed with hot pain. Dizzy, I swayed as the land shifted beneath my feet and blurred.

I gasped for breath. The plain became clear again. The riders were closer, riding massive horses. To the left, a lone rider, one of the Dead, rode hard away. The lead rider broke from the pack and came toward me. His essence solidified in my vision, a cool bright blue, not like the Dead, but like home. A plain black helm obscured his face. I held my sword at the ready.

The rider closed in on me, his strange horse lit with its own eerie essence, not truly of TirNaNog, but not of home either. It moved oddly, somehow higher above the plain than it should have been. It wasn't touching the ground. It was only riding in the smoke around it. Only one animal looked like that, a dream mare, a creature out of legend, the Teutonic talisman for riding the Ways.

The rider pulled the reins, and the horse shied sideways. He held his hand up, and the line of riders behind him stopped. As he removed his helm, long dark hair fell to his shoulders. My gut felt like it had filled with ice water.

Bergen Vize.

He stared with amusement and surprise. The dream mare danced on its feet in a smoke cloud that billowed like steam, thick, rippling vapors that dissolved in the air a few feet from its hooves. "This is unexpected," he said.

"Nice little army you have there, Vize."

He twisted in his saddle, looking back at his companions. "It's a start."

"Where's Meryl Dian?" I asked.

Vize pursed his lips, appraising the company. "No one by that name is with me."

I gripped the spear tighter, feeling it go cold with my anger. The dream mare neighed, its fear vibrating in my gut. "A druidess. Your friend ap Hwyl brought her here."

Vize considered, his eyes on the retreating rider. "My business with ap Hwyl is nearly concluded, but I know nothing of this Meryl Dian."

I scanned the several hundred riders behind him. The spear amplified my sensing ability, allowing me to pick out the nuances of individual essence signatures. Some I vaguely recognized, associates of Vize whom I knew from the days I was tracking him. The one essence signature I cared about wasn't there.

I relaxed into a fighting stance. "Then we have other business to settle."

He arched his eyebrows as if the idea amused him. His gaze went to the spear. Recognition flickered. He knew what it was. Meryl said it had traveled to Alfheim. Vize obviously knew the spear. "I have other plans today," he said.

"I know. So does the Guild. They're going to stop you if I don't."

"They may. Someone else will accomplish my goals instead."

"You accomplish nothing but destruction and murder."

His amusement shifted to impatience. "How simply you view the world, Grey. Sometimes you have to destroy one thing to save another. The fey destroyed Faerie. They're going to destroy their new world. It may cost some lives, but it will be worth it if I can stop them."

I shook my head. "The only one destroying the world we live in is you, Vize."

He saluted me with his sword. "Spoken like a true slave."

I held my sword level with the ground. "Where's the ring?"

He rotated his sword to show me the hand that gripped the hilt. On the index finger was a thick, wide ring. Last time I saw it, it had been gold. It was black now, dull and pulsing with a darkness that made my skin crawl. The dark mass in my head shot pain through my forehead.

"I'm afraid it won't come off," he said.

I smiled grimly. "I can think of a way."

He chuckled. "Yes, well, I've considered that option, but the ring had other ideas."

I trembled with anger. He was right there. After more than two years, he was right there in front of me. The spear reacted to my emotion, hungering to be free, wanting to fly at Vize. The distance between us wasn't much. I could take him out. I'd have only one chance, assuming he didn't parry the throw, or I missed. I had a feeling this spear didn't miss. The moment I threw it, though, his army would be on me. I wouldn't be able to cut the ring from his hand, retrieve the spear, and get away with my life.

I didn't care. Dying to stop Vize didn't seem inevitable. I leveled the spear at my shoulder. The dream mare reared, and Vize flashed on his body shields. Several riders behind him broke toward us. The horse wheeled as Vize fought to control it. I caught a full view of Vize. His body shield was in fragments, patches along his back and up one side of his head, useless patches on his legs. His right side, the side he wore the ring on, had no shield at all. The damaged body shields told me all I needed to know. I lowered the spear.

The dream mare calmed, though her eyes rolled in fear. Vize held his hand up to the oncoming riders, and they checked their advance. Curious, he looked down at me.

"You didn't attack me," I said.

His face went neutral. "Perhaps I am not the murderer you think I am."

"Bull. I've screwed your plans twice now, and you're not even trying to take revenge here. I don't think you can. You've lost your abilities, haven't you? You lost them that day we fought."

He narrowed his eyes. "I see now. You're Powerless. I have wasted enough time, then." He thrust his hand up in a fist, then swung it forward. The riders behind him burst into motion, bearing down on us. On me.

"This isn't over, Vize," I said.

He goaded the horse closer, but not close enough for my sword. "Give me the spear, druid, and I will guarantee your life."

"No deal," I said. I closed my eyes as the first rank of oncoming riders reached Vize. I thought of Meryl. She was why I was there, she alone. A tunnel formed in my inner vision and a brilliant core of green essence blossomed in my mind. It wasn't a memory. It was real. The spear had opened my vision to Meryl's essence signature. I let the spear feel my desire to be there, be with her, wherever that mote of green essence was. My gut and brain twisted as the spear responded. The dark thing in my head pushed like razor blades, and I let the pain in. Everything fell away until only the green point of essence remained. Weightless, I soared through an inky darkness, the spear burning the way before me. The mass in my head strained against it, trying to pull me away, but I fought back, drawing energy from the spear. The darkness clawed at my mind, resisting the white flow of essence. I fell into nothingness. Again.

32

Ancient trees surrounded me, great gnarled beasts with trunks twenty feet across and deep violet moss swaying lethargically from enormous branches. As dim light filtered greenly down from high above, dark birds winged through the leaf canopy with muted calls. Brief bursts of essence flashed here and there in the deep shadows of the underbrush and faded away like spent glow bees. The air was thick with an eerie stillness broken by the occasional snap of a branch or soft insect whirr.

I leaned on the spear. Having a sturdy stick of wood was coming in handy. Sweat ran freely along my lip and down my cheek, and I wiped my hand across my mouth. It came away red. Not sweat, blood. Blood seeped from my nose and my ears. A tickle in my throat turned into a cough, and I spat more blood on the ground.

I picked through twisted roots and dense foliage toward a brightness winding through the trees that indicated a trail. Someone had walked it recently, kicking up a staggered path, like something had been pulled along behind. Or someone. Meryl's essence hung thickly in the air. I followed it down the path, all my senses on alert. Not far off, sunlight shone more brightly where the trail broke through the trees.

I slowed my pace to soften my footsteps. At the trail break, the trees pulled back to form a shallow clearing. In its center rose a lone standing stone. Sharp ribbon lines of a binding spell held Meryl against it. I released the breath I hadn't realized I was holding. She was alive. Even better, she was awake and alert. Powell paced nearby, muttering under her breath.

They wore the brooches from the Met, Powell the apple tree and Meryl the horned serpent. Powell had scored not one, but two true silver branches out of the robbery. My sensing ability picked up the fluttering of numerous sendings. Little spots of essence shot from Powell's fingers as she made glow bees on the fly. I thought of the lone rider I saw racing away from Vize's people. It didn't take a rocket scientist to know who it was. I had no idea how far I had traveled, but I doubted I had much time before Viten showed. I poked my head into the trailhead to attract Meryl's attention.

About time, she sent immediately. I ducked. A cranky mood instead of a bad one was a good sign. I crept along the edge of the clearing until the standing stone was between me and Powell. When she faced away, I carefully broke cover from the trees and scrambled to the stone, pressing my back against it. Ribbons of essence around the stone held Meryl in place. They tingled against my back and came alive as they shifted position to loop over me. The dark mass in my head pressed pain against the backs of my eyes.

Powell stopped her sendings. "What are you doing?"

I froze. She had sensed the disruption in the bindings.

"Falling asleep from boredom," said Meryl.

"You won't be soon," she replied. The sendings began again.

I faced the standing stone. My sword felt warm in my hand as I lifted the blade to one of the ribbons. Bindings are directed essence with no will of their own. Sharp metal can disrupt them. The first ribbon literally melted as I brought the blade near. One of the rune charms glowed on the sword. The remaining bands shifted and tightened, and Meryl sucked in a breath. The damned things may be mindless, but they still hurt like hell. Cutting each successive band would cause the remaining ones to tighten. I swept the sword across the stone, the blade making a metallic shriek as it scraped. The ribbons parted, waving in the air as they lost purchase, then snuffed out.

Sword up, I jumped from behind the stone. Meryl was free. A flash of green filled the clearing with the ozone odor of an essence strike. Powell spun, tripping back on her heels, and fell flat on her back. Meryl extended two fingers like a gun barrel and blew on them. "That'll teach her to turn her back on me."

I wrapped my arms around her. "Sorry I didn't get here sooner."

She hugged me back, her orange mop of hair pressing into my shoulder. "You need to work on your sprinting."

I kissed the top of her head.

Powell was out cold. Meryl chanted lines of essence in the air that dropped on Powell and twined around her. Meryl nodded as she examined her work. "One good binding deserves another."

Powell's eyes fluttered open. She sat up and screamed as the binding spell cinched, sending shock waves through her.

"Oh, shut up, Winny," Meryl said. She gathered the ribbons of the spell in her fingers and twisted them into a knot, tugged at them to make sure the spell held.

A sharp point pierced the skin at the base of my skull. I froze.

"Do not move, please. I can easily sever your spinal cord before you even realize it." Viten. We had run out of time. He was close, his breath on my ear, a smooth honey voice that did not sound the least bit nervous. I never heard him coming.

Powell struggled into a seated position, letting out growls of pain. "Liddell!"

"Surprised and happy to see you, m'love," he said. "Will someone do the honors and release her?"

I had my sword and the spear. Viten made the mistake of closing the distance between us, which made me more dangerous to him. He probably had sensed he had two druids to deal with, not knowing one of them had no abilities.

"Do it," I said. As long as they didn't bind Meryl again, I wasn't worried. Yet. Meryl looked like she was going to argue. With a shake of her head, she released the spell. Powell jumped up and locked her arm around Meryl's neck, pressing a knife to her neck. It was the Breton dagger from the Guildhouse. The real one.

"Let us go, and no one gets hurt," I said.

"I don't think I can do that," Viten said.

He scratched the tip of his sword along my neck as he circled around me, and I met Liddell Viten—con artist and murderer—face-to-face. He stood a foot shorter than me with the pale complexion all kobolds had. His features were smoother than average, which made glamours that much easier to use. For a dead guy, he didn't look any the worse for wear. He wore fine clothing, archaic in a vaguely Teutonic court style, but made from an expensive-looking material. Being Dead seemed to agree with him.

He compressed his already-thin lips together until they disappeared. "Drop your weapons, please."

At least he was polite. "No," I said.

Laughter danced in Meryl's eyes, and she tossed me a sending. *Go for his sword when I move.* She didn't give me a chance to think about it. She activated her body shield at full strength. Its sudden appearance tipped the dagger away from her neck. With impressive speed, Meryl dropped back on her hands and let loose with a flying round kick, knocking Powell off her feet. Distracted, Viten turned toward them, and I parried his sword out of his hand with the spear. Meryl stomped on Powell's arm and grabbed the dagger. It was over in seconds.

With smooth grace, Viten leaped out of reach. He brought his own body shield on, weak in comparison to Meryl's, but his fingers were charged with the unnatural essence of Tir-NaNog.

Meryl prodded Powell. "Tell him why I knew you weren't going to stab me with the dagger."

Powell glared up at her. "It's a soul blade, Liddell."

Meryl kept her eye on Powell. "If you used it to kill me,

the souls would have released and wrecked your little plan to get him out of here. You always assumed that you knew more than I did, Winny. You were a lousy boss, by the way."

The strange mix of surprise and tenderness that crossed Viten's face fascinated me in a revolting kind of way. He met Powell's eyes with an intensity that could only be interpreted as love. The realization that this woman had killed two people to create a soul blade for him so that he could kill yet another person to get out of TirNaNog touched him just as if she had just told him she made his favorite dinner.

Powell flashed a fervent smile. "Kill her, Liddell. She can't hurt me."

"Oh, I don't have to kill you to hurt you, Winny," said Meryl. She shoved Powell toward Viten. I don't know who was more surprised, me or Powell. Meryl twirled the knife and smiled. "I've already killed you once, Viten. Let's make a wager. I bet that I can kill you with this knife before you can get a shot off. Consider this before you decide: I will only die, but you, my friend, will be obliterated by the souls in the knife. That's how this thing works against the Dead."

"She's lying," Powell snarled.

Meryl arched an eyebrow. "You think? I'm willing to stake my life on it."

Powell drew herself, haughty and assured. "Then I will kill you, Meryl."

"You took me by surprise, Winny. I will win one-on-one with you," she said.

Powell looked smug. "I've already died once for Liddell. I'll do it again. The Guild will protect my soul stone as long as it thinks it can arrest me. I'll come back here next Samhain and destroy you."

I pulled Powell's soul stone from my pocket. "Would that be this stone?"

Powell let out a growl of anger from deep in her throat. Viten lifted his hands, charging them with the pale essence of TirNaNog.

"It's over, Viten. Step away."

Viten set his jaw with smug assurance. "Kill her," he said.

Meryl and I exchanged glances. "What?" I asked.

"I said kill her." Viten pulled Powell into a tight embrace, nuzzling the side of her head and murmuring in her ear. "I have missed you every day, m'love, dreamed of you every night. Not having you at my side has been a torment. Every minute spent here is a minute I wished you could see this place."

Meryl rolled her eyes. "I think I'm going to be ill."

She looked stunned when I tossed the stone to Viten. "We don't have time for this. The fairy ring is surrounded by cops and Guild agents. She'll be detained as soon as she crosses the veil."

Powell clutched at Viten's coat. "The knife, love, get the knife."

He smiled down at her and caressed her face. "We have no need of it. I appreciate what you've done, m'love. I do. I truly do. But you've accomplished more than you realized. I have some power here. Here is where I wish to stay. It's beautiful, Rhonwen. It's glorious. I don't want to go back. You mean everything to me. I want you to stay. Here. Always. With me."

She stared up at him, tears in her eyes. "Yes, love. Yes."

They kissed with the pent-up passion of ten years apart. White essence burst in Viten's hand followed by a loud crackling. With a sharp gasp, Powell pulled her lips away from his. She struggled for breath, her chest heaving as the dust of her soul stone poured through Viten's fingers. Her mouth broke into an ecstatic smile, then her eyes rolled in her head. Viten caught her as she went limp and lowered her to the ground. He cradled her across his chest, smoothing her hair back from her face, a repulsive, satisfied smile on his lips. He kissed her again. "Tomorrow, m'love, tomorrow you will wake up here, and we will spend eternity together."

Meryl's jaw dropped. "Wow. Was that the most romantic and sick thing you've ever seen or what?"

33

Viten rocked Powell's body. I leaned down and ripped the silver-branch brooch from her coat. The colors leached out of her skin and clothes as she lost her physical substance, then she faded out into the air. Stricken, Viten clutched at her disappearing form until his empty hands groped at nothing. Somewhere in Boston, her dead body would turn up. He lifted red-rimmed eyes toward me. "You could have given me a few more moments."

I slipped the brooch into my back pocket. "You've got eternity, right? Get out of my sight before I shove this spear through your chest."

He rose with an imperious look and stooped for his sword. I stepped on it. "You won't be needing that."

Viten tried to stare me down. Like I said, that doesn't work much with me. "Someday, sir, you will find yourself here. I will be waiting."

"Thanks. Be sure to tell your funeral director I like Guinness," I said.

Viten sauntered down the trail.

I picked up the sword and made a few swipes with it. It had a fine edge, the grip a little small, but a decent balance. I held the pommel toward Meryl. "For those times when an essence shock to the head is not enough."

She tested its balance, then batted her eyes at me. "How thoughtful of you. Too bad you didn't take his sword belt, too."

I slid my belt off. "You're just trying to get my pants off again."

She snorted. "Trying? You're a guy. A simple 'take your pants off' works." She coiled the belt around her hips, looping it around the steel buckle to form a frog to slide the sword through. She tested the draw a couple of times, then rested her hand on the pommel. "I'm good."

I don't know what it is, but a woman with a sword works for me. Always. Granted, the pumpkin orange hair is unusual, but with Meryl, it completes the package. And the boots. The boots work, too. Meryl walked to the opposite side of the clearing, where the path took up again.

"This is the way to the henge?" I asked.

"You didn't come in this way?"

I shook my head. "I sort of teleported."

She chuckled. " 'Sort of'? Okay."

Pink essence burst in my face. I was so on edge, I fell back with the spear up and my sword ready. Joe hovered away in outright panic. "What the hell is going on?"

I'd been trying to get Murdock not to overreact when Joe shows up, and here I was startling like a newbie in the Weird. I relaxed like nothing happened. "Hey, buddy. Fancy meeting you here."

"Me? You're in Anwwn, then I felt you teleport, and *you're* surprised?" I couldn't even begin to pronounce the Cornish word he used for teleport.

We made our way up the path. "Long story, Joe. How the hell did you get here?"

He flew a random pattern beside us that he used when he was on guard. His hand clutched the empty air at his side, which meant he was ready to pull his glamoured sword. "Flits always get into Anwwn on Samhain. Well, not always, but before, when the world made sense, and we could visit our dead friends proper every year. Except the Way finally opens and everybody's running this way and that trying to get out and people not where they're supposed to be. I almost wish I stayed home tonight and went to a bar. Hi, Meryl."

"Hey, Joe." She grinned, like they had some mild secret they weren't sharing. I haven't figured out what she thinks of Joe. He doesn't come around much when she's with me, but they each seemed amused at the other's existence.

He twirled in front of us. "Are you guys Dead?"

"No, dead tired, though. You never mentioned teleporting is tiring," I said.

Joe shook his finger. "And that's another thing. What the hell is that? All of sudden, I felt you in this horrible rush of nothing, then I go and look and here you are." He narrowed his eyes at me. "You're really not Dead, right?"

I shook my head. I held the spear out to look at it. "I have it on good authority that this buppy is called a sliver of the Wheel."

Joe's eyes bulged. "Where did you get *that*?"

I shrugged. "A fairy queen. It's the traditional method if I remember correctly."

Joe pounded his fists against his forehead. "I'm either too drunk or not drunk enough."

"Story of my life lately," Meryl said.

The sunlight dimmed as we hurried down the trail. A bank of clouds moved in, charcoal and thick, materializing in the sky with an unnatural speed. "I thought it didn't rain here," I said.

Joe checked the sky. "Sure it does. Usually at night, though, and it always smells like fresh."

"Fresh what?" asked Meryl.

He dropped his eyebrows at her. "Fresh like fresh. It's not a difficult concept."

"Well, it wasn't night a minute ago, and those clouds don't look happy," I said.

Joe fluttered up to get a closer look through the break in the tree canopy. "Something's not right." He flew higher until we couldn't see him above the trees. When he popped back in our faces, his face was troubled. "I don't like it. I can't see behind us. There's a nothing like nothing. It's just . . . nothing." He looked over at me, his eyebrows shooting up. "Oh! It's like the nothing in . . ."

"I got it, Joe. Let's just get out of here," I interrupted. I knew what he was going to say. Joe had talked about nothing like that once before with me. It was what he called the darkness in my head.

We moved faster, concentrating on the path. After several tense minutes in the unchanging forest, the trail ended at the broad expanse of the grassy plain. Joe stopped so abruptly, I bumped him into an aerial stumble.

In the gray twilight of the overcast sky, clouds of blue and mauve did a slow churn, heavy with the threat of rain. Miles distant, a smudge of gray essence marked the position of the stone circle. A mass of people pressed toward it from every direction, hundreds, maybe thousands, of the Dead. The air vibrated with a riot of species signatures. The Dead moved in a vast ring that contracted as they advanced on the stone circle. In the gap between their front line and the end of the portal entrance, a company of riders burned with a brighter essence. They weren't locals. I recognized the essences of living people. "That's got to be Bergin Vize down there."

Meryl shaded her eyes to see what I was talking about. "What the hell is he doing here?"

"He's going after Tara," I said.

Joe snickered. "Not if they get caught."

At a glance, the massive crowd looked like it was making for the stone circle. Joe had pointed out what wasn't immediately obvious. The crowd was closing in on Vize, not the henge. "The Dead are chasing them."

Joe flew slow arcs in front of us. "Yep. Lots of people like it here, but lots don't. If a Dead person kills a live person in Anwwn, they get to change places."

Meryl looked intently across the plain. "Yeah. I was supposed to be Viten's Get Out of Jail Free card."

A mile off, the edge of the crowd nearest us shifted and

broke from the rest. It was pretty clear where they were heading. I stopped. "How do they know if someone's alive, Joe?"

He laughed and looped in the air. "Living essence lights up like a Beltane fire here. The chase is fun."

Meryl stopped, too, realization sweeping over her face. "Everyone's essence?"

Joe hovered between us with a puzzled look. "Of course. They never catch flits, though. Well, almost never."

"But you can get away, right?" I asked.

Joe fluttered to the ground and shrugged. "Depends on how good you are at fighting and running. They ignore you only if you have the blessing of Anwwn to be here."

Meryl and I looked at each other again. "I missed the queue for a blessing, did you?" she asked.

The frayed edge of the crowd had become a wedge pointed right at us. "We've been spotted."

"What do you . . . Oh!" Joe said, jumping back into the air. He finally got it.

Meryl unpinned the serpent brooch from her jacket. "Let's dump the silver branches, Grey. We'll fade back."

I gestured with the spear. "I don't think leaving this lying around is the smartest idea."

Joe peered at the spear. "I'll take it back if it will let me."

"That only solves one problem." I held my arm up. The silver filigree from the spear wound around it in a branching vine pattern. I pushed at it with my body shield. It became colder but didn't move. "It's bonded to me."

Meryl blanched. "Your entire arm is a silver branch?"

Smiling weakly, I held my arm up. "Technically, I think just the forearm, but it's all kind of connected."

Meryl whirled toward the open plain. The crowd was within a half mile. I came up behind her and hugged her close against my chest. "Go, Meryl. I'll avoid them as long as I can and make my way to the henge."

Joe flew toward us, his face upset. "You won't have much time if you don't go back direct-like. Samhain is almost over. I can feel the portals closing."

Meryl broke my embrace and reattached the serpent brooch to her jacket. "Come on. I'll shield you, and we'll run for it."

I shook my head. "It's got to be five miles to the henge, Meryl. I know you're strong, but even you can't maintain a shield for both of us that long. Besides, the moment we set foot in it, that mob is going to turn into a mosh pit with us in the center. I came to get you out, and you're getting out. Go. Please. I'll be fine."

She had that look in her eyes, the one that says she won't take no for an answer. "I'll believe that when I hear a better plan."

"I've never seen such a storm here. It's almost like Anwwn itself is angry," said Joe. The forest behind us had gone dark. The clouds deepened from dark gray to black, streaks of rain rippling like curtains in the distance. A strange darkness was behind it, a negation of space that felt devoid of essence. I shivered at the familiarity of it. It felt like nothing. Joe was right. It felt like the thing in my head. Lightning flickered, followed by a long roll of thunder.

I pursed my lips. "Great. Now I've managed to piss off an entire otherworld dimension."

"Teleport!" Meryl exclaimed.

"What?"

She grabbed me by the arms and shook me. "You said you teleported. Teleport us back to Boston."

Joe shook his head so vigorously, his hair splayed out. "You can't. You have to use a portal."

"You lost me," I said.

"Teleporting is one of the Ways. It's a place, not a portal."

"Then teleport us to the henge. We can skip over the plain," said Meryl.

Joe grinned. "Now you get it."

I looked inside myself, testing my inner vision, letting the spear feel my desire. It vibrated in my hand, and the misty tunnel opened in my mind. Far off, a gray light smoldered, vague and indistinct. "I think I can do it."

Meryl glared. "What do you mean 'think'?"

I shrugged. "I missed you by a few hundred yards when I did it last time." I gazed at the Dead, estimating the distance between their front line and the entrance to the henge. "That'll be close enough. I can outrun them."

"That's not good enough. Take me with you. I can shield us if you come up short," she said.

I looked at Joe. "Can I do that?"

He shrugged. "She's too big for me, but she's small enough for you."

I compressed my lips as I thought. "Let's do it."

"Meet you at the henge," Joe said. He saluted and popped out.

Meryl hugged me with a fierce grip.

"Ready?" She didn't speak but nodded into my chest.

I closed my eyes. The misty tunnel spiraled off in my inner vision, a streak of pink vanishing through it. The spear trembled as it felt my desire for the gray essence of the standing stones. The dark mass in my head shifted, as if trying to avoid the light. It hurt. The damned thing always hurt. I ignored it and visualized moving through the tunnel toward the gray smudge. The spear reacted by pulsing with a violent white light. I tightened my grip on Meryl as my head spun with dizziness. The dark mass sliced sharply in my head, and the spear pumped white light into me. I screamed. My body wrenched forward, harder and more painfully than before. Everything twisted to a smear of color, light and sound merging into something new and its own, as a dark fire clawed at my mind.

The pain subsided. My eyes burned, and I couldn't see. I stumbled on firm ground, sinking to my knees. The pungent odor of grass filled my nose. Everything hurt. Everything. Hands grasped my shoulders, pulling me back. I lay against something warm and soft. Black spots flashed as consciousness threatened to leave.

"Dammit, Connor. You're hemorrhaging." Meryl sounded far off.

Something pressed down on my chest. A hand. My body

shields fluctuated on and off as essence flowed into me. A warm tide of light spread from my chest, up my neck, and into my head. The dark mass spiked against the essence. Pain pierced my head as the light and dark grappled. The light winked out. I came to, nestled in Meryl's arms. I felt damp. It didn't smell like sweat. It was the raw tang of blood. I was saturated with my own blood. "I want a shower."

She tracked a finger on my cheek and showed it to me. "Your face is a mask of blood."

Blinking more blood out of my eyes, I tried to smile up at Meryl's concerned face. "I hope this gets easier with practice."

She laughed. "You're stable. I hit you with a healing spell, but I had to use essence from the henge. It might not be enough."

Joe flew position over our heads, his sword out as he stood guard. I took the fact that he was concentrating on something instead of talking to mean we weren't out of the woods yet, so to speak. I pushed myself up.

We had hit in the center of the stone circle like a bull's-eye and landed beneath the pillar stone. On one side, several Dead clustered, calculating looks in their eyes as they observed us from across the circle. More Dead trailed in from the avenue entrance.

Two portals in the circle showed clear night skies crisscrossed by searchlights. People were rioting around standing stones. Stonehenge in England was unmistakable, and the other had to be Carnac in France. In both portals, panicked Dead faced us from the living side, pressing against the openings. They had crossed and couldn't get back. The veil was closing as the sun rose. That wasn't the way it was supposed to work. When Samhain ends, the Dead go back to TirNaNog. Apparently, though, not tonight.

Another portal showed a place I recognized. I had been there once a long time ago. A bonfire burned high into the sky. Druids in court attire and Danann fairies in battle armor moved in smoky torchlight. To either side, ranks of Celtic warriors faced the portal, swords drawn and shields up, guarding Tara.

Only one other portal showed through to the living side. Boston Common was empty of everyone except the police and Guild security. In front of the portal, on the TirNaNog side, Ceridwen stood. She no longer hid behind a glamour, revealing golden wings in their full brilliance. Her eyes glowed with a wild white light as she guarded the Boston portal, the prone bodies of the Dead at her feet.

34

Ceridwen's face hardened with anger when she saw me. She walked over the bodies around her. The Dead standing near backed away. A Dead elf tried to slip to the Boston portal behind her. She casually shot an essence-bolt at him. She didn't hold back, but hit him with a full blaze meant to kill. He fell in silence, and his essence winked out. Tomorrow, he would wake up somewhere in TirNaNog as if death were only an inconvenience.

"Nice shot," said Meryl.

"You have doomed Tara over the life of one person," she said to me, not bothering to acknowledge Meryl.

"Nice to see you, too," I said.

She held her hand out. "Return the spear. I need to bring my warriors into TirNaNog to protect the Tara portal."

I handed it over. "All you had to do was ask nicely."

Ceridwen examined it, glancing once at me before throwing it at one of the Dead standing nearby. The spear left her hand at speed, stopped in midair, then dropped like a stone. As she crouched to retrieve it, it faded from sight and reappeared several feet away.

Ceridwen looked devastated. "It no longer responds to me."

"I noticed," I said. The spear shone in my mind, a line of

white essence, as if it were an extension of me, bonding to my essence beyond any words of command. I held my hand out. The spear lifted and returned.

Ceridwen's eyes flashed brighter. Fearfully, she looked to the dark portal with the bonfire. Figures moved in and out of the frame, soldiers in silhouette against the flames. "That's Tara, isn't?" I asked.

Ceridwen nodded.

"They don't look unprepared," I said.

"They are not, but they are underdefended," she said. "I was to bring the New York and Boston warriors here to act as a first line of defense. I needed the spear to activate the spell to bring them here."

"You got yourself in all right," I said.

She drew herself up, doing the imperial monarchy pose. "We are a queen of Faerie, druid. We need no talisman to walk the Ways. You command the spear. I will give you a spell for you to bring my warriors in."

"I know you read my file, Ceridwen. It's no lie that my abilities are blocked," I said.

"The spear responds to your command. You must put aside your petty anger and do as I say."

I held the spear up. "You don't know what you're talking about, Ceridwen. You think you commanded the spear? You're wrong. The spear doesn't do whatever I want. It reacts when what I want serves its purpose. I can feel when I'm doing something it wants me to do."

She didn't respond. She didn't have to. We could hear riders approaching, the pounding hooves like rolling thunder, growing louder and louder. I looked around the stone circle. The Dead that remained moved toward the entrance portal, probably deciding Ceridwen was difficult enough alone and now that she had friends, they might have better luck with Vize's people. At least they would slow Vize down. Once he reached the inside of the circle, either Tara or Boston would be easy pickings. Neither alone could hold his riders off. "Tell Maeve there's been a change of plans. She's the front line now. If she wants to survive, she needs to bring her own warriors in. I bet she knows how to do it without the spear."

Ceridwen's wings rippled in agitation. "You do not tell the High Queen to do anything."

I shrugged. "Okay. I'm sure Vize will be happy to give her a heads-up."

Her nostrils flared. She spun on her heel and stalked toward the Tara portal. As she stood on the threshold, her golden essence interacted with the veil in a static prickling. On the other side, people shifted in a flurry of activity. The warrior ranks parted, and a tall, slim woman appeared.

As she drew closer to the portal, firelight reflected off her armor, white leather with a crowned helm of silver. She kept her distance, but her pale features glowed, her cheeks long and chiseled and the line of her jaw firm. Blue highlights shone in long ebony hair that framed dark eyes. Even at this distance, the fathomless eyes of an Old One, a fey that had seen centuries of life, glittered with the deep experience of time. I had my first direct look at Maeve, High Queen of the Seelie Court at Tara.

Neither queen spoke aloud as they faced each other across the veil. Intense sendings vibrated over the competing essence of the stone circle. Their speed increased, the flutterings getting stronger as the exchange became heated. Ceridwen bowed her head just a bit and stepped back, allowing the High Queen a view into the circle.

Maeve's eyes flared with an eerie pale light as they locked on me. A palpable presence reached out through the portal, a gripping pressure against my skin. Her face swam closer, filling my sight, her eyes boring into mine. It was an illusion—she hadn't moved. I felt like I was being examined like a bug under a microscope. I couldn't tear my gaze away, mesmerized by the way her own eyes glittered, her face shockingly beautiful, a cold, untouchable beauty that had as much to do with a woman who knew her own mind as it did a woman who knew her own attraction. I shivered under the scrutiny, oddly shy and, dammit, insignificant. The pressure released, and Maeve was where she had been all along on the opposite side of the portal.

Another brief exchange occurred between the queens. Ceridwen's body stiffened in response to something as their conversation broke off sharply. She stumbled from the portal. A blossom of light flared as essence flashed in a noiseless explosion. It filled the space between the standing stones framing Maeve until she could not be seen through boiling clouds of essence. It solidified into a solid wall of white, hiding the view of Tara. A moment later, it rippled and imploded. Nothing remained. The portal to Tara was gone, replaced by a view of the grassy embankment outside the standing stones.

Ceridwen rejoined us, struggling to keep her shock under control. "Maeve does not have the power to enter. She destroyed the fairy ring to protect Tara. We're on our own."

"Okay, that's a problem," I said.

A thin haze sprang up in the portals to Stonehenge and Carnac. Samhain was ending with the rising sun a continent away. The veil was closing. With Tara gone, only the Boston portal remained open. At the far end of the entrance avenue, Vize and his riders were close enough to distinguish individuals. The lead company rode dream mares wrapped in a mist lit by an amber gleam from the horses' eyes.

Ceridwen moved up next to me. "Our sources told us Vize planned to enter Tara to attack Maeve. He was then going to return here and escape through a Teutonic portal hidden somewhere in TirNaNog. I was expecting him sooner, but something seems to have delayed him."

I watched them coming on. "Vize was working a deal with a woman named Rhonwen ap Hwyl. He must have been looking for her, but she had her own agenda and is a little dead at the moment."

Ceridwen looked back at the Boston portal. "Samhain is almost over. I don't think Vize will be able to get back to his own portal before the veil descends for another year. That leaves Boston his only escape now. I will not let him through."

"Let's get out of here and destroy the Boston fairy ring like Maeve did," I said.

Ceridwen shook her head. "After you entered TirNaNog, the Taint bound itself to the veil. We don't know how to break it, thanks to you two."

Meryl whirled on her. "For the last time, Ceridwen, there is no damned druid conspiracy. We don't know how to stop the Taint. You want to point fingers at traitors, take a look at Tara. Maeve destroyed her own portal and left us high and dry. Nobody made her do that."

Ceridwen drew herself up, towering over Meryl. "You may not address me in such a familiar tone."

"After being thrown in a cell because of your stupidity, I'll address you any way I damned well please," Meryl said. Ceridwen clawed her hand full of essence. Meryl triggered her body shield and pulled her sword.

Joe swung himself upside down between them. "Uh, ladies? I'm pretty sure we should be pointing our stuff at the bad guys."

Meryl glowered and gave Ceridwen a cold shoulder. Ceridwen hesitated, and I thought she might shoot Meryl in the back. Joe gave her the big grin, and she tossed the charged essence at one of the nearby Dead. If she kept killing them off like that, we'd probably have enough to block the portal.

She adjusted her helm as she faced the riders. "Aim for the dream mares. If the riders touch the ground, they will fade back into the world of the living. This far from their own portal, they may not get back at all."

"I'm not killing horses," said Meryl.

Ceridwen shrugged. "Then die."

Meryl threw her a look with all the warning signs of a small nuclear device.

Vize's riders bunched together within the entrance. The avenue could hold no more than two or three of them abreast.

Screams carried on the wind. Some of the Dead attacked as the riders jockeyed for room in the narrow lane.

"We need to delay them as long as we can." I pulled Powell's brooch from my pocket and tossed it to Joe. "Get Dylan, Joe. Tell him ASAP." Joe plucked the silver branch from the air with a smooth catch and vanished. He flashed into sight in front of the Boston portal and flew through.

"What's the plan?" Meryl said.

"Ceridwen said defend. So, we defend as long as possible."

Dylan stepped through the door wearing the silver branch. He paused at the threshold, intense curiosity on his face as he took in the scene. He jogged the distance between us, but I pointed him to the entrance of the stone circle. "No time to explain, Dyl. We need an *airbe druad* right there as strong as you can make it."

He didn't pause, but kept going to the entrance stones. The air trembled in his wake as he pulled essence from the ground. Before he reached the entrance, his barrier spell was executing, lines of essence curling around the standing stones, knotting and weaving to form a shield.

Ceridwen surveyed the work, unimpressed. "Teutonic warriors know how to counter an *airbe druad*," said Ceridwen.

I nodded, assessing the approaching riders. They had killed the Dead from the circle, but more were catching up behind them. From the rear, essence-fire and swordplay echoed off the standing stones. "It'll take them some time. Ceridwen, do a sending to Keeva and make sure she has the Guild agents ready for anything that comes through that portal."

"I do not take orders from you," she said.

I stared at her. "Look, I'm going to say this once: Either do what I say, or get the hell out of my way."

She made a pinched face, and the sending shot off her head like an arrow. Keeva was going to have a headache when she got it.

"Now. You and Meryl back up Dylan as long as you can. Let Vize through. Take down anyone else who tries to follow.

Watch your time. Dylan and Meryl can drop their silver branches, but you and I need to run for the portal before it closes."

The air crackled with streaks of golden light as Ceridwen followed Dylan across the field. "This is madness."

"Welcome to my world," I said to her back.

Meryl looked up at me. "I am not going to let you kill yourself."

"I don't intend to," I said.

Her face became set. "Don't think I'm stupid, Grey. Dylan and I only have to drop our silver branches to get out of here, but you can't shake that silver off on your arm. Ceridwen can reach the door before those horses. You can't outrun them. You are not dying here."

I shook my head. "I have no intention of dying here."

She poked me hard in the chest, but her eyes were glistening. "You owe me a lobster."

I reached for her. She backed away. "Uh-uh," she said. "You don't intend to die; I'm not giving any good-bye hugs."

"How about a good-luck one?"

She pursed her lips, dropped her chin to her shoulder, and held her arms out. "Okay."

We hugged. I kissed the top of her head, then tilted her face up for another. She pulled away. "No. You get your good-luck hug, but I am not going to kiss you. Besides, you're face is a sheet of blood, and it would be icky."

She danced away from me, then ran after Dylan and Ceridwen. Joe circled in front of me, facing toward the henge entrance. He held his sword ready for swinging.

"Is my face that bad?" I asked.

Joe considered me for a little too long. "Well, you have that little scar by your eye from when you fell in the bathtub when you were five."

I frowned at him. "I meant the blood."

He smiled as if it just occurred to him I didn't normally walk around with blood on my face. "Oh! No, the blood's cool. You should keep it."

"Thanks." I looked at the little guy, hovering all tough and mean in his loincloth. "Joe, promise me you'll bug out if this falls apart."

He didn't look at me. "Nope."

"Joe . . ."

He kept his eye on the entrance. "Connor, I've stood by your family for generations during some very dark times. Dark, dark times. Even Seamus Ogden macGrey, who was a huge prick. I think he was your great-great-great-great-grandfather. The only reason I stayed with him was his wife made a most excellent mead and was a long-suffering waif. And a looker. Boy, was she a looker. She's where your brother Cal gets his red hair, if you ask me. I remember this one time . . ."

"Joe . . ."

He shook his head. "I ain't leaving."

"Fine. No more cookies for you."

"I left a reminder for you to pick up more."

"You mean you left the empty bag on my pillow."

He laughed his maniacal laugh. "Yep."

"Here they come," I said.

35

Vize led the charge. Long black hair streamed from under his helm as he bore down on the entrance. He rose in his stirrups, holding the reins with one hand as he raised a spear with the other. My heart skipped a beat. I flashed open my sensing ability. Relieved, I read nothing more than oakwood charged with elf-shot. It wasn't a match to my spear. I knew damned well I didn't want a splinter of the Wheel in his hands.

He launched the spear. He knew how to use one. It sailed straight and true, piercing Dylan's *airbe druad* with a burst of emerald essence. That was all it was meant to do, punch a hole to test what they were up against. Dylan patched it without effort. The spear peaked and dropped toward the center of the circle. It had no more charged essence, so it was a simple wooden spear again. One aiming for my chest, but still pretty simple. I lifted my sword. A streak of pink whirred by, and Joe knocked the spear to the ground.

"Thanks," I said.

"De nada," he said, returning to his aerial perch.

A stunning assortment of fey rode behind Vize. I hadn't realized that the animosity to the Seelie Court was so widespread. Things had become much worse since I had left the Guild. Elves in the same black leather tunic Vize wore, unemblemed. Dwarves rode with him, too, surprisingly. Their loyalty to the Elven King was moderate at best, but aligned with Donor Elfenkonig's henchmen was the last place I'd expect them. If the Elven King wasn't supporting Vize, they had much to lose. Plenty of solitaries joined him, all shapes and shades, malevolent and wild looks in their eyes. The scary part was the Celts. He had Celtic fey with him, mostly subclans of the major races, but more Danann than I would have guessed flew air cover. I had no idea what that was about.

Vize rode far ahead of his comrades. He might be as damaged as I was, but he wasn't going to let his followers see him cower in the rear guard. The Teutonic fey put a lot of stock in crazy bravery. Even so, Vize had to be nuts to put himself in that much danger. As he neared, a heavy-duty body shield on him confused me. He didn't have one earlier. A blue-skinned solitary clung to his back like a climbing animal, all sharp teeth and claws and tangled white hair. A nixie. The shield was hers.

Vize checked the dream mare at the barrier. He cocked his head up, staring transfixed at Ceridwen. He shouted something to his lead riders, but I couldn't hear what he called.

Dylan sliced a hand through the air, rending a space in the *airbe druad* between the entrance stones. He made it look like a tactical error and frantically threw useless bindings at the gap to repair it. Vize waited for his company to catch up, then spurred his horse forward. He lunged through the opening, the dream mare lifting in an impressive leap, smoke trailing after it like exhaust. Dylan yanked his fist down, and the barrier snapped closed. Meryl moved in and amplified the charge on the entrance before anyone else could get through. Vize's immediate followers slammed into the barrier, and the ranks behind them crashed into them in a satisfying knot of confusion.

Vize was nicely surprised when he realized he was alone. He pulled forcefully on the reins, his solitary friend dangling precariously from his back. He managed to bring the horse to a halt, and the great beast danced in a circle as Vize looked back. His followers had stopped tripping onto each other, spacing themselves as best they could to make room. As they reorganized, they threw lightning strikes of essence against the *airbe druad*.

Ceridwen soared overhead in a pulsating golden aura. Single-handedly, she fended off dozens of the airborne fairies and winged solitaries who tried to fly over the barrier. Her power amazed me. UnderQueens packed more of a wallop than I would have ever guessed.

The narrow space of the entrance avenue worked in Dylan's favor. No more than three or four fey could attack the shield without hitting one another. Between the extra charge Meryl gave him and his own considerable skill, the barrier held the riders off. Bergin turned the dream mare toward the Boston portal

"Vize needs some prodding in this direction, Joe," I said.

Joe grinned deep dimples into his cheeks. He flashed out and reappeared with burst of pink essence in Vize's face. He slapped Vize on the nose and disappeared. The frustrating thing about fighting with a flit is that they're too small to target a hit well, too fast to chase, and too unconventional to anticipate. A slap on the nose is the last thing you expect anyone to do. And it hurts, to say nothing of humiliating.

Vize wheeled the horse. Joe appeared and hit him on the back of the head. The dream mare shied sideways, confused by Vize's shifting and turning in the saddle. Joe flashed in and jabbed the beast in the haunch. The mare reared with an angry neigh and bolted across the stone ring.

Joe popped in next to me. "Careful, he's got a nixie with him."

Reining in the horse, Vize realized I was there and cantered toward me.

"You're too late. Maeve destroyed the Tara portal," I said.

His eyes shifted among the portals. "That's better than I hoped."

Dylan's calm voice filled my head. *We can't hold this much longer.*

The Boston portal started to mist like the other doors had when Samhain ended. I pointed at it with the spear. "You're trapped, Vize. Order your people to stand down. Surrender to the Guild authorities, and no one gets hurt."

Vize leaned forward on his saddle, chuckling. "I appreciate your intent, but, unfortunately, that would be inconvenient."

"They follow you. If you die, they'll get the message where this is heading for them," I said.

He looked down at the sword, then at me. "Since when does the Guild act as executioner?"

"I'm not Guild anymore, thanks to you. My perspective has changed."

I brought the spear to my shoulder. I meant to use it for what it was—a spear—but something happened. Something I didn't do. The spear shuddered in my hand, drawing in essence on its own. The air thickened with pressure, and the spear glowed white. Vize's dream mare screamed and backed away. Vize grappled with the reins as the ground trembled. A wave of dizziness hit me, and my vision narrowed. Pain stabbed behind my eyes, the dark mass scuttling like a crab across my brain. Shouting, Vize clutched at his temples. A roaring filled my ears, a howling of wind. The light of the spear faltered, and the pain in my head subsided. The darkness swelled in my head, a dark blot driving away the light.

Vize looked dazed. Fear etched across the nixie's face as she clutched his back. She pointed over my head. Outside the stone circle, a blank wall of darkness hung above the horizon. The nothingness from the forest had grown, stretching across the sky in a silent curtain of deepest black. It had no depth or dimension, stretching in all directions beyond sight.

They're breaking through.

Dylan's sending drew my attention back to the portal entrance. More winged solitaries filled the air, the Dead joining Vize's companions. Excitement built among the fighters as Dylan's shield barrier collapsed. Riders on horseback and the Dead on strange beasts spilled through the entrance and flooded into the field.

Fall back! Fall back! Ceridwen sent. She retreated from the entrance stones, a host of solitaries and Danann fairies pressing her back. A continuous discharge of essence-fire exploded from her hands as she drew strength from the air. I had no idea how long she could keep that up. Even Faerie queens had to have their limits.

I ducked away from a flash of movement in my peripheral vision. Too late. The nixie sailed through the air and dug her claws into my shoulder. I dropped my sword and spun in place, trying to pull her off. I yelled as she sank her teeth into the back of my neck. Joe dove in, sparks flying from his sword when it slammed against her body shield. I jabbed at her with the spear, but the angle was wrong. I stretched my arm out as far as I could for another stab when the spear yanked out of my hand. The nixie's claws dug deeper, and she leaped away.

Joe chased her as she spun over a knot of fighters battling the Dead. With a squeal of manic joy, she caught the mane of Vize's horse and swung herself onto its neck. The Dead and Vize's riders swirled between us in a confusion of fighting. I lost sight of them. The air became thick with essence and war cries from across time. Strange dark animals scurried across the grass or launched themselves into the air, horned and scaled things I didn't recognize. I grabbed my sword from the ground. Frantic, I searched for the spear.

The fight churned, the heads of the mounted riders rising and falling in the melee. Dream mares screamed as the Dead pressed the advantage of close quarters. The darkness in my head recoiled enough for me to sense essence again. I felt the spear nearby. The mob shifted, and Vize appeared lunging his way through the battle. In a raised fist, he had the spear. He had taken it from me.

I opened my mind for the spear. I pictured it in my hand, let it feel my desire for it. I had a strange double vision, the spear in my mind flaring and the one in Vize's hand twirling away from him. But it didn't come to me. The image in my head slipped away, its burning white essence fading. Vize had the spear, or the spear had him. The bright light in my vision dwindled while the dark mass pulsed with renewed strength. The spear was no longer bonded to me.

A shaft of essence tore through the throng. Meryl charged through in its wake, her eyes blazing yellow. She cut a path forward, swinging the sword with one hand and firing essence with the other. When she reached me, she pressed her back against mine and kept fighting. Joe returned in a whirling frenzy, the blue flame of his sword burning in the air.

Move toward the portal, Meryl sent.

"I can't. Vize has the spear," I shouted. There was no way I was leaving it with him. I tried not to laugh at the string of cursing Meryl let fly. Swords flailing, we pushed across the field, moving closer to Vize. He reined in the horse, managing to keep it still. Standing in the stirrups, he leaned well back. He threw the spear.

The sounds of battle faded from my awareness as I watched the spear rise, unable to stop it. It seared a streak of flaming orange essence across the air, not toward me, but up. With a concussive blast, the spear struck Ceridwen between the shoulder blades. She heaved upward with the force of the blow, and the spearhead erupted from her chest. A golden halo flared around her, bursting outward in a shock wave. The wave front knocked her airborne adversaries out of the sky and threw everyone to the ground. As we fell in a tangle, Meryl instinctively hardened her body shield around us. Heat scorched the air, and I screamed as the thing in my mind spiked.

Ceridwen fell. Her essence wave collapsed with a sonic boom, and she fell with a sickening slowness, her lifeless wings flapping and ballooning like limp sails as she twirled down on currents of essence. She hit the ground near the pillar stone in the center of the field. The circle's essence flickered, and the ground rippled like water.

I struggled to my feet and helped Meryl up. Bodies lay

around us in a blasted circle of scorched earth, the Dead as
well as Vize's own fighters. His own fighters. He didn't care
about his own people.

"Good Mother," Meryl whispered.

Across the field, Vize's mount churned in a mass of panicked fighters, the nixie's body shield a shimmering halo of
blue light around them. The dark thing in my head jumped,
spiking again. Incredible pain fanned the rage within me. A
muddy red blurred my vision as I swung my sword. Everyone
and everything fell back from me, the Dead and riders alike.
My sword grew hot, its plating darkening, and my arm
throbbed with the heat.

As people scrambled away, Dylan appeared out of the confusion on the field. He was closer to Vize, close enough to
reach him first, and he hit him with essence-fire. It crackled
across the nixie's shield. The mare shied and bucked from the
scattered overflow fire. He hit them again, but the nixie deflected. Dylan gathered white-hot essence in his hands and
ran at them. With an amazing leap, he became airborne for a
moment, hands burning through the nixie's shield. When his
fingers tangled in her hair, he ripped her from Vize's back.
They fell grappling, arms and legs in a frenzy. He shook her
off and flung her away. As she landed, she rolled hard on the
ground and vanished.

Unprotected, Vize charged through the fighters, the dream
mare knocking people aside as he pressed toward the Boston
portal. I cut across the field into their path and faced them
head-on. The startled mare reared over me, her hooves flailing at my head. I dodged as she came down and bucked.

Vize lost his helm. His hair whipped around him as he
fought to control the horse. I darted in and grabbed the har-
ness. The mare jerked her head back, lifting me off my feet. I
swung my sword as the momentum brought me within range
of Vize's exposed face. His sword came up under mine and
parried me away.

A shock jolted us both when our blades met. Black vapor
burst into the air between us. I fell, screaming, as the dark

thing in my head writhed. I landed on my feet, fighting for balance and pivoting on my heel. Vize dangled from the saddle with his ankle caught in the stirrup. The horse lunged forward, and Vize slipped farther, his head and shoulders hitting the ground. My vision turned dark, pain bleeding from my eyes. The dream mare screamed again and reared. As his leg pulled free, Vize flipped into the air. He landed on his back at my feet, and I raised the sword over my head, blade down.

I flinched as a white streak of essence blossomed in my mind. The spear had returned to me, bonding to my essence and driving back the dark mass. I looked down at Vize, his eyes wide with the knowledge I was going to kill him.

"Your face!" he said.

I plunged the blade down. It struck barren earth as Vize faded away. I staggered back, my breath ragged as the sword shuddered in the ground. I inhaled and pulled it free. Beside me, Dylan had the dream mare by the reins. She stamped in place, but didn't pull away. He stared at me with a look of horror. "Connor?"

I heard him. I heard him, but couldn't speak. It took every ounce of energy to fight the pain in my head. My left arm shook as I focused on the darkness, refusing to give in to it. The mesh on my arm burned with cold, the essence of Tir-NaNog pouring into it, the essence of the Dead. The darkness receded.

"Connor?" Dylan said again.

I didn't get a chance to answer him. Screams went up across the field. The Dead fled from the center crescent of stones as fierce bolts of golden essence scoured the ground.

"She's alive," I said in disbelief. I didn't recognize my own voice. "Ceridwen's alive, Dyl. Get me over there."

Whatever he saw in my face, he seemed relieved to hear me speak. He mounted the dream mare and pulled me up. We rode back to the center. Vize's remaining riders clustered on the opposite side of the trilithons, fighting off the Dead.

My gut twisted when I saw red armor. Flanked by Meryl

and Joe, Ceridwen lay faceup, the point of the spear protruding from her chest above her heart. The length of the spear held her twisted off the ground. Her body essence shone with a pale light, cycling dimmer and dimmer with each breath.

I jumped and sank beside her. "Ceridwen? Can you hear me?"

Her eyelids fluttered open. "What happened?"

"Vize tried to kill you."

She inhaled with a wet sucking sound. "He may yet succeed."

"Hang on, Ceridwen. We're going to get you out of here."

"Don't leave my body here, macGrey."

"I won't. And I told you, my name is Grey."

Ceridwen grabbed my shirt. "Listen to me, Grey."

"Ceridwen, don't move."

Her eyes became brighter. "I lied, Grey. Maeve betrayed us. She refused to lead her warriors in and leave them with me. She could have done it and left unscathed, but she refused, Grey."

I stared down at her in shock. "She refused?"

Ceridwen grimaced as she nodded. "She said your city's sacrifice would serve Tara's security. She doesn't care if Vize gets through to Boston."

The dark mass roiled within me, anxious to be released again. I kept it back by sheer willpower, letting the light of the spear in my mind keep it from growing again. I grabbed Ceridwen's hand and leaned in close. "Stay with me, Ceridwen. I'm going to get you out of this, and then we are going to kick some serious Seelie Court ass. Deal?"

She tried to laugh. Blood speckled her lips when the laugh turned into a cough. Not a good sign. "Deal, macGrey."

If I had never had reason to despise Maeve, I had one now. I marked the distance to the Boston portal. Vize's remaining riders and some of the Dead pushed toward it. A long way to go through more fighting. The haze in the portal had deepened. I could make out city lights on the other side, but morning was coming to Boston. Samhain was ending, and the portal would close with the dawn.

I lifted Ceridwen gently. "Take her out, Dyl. Find Gillen or Briallen. We need her alive."

Dylan generated a levitation spell to lift her. We positioned her sideways in front of him, the spear jutting out to either side. A small hope rose in my chest when Ceridwen lifted a hand to hold Dylan's collar. It slipped off. Her head slumped against his shoulder, her essence sputtering.

"Get on!" Dylan yelled down to us.

"No, you need speed. Get out of here." I slapped the mare hard on the rump with my sword. She bucked forward before Dylan had any more say in the matter. The fighters fell back at his approach, frightened by the wave of essence he fired in front of him. They swirled into the wake of his passing.

Meryl leaned against the pillar stone watching Dylan ride off. "We're never going to get through that," she said.

He reached the portal. The dream mare's hooves lit with fire as they lifted from her smoky essence. They dove through the haze. A boiling rush of green flame erupted from the door as the Taint from the other side seared through the riders and the Dead. A wind filled with screams roared into the circle. Meryl and I clung to each other as the pillar stone shifted.

"Get out of here," I shouted.

She tilted her head up to me and smiled. *No one should die alone.*

I searched her face, traced every curve and line of it with my eyes. I stared down at this person who had done everything I ever asked of her. And more. I saw something, something beyond physical attraction, this brilliant glow of uncommon beauty I couldn't begin to put words to. My chest ached as I closed my eyes and kissed her, feeling her lips against mine, not with the hunger of sex but the essence beyond it.

I broke the kiss. Meryl smiled from under her bangs. I leaned down and kissed the top of her head, then ripped the silver branch from her jacket. Even with the storm of sound around us, the brooch made a metallic ping as I flung it among the trilithons. Meryl's eyes went huge with realization. She lunged for me, trying to use me as her anchor in TirNaNog, but I stepped out of her reach.

"Connor!" Meryl screamed as she felt whatever the sensation was that dropped her out of TirNaNog. She vanished. Somewhere on the other side of the Boston portal, the true side where Boston was and my life had been, a supremely angry druidess was reappearing. I didn't care. No matter how pissed she was at that moment, she was damned well alive, too.

Joe hovered by my shoulder and spoke very quietly in my ear. "I hope you realize I can't shield you like she could."

I nodded. Another gust of Taint blew from the door. The force of it sent Joe into a spiraling tumble as a sliver of intense white light pierced the mottled green. It shot hard and true at me, burning in my mind, the bond solidifying with a brilliant spasm in my head. I caught the spear one-handed, and it pulled me off my feet. It burned in my hand, not with the intense cold it once had, but with a white-hot fire. It stabbed the ground at the foot of the pillar stone, twisting and writhing as it sucked essence from the ring itself, great waves rippling through the stone circle. The Taint channeled into me, coursing down my arm and into the spear.

Standing stones cracked. The entire circle warped and swayed. The stones on the sides of the entrance avenue caved inward, pulling down the standing stones and lintels to either side. The adjacent stones fell next, pulling the next set with them. Standing stone after standing stone after standing stone buckled and fell.

Joe tugged at my ear. "Come on! The Way is closing!"

It was more than closing. It was collapsing. As the standing stones tumbled into the circle, they released torrential waves of essence. The circle was half-gone, a tangled heap of crumbling stone. A boulder came flying through the air. Joe screamed as his body shredded into ribbons of pink. The boulder tore through him, and the shreds scattered outward.

Joe was still screaming when he snapped back. "I can't teleport. The Way is closed!"

"The portal! Get out of here, Joe!" I yelled.

He buzzed into my face. I had never seen him so angry and so afraid. He trembled as he turned this way and that, as if looking for an answer to the destruction around us. He flew off, essence waves knocking him about like a leaf on the wind. He dove at the ground and looped back up. He reached the Boston portal as cracks bled up the standing stones to either side of it. Our eyes met one more time as he paused in front of the haze. He flew through to Boston.

Everyone was safe. I was alone.

36

I might have made everyone leave me to die, but that didn't mean I was going to accept my own end sitting down. I'd never get to the portal in time, but simply watching it close felt too much like passive suicide. I had to at least pretend I could reach it, click my heels, make a wish, drop the silver branch, and be transported home sweet home. If I wasn't going to die in my sleep, I'd be damned if I leaned back, tapping my foot to the ol' ding-dong of doom. Sometimes delusional thinking has the nice side effect of letting you feel better about yourself. I pulled the spear from the ground.

Essence whipped the air. The standing stones toppled as the ground undulated like viscous liquid. I staggered and stumbled across it, even crawled at one point when the earth welled up in my face. The fallen stones became elastic, oozing into each other in a sludge of moldering essence. The henge outside was a gray-green smear, no discernible features or landmarks. Even the Dead were gone, their body essence absorbed by the maelstrom.

Everything disintegrated, but the spear became more real than ever, a firm purity that drank in waves of released essence. I no longer felt pain from it, not in the physical sense. It radiated through me, a force of light, neither hot nor cold, but a thing of energy, eating up whatever passed for substance inside me. Even the dark mass in my head retreated, not disappearing but shrinking to a mote of nothingness. The forgotten pathways to my abilities unfolded like a lost flower, but the spear's light rushed in, blocking my ability to manipulate essence as completely as the darkness had. At least I didn't have a headache anymore.

The earth groaned. The ground heaved, raising me on a hill high enough to see the last portal standing. It glowed a molten blue-white, essence pulsing and flickering as the haze thickened. The groaning deepened to a rumble that rose in volume. A higher-pitched sound sliced through the rumbling, louder and more variable, oddly familiar, but elusive. With a rush of power, it pierced through all the other noise around me until there was no mistaking the distinct sound of an engine.

Crimson essence exploded from the portal. The whine of the engine broke free, no longer muffled, and a police motorcycle soared through the portal. It hurtled upward in an aura of flame, trailing a streak of burning essence. The bike came down fast, landing in front of me, its rear wheel skidding out sideways. Essence billowed over me.

"Don't just stand there. Get the hell on!" Murdock shouted.

He spun the bike toward the portal. A wave propagated through the ground, and the hill became a gully. Murdock revved the throttle in the face of a growing peak of earth. I barely swung my leg behind him before he let out the clutch. The engine sang as the front tire lifted, and we tore up the hill. We rode the ground swell like a boat riding a wave. At the crest, we went airborne. The engine screamed as the tires spun free.

The portal twisted toward us, the lintel stone cracking and throwing fist-sized chunks of stone. The last of the circle collapsed, and the portal heaved over. Brilliant essence sprang from the spear and tore open the veil.

Images cascaded across my vision, buildings and trees and people, as the bike flew out of the fairy ring. We hit the ground, and the bike skidded from under us. Murdock's body shield took the brunt of the initial impact, but I rolled free, falling down an embankment until a tree stopped me.

I winced as I propped myself up to catch my breath. Several somethings felt broken inside. The air vibrated with essence, a steady, bass throb against my skin. The wind carried the rich, flinty odor of essence-fire. Flames burned everywhere, and the damaged landscape showed evidence of major exchanges of essence-fire. The great oaks at the top of the hill lay broken and uprooted.

So many people on the Common earlier had set off my riot radar in my old security muscles. The destruction around me confirmed it hadn't been wrong. The entire Common was in lockdown, empty of the crowd that had streamed to the fairy ring. The only people remaining were fey from the Guild or human police. Even at this distance, Keeva's essence signature was identifiable up near the statehouse dome. Danann security agents flew in line formations along the surrounding streets, more than I had seen even in the Weird, which was saying something. They weren't too circumspect about using essence either.

The fairy ring had changed. What had been a hazy funnel of essence had become a soaring column of light, a rich yellow shot with white. The Taint burned along its edges, green and black. Essence trembled the air, radiating from the column with an intense heat. The pillar of the war monument warped under the pressure, the bronze statue of a female warrior at the top leaning forward as though she was going to jump. Municipal emergency vehicles—police cars and motorcycles, EMT vans, fire trucks, and ambulances—raced from beneath its impending fall. Two communications vans had become too deformed to go anywhere.

Murdock picked himself up, looking no worse for wear. Of course, he had the body shield, not me.

"Thanks for the save," I said.

He shook his head at me like we had done something amusing and embarrassing. "It's not like I could just leave you with a bunch of dead people."

I smiled, too tired to argue with him. "No, only a jerk would do that."

He gestured at my hand. "Does that hurt?"

Essence radiated out of the spear, too powerful for a simple wooden shaft to maintain. I didn't think the spear was even there anymore, not in any physical sense I could understand, white fire taking on the spear's shape as it bled through from wherever the light was coming from. The essence coiled up my forearm, igniting the silver mesh like a tattoo of light. I couldn't see or feel my hand. I didn't know if I still had a hand. "Surprisingly, no, but it probably will as soon as I remember to feel."

The ground shook. The column of light soared higher, its bottom edge expanding across the remains of the fairy ring. "Is that supposed to happen?" Murdock asked.

"I don't know. I've never seen anything like it," I said.

If I wasn't sure of my hand, the dark mass in my head decided to remind me it still existed. It shifted, probing into the essence of the spear, both essences pushing for dominance. I closed my eyes, encouraging the spear to feel my desire. It was not like ability control—I didn't even think it was an ability, at least not one I understood. It didn't hear me during Vize's throw; otherwise, it would not have injured Ceridwen. No, the spear had its own agenda, responding to me only if it chose. Whatever it was doing, it caused a hell of a lot less pain than the dark mass, and I welcomed it.

"I failed," a voice said.

Startled, Murdock and I moved together but saw no one. The air rippled and Vize appeared in a relaxed posture, his sword in his hand but down at his side. The nixie squatted on the ground chuckling, her hand clutching the hem of Vize's tunic. Chalk up cloaking as another of her abilities.

Murdock called up his shield. My sensing ability detected no metal on him at all. He had lost his gun somewhere.

I pointed my blade at Vize. "Drop the sword."

"Do I have your word you won't run me through?" he asked.

"You mean like you did Ceridwen?"

He held both hands up, the sword high in his right. "What needed doing is done. I did what was demanded."

I gestured. "Drop it."

He relaxed his knees, keeping his eyes on me as he crouched, lowering the sword parallel to the ground and placing it on the grass.

The nixie grabbed at it, and I focused my blade on her.

"No! No! Keep it, Berg! He has two teeth, and you have none," she said in an old variant of German.

Vize straightened, stroking the nixie's matted hair. "Hush, Gretan. We have more to achieve here than our lives," he replied in the same language. Loathing filled her eyes as she glared at me. She released the sword and clutched Vize's leg again.

"The Wheel could have dropped me anywhere, Grey. It chose here," Vize said.

"The fact that you want the spear might have something to do with that," I said.

He shrugged. "Perhaps. But I didn't cause this, Grey. You did."

"I have a different interpretation of who caused this, Vize," I said.

He gave me his back, watching the column in the sky grow wider. "Yes, well, I'm sure you will take great solace in that as we all die. Can you read the runes on the spear?"

The runes. They were there, faint, almost lost in the white essence in my hand. *Way Seeker. Way Maker. Way Keeper.* I pressed the spearhead against Vize's neck. He didn't flinch. "What do you know about them?"

He tilted his head to see me over his shoulder. "What they say. The holder of the spear seeks the Way of the Wheel, makes it and keeps it. And the spear seeks whoever the Wheel decides will make and keep the Ways. It seeks someone to execute the will of the Wheel, like it did when it came to me in TirNaNog."

I exchanged glances with Murdock. I didn't believe Vize. "The Wheel of the World wanted you to try to kill Ceridwen?"

Vize returned his gaze to the column. "I dreamed a figure in red would destroy everything I sought to achieve. I tried to eliminate that threat, and the spear seemed to will it. I tried three times and picked the wrong person each time. I misunderstand the metaphor. You are the red figure, Grey, you with the spear in your hand and a bloodstained face."

"Then I've stopped you. I've won."

He gestured at the sky. "Have you? Congratulations."

"I don't believe you."

"I don't care. The spear left me, and the Wheel turns, Grey. Some say we do things that change Its direction. Some say we can't. Doing nothing is the same as doing something. We always choose. In the end, the Wheel turns. I can accept the choices I've made. Can you?"

A sending fluttered through the air. The nixie grinned up at me, and Vize bowed his head. They vanished.

I swung my sword through empty air. "Dammit."

"What happened?" asked Murdock.

I shook my head. "I'm stupid, that's what happened. He told the nixie to cloak them. I assumed he couldn't do sendings because I couldn't." I stared up at the column. "I don't believe that religious crap."

Murdock frowned, looking down at his feet. "I do."

"What?"

The column glowed as Murdock stared up at the sky. "I don't know what that place was I just pulled you out of, Connor, but it was real. I don't know what that means, but I do know I have to have more reason to wake up every day than to watch shit happen."

"What the hell do you expect me to do?" I asked.

"I don't know. I just don't think we can do nothing," he said.

The column was growing. If I didn't believe anything else Vize said, he was right that whatever had happened in Tir-NaNog was spreading. "I have to go back up there," I said.

Murdock nodded grimly. "Don't fall in. We don't have another bike."

I started up the hill.

"Connor," Murdock called out. I looked back. He nodded once. I saluted him with my sword.

I approached the damaged fairy ring, the spear vibrating in my hand. Scattered about the remains of the hill, gargoyles faced the column. Some slumped in the face of all the essence that had spilled over them. Their unintelligible, dry voices hummed in my head, several at once in tones that could only be described as both hope and sadness. I stepped over crushed mushrooms, their broken flesh pungent in the air. The spear pulsed, the runes visible, a dark burning blue. Essence streamed over me, my hair bristling with static charge. The column stretched above, pulling at me while the dark mass in my head clung with tenacious claws to my body essence. The column was a roiling mass, mostly white, with shades of indigo, amber, and emerald. It reminded me of standing in the veil. Maybe it was the veil, unleashed.

A flash of pink spiraled down, and Joe landed smoothly on my shoulder.

"Hey," he said.

"Hey."

"Thought I bugged out, didn't you?"

I jostled him as I shrugged. "Not really. I don't always get what you're up to."

He chortled with an incredibly smug look on his face. "Somebody had to take Murdock the silver branch you threw away."

"Oh. That explains it." I hadn't thought to ask.

"What are you doing?" Joe asked.

"Thinking about the consequences of nothing."

"Ah, it's come to that. I was afraid that thing would kill you eventually," he said.

So Joe. I wasn't sure we were even having the same conversation. He was fascinated and repelled by the thing in my head, the thing he called the nothing. I shivered.

"That's the choice," I whispered.

"What?"

"Nothing. That's what you called it when I asked you how you found me when you teleported. You said you looked for the spot with the nothing in the middle of it."

He craned his face around to look at me. "Isn't that what we've been talking about?"

I answered him with a laugh. He really was crazy. Brilliant crazy, but still crazy.

Whether Vize intended it or not, his final words made sense to me. If I did nothing, the column would keep growing. But if I *used* nothing, it might stop. Or it might turn everything to nothing. Between the known nothing and the unknown nothing, I took the unknown.

When I held out the spear, electrostatic sparks arced between it and the column. Power surged within, and my body shook as the dark mass flared in response. After fighting against it for three years, I embraced the darkness, filled my mind with the desire for it to grow. It responded like the spear, only painfully. Taint seeped down the spear toward my arm, no longer pulling the column wider, but spiraling down into a nexus that was forming between the light and the dark.

My mind screamed as I pushed at the dark mass within. The nothingness of it seared through the mesh on my forearm. A dark streak oozed down my arm, a fierce course of nothing, a complete absence of essence. The light and the dark met where my hand clutched the spear. I pressed harder, the thing in my head crushing against the inside of my skull. The column wavered and paused its motion. I forced myself to continue, willing the essence through the conduit that formed within my arm. After a faint hush, the essence in the column brushed against my face, pulling back to form the veil.

The black nothingness crept along the spear. It bucked in my hand, spitting the Taint out. The flow of essence from the column diminished, surged, then diminished again. I forced the darkness against it. It receded and returned. Each time I pushed, it gave back weaker until, finally, it changed course. It turned, folding in on itself, reversing its momentum. Joe yelled in my ear as he pounded my shoulder in excitement.

Elated, I opened my eyes. Darkness consumed my arm and permeated the spear. It reached for the column with a gnawing hunger. Above, the victory monument swayed violently and rebounded. Essence and darkness twisted it into a sinuous line of granite dancing in the air. With an ear-piercing screech, it pulled from its foundation, and the column of light sucked it in.

The column shrank. Enough. It was enough. I took a deep breath and willed the darkness to withdraw. It raged up my arm, swelling into a restless mass in my head again. It slammed against the back of my skull, and I went airborne. I landed on my back and gazed up at the sky. With a loud screech, the column contracted, stretched into the shape of a pillar, and collapsed.

Joe floated above me, the rising sun glistening gold on the edges of his wings. He circled, a reflective expression on his face. "I think I need to change my loincloth," he said.

Things shifted in my body. More cracked ribs, probably a broken one or two; aching joints; a soreness in my lower back, probably was a damaged kidney; and every square inch of my skin felt abraded. My forearm throbbed with heat. Vapor wisped over the silver filigree. The metal darkened and sank into my arm, leaving behind a faint indigo ghost image of the swirling pattern. I flexed my fingers, my skin tight on a smooth pink hand.

At the bottom of the hill near Beacon Street, the inert body of a dream mare lay on its side, the light gone out of it. Next to it, unmoving Danann security agents stood in a circle facing outward. Between them, I caught glimpses of a red figure on the ground. My sense of elation fell. Only a Danann honor guard stood like that. Ceridwen hadn't made it.

"They died coming through the veil," Joe said softly in my ear.

Sadness and small guilt swept through me. If I had not been so cocky years ago, Vize would have been in custody, and Ceridwen would not have died. She had fought to protect a place she had no reason to protect, people she didn't know, following orders from a High Queen who had betrayed her. At least she knew she had been duped. I would make sure everyone heard what she told me at the end. We might not have liked each other, but Ceridwen deserved to be honored. I walked down the hill to pay my respects.

Except for a lack of essence, the dream mare appeared asleep, crouched on her haunches with her long neck stretched out on the ground. One of her eyes was open, a milky white glaze. She had had some kind of essence reaction. The veil or the Taint, or probably both, killed her.

As I came around the horse's body, Ceridwen became visible. The honor guard kept a distance of several feet. Her body had been arranged on the ground to await transport. She lay on her back with her armor and helm on. Someone had placed a sword on her, blade down, and wrapped her hands on the hilt.

I stopped. Beyond the honor guard, more people gathered, Danann security agents, and several Guild personnel. A small group surrounded Briallen, her body rigid with emotion. She must have sensed me because she turned and held out her hand. My stomach lurched at the look on her face. I forced myself to move, denial warring with realization as I approached. I took Briallen's hand and folded my arms around her. She wasn't crying, but the grief radiating off her was palpable.

I held her tightly against my chest as I stared down at Dylan's dead body.

37

I leaned against the door of the room high in an isolated tower of the Guildhouse. The domed chamber had a complex truss design reminiscent of Renaissance architecture applied with druidic sensibilities. Thick oak beams crisscrossed the ceiling and reached to the floor. A Palladian window filled an entire wall with an expansive view to the east. The stained glass along the frame of the window was done in multicolored geometric shapes, some clean, clear colors, some rich opalescents. The center pane had a stunning image of an oak grove in bloom, complete with representations of mistletoe hanging among the leaves. Louis Comfort Tiffany had made the window himself under a direct commission of the Seelie Court. I couldn't image what its value was.

I rolled the sphere in my hands, admiring the craftsmanship. The knotwork of the outer shell patterned with meticulous fine lines to resemble a flat, braided rope. The interior orb moved freely with a faint sound as I spun it with my finger. The precise incisions of ogham script on the orb appeared and disappeared beneath the knots as it moved, the light catching the various aphorisms and poetic triads. I used to think the words were sentimental, in a derisive sense. It's funny how a charged emotional state can transform something maudlin into something profound.

Dylan's body lay shrouded on the funeral bier draped in a ceremonial robe, the indigo and gold Celtic weave of its hem pooling on the floor. The brilliant white cloth was placed so that three vibrant yellow suns with flaming red borders rested on his chest. His face looked handsome in repose, no indication of what he might have felt when he died. Leaving a good-looking corpse fit his style.

I waited in the dim predawn silence. A small fluctuation of essence in my chest prompted me to look up from the sphere. The window brightened as dawn arrived, the sun's essence seeping into the sky in feathery touches. In the clear space above the grove image, the sun appeared in full, perched on the horizon. Light bathed the room, Dylan's shroud a sudden field of colors reflected from the stained glass.

"It would serve you right if I walked out the door right now," I said.

I didn't mean it. Not really. I moved to the bier and held the sphere over Dylan's face. The sun warmed the sphere, and it awakened. I lowered it gently to his forehead as the inner orb began to spin on its own. Faster and faster it turned, glowing with a soft white light. Essence welled out of the spaces of the knotwork and overflowed onto my hand, spilling out warm and soothing, running down Dylan's face. The shroud glowed as essence ran under it, the shape of his body burning under the cloth. The orb slowed as the light faded, then stopped. I stepped back.

The cocoon of light faded as Dylan's body absorbed the phosphorescent glow. Shafts of sunlight crisscrossed the room, a hushed, reverent silence of light. The shroud moved, a subtle shift across the sun emblems.

Dylan gasped, lurching into a seated position. I wrapped my arm around his shoulders and lowered him back down. With his eyes focused on the ceiling, he took deep, ragged breaths, filling his body with air and essence. His breathing slowed, becoming controlled and normal. He closed his eyes.

I crossed my arms and waited. He opened his eyes again and smiled. As angry as I was, I couldn't help smiling back.

It's something uncontrollable after you think someone is dead.

"You're an asshole," I said.

His smiled broadened. He started laughing, which led to coughing, and he sat up to clear his throat. Eyes tearing from the effort, he shook his head, still smiling. "That's not the welcome back I was expecting," he said.

I tossed him the sphere. "I am so angry with you right now. We thought you were dead. *I* thought you were dead. Then I get home and that thing is glowing in my study."

He looked sheepish. "I was going to tell you, but things got complicated."

I snorted. "Complicated? More complicated than 'oh, by the way, hang on to my soul for me, I might need it?' That's crazy, Dylan. I could have thrown that thing out."

He tilted his head down. "But you didn't. I had faith you wouldn't, or I would have come back for it."

I shook my head in disbelief. "You're lucky I called Briallen instead of using it for a night-light."

He spun the orb and held it straight out so I could read an ogham script: *Life is a series of trust moments.*

"Danu's blood, as you like to say, Dyl. That's some freakin' trust."

"And not misplaced, obviously," he said.

"You have a very angry Auntie Bree, by the way."

He nodded, working the stiffness out of his jaw. "She'll understand. She never stays mad at me for long."

"Lucky you."

He stretched and yawned. "Wow. Being dead really knots up the muscles."

"You should get as much rest as you can. The Guild is in an uproar. They're going to be all over you about what happened."

He grimaced. "Actually, Con, I don't want anyone to know I'm alive."

That took me off guard. "Why not?"

He gave me a sly look. "Believe it or not, I was planning

on dying in a couple of weeks. This whole scenario saves me the trouble."

Realization dawned. "The Black Ops job."

"Yep. Dead's always the perfect cover."

"Please tell me I don't have to keep that a secret from Briallen," I said.

"Oh, no. She knew my plans. She'll agree this is perfect. I mean, after she stops being mad at me for dying for real. Sort of," he said.

I shook my head, laughing softly. "Gods, Dyl, we lead crazy-ass lives, you know that?"

He nodded, amused, too. "Yeah, we do. You should go before anyone else comes in. I don't have much time to slip out of here."

I held my hand out. "Good luck." We shook. On impulse, I pulled him up and gave him a hug. "Don't do that again."

"I'll try not to," he said in my ear.

I left him sitting on his funeral bier, head tilted back to catch the warmth of the sun. Outside the room, Meryl waited on a bench in the corridor, empty except for two Danann agents standing honor guard. She looked curious as she hugged me. "You're oddly happy for someone visiting a deceased friend."

I wrapped her under my arm as we walked to the elevator. "I can't believe what a jerk I used to be."

"You could have just asked me," she said.

"But I've gotten better, right?"

She rocked her head from side to side. "Well, let's say things look promising."

"But I'm much better, right?"

She looked at me from under a head of ice blue hair. "Buy me the lobster you owe me, and we'll talk."

I huddled in my jacket against the late-night cold. Winter was coming on strong. I burped lobster as I crossed the Old

Northern Avenue bridge into the Weird. The lone police car at the checkpoint had turned into three. After what happened on the Common, the city dropped all pretense of calling it a safety measure for everyone. The entire neighborhood was closed off. Jersey barriers were thrown down everywhere to control traffic in and out, not just on the bridges. It wasn't martial law, but it was only a matter of time before they figured out the legal niceties.

I turned onto Sleeper Street. The thing I liked about my street was that it wasn't filled with late-night partiers unless something was going on in my own building. The thing I didn't like was that it wasn't filled with late-night partiers and was creepy and desolate late at night.

A flutter of essence washed over me, and my fragmented body shield kicked on. Someone casting a sensing spell. It wasn't nasty or threatening. I stopped. If whoever had cast it didn't know exactly where I lived, I didn't need them to see me enter my building. I scanned the street. The warehouse across from my building had garage doors that spent a lot of time closed. At the far end of the block, someone lingered in the darkness of a recessed loading bay. I opened my sensing ability again to do my own scouting and got the surprise of the day. The essence wasn't normal, as if anything in the Weird was normal. Between the seething anger of the people who lived down here and the damned Taint, the last thing we needed was the Dead of TirNaNog roaming around.

A tall, cloaked woman stepped into view under a streetlight. Neither of us moved, but stared at each other for a long moment. She beckoned me closer. I joined her under the pool of light, her essence resonating with the feel of TirNaNog.

"You aren't surprised to see me," she said.

I shrugged. "You have no idea how much nothing surprises me anymore, Ceridwen."

She laughed, low and comfortable. "I'm Dead."

I nodded. "I can feel that. Why are you here?"

"The Way was closed," she said.

"Ah. At least you said closed and not gone. I'm not sure if TirNaNog was destroyed."

She nodded. "A fair concern. I choose not to believe it is gone. I think I would feel it. As I did not believe Faerie was gone when I lived, I do not believe TirNaNog is gone now that I'm Dead."

"You Dead people are so optimistic."

She laughed, an oddly pleasant sound under the circumstances. "Under different circumstances, I think I might have liked you, Druid macGrey."

I nodded in courtesy. "I think we would have found something to talk about."

She worried her hands together and removed a ring. "I want you to have this."

I tilted it toward the light. It was an ornate gold band set with a large carnelian. "This isn't necessary."

She smiled, turned slowly on her heel, and walked away. "It will be. Tell no one I gave it to you. Remember we have a deal."

She disappeared into the darkness. I tossed the ring in the air and caught it overhand. As I slipped it in my pocket, I hoped I didn't regret words said in anger.

I backtracked to my apartment. The Dead who had made it into Boston through the veil found themselves in the same dilemma as Ceridwen. They couldn't get back and had no place to go. Naturally, they were gravitating to the Weird.

A darkness was gathering around me. I felt it as palpably as I felt Ceridwen's ring in my pocket. The dark mass in my head had an awareness or at least something very close to it. I didn't know anymore if I was responding to it or it was responding to me. Like the spear. For one brief moment, it became a fierce white thing in my head, but it felt like something more, something important, yet mutable. I could believe it was a sliver of the Wheel, or at least Its instrument. And I, in turn, had been the spear's instrument before it vanished in the collapse of the veil.

And so was Bergin Vize. Like I was bonded, so he had been for a brief time. All this time, I'd thought he had done something to destroy my abilities, but now it seemed that whatever happened had destroyed his, too. Whether he'd caused it or not was still a question, but the fact remained that our paths kept crossing. Whether that was his doing or the Wheel's didn't matter. It just was. And would be again. Especially now that he was loose in Boston.

I wake up every day thinking about the past, the things I remember and the things I don't. Everything is there, just on the edge of my thoughts, things I've said or done. People I've loved or killed. Actions and events reach out to the present and change the future. All there, waiting their turn on the Wheel. Memories lurk in dark recesses. Old friends become new again. Dead things are reborn, marching forward out of the past into the future, standing tall and sure, refusing to lie down and rest, unfallen dead things that claim a piece of the Wheel for themselves, claim a piece of me. Where they lead, only the Wheel knows, and It reveals Itself with grudging hints, confusing metaphors, and inevitability.

And the dark mass in my head complicated everything. It kept me out of the Guild. It kept me from remembering. I thought it was killing me. Which might be true, but what also was true was that without it, I would have died a few times recently. What happened in TirNaNog changed it. I felt it. It was time to try again to figure out what the hell it was. I had exhausted my resources. Neither Briallen, Nigel, nor Gillen Yor had been able to figure it out. Maybe it was time to start looking for answers in unlikely places.

Joe popped in, humming with a particularly proud and smug look on his face.

"I take it the mission was a success?" I asked.

He snapped his fingers. "It was a cinch."

"And no one saw you?"

He thumped his chest. "No one sees a flit when he doesn't want to be seen."

I'd worked with Keeva long enough to fake her handwriting to the casual eye. I couldn't wait to see what happened when her boyfriend showed up at the Guildhouse board of directors meeting tomorrow wearing the good-luck gift "she" had left in his office. The only downside was I wouldn't see Ryan macGoren's face when he realized he was proudly wearing an expensive gold torc that had been stolen from the New York Met.

I smirked. "Good man. I'd say this calls for a drink."

He grinned back. "No port."

It's been a century since the peoples and magic of the Faerie realms mysteriously appeared in our world, an event known historically as Convergence. Humanity has learned to coexist with fairies and elves, but sometimes it seems Convergence has only brought new breeds of criminals—and new ways to fight them.

meet laura blackstone

In Washington, D.C., Laura Blackstone is the public relations director for the Fey Guild. Janice Crawford is a druid who helps out when the D.C. SWAT team needs magical backup. Mariel Tate is a lead investigator for an international intelligence agency. But what most people don't know is that they are all the same woman.

Laura has been juggling different identities for years, using her ability to disguise herself with magical glamours to gather intelligence. Now, as "Laura" puts together publicity for a special fey exhibition at the National Archives, "Janice" is almost killed in a drug bust gone bad . . . and "Mariel" discovers a possible connection between the drug raid and threats against the opening of the exhibition.

Laura's different worlds are about to collide, and if she can't keep it together, she'll have more to worry about than having to retire an identity. She may lose her life.

Look for the first Laura Blackstone novel
***SKIN DEEP* by Mark Del Franco**
Coming in August 2009 from Ace Books